VARNEY THE VAMPYRE;

or,

The Feast of Blood

A Romance.

Book Five

The Fate of the Vampyre

Other works by James Malcolm Rymer

Phoebe; or, The Miller's Maid.
Moreton; or, The Doomed House.
Grace Rivers; or, The Merchant's Daughter.
The Black Monk; or, The Secret of the Grey Turret.
Don Caesar de Bazan. A Romance of Old Spain.
The White Slave. A Romance of the 19th Century.
The Black Mantle; or, The Murder at the Old Ferry.
Paul the Reckless; or, The Fugitive's Doom.
Jane Shore; or, London in the Reign of Edward IV.
Ada the Betrayed; or, The Murder at the Old Smithy.

VARNEY
THE VAMPYRE

James Malcolm Rymer

Book Five
The Fate of the Vampyre

WILDSIDE PRESS
Doylestown, Pennsylvania

Varney the Vampyre;
or,
The Feast of Blood
Book Five:
The Fate of the Vampyre
A publication of

Wildside Press
P.O. Box 301
Holicong, PA 18928-0301
www.wildsidepress.com

TWENTY-FIRST CENTURY EDITION

*— "How graves give up their dead,
And how the night air hideous grows
With shrieks!"*

Introduction

Del Howison

What you hold in your hands is the final installment of the Wildside Press edition of *Varney the Vampyre; or, The Feast of Blood.* Although in length this novel certainly resembles *War and Peace,* it is nowhere near the literary tome that Tolstoy wrote. Unsurprisingly, both authors were getting paid by the word. Coincidence? Perhaps not. Clearly, though, Leo had better words.

In fact, *Varney* author James Malcolm Rymer was somewhat ashamed of his effort and tried to hide his identity as its author. He was quite successful in this regard — he was able to disguise himself as the author not only during his lifetime but for another hundred and twenty years! In fact, it was not until 1963 that Louis James found conclusive proof that Rymer was indeed the author of the work.

Rymer was an editor and had published his first novel, *The Monk,* in 1841. He had a reputation to uphold. But times were tough, and he was forced into popular fiction somewhat reluctantly due to his failing financial condition. His weekly installments of *Varney* were a quick buck over several years during the mid 1840s. When his Pennydreadful installments ended they were collected together and published as a novel in 1847. Rymer received a lot of mileage out of *Varney* (or Mortimer, as that was the character's real name).

Although it wasn't the first English language supernatural story ever written, it was the first full-length English language vampire novel. It tells the tale of what is essentially an inept vampire. In the second half of the novel he attacks young woman after young woman. They scream. People come to their rescue and Varney must flee. This ineptitude is probably due to the fact that he is really a reluctant vampire, merely caught up in this undead state as punishment for a crime from a higher source.

The novel is not without its nice touches. Rymer helped establish the vampire as someone with great strength, long fanged teeth, shining eyes and white skin that blushed whenever he fed. Many of these characteristics were used over forty years later by Bram Stoker in Dracula. However, Rymer's being could walk in the sunlight. He didn't need to feed every night and when he did he did not pass along his vampiric condition to his victim. The most unique point, as you have started to discover at this point in the novel, is that even though Varney is an evil being, needing to kill to live, he has a more complex nature than one might imagine and actually emerges as an honorable person with feelings for others. This undead has a touch of the Tin Man's heart.

The major problem with the book, and probably the main reason Rymer tried to distance himself from it, is that it is very poorly written, having been done so hurriedly and only for profit. The timing of its publication is really what has allowed this story to stand the test of time. Because of its poorly written nature copies were not saved, but instead were read and tossed aside like a modern day beach or airplane paperback. Thus copies became rare.

Unlike Stoker's *Dracula* (which has never been out of print since its initial publication) *Varney* was not published again until 1970 and once again in 1972 in two volumes by Dover press. Thirty years later new generations of genre readers want a copy of one of the basestone vampire novels. Luck for us Wildside Press has taken up the challenge which you now hold so tightly that the blood is draining from your fingers. I hope you enjoy this final installment of *Varney the Vampyre; or, The Feast of Blood.* But remember, I warned you.

– Del Howison
Dark Delicacies
Burbank, CA 2002

Chapter CLVI.

THE STORM. – A SHIPWRECK AT SEA. – THE HAPLESS FATE OF THE MARINERS.

*T*he morning was ushered in with wind and rain; a tempest was howling over the main; the seas lashed the shores with a fury that made it dangerous for even such vessels as were moored; and great fears were entertained that many wrecks would be seen before the night set in. The roar of the ocean and the bellowing of the wind was almost deafening; and the few fishermen and sailors that now and then showed themselves; as they came towards the shore to ascertain the safety of their little barques, could scarcely make themselves heard.

The sky was too heavy, and the rain too incessant, to permit them to see very clearly or very far; they could not see any ships in the offing.

"Neighbor," said one, "did you hear the wind in the night?"

"Hear it!" replied the man spoken to; "could I help it? Who is there that could sleep, while such a tempest was blowing great guns. I never heard anything like it in all my life. God help those poor fellows who are at sea such a night as this."

"So say I, neighbor, so say I; if there be any upon this coast – if any awake with the morning dawn and find themselves upon a lee shore, they will never get off again, depend upon it; they are all lost men."

"So they are; there's no hope for them on this shore; every vessel must, indeed, come upon it, and no aid could be rendered to them."

"You are right, neighbor. I am glad our boats are high and dry; for, if they were not, they would never be on the sea again, except as fragments; every timber in them would be broken to pieces, and scattered about the beach."

"Ay, ay, 'tis an awful day. I propose, neighbor, we should make an attempt to get our boats still higher on the beach; see, the sea comes now within a few boat-lengths of them; a few more waves heaving one upon the other will at last reach them, and, if so, we are, indeed, poor men, neighbor."

"With all my heart; we have no time to lose, neighbor — see, the waves have got nearer yet — come on, come on."

The two fishermen hurried down to the beach; and, with the aid of one or two more, who had hurried onwards with the same object as themselves, that of putting the boats out of danger from the waves, they succeeded; and then they returned, leaving their boats, their only wealth, high above the reach of the most tempestuous sea.

"There, neighbor, I never heard such a sea. I will go and see what can be done in-doors by the fire-side; this is not a day to be out in; you are wet through in about ten minutes, and nothing to do but to look on the black clouds."

"No, neighbor; though I don't think in-doors much better, for I expect our roof to come off, or the chimney to fall over; and must consider myself very fortunate if I do not have the whole house blown down."

"Ay, ay; but I expect to hear of a few accidents. I don't see any vessel coming in the horizon at all — do you see any?"

"None."

"Well, I hope there may be none. I'm for the house; too much of this may be hurtful to a fisherman; so, good day."

"Good day, for the present. I dare say we shall see each other before the day's out, if anything may happen in the shape of wreck."

"Safe and sure to be out."

"If you hear a gun, let me know, if I should not be out; for the wind blows and the sea roars so loudly that I can scarcely hear at all."

"I'll be with you; and do you the same for me, if I should happen to miss it; though I can't tell how that can be, as the wind blows dead in shore."

"It's a bargain — I'll do it."

The two fishermen parted from each other, and entered their own dwellings to escape the fury of the elements; for there was nothing to keep them outside, but there was everything to induce them to stay in-doors — a warm fire and freedom from the wind and rain, though that howled and roared in the chimneys in a frightful manner.

*I*f the aspect of the affairs was bad on the land, it was much worse at sea; for there a vessel rode out the fury of the storm gallantly enough, and resisted the force of the winds and waves for some time; but she could not resist the impetuosity of the elements, though she strove hard and resisted long.

She strained, and timber after timber started, masts were gone, and the rudder became damaged, and at length no hope was left.

The crew was not a large one, and the pumps had become completely choked and useless; while the vessel was drifted hither and thither without any means of guidance whatever; she was at the mercy of wind and waves.

"We are drifting towards the shore," said the mate to the master; "we cannot keep her head out to sea at all."

"I know it," answered the master, gloomily — "I know it; she has been making land for some time now, and as we have neither rudder, nor sails, nor masts, we may as well make our peace, for the worst must soon come."

"I expect that some time ago, when I found that the wind was set dead on shore, and the rudder was gone."

"Surely, we haven't much time to lose; let the guns be fired, as a signal of distress; it may give warning to those on shore."

"We cannot expect assistance."

"Not here, I know."

"Certainly not; no boat would live for a moment in a sea like this."

"No, I know it would not; but it may put them upon the look out, and some of our poor fellows may get picked up; for we don't exactly know how far we may be driven towards the land, and we may be sent right on to the beach, for aught we can tell."

"So we might."

"I hope we may."

"Are the guns ready?"

"Yes, sir, they are loaded; but there is only one barrel of powder dry."

"Let it be cared for; fire the guns."

The order was promptly obeyed, for the men had left off pumping, conceiving it useless to continue it any longer; indeed; they could not, for the pumps were no longer serviceable, and they saw the land ahead, and each man made up his mind that the struggle for life was about to commence; while the firing of the guns was a measure of precaution which might, or might not, be of use; and as every one clung to hope to the last, the order was obeyed with alacrity.

The guns were fired in minute intervals, and at length every half minute while the powder lasted, and then they ceased.

There was not more than from fifteen to twenty souls on board; but there were several passengers among them; one in particular was remarkable for his height, and the singular pallid hue of his features.

He was reserved, but of gentlemanly deportment; he was well aware of his danger, but it did not appear to render him incapable of seeing and understanding what was going on; but he was grave and melancholy.

"How long, captain, do you think it will be," he said, approaching the master, "before the vessel will break up; for I see that we shall be wrecked, that is no secret at all to any of us, and certainly not to me."

"I don't know," replied the captain; "it is impossible to say."

"Cannot you form an opinion upon the subject?" inquired the stranger.

"I can; but it is only an opinion. I can give you no information," replied the captain, who did not wish to give an opinion upon such a subject.

"Certainly, I am aware of that. I asked for an opinion; if you have one, perhaps you may be good enough to favor me with it, if it be not too great a favor to expect from you, sir. I thought you had experience enough to enable you to form an opinion, and it was for that reason I asked you."

"Well, sir, we strike in five minutes, perhaps in twenty; it depends upon wind and waves, our course, and how far we may go ashore."

"I understand you; if we are forced in upon the shore in a direct line, we may expect the shortest time."

"We may."

"And if we should not meet with any obstruction, we may be thrown far on shore."

"Yes; if we had but the means of guiding the vessel, I could steer her within fifty or a hundred yards of the shore, where she would strike, and a better chance would then be had of some reaching the shore."

"Which is now rather more than uncertain."

"It is so," said the master.

At the moment there was such a shock from the vessel striking upon a sunken rock, that they were all thrown down on the deck, and the sea made a clear breach over her, and swept away several of the crew.

The master contrived for a moment or two to secure himself to a spar, with the hope that he would be able to float off; but this was a vain hope, for a moment after he was lifted up by a sea, and dashed against the stump of the mast, and crushed in a horrible manner, his blood dying the deck for a minute, and then it was washed away, as he himself was by the same wave, and was not seen again.

The master no doubt had been killed, and there was nearly all of the crew swept away; but among those who yet survived, was to be seen the tall stranger, who stood in the storm, and held on by a portion of the vessel; he still braved the fury of the waves as they broke over the deck clearing all before them.

Each breach of the sea made away with some one of the unhappy mariners who yet clung with hopeless desperation; but yet they feared to quit their last hold, and to throw themselves into the foam that was boiling around them.

In the meantime the vessel heeled about, and every now and then, being in shallow water, a great wave would come and lift her up, and then leave her higher on the rocks, but giving her each time dreadful shocks, and breaking her keel up.

The only hope the unfortunate men had, was that some portion of the wreck upon which they might chance to be, would be floated to the shore before life was extinct; but this was more and more hopeless, for the breakers over which they would have to float would probably be their destruction, for they would be dashed to pieces.

The wind and the waves howled and roared, and drowned all noise – nothing could be heard, and nothing seen, for the waves broke over them so furiously, and raged so high above them, that they neither could do so, nor even see the shore. Nothing but a white sea of foam and spray met their eyes, whenever they cold raise them, and free them from salt water.

At length an immense wave came rolling towards them; the men shrieked as the flood came onwards. In a moment afterwards they were lifted up, vessel and all, and carried a few yards further onwards and then left, with a report that seemed like that of a cannon to them; but they felt the shock, and when the wave left them, the vessel was no more; a mere mass of boards and other matters floated about; she had been utterly and entirely destroyed; no vestige of her was left, and nothing but a confused mass of planks was to be seen, with here and there a human being clinging to them for life. But, alas! their efforts were vain – they sank – they could not sustain the battle with the waves and the breakers; they were dashed to mummies, and every limb broken on the foaming, raging breakers.

Chapter CLVII.

THE FISHERMEN. – THE DESPAIRING CRY OF THE MARINERS. – THE BREAKERS FROM THE SHORE.

On shore the day wore away; the wind blew furiously, and the oceans roared to such an extent, that no other sound was audible; and the fishermen who lived upon the coast kept within doors, knowing that nothing could be done out of doors on such a day; and each one seated by the fire, began to recount some wonderful tale of death and shipwreck, or of happy escapes from the boiling sea, until noon had long since passed, and the turn of the day showed a decided approach towards evening; but no abatement of the tempest.

The principal fisherman on the coast, a man whose poverty was less, rather than his wealth was greater than his fellows, sat by his fireside, with one or two others of his class seated with him.

"I never saw a worse storm," said one of them.

"I have," said Massallo, the fisherman.

"You have?" said one of his comrades, in his turn.

"I have, I can promise you — one that blew me upon this coast, where I have ever since remained, and intend to remain."

"I have heard you say so; but I never heard the particulars of that story; it must have been many years ago, I fancy."

"Yes, it must have been fifteen years ago," said Massallo, speaking; "fifteen years ago at the very least, if not more than that."

"Well, I think it must be quite that time; for my old man has been dead these fourteen years, and he remembered you very well, and used to speak of you; and, as I thought, you must have known him more than a year."

"Aye, two."

"Well, it must, then, have been more than sixteen years ago since you came here."

"I dare say it was; very nearly seventeen years ago, now I come to think of it. The storm, if possible, blew harder, and the waves beat higher than they do now; the rain was heavier than it rains now; and, in addition to all, the thunder and lightning were tremendous, not a sound could be distinguished. The speaking-trumpet was useless — no sound issued from it — all was confusion and danger."

"It must have been a rare time, certainly."

"It was a time for devils to be abroad, and not for men; but we were compelled to pump, and cut away the wreck. Why, you see, we had been chased by the Algerines, and we had got nearer to the land than we would have gone, but for the fact that we desired to escape from a superior and formidable enemy, who knew no mercy.

"Yes, the Algerines, if they had spared us, would have made slaves of us for our lives, and there would have been little wisdom in being caught by them, if we could help it."

"I should imagine no one would ever do it."

"Well, that was the cause of our being in shore nearer than we ought; but we noticed that the Algerine sheered off at a moment when there was but little chance of our escaping him; but we could not tell the reason; but we concluded that he saw some danger, of which we were at that moment ignorant.

"Well, we had not time to haul out a little before we were surprised by a tremendous clap of thunder and lightning, as vivid as if it had been brought from all quarters of the world, and loosened at one and the same moment."

"It must have added to your terrors."

"It was the main thing that wrecked us on this coast."

"What, the lightning! why, I suppose it struck you, then?"

"Yes; we could have held off, or run the vessel bump ashore — almost dry — but we lost all command over her, when the lighting shivered our mast to atoms and left the stump burning in the vessel; then, more than that, it killed two of our best hands at that moment, and most of us were knocked up and unable to work at the pumps; but it was of no use; we came ashore, crash went the vessel, and we were all in the boiling sea in an instant, and a wave or two more threw me on the beach, without any fatal injury, and I scrambled up out of their reach."

"And then you remained by us."

"Yes; I did not find means to return whence I came for some years."

"Perhaps you had reason."

"I had; I was a rival for a girl; I was then endeavoring to win money; I had entrusted some money in the vessel — all I had; and with her I lost all, and with that all I lost even hope, and never returned to my native home."

"Did the girl love you?"

"She liked me well enough to have me, if her relations would consent, but they would not, unless they saw I had more money than I could obtain; and, in default of that, they would marry her to another, who had more money than I; and I only obtained time to get money by the girl's intercession; but I was baulked."

"Well, that was bad; but I suppose you were well assured that you would be rejected if you had not money."

"I was, by her family."

"And herself——"

"That was not so sure; and yet they had great influence upon her; but I could not have the courage to go back and ask her to wed poverty; a man without even the means of purchasing a wedding garment."

"You did right, neighbor."

"I did, and I knew it," replied the fisherman, bitterly.

"But you have prospered since; and you have been happy, if I mistake not."

"Yes, I have been prosperous, and tolerably happy; it is wonderful how men adapt themselves to the circumstances around them."

"They do; if they did not, how insupportable would life be."

"You are right; I should have been miserable for ever; I should never have recovered my feelings, and should never have been what I am now."

"The storm seems as furious as ever, neighbor," observed one of the fishermen, after a long pause, for they were meditating upon what they had heard, "and I think we shall have but a very rough night of it."

"Good; we shall have a night of it."

"I think," said another, "I must be getting near my own fireside by this time; they will expect me home, or think some accident has happened."

"And I will step out to see how the weather looks before it grows dark; there appears no change."

"Hark! what is that?"

There was a moment's pause, and in about a minute, in one of the lulls of the wind, they thought they heard a gun; but the storm increased so as to leave them in great doubt of what it was.

"It was a gun, I think," said the fisherman. "Such sounds as those I have heard before; but 'tis hard to tell them form the sounds of the elements."

"We can tell when we get outside, I dare say; but the wind sweeps all sounds past so rapidly that it is scarcely possible to tell even there; but there is yet light to see, and as the sun sets in the horizon, we have a chance of seeing a sail if there be one."

"We have, but not of helping her."

"True; there is no help for those on board."

"May Heaven have mercy upon the poor mariners," said the fisherman's wife. "It is hard times with them now. Life is dear to all, and they will cling to it. Do what you can for the poor beings."

"There's no doing anything," said the fisherman, gloomily. "Neither boat nor ship can ride through such a sea, on the ocean or at anchor."

"But they may be cast ashore, and they may not be quite dead, you know; instant aid might avail much, when even they had ceased to feel."

"We will not fail in that particular. We are going down to the beach now, and shall not neglect any means that are in our power, at all events; more we cannot do, but that much shall be done, and I hope it may be of some service."

"Hark! the same sound again," said his companion.

"I did not hear it."

"Nor I."

"Come on; we shall now know better in the open air," said the fisherman, as he wrapped himself up in a large rough coat, and pulled his hat over his eyes. "The rain is as heavy as ever, and I think it will soon fill the sea to overflowing."

The fisherman left the hut and proceeded towards the beach; at least, they did not go down, for the waves ran so high that they beat a long way inland — more so than they had ever done before.

"What do you think of our storm?"

"It is a complete tempest — furious; and the wind blows the waves towards the shore, and that is the cause why we have the sea so high; and should the wind continue in that quarter for a day or two, even our cottages will be in some danger."

"I dare say they would; but it would be without example if the winds were to continue in that quarter for so long a time, blowing a complete hurricane without any intermission. I should almost think the world about to end."

"Do you see any vessel out in the horizon?" inquired one of the fishermen.

"Not I."

"But I can hear the gun."

There came booming across the waters the sound of a piece of artillery. There was no mistaking it — it was plain and evident to all that there was a vessel in distress somewhere, but they could not exactly tell where.

Again the sound reached them on the wind, accompanied by the roar of the elements; but it was enough to distinguish it by from the rest of those awful sounds, which spoke plainly to them of the dreadful fate of the unfortunate men who were on board the vessel in distress.

"Can you make them out?" inquired one of the fishermen of his companion. "I cannot see her, though I hear the guns, and can almost imagine her whereabouts."

"No, I can't see her," replied the man spoken to.

"I can though," replied the first fisherman; "she lies close in shore, not a mile out, nor yet that. I think she's dismasted."

"I see her now, myself. I looked about in the horizon, above her there. She labors much, and the sea breaks over her."

"She has lost her rudder, I have no doubt, and is drifting right in shore. What will become of them, I cannot well think."

"It is too easy to think."

"Do you imagine that one man among the whole crew can be saved?"

"Hardly, on such a shore as this, with rocks on all sides; every man that is swept overboard will be dashed to pieces, and disabled, even if lashed to spars."

"You are right; for if one man survives this wreck, it will be a miracle, and I can hardly believe it to be possible."

They now watched the course of the vessel. The guns had ceased to fire, and daylight was fast departing; and though she came nearer, yet she became less distinct; but still they could see her, and note her progress well through the surf that rose up around her as it dashed against the laboring vessel's side.

"She strikes," cried one of the men; "that shivering action is her first shock."

"Yes," said a companion. "Poor wretches, they have but a short time now. She will go to pieces on those rocks as sure as they are there."

"May she not hold together?"

"No; see, she heaves up again! No; as there are but bare rocks under her, and she will not settle into any place, but continue beating and bumping upon them until she will break and split to shivers, not a timber can hold."

"Too true — too true," said his companion.

The fishermen now bent their eyes upon the ocean, where this exciting scene was going on, but they spoke not. It was growing yet darker, and yet they gazed steadfastly, heedless of the beating and overwhelming rain; but they could hardly see the vessel, until at length a loud shriek came to them, borne to them upon the hoarse winds, and heard distinctly above the roaring of the ocean.

The fisherman knit his brows, and compressed his lips, as he heard the sounds, and then, clasping his hands, he said, —

"Heaven have mercy on them! for I fear the sea will have none. It's all over, and they are dead and dying. Follow me!"

Chapter CLVIII.

THE ONE BODY WASHED ASHORE. – THE FIRST REQUEST. –
THE SHIPWRECKED STRANGER.

*T*he fishermen followed down towards the beach, for they had been standing upon some cliffs which commanded the sea below, which now was one dark boiling mass, in which nothing at all was distinguishable; and, therefore, they could not tell what went on below.

They soon arrived at the little bay, in which their fishing-boats used to ride; but they had been drawn up beyond the reach of the sea, though the sea now ran quite up into the land, and they stood watching the waves as they rolled upwards.

"Had we not drawn our boats higher," said one "they would have been wrecks by this time, and we should have been beggars."

"Ay; so we should, neighbor."

"Don't you see the waves beating over the very spot were they lay?"

"I do; and they ain't far from them even now, and I am in some fear lest they reach them; but they have been moored as well."

"They are doubly secured."

"Do you see anything upon the water yet?" inquired the first fisherman.

"Nothing."

"Nor I, and I have strained my eyes to their utmost. They are most likely all dashed to pieces, and they are not likely to live through such a sea."

"No, no; they must be overwhelmed with water. God help them, poor fellows! and if they are not to be saved, may they soon have an end to their tortures, for the strife after life must be dreadful."

"It is dreadful," said the other; "but you must know that the sufferings are endured under excitement, and therefore not so much felt as when they have been saved. To have passed the barrier of life, and to become insensible to all, and then to be recalled to life, is an agony not to be described. I have seen men who have been restored to life, and who have solemnly declared that the pangs of death they could encounter, and not those of a return to life."

The fisherman made no reply, but stood listening to the howlings of the storm, and watching the waves; but this was productive of nothing – they watched for more than two hours, and yet nothing came ashore.

"I don't see we can do any good here," said one.

"Nor I. Those who were alive, must now have been dead some time."

"Yes; the sea don't wash them this way."

"Most likely," added another, "they are washed among the breakers, and dashed against the cliffs, and therefore cannot reach this place, where they can reach the land."

"It usually happens so."

"It does; but we may as well return. There is a wreck, no doubt."

"That is quite settled."

"Quite, as you say; but there are no signs of it."

"Save such as you saw."

"Yes; we have evidence enough of the fact. We saw her go to pieces, and we have heard the death-shriek of the mariners, and more we cannot have seen. When we come down here in the morning, we may indeed see the bodies, and the broken and severed planks of the unfortunate vessel, strewn over the sands."

"I shall return again after I have had an hour or two's turn in," said the fisherman.

"Give me a call," said his companion, "and I will go with you."

"And I."

"Agreed. Then about midnight we will again visit the beach, and see if any of the men are ashore."

*T*here was no one now by the shore, and naught save the sounds of the turmoil of the elements could be heard. What other sounds can be any possibility be distinguishable at such a time? There was nothing that could be done there that would sound. The loud roar of the breakers was tremendous; the dash of the waves against the cliffs, and the steady bellowing of the wind, which sounded not much unlike a steady and continued report of great guns fired at a distance, were as but one sound and that sound of a strange, awful, and furious character – perfectly dreadful.

There was one body, however thrown up by the waves, as if they would yield that one alone, and no other, or as if that one was the only one they refused to swallow; it floated about for some time, and was thrown hither and thither, now thrown on shore by one wave, and withdrawn by another.

At last a high wave came rolling onwards, and falling upon the shore, it lifted the body up, and carried it further upon the beach and there left it, and no subsequent wave came so far as that, and it was left unmolested.

That body was the carcass of the stranger, who of all the rest had been swept towards the little bay, and deposited there alone.

*T*he fisherman left his hut to call his companions, and having done so, they came towards the beach, while they conversed together.

"Well," said one, "I did not expect to see the storm abate so soon."

"I did not," replied his companion, "though, I dare say, it was much too violent to last much longer; and yet I can scarcely credit my senses that it is really gone, and that the deluging rain has ceased altogether."

"Yes; and there comes the moon peeping behind that mass of clouds."

"The wind blows stiffly yet; but it has greatly moderated, and I think it will continue to do so."

"I hope it may; but the sea does not abate a bit, and will not for many hours, even if the wind was to go down."

"Oh, dear, no; the waves will keep on in this fashion for some hours; and I dare say it will be useless to get our boats out; we shall not have any more fish for some days to come."

"Most likely not; but I would not venture to go out while the sea is heaving, after such a storm as this; there would be but little use in doing so, I am quite persuaded; but what is that yonder?"

"Where — I see nothing?"

"There, lying a few yards from the reach of the waves; to me it looks like a human body. It is quite quiet and still — no motion — it is, I fear, dead; there is no motion, and the attitude is that of one who has not moved after he was thrown there — I think not, however; but let us see what it is."

The fishermen now went down unto the beach, where the body lay, for such it really was; and, when they reached it, at once saw it was a human body, and they all paused before it.

"Bring it higher up on the beach; the waves may come upon you presently — they are high enough. Bring him up higher on the beach, and you will then see what state he is in; for if his limbs are broken, and his body otherwise injured to any extent, you may spare much useless labor."

The fishermen drew the body up higher; they then carried him to a dry and sheltered spot, and examined him, but found no particular injuries to speak of, but that he was apparently drowned.

"What course to pursue," said one, "I don't know; no doubt but he is quite dead; he must have been in the water several hours, besides being knocked about on the breakers, which is enough to destroy life itself."

"I should imagine so; and yet, we had better take it up to the cottage, and place it under cover; indeed, we cannot tell how long it has been thus; therefore, I say we had better make some attempt to recover him; he may yet come round, though there may be but little hope in it."

"We will try; stand out of the moonlight — we shall be able to see presently better what he is, than we can now."

The moon was now freed from the mass of deep heavy clouds that hung over it, like a curtain before that luminary, and which now shed a brilliant light upon the earth. The fishermen stood round gazing upon the body of the stranger.

"Ha! it moves," said one.

The body did move, and no sooner did the moonlight fall full and fair upon its form, than it slowly raised itself upon its elbow, and gazed around. A deep inspiration took place, almost a groan, and some sea water was vomited.

"He lives — he lives!" exclaimed the fisherman.

"Take him to the hut," said another.

They all stooped down to aid him, and began to lift him up.

"He lives — he lives!"

"Away with him to the hut," said several of the fishermen. "Before a warm fire, and with some warm drinks, he will get better."

"A little more light — a little more light, if you please," said the stranger, in a bland but broken voice, as he attempted to move his hand.

"He speaks!" exclaimed the fishermen in a breath, and at the same time they removed a pace or two, and looked at each other with amazement, and then again at the stranger, who gradually rose up, and sat upright in the light of the moon.

"Are you any better?" inquired one of the men who had looked on in silent amazement, not unmixed with awe, as they gazed.

"Yes; much better. What a vile thing is sea water," said the stranger, turning such a ghastly face upon the men that they shrunk in horror, and yet they were not men used to fear or any like passion.

However, they soon approached him, muttering to each other, —

"What manner of man is this?"

They did not long consider what was to be done, for one of their number replied, —

"Poor fellow! he is not used to the rough usage of the waves, and therefore does not improve upon their acquaintance. But let us lend him a hand."

"With all my heart," replied his comrades.

"Will you come with me to my cottage?" said the fisherman. "You will benefit more by a good fire than by the cold moonlight, I'll warrant. I never throve upon night air and wet clothes, and I cannot believe you will."

"We all know our constitutions best," said the stranger; "but if you will grant me the accommodation you speak of, it will be welcome."

"Come, lean upon me; never mind your clothes being wet."

The stranger rose, and, to the amazement of all, he appeared to walk as well as any of those present; and the only difference was, he was ghastly pale, and he was dripping with sea water, which left a track after him.

"Had you been long on the beach?" inquired one.

"I don't know," replied the stranger. "I was insensible."

"Can you form any idea how long you have been in the water?"

"I really cannot tell even that; for I was insensible immediately after the ship went to pieces, which she did about the close of the day; and I only remember receiving a hard blow by being struck against a rock, or a piece of timber, I cannot say which."

"You must have been insensible for some hours."

"I dare say I was."

"I never heard of such a miraculous preservation."

"Nor I."

"To come to life, too, without any aid to recover you, that is what entirely bothers me."

"Well, they do say, those that are born to be hanged will never be drowned," added one of the fishermen, in an under tone, to his companion.

They soon arrived at the hut of the fisherman, in which there was a good fire, and the wife and daughter were ready to do all that could be done for the unfortunate stranger.

"You have saved a mariner, then?" said the wife.

"We have picked up one from the wreck, wife; but we cannot call him a mariner. This gentleman was, no doubt, a passenger."

"Welcome, sir! I did not expect to see any one alive from the wreck, much less in condition to walk an speak."

The stranger paid them some compliments; but contented himself with sitting by the fire, and being entirely passive in their hands, and eventually retired to rest well wrapped up and warm.

Chapter *CLIX.*

THE FISHERMAN'S COTTAGE. – THE FIRESIDE, AND THE TRAVELER'S BED.

*T*he fisherman's hut was large and roomy. There was no choice furniture, though there was enough of the homely conveniences that were to be found in such habitations — much more so than is usual. There was a large fire-place, upon which some faggots had been newly laid, and which now blazed away most cheerfully.

"Our home is humble, sir," said the fisherman; "but such as it is, you are welcome to it, and may it serve you instead of a better."

"I am much beholden to you," replied the stranger; "much beholden to you, and cannot thank you enough. This change is most valuable. I do not know in what state I should have been, had you not come forward and offered the shelter of your house to me. I am very cold, indeed, and the warmth of your fire is grateful to me."

"I am glad of it, sir. You are the only one, I fear, as far as I know, that is saved. Was there many on board?"

"About twenty, I think."

"Poor fellows! they have met with a watery grave."

"Yes, they have, I fear. They have had a fearful struggle, for many were lashed to spars, hoping they might be washed, or floated, ashore. I hope I am not disturbing, though I fear I am, your wife and daughter — that is your daughter, I presume, if I may judge from her likeness to yourself."

"Yes, sir, that is my daughter; she's a good girl, sir, though I say so, that am her father; and if a secret must be told, in another month she will exchange a father's for a husband's control and care, which will I hope, be a happy change."

"They have long loved each other," said the mother, "and, to my mind, it is cruel to keep them apart. Times will never be better, and I don't see but they may begin the world as well as others, with little more than a will to work."

"You are right," said the stranger; "you are right; it was never intended that mankind should wait till circumstances were propitious, or it would have made the desire dependent upon circumstances, too."

"You have hit the right nail, sir — you have spoken the truth; but still we must recommend caution."

"Very right. I wish them joy and prosperity," said the stranger.

There was now a bustle in the cottage. Some of those who had accompanied the stranger into the hut, now departed, while the remainder left a few moments after, in company, leaving the fisherman and his family with their guest.

"Well," said one, "of all the odd looking fish that ever I saw come out of the sea, I think he beats all; not but what I make every allowance, but I cannot make any in such a case, because he has not been drowned."

"He was quite insensible, and had been so for a long time. Don't you remember what he said about his becoming insensible immediately after the ship struck."

"Yes; I heard it all, but hang me if I can understand it. He is as if he had been bled to death, and then came to life."

"He ain't got much of a color."

"No; but more than that, the dreadful deathly, or ashy paleness is fearful; and then his peculiar features, his long hair, flattened to his head by the water, and the teeth in his head, which appear as if they had been set with the express intention of enabling him to catch otters."

"That would be no easy task, either; but I must say, as you say, that there have been better looking men than he, at all events."

*I*n the fisherman's hut the stranger was willingly attended to by the fisherman and his family, without any invidious attention; and when he had changed his habiliments, he seated himself again by the fire, when some warm drinks and other refreshment were given him.

"I did not think to find any one alive when I went down to the beach," said the fisherman. "I thought all were lost."

"And I doubt not but they are all lost, save myself," said the stranger, blandly; "and though I do not appear much hurt by the occurrence, yet I feel as if the whole mass of my blood was changed, and that I should never again be what I was; that, in fact, I shall always carry about me the appearance, and certainly the feeling, of a man torn from the arms of death, and made to live."

"It does affect some people strangely," said the fisherman. "I know what shipwreck is myself, and, therefore, can easily guess what it is to those who are unused to the sea. I was the only one saved out of a whole crew."

"Indeed! then your case is identical with mine."

"In that respect it is," replied the fisherman; "but I was used to the dangers of the sea; and, though that makes no difference when you find yourself in the boiling waters, yet a man who has the fear of wreck constantly before his eyes, can see the danger — take more precaution, and is not so likely to lose that presence of mind which at such times is so valuable."

"So it is; though I took it very quietly, and stood still until I was thrown down by the first shock of the vessel."

"She struck more than once?"

"She did; four or five times; she was thrown upon the rocks in shallow water, I believe, as I understand these matters."

"Yes, it was so," said the fisherman — "it was so."

"Well, it was only when the waves left us that we came down with a dreadful crashing shock, which caused the vessel to shiver as if she had been but a leaf. Well, every time a wave swept towards us, it lifted the vessel off the rock, and carried her a few yards further, sometimes scraping and scratching her keel as she went along; at other times, she was lifted clear of the rocks, and then suddenly thrown upon them with great force, and then every timber separated."

"Just what might be expected."

"And just as it occurred," said the stranger.

"And, of course, the crew were carried into the sea, and drowned."

"Yes; but what became of them — I mean where they were carried to — I cannot tell; but I suppose among the tall rocks that I saw before the wreck. But why was I not carried there and left?"

"It is something that neither you nor I can tell," said the fisherman.

"Perhaps so; but I am safe, and only so to tell the disaster to others, not for a warning; for it can be none, but I am saved."

"You are. Perhaps you would like to lie down for an hour or two before daylight comes, and then we will take a walk down to the shore in the morning, and see if there is anything washed ashore."

"I am tired, and think that it would be of some service, if I can sleep; though I dare say I shall be dreaming of what I have seen and felt, and hardly dare to sleep, so great is the disturbance in my mind."

"Sit up, and welcome, by the fire," said the fisherman; "you can do so; it may be as well, perhaps, too — you may be able to sleep that way."

"No, no, I'll lie down on the boards — I am not particular upon such an occasion; and, as it has turned out, I shall be too much in need of rest to sit up. The warmth of the fire, too, draws me off, I can find, and I dare say you feel it too."

"It has that effect, as much as I am used to it," replied the fisherman; "but do what you please; I shall turn in till daylight, unless you want anything more."

"Nothing, thank you, my good friend, but a place to lie down on, and then I am quite content for the remainder of the night."

"There is a settle up in yon corner where you can sleep; it is rough and homely, but we have nothing otherwise here."

"No apology; I am too thankful for what I have escaped from, and for what I have received, to look hard at the mercies afforded me."

*T*he stranger said no more, but took the fisherman's advice and walked to the settle, and then lay down with his face towards the fire.

"Good night," said the fisherman; "pleasant slumbers."

"The same to you, my friend; I hope I have not dispossessed any of your family of their means of rest. I have, perhaps, deprived them of their bed."

"No, no; sleep in peace; we are all provided for. I sleep here," he said, as he was about to open the door; "and my daughter sleeps there," he added, pointing to a small door. "So, you see, we have our appointed places, and that on which you now sleep is retained for the use of any strange traveler of friend that may need it."

"Then good night," said the stranger, which was returned again by the fisherman, who entered his own room, leaving his guest lying on his bed, and looking around him by the light of the fire, which burned yet for some time.

Chapter CLX.

THE NIGHT IN THE FISHERMAN'S HUT. – THE MIDNIGHT
FEAST OF BLOOD. – THE CHASE, AND THE GUN-SHOT.

*T*he stranger, as he lay, listened to the sounds that were emitted by, and occasionally opened his eyes to gaze upon, the flames, as they ran upwards; he watched the forked tongues as they played about the faggots, and then turned his eyes towards the various parts of the apartment as it was now and then illuminated with its warm glare.

What might have been his feelings after his escape it is difficult to conjecture, for he appeared not inclined to sleep, but to gaze about him and keep watch over the fire, which every now and then blazed up afresh; and his mind appeared to be intent upon something else than merely thinking of the past — there was too much of inquiry and curiosity about it.

"The time has come round again," he muttered; "my blood requires renewal, my strength renovation, and no aliment will do that but maiden's blood."

A horrible expression of countenance came over him that must have caused a feeling of horror to have crept through the veins of any one who might have been near to see him; but, as it was, he was alone, and there was no one to be terrified.

"Yes, yes; I must have that supply, else though the sea may give up its dead, and the earth refuse to cover me, yet I may sink into that sleep I would so willingly escape from; then, indeed, I should suffer what I cannot bear to think of.

"Yet how near have I been to that death from which I have believed it impossible to return; but yet the moonbeams have found me, and I have again been re-animated, and the horrible appetite has returned which must have its periodical meal — its terrible and disgusting repast. It must be done, aye, it must be done."

As he muttered, his lips met, and his long tongue was occasionally thrust out, as if he were anticipating the pleasures of the feast.

"Yes, yes; this very night must renew the life that has been this night restored to me. I must make a fresh attempt. I think he said his daughter lay in yonder chamber; in another hour I will adventure upon this scheme."

His eyes were fixed upon the door, which he appeared to watch and examine with the utmost care and avidity.

He watched, however, for some time, and the flames appeared to subside, and the embers gave out a dull, red glare, and some warmth.

"Now is the moment," he muttered, as he rose softly from his bed; "now is the moment — all are asleep, and stillness reigns around me. I will go and ascertain if all be quiet, and then to my midnight orgies — a feast that shall restore me to my life — my former self."

He crawled out of the bed, and stood upright for a moment, and listened, and then, with a noiseless step, he crept to the door of the fisherman's bedroom, and then listened for some seconds, and muttered as if he were satisfied, —

"Yes, yes; they sleep sound enough, and will not readily awaken."

He then took a small cord, and tied the handle of the door to a nail on the post, so as to offer an impediment to egress from the sleeping-room, and then he went towards the other which the fisherman had told him belonged to his daughter. He paused, and listened at the door for a few moments, and then he said, —

"Yes, yes; that is the maiden's chamber — that is sure to be her chamber — her father said so, and I have no reason to doubt he told the truth, since he had no cause to lie; here, then, is the casket that contains all my treasure — the elixir vitae of my life — the undefiled blood of a maiden's veins."

He tried the door, but it was secured on the inside.

This, for a moment, disconcerted him, and he took a moment or two to consider what best could be done; and at length he saw a small chink in the wall, which he approached; then, peeping in, he saw that if he could enlarge the hole, he might push his hand in, and open the door by undoing the fastenings.

This was effected by means of a chisel which happened to be lying near at hand; then he opened it, and thrust in his hand and withdrew the bolt that held the door, and quietly opened it.

With cat-like caution he approached the bed where the fisherman's daughter lay. She was a beautiful girl, scarce eighteen, and, by a consent of all, the queen of the place, in respect of beauty.

With greedy eyes the vampyre approached the bed on which lay the form of the sleeping maiden, and gazed upon her fair white neck and bosom — heaving with the sleeper's breath; and then, as if he could contain himself no longer, he eagerly bent down over her, and then, as her face was turned on one side, his lips and teeth approached the side exposed.

A scream ran through the fisherman's hut that awoke its inmates in an instant, and which, though it banished sleep, yet it gave not the power of thought.

"Help! help! help!" screamed the maiden.

"'Tis Mary!" said the fisherman; "surely——"

"Hasten, and see what 'tis that ails her. She never would scream so, unless in utmost peril; hasten, and see."

"Help! help! again screamed the maiden, as she struggled in the arms of the monster, who kept her in his powerful grasp while he sought the life current that crimsoned her veins with horrible desire.

"The door is secured; d——n!" muttered the fisherman. "What does this mean? Give me my gun down, while I force the door."

The old woman handed down the gun, while the fisherman put his strength to the door, which quickly gave way and flew open.

"Here is your gun. Be quick; but do not be too hasty in its use. See to Mary and the shipwrecked voyager."

"Who secured my door, dame, but he?"

"The door! Ay, I remember — hasten!"

"Help — help!" again shouted or screamed Mary, but not in so loud a voice as before; she was getting weaker, and just as the fisherman emerged into the large room, the faggots fell together and gave forth a sudden blaze, and in an instant the whole place was lighted up, and the fisherman's eye sought the couch of the stranger whom he had lodged, but the bed was empty.

"Gone!" he muttered — "gone!"

He turned his head in the direction of his daughter's bedchamber, and saw the door was open, and he heard a struggle and a sucking noise.

"Ha!" he muttered, and rushed in exclaiming — "What means this noise? Who calls for help?"

The appearance of the fisherman was so opportune and so sudden, and so intent was the vampyre upon the hideous meal, that he did not hear the approach of the fisherman, and it was not until the latter shouted that he turned and saw him.

"Treacherous and ungrateful villain!" said the fisherman, who was almost powerless from terror and astonishment.

The vampyre turned and dropped his victim on the bed, while he endeavored to pass the fisherman; but the act recalled him to himself, and he made a blow at him with the but-end of the gun; but the vampyre jumped back, and the blow missed its intended object, and they both closed for a struggle.

The fisherman, however, found that he had one to do with whose strength was even greater than his own, however great that might be; and in a moment more he was thrown down, and the monster rushed across the outer room, oversetting the fisherman's wife; and forcing open the outer door, he fled.

"I am thrown," said the fisherman, rising; "but not done for. Mary, are you hurt?"

"Oh, my God — my God!" exclaimed the poor girl. "He had begun to eat me and suck my blood! I have the marks of his teeth in me."

"I'll have revenge upon him yet."

"Nay, father. He is some monster — do not go!"

"No, no," said his wife — "no, husband, do not attempt it! strong he is; he may do you a mischief."

"I know," said the fisherman. "He has thrown me, and he has abused my hospitality; he is not fit to live. He has not, however, any means of fighting against the contents of my gun. I have got that loaded, and will punish him. Be he man or devil, I will make the experiment of following him."

All this took place in less time than it takes to relate it, and the fisherman rushed out of his hut to follow the stranger who had acted so badly.

It was now early dawn; and, though the waves still lashed the shore in angry violence, and kept up a ceaseless roar, yet the sky betrayed none of the signs of yesterday's storm, but was serene and calm, and not a cloud was to be seen — nothing but a dim, grey night pervaded all space.

There was just light enough to see objects moving about, and when the fisherman got outside the hut, he saw, about a hundred yards or better before him, the form of the stranger, making for the woodland at the height of his speed.

The fisherman hastened to intercept him which, however, was unnecessary, for another, coming from that quarter, turned him, and he fled towards the sea, whither he was followed, and, when upon the cliffs, the fisherman fired, and the vampyre fell over and was supposed to have been drowned.

Chapter CLXI.

THE ASSASSINS ON THE RIALTO. – THE ATTACK AND DEFEAT. – THE STRANGER.

On the Rialto, one evening, as the sun was sinking in the golden west, a stranger was seen walking to and fro in deep musing, apparently unmindful of what was passing around him, or of the approach of evening, an hour when the remorseless assassin is known to stalk abroad in the streets of Venice, and there the dagger finds is victim.

Several individuals looked hard at the stranger in the cloak, but no one approached him, save those who passed him, and in doing so bestowed a passing gaze upon him, which was not returned, for he heeded no one. But he was not much open to recognition even if he were known, for the cloak with which he had enveloped himself was of such ample dimensions that it completely concealed him from the curiosity of the many; indeed, his face was hardly visible, for the fur collar he wore hid all save the bridge of a prominent nose, and his eyes, which had a peculiar luster.

The evening still grew darker and later, and the passengers were fewer and fewer, but still the tall stranger walked slowly up and down; but no one ventured to say anything, though more than one had the inclination to speak; but the tallness of the man, and the point of the long rapier which appeared beneath the cloak, checked any inclination to familiarity, and induced a more voluntary courtesy than might at all times have been accorded.

There were, indeed, a small knot of three individuals, who kept near the same place, and whose eyes every now and then directed their glances towards the stranger, as if they regarded him with impatience.

These men were of a suspicious character; they all wore cloaks and slouched hats, but they had all seen some service, and were somewhat the worse for it. They conversed together, and walked away for a short space, but they returned presently, and still found the stranger as before at the same spot.

"Well," said one of the three, as they again met at a certain spot, "what think you now — is he a spy or not?"

"I don't know what to think, Rubino. Spy or no spy, he will interfere with our duty tonight. I wonder what is best."

"What do you mean?"

"Why, would it be better to chance his presence, or shall we put him away? He evidently intends remaining there, the devil only knows how long."

"I believe you; but it appears to me that both plans are objectionable to the last degree, though I confess I can see no alternative whatever."

"Which do you consider the least objectionable plan? — that is what we have to consider, for there are but two plans, and we cannot fail to do our business; should we do so, we should lose something, and we should never get any more employment."

"Good. If we attack him, we shall lose our chance with our better customer. We shall lose our man, at the least, if we get clear."

"He wears a long sword, and is a tall man. If he has any skill, and I dare be sworn he has, he will prove an ugly customer."

"We are three."

"That is very true; but an encounter only makes it the worse, and even if he be killed, which, if we are true to ourselves, he must be, we shall be obliged to quit the spot, and our main object defeated."

"That is most true; but shall we risk the attempt when there are two?

It will make it too many odds; we shall not be so sure of success as we ought to be."

"We have the advantage of striking when we are not seen. A blow is sure when no hand is raised to ward it off."

"Ay, we should dispose of one before he has made any resistance, and before the other can offer any opposition or attempt any assistance, should the first have life enough to call out. Come, come, let's have no fear of the result; it is all in our own hands."

"Shall we not run more danger during the encounter of being taken by others who may come up, attracted by the fray? There is much to be said about making an alarm, because numbers will then be drawn upon us, and you know we have little sympathy among the multitude."

"No, no; we must make all possible haste, and then we may elude all possible chance. Strike the blow home, and then we may baffle all; for if he cry, he will fall, and those who help him, will raise him, and we shall have time to make our escape."

"No doubt — no doubt; 'tis a good plan — a very good plan, and one that I think will succeed; at all events, it only wants a good trial to make it succeed; you see, a strong arm, quick eye, and swift foot, is all that are necessary."

"I see; and one more quality."

"What is it?"

"Good luck."

"Granted; but that often comes from the manner in which a thing is done, and sometimes from the want of skill in those who should make it the reverse. Confusion for a moment gives us our luck, and then we are safe."

"So we are."

"How goes the time, Rubino?" inquired one of the assassins, for such they were.

"Oh, it yet wants one hour of the time in which we are to meet him."

"Well, then, we have more than a chance yet of our being undisturbed here, and the stranger may leave for some other part of the city; but our plan is fixed whether or no. Shall we turn into a vintner's?"

"No; we have no time for that, as yet."

"No time! What mean you Rubino?"

"That we have no time," replied Rubino, "to quit this neighborhood, because you will perceive he may come any time these next two hours, which is a matter of some importance; for if he reach home alive, we have miscarried, and incur great displeasure, if not vengeance."

"We care but little for the vengeance of another."

"We may not individually; but you must know, this one knows too much of us and our haunts to be a safe and pleasant enemy; besides, we shall lose a liberal patron — one who has given us some gold and promised us more."

"Ay, ay; he's the man to serve, and we will not disoblige him; we'll deal fairly by him, and he cannot expect more."

"And he will reward us liberally."

"Amen, say I. Now we have waited long enough, let us walk down the Rialto, and when we get to the other end, we can plant ourselves in such a position to watch his advance towards us, and then we can walk to him."

"Had we better not remain somewhere nearer at hand, because we can then start on him unawares, and thus have a blow without alarming him; and, if that be a deadly one, why, then we are safe. No one will know the mischief is done."

"So much the better; but come, we will continue our walk; it will lull suspicion, and when we come again, one of our number can creep into one of these alcoves, and there wait against his coming."

"And you will be at hand?"

"Of course; we shall keep upon the look out, so as to be near at the moment you commence the attack."

"But suppose I should fall?"

"Then you must continue the attack in a sharp and rapid manner, engaging all his attention to defend himself."

"Ay; and leave me to myself to the attack of that man yonder, should he be at hand at that moment."

"Oh, no, no. Do not hurt yourself. You need be under no fear of that sort, for you see it will only be man to man, and a fair encounter."

"It has never yet been fairly done, and will not be with me in this matter, don't you see. If help arrives, I'm lost; and, if I be lost without help, it will be the worse for you. I'll take my share of danger and mishap, but I won't be imposed upon by a comrade, and so you will understand it first."

"Who was desirous you should? Shall we not be at hand?"

"At your heels, I expect; but don't you see that, by giving a minute's time, you endanger all; for, if my first attack fail, he ought not to be allowed rallying time; he ought not to be permitted to recover himself, and attempt defense, indeed, because that gives time, and we may be beat by others coming from whatever quarter we may go."

"We do not intend it. We only are desirous that one of us should be prepared to make the attack, while we are walking to and fro, and perhaps attracting his attention, and drawing it from you. Then we aid you; but, should you be foiled, why we will hasten as if we were coming to help him."

"I see; well, let it be so."

"Good. We can then act effectively, and we are the gainers by this stratagem. Now then, Roberto, do thou hide thyself in yonder alcove."

"I will. My dagger is sharp, and you know my arm is not usually a weak one, and that I have done some service with it ere now."

"Thou hast."

"And it will again do more."

"Hush! hasten in. I hear footsteps yonder. 'Tis he, I think. We will not go far, but within the reach of your eye; fifty yards, at most, will be the distance. We will take and come towards you the moment we find he has reached you."

"Good. Begone – he comes."

The assassin stole into an alcove, and then paused in the deep shade of the place where he had concealed himself, and the other two walked down a short distance – about a hundred and fifty yards or so – and then paused and looked back.

"Do you see anything of them?"

"No; I don't at this moment. It is getting very dark."

"We had better return and see what happens. We shall get up in the very nick of time, and be able to take part in the fray."

"Well, be it so," replied the other. "I'll go with you; but we run some risk in encountering the stranger in the rapier and long cloak."

"Most true; but we shall not have taken any part in the affair; that will clear us of anything that may tend to inculpate us. We are right; and, if we find our comrade hardly pressed, we can aid him, and that at a time when it is unexpected by the other party. Hark! they are at it already."

"Come on."

They both hastened towards the scene of combat, towards which they both ran, for they knew their comrade's voice.

The other villain awaited the coming of the stranger, whom he was waiting to assassinate, as soon as hi comrades had left him.

The unconscious stranger walked down the Rialto with a slow and steady gait, humming an air from some opera as he walked along, well pleased in his own mind. He wore his cloak open in front, and his sword dangling at his side, and altogether most unsuspicious of an attack.

Scarcely, however, had he passed the assassin's hiding-place, than the fellow rushed out and made a desperate blow at him with his dagger, which, however, miscarried, on account of the loose manner in which he wore his cloak; the blow was foiled by the folds of the garment, and the wearer turned round.

"Villain!" he exclaimed, "thou shalt have thy deserts;" and, as he spoke, he drew his sword, and became the assailant in his turn.

"Help! help!" shouted the villain, who found himself beset by one who would quickly make him repent his temerity.

At that moment the rest of the assassins came up, and commenced a furious attack upon the single stranger, who, of course, from being almost a victor, was immediately compelled to give ground to the three.

"Help! help!" shouted the stranger, as he was forced on one knee, and that with a wound; but at that moment help was at hand, and the tall stranger stepped up to his side, and casting his cloak on one side, and drawing his rapier, he ran one of the assailants through the body and he fell backwards dead.

A furious combat ensued between the stranger and the other two assassins, who were compelled to fight, so closely were they pressed by the stranger; however, after a few moments, they turned and fled.

The stranger then turned towards the wounded man, who was rising from the ground by the help of the pillar that was supporting the sides of the alcove, and then endeavored to stanch the wound he had received.

Chapter CLXII.

COUNT POLLIDORI'S PALACE. – SIGNORA ISABELLA, THE COUNT'S DAUGHTER. – THE INTRODUCTION.

*T*he stranger walked up to him and offered his services, saying, – "Are you hurt, signor? – you bleed!"

"But slightly hurt, signor, thank you for that; you have saved my life. I had been cold meat, indeed – a bloody corpse for all Venice to look upon tomorrow, but for your valor and stout assistance."

"Name it not, signor; but the rascals have been well paid. There lies one of them – the others have escaped; but permit me, signor, to say, that the sooner you get away from this spot the better, for the knaves may return in greater force than before, or they will wait till you leave; by that time they will have rallied, and dart out upon you as you pass along."

"I do not fear that, signor, much; but the fact is, I am almost too weak to walk unaided."

"Permit me to render you the assistance you require. I am a stranger in this place, and therefore unused to your ways; but —"

"Say no more, signor; I will accept of your services if you will accept of a lodging at my poor home. I have that which shall make you welcome — heartily welcome; and the signora, my daughter, shall make you welcome, too."

"Signor, if I can be of service to you I will do so with pleasure. Lend me your arm, signor; but your wound is not stanched — let me bind it more carefully and securely; you ought not to bleed from such a wound when bandaged."

"Perhaps, signor, you have had more to do with these matters than I. I am a peaceable Venetian of rank, and neither afraid nor unwilling to draw a sword in a good quarrel, shrinking not from some odds, but I have had no practice in these matters; times and circumstances have not been propitious."

"It matters not," replied the stranger; "you shewed what you were when you had nearly defeated one, and afterwards kept at bay three. He must be a man who can behave thus, sir; he must have the heart and conduct of a soldier — you would be one did occasion serve — no man can be more; but I have seen many climes, and have therefore some knowledge in these matters beyond the mere inward power and courage. I have, from sheer necessity, been compelled to mix in *melees*, and not from inclination."

"I thank you for your skill as a surgeon, for truly you have stopped the bleeding, which I had not been able to do myself."

"Lean on my shoulder, signor; it will enable you to walk better. Have you far to go?" inquired the stranger.

"No, signor; but we will take a gondola, it will be the easier traveling, and, moreover, it will land us at my house, where you shall be most heartily welcome. If we turn down here, we shall soon obtain the aid of a gondolier. I had intended walking, but I have enough of that for one night, even if I were able to walk, which I am not."

"As you please, signor."

As the stranger spoke he walked towards the place indicated by the wounded man, and in a few moments more they reached the grand canal, and finding a gondolier sleeping in his gondola, the stranger left his wounded companion to wake the sleeper to his duty, by shaking him.

"Hillo!" said the stranger, "will nothing wake you — get up instantly, and about your duty. Do you always sleep here?"

"No, signor," said the man, sleepily.

"Well, then, are you engaged?"

"Yes, signor, if you engage me."

"Well, then, I do."

"Where to, signor?"

"Come with me to bring a wounded gentleman into the gondola, and he will tell you where to. Come, quick — have you not yet awakened?"

"I'm awake, signor, and willing," said the gondolier, following the stranger to the spot where the wounded man was standing, and, by direction of the stranger, he aided the wounded signor into the gondola.

"Now, signors, I have but to know where you desire to go to."

"Row on until I tell you where to stop. Follow the course of the grand canal, and you will go right enough."

There was some time spent in silence, while the gondolier rowed as desired up the grand canal, until they came to a large mansion, which the wounded man gazed upon, and, after a moment's pause, as if he had a difficulty in speaking, he said, as he pointed to the building, —

"There, row up to yonder steps; there I will land — that is my house."

The gondolier immediately obeyed the injunction, and pulled for the stairs, and when they reached the place, the gondolier stepped out and secured the gondola.

"Call out some of my people," said the wounded man, "call them out. I am very stiff, and not able to get out."

The gondolier obeyed, and in a few minutes more several men, all in livery, ran down the steps to the gondola, and lifted their master out, who appeared to be unable to do so of himself.

The gondolier was rewarded according to his deserts, and the stranger followed the wounded man into his own house, which was a most extensive building, and filled with servants, and furnished in the richest manner, displaying magnificence and wealth to a degree that was scarce to be surpassed in Venice.

They were shown into an apartment replete with every appointment that wealth or luxury could suggest, and the wounded ma was placed on a sofa, and his attendants stood round him as if waiting his orders.

"Signor and stranger," he said, "welcome to my house, as the preserver of my life. All I have here is at your service."

"I am obliged," replied the stranger, with a dignified acknowledgement of the courtesy — "I am obliged; but I cannot recognize on my part any such right. If I have done you service — as I will not affect to believe I have not — still you overrate the amount of it. But I will accept of your hospitality for this night; for I am a stranger in Venice, and have little or no knowledge of the best course to pursue."

"Remain here."

"But you had better dispatch some one for aid," interrupted the stranger. "You are in pain, at this very instant; send for some assistance. You require the aid of a leech immediately."

"I am faint — very faint," he replied.

"Hasten," said the stranger — "hasten some of you to fetch a leech, instead of losing your wits in silent astonishment."

The servants immediately bustled about, and seemed to have awakened from a trance, and were seen running in different directions. The room was soon cleared, and the tall stranger seated himself by his wounded host.

"In me you see the Count Polidori."

The stranger bowed.

"I am not a native of this city, though now one of her favored citizens. I have left the land of my birth because I and my rulers could not agree, and I ran some danger in staying against their will, and I have settled and married here."

"Our adopted country is that which demands our care and preference," replied the stranger. "That, at least, is my opinion."

"No doubt. I am now," he continued, "a widower."

"Your lady is dead?"

"Yes; I am sorry to say so. I have, however, one child living at home, and one who is serving his country in her fleets, an honor to our house; but my greatest comfort is the dear image of my lost wife — my daughter."

"Is she here now?"

"Yes; in this palace. Signora Isabella is devoted to her father, and would not for the world do aught that would give me a moment's pain; indeed, she would die for me rather than I should feel displeasure."

"Such a daughter must be a treasure."

"She is a treasure."

"And what an inestimable jewel would she be as a wife."

"She will be when the day comes when she will mate, which I hope will be before I die; for I should be too anxious respecting the worth of the man who was to be her husband, to permit me to die happy, unless I saw and approved of the choice, or chose the individual myself."

"I see you are more anxious," said the stranger, mildly, "in providing future happiness for your daughter, rather than in hoarding wealth or titles for her."

"I am," said the count.

"And a most laudable ambition, too; an ambition that few parents do not neglect in the pursuit of one of a different character — either some young love, or some one who is endowed largely with worldly goods or titles."

"My Isabella will have enough of both; and, therefore, she will not need to seek for them; but she will not throw herself away upon any nameless adventurer who may love her fortune better than herself."

"That would be as cruel a neglect as the other," replied the stranger; "and, in my opinion, more culpable of the two."

"So it would."

At that moment the door opened hastily, and a light step was heard, and before the stranger could turn round, a lovely young female rushed to the side of the count, throwing herself on her knees, saying, —

"Oh, heavens! my dear father, what has happened? Are you hurt? For Heaven's sake, my dear father, what is the matter?"

"Little or nothing, my dear Isabella."

"But you are wounded. Ah! there is blood! My God! my God!"

"Hush, Isabella. I am wounded, but not hurt seriously."

"I pray Heaven it may be so. But what sacrilegious hand could be raised against you? You have wronged no one."

"I am not aware of having done so, certainly," said the count; "but that does not always give any security to the wealthy. They will sometimes destroy them from motives apart from individual revenge."

"The monsters! But have the villains been secured?"

"One has paid the forfeit of his life for his temerity and villainy; the rest fled."

"Ah! what will these assassins not risk?"

"Well, my dear Isabella, I have answered your inquiries, and now, perhaps, you will see if you be alone with me."

"Alone with you!" repeated Isabella, not quite comprehending the words; but she looked up, and her eyes encountered those of the stranger, who was gazing earnestly upon her, and she started, as she rose and said, —

"Excuse me, signor, excuse me — I knew not any one was present."

"Nay," said the stranger, "filial love and respect need no excuse, signora. Do not think so badly of me as to imagine I can think otherwise than you were actuated by the tenderest impulses."

"Your kindness, sir—"

"Isabella," said the count, interrupting her, "but for this gentleman's timely and efficient aid, I should at this moment have been a corpse in the streets of Venice."

"You, my father?"

"Yes, my child. This signor came up just as I was wounded and beaten down, and saved me from death. He killed one of my assailants, while he put to flight the other two, who left their dead companion in the streets. Thank him, my child, for he is my preserver, and he deserves thanks for the deed as well as for the bravery with which it was done, for he ran great risks in such odds."

"He must. Signor, I know not how to thank you or what to say; the greatness of the obligation paralyzes me, and I have not words to tell you how grateful I feel for your goodness and courage; but 'tis an obligation that can never be forgotten or ever repaid — it is impossible."

"My dear signora, permit me to say you rate my services too highly."

"Nay, that is quite impossible; for my father's life I prize far before my own – before anybody in the world; and to save that is to lay me under the heaviest obligation it is possible to impose upon me."

"Say no more, signora; I will not underrate it after what you have said; but you must say as little about it as you will. I am happy, however, to have done any act worthy of your thanks."

Chapter CLXIII.

THE OPINIONS OF DOCTOR PILLETTO. – THE STRANGER'S ACCOUNT OF HIMSELF. – THE WELCOME OF THE SIGNORA.

*A*t that moment the door opened, and a servant announced the arrival of a leech, the famous Doctor Pilletto, who forthwith entered the apartment, and advanced towards the couch on which the wounded man lay.

"Oh, doctor, do what you can for my father," said Signora Isabella.

"I will, signora," replied the doctor. "I will; but what are this hurts or his disease? for I see he has been taken very badly; but why this paleness? You appear to have lost blood."

"I have bled, doctor, and I want you to dress my wound. I am hurt in the side here, and but for my friend here I should have been hurt mortally."

"It was not a duel then?" said the doctor.

"No, no, doctor, no, no; it was an attempt at assassination, and I have escaped the death some one with more enmity than courage had doomed me to; but, at the same time, I am free, and one of his agents has perished."

"'Tis but just," said the doctor; "but I must now see the wound; with your good leave, we'll strip the wounded part and apply bandages to it, so as to secure it; after which something else must be done."

The wounded Pollidori was stripped, and, after some exertion, the wound was dressed, and all bleeding stopped.

"What is your candid opinion concerning my wound, doctor?" inquired the count, "What do you think will be the result? I would be truly informed of whatever probability of danger there may be remote or immediate, as the case may be; tell me, I beseech you, doctor?"

"I will, count."

"I have those things to do which are important, and the execution of them depends upon your answer; so do not mislead me."

"I will not; I cannot form so clear a judgment of your case as I can in a few days hence, when I may see the progress of the wound towards healing; though at present I see no signs of danger, yet some may come."

"You do not consider the wound dangerous of itself?" said the stranger.

"No, not of itself; but it is so close to a mortal part that it cannot be considered free from danger; indeed, it may become so. A little more on one side would have made it quickly fatal; but, as it is, if it heal well, there will be no danger. You must keep your couch for some days."

"That will be a lighter evil than any other," replied the count.

"You have lost much blood, and that alone will make you very weak, and it will take some time before you will be entirely recovered from your present state, and then your wound will probably be healed."

"And what you appear to think may be dangerous, is only any possible interruption from the wound itself."

"It does so happen sometimes from bodily infirmity, it shews itself in healing, and the wound, which now appears healthy, may turn to gangrene, and then the worst may be apprehended."

"It may," said the stranger; "but these things are only the worst that may happen in extreme cases."

"Exactly," said the leech.

"And you have seen nothing in this case to induce you to anticipate any such result as this — it is only what may happen."

"That is all. It appears to me that all is well at present."

"Then I think the count had better be left to himself in quiet, and he may have a good mind upon his recovery."

"It will be best," said the doctor.

"I am fatigued and sleepy," said the count; "I would be alone. Daughter, you must entertain this gentleman as I would do were I able to do so. Signor, the signora will do the office of hostess — excuse so cold a welcome."

"Name it not," said the stranger. "I am well cared for. A welcome from such a one is well worth the acceptance of a prince, much less that of a stranger unknown in Venice. I thank you for it."

"Say no more on that head," said the count. "I came here almost a refugee, and quite a stranger myself."

"Will you come this way, signor," said Signora Isabella; "we will leave my poor father to himself, he will sleep."

The stranger rose, and Doctor Pilletto also, both following the signora, who led them into a separate, but splendid apartment, and entreated them to sit down, and apologized for her own want of spirits to entertain them suitably.

"For that matter," said the doctor, "I am by no means surprised; for such a mishap can never be heard of without producing lowness of spirits."

"And such a misfortune is always productive of grief," said the stranger. "Signora, say no more, I would not interfere with your grief. I do not wish to stop it, and shall feel myself a bar to your own feelings if you say any more. I am made welcome, and feel myself so."

"You are, sir — your kindness deserves no less; but I pray you tell me how this affair occurred, in which you have been of such signal service to my father, in saving his life?"

"To tell you that, signora, I must first tell you who and what I am."

"I do not wish to be thought unduly curious," replied signora.

"Not at all. I am bound to acknowledge you have a right to it, for you have no introduction with me which usually supplies the place of an account of who and what we are; therefore I'll tell you, though I cannot boast of being more than a simple chevalier of now no fortune, having left my country because I raised my voice against the abuses of state; therefore I am but a nameless and fortuneless stranger."

"Many a worthy gentleman has been in such a plight before now," observed the doctor. "I have known many such."

"And I am one. Not that I am without means," added the stranger; "I have been lucky enough to provide against such a calamity as that which has befallen me, though not to the extent I could have wished."

"You are fortunate, chevalier."

"I am so far. I came but this morning to Venice; I landed here, and agreed to meet the captain of the vessel, who promised to meet me on the Rialto, to conduct me to some quiet and respectable changehouse where I could lodge."

"And he met you not?"

"No. While I was waiting for him, I heard a cry for help, and found, upon running up, the Count Pollidori beaten to the earth, beset by three villains, who had already wounded him in the manner you have seen; and I at that time stepped up, and, being unexpected, the men were confused, and one of them fell, mortally wounded; and, after a little further desperate fighting, they all fled."

"It was fortunate you yourself were not beaten down too with such odds; for these men are usually desperate."

"True; but, you see, one was gone, and they could not tell how it might be with the count — they did not know how far he might be able to join in the fray again, and if he were to do so, there would immediately be an equality between us, and such men do not seek such a fight."

"Truly not, chevalier," replied the signora — "truly not. When they are safe and secure in their deeds of blood, they will perpetrate them; but in fair contest such men never shine — their deeds are of darkness."

"Most true — most true."

"But they have a deal of ferocity," said the stranger; "and, when they can, will pour out blood like water; but what amazes me is, that one like the count, your father, should have been beset by such villains. They must have had some object to accomplish in getting rid of him by such means."

"Private enmity."

"Indeed! It must be a bad state of things."

"It is, chevalier. It is a sign of great degeneracy in the state; but it is so. For gold you can procure the death of any man in Venice."

"Horrible!" said the stranger. "I have heard of such things; but I deemed them fabulous, or, at least, overrated."

"No, no — I fear not; and yet, who could have an enmity so deep as only to be healed by blood? and yet, the good and great have as many enemies as the wicked, for they are always opposed to each other."

"Undoubtedly," said the doctor; "good and bad are always antagonists."

"Exactly. What, however, is the worst in these cases is, the bad very often get the better of the good, which is the reverse of what ought to be done; because, you see, if we are to suppose that there is a power above that rules men's actions, surely we might expect to see goodness manifest in the majority of cases; whereas, we usually see, to a much greater extent, the success of evil."

"Not always."

"Not always, certainly," said the doctor; "but the exception proves the rule. Goodness ought to be the great object of men's lives; but it is not; yet it ought to rule, and we must endeavor to be ruled by it, despite the way of the world, which is often, as we daily see, the reverse of what it ought to be."

"But," added the chevalier, "when ambition rules the minds of men, you will find that all other principles give way."

"It is so; but why, I cannot see."

"Because 'tis the master emotion of the mind," said the stranger.

"And ambition appears to possess the souls of those who govern, whether for good or for evil," said the signora. "Some are ambitions of being rulers — some of being conquers, and some of politicians; but they are all moved to it by ambition."

"Aye," said the stranger, "the lover is ambitious of the smiles of his mistress, though ill fortune will, now and then, deny him the good luck to win them."

Chapter *CLXIV*

THE COUNT POLLIDORI'S RECOVERY. – THE INTERVIEW WITH THE SIGNORA ISABELLA. – THE CONSENT.

A few days' confinement placed the count beyond the reach of danger. His wound healed rapidly and favorably, but which was more than anticipated by the cautious leech, who abstained from saying so, but took his daily seat beside his patient's bed, and, with his prosy and imperturbable gravity, he continued to give his advice.

"Count," he said, " your wound is healing."

"I feel it is so," said the count.

"But you must be cautious. I would not have you be too sanguine, or trust your feelings too much."

"I do not; but I may take wine?"

"Indeed, I would recommend you not to do so; for wine is inflammatory, and you are likely to suffer for it."

"And yet I took a bottle last evening."

"Last evening, count?" said the physician.

"Yes; I speak truly."

"I doubt it not; but it was very imprudent — very imprudent, indeed; for, though half a bottle may do no hurt to a man in full health, yet a whole can do him no good, even if it do him no harm; but, in your case, it is dangerous."

"It might be; but surely the danger is past now?"

"If you have taken it over twelve hours — though four-and-twenty would be better."

"It is over twelve hours."

"'Tis well; but it was hazardous; you are fast getting well, and, as it happens, you have no fever, or other evil changes about you; therefore, you may continue your wine, but not in such quantities."

"I will be more cautious; but, Pilletto, what is your opinion of my guest?"

"Your preserver?"

"Yes; the same."

"He is one of the most learned men I ever met with; even professed scholars have not been found so full of knowledge."

"That speaks something for his youth."

"Most undoubtedly."

"But what think you of him as a man of the world?"

"I think he has a vast fund of information; he has had an enlarged experience of society, and has visited, I think, all the continent of Europe; he understands their languages and manners, too, and has the appearance of a traveler, and a man used to the best and most distinguished society."

"That is just my opinion of him."

"I understand he is from France."

"Yes."

"A refugee, in point of fact, I suppose, without means."

"No, he appears to have means, and hopes that times my so alter to permit his return, and the resumption of his former fortune."

"I understand as much, and he has spoken of people whom I know well in France, that would not associate with any beneath their degree; and he has told me things they would have divulged to none, save their equals and families."

"It is my opinion of him."

*T*he doctor took his leave, and the count was again left to himself, and he began evidently to ponder over something in his mind, which appeared to demand his attention, and he, for some time, sat immoveable.

"My daughter," he murmured, "is a rich reward even for such a deed. I do not pit my life against hers; no, no; she is by far the most valuable; she I love more than life, and would provide for her in a manner that shall procure her future happiness, rather than her immediate approval.

"The dear girl does not well understand these matters; she does not know that present pleasure may be followed by future pain. She knows not that we should forgo the present, to ensure future happiness."

He paused a moment, and then he continued, —

"But I cannot be mistaken in this man. No, he has done a deed, which, though I value it not at so high a price, yet gratitude impose upon me the necessity of showing the highest consideration. She is fancy free; and I do not see there will be any difficulty in the way whatever."

At that moment the door opened, and Signora Isabella entered, and advanced towards the couch on which he lay.

"My father!"

"Ah, Isabella, I was but then thinking of you."

"Of me, father? I come to see how you are. Our good guest and preserver had been telling me he is quite sure you are much better than Doctor Pilletto will admit; for he is slow and cautious to a degree."

"My dear, he is quite right – I feel it."

"Oh, how joyful I am!"

"What think you of our guest, Isabella? Do you not think him a man well worthy of our warmest esteem and gratitude?"

"Indeed he is, father – he is noble."

"I think so – the true nobility of soul can be seen in him; to such a man as the chevalier, would I see my Isabella united; to such a man could I confide my daughter's happiness, for he would secure it."

"What mean you, father?"

"That the stranger, of whom you speak so highly, is to be your future husband; the preserver of the father will not act unkindly by the child."

"My father, I am stunned."

"Yes, my dear daughter, I have fully settled this matter in my own mind; he has asked your hand – go see him – you have my blessing. I am sure he will be happy. Isabella, you never disobeyed your father; such an act would be the cruelest stab that ever was planted in my bosom."

"But when," said Isabella, almost trembling; "but when will this be? When am I to be given away, father, as you would a present of flowers?"

"Isabella, when have I deserved, when have I had such an answer from thee? Let me have no more of this."

"But when have you fixed as a time upon which I am to be sent away from home to strangers?"

"You will not leave this palace, Isabella; you and your husband will always be here, and I shall have the satisfaction of seeing the happiness I have planned and made. He will be a father to the child, as well as a husband."

"I do not wish for any such change. I am happy, but shall be otherwise, if I am compelled to wed."

"Compelled, Isabella, compelled! Do you speak of being forced, when I wish it? Now that I have settled it in my own mind, love and duty to me, and gratitude to this gentleman, all conspire to point out how you should act."

"But when, father, when?"

"Tomorrow."

"Tomorrow!" repeated Isabella, in mournful accents.

"Yes, my child; 'tis better done at once — 'twill, at all events, save any of those unnecessary thoughts that might disturb you."

"My father! my father!" said the young lady, as she sunk upon her knees before him.

"Well, my child?"

"Pardon me for once begging a favor of you."

"What mean you by such words?"

"I wish a longer interval to be allowed me before I am — I am——"

"Married," said her father.

"Yes, father; that is the dreadful word."

"Isabella, mind, my love, what my wishes are."

"I have heard them, father; but give me a week — indeed, you cannot decently bring this matter to a conclusion before the end of that time. I have had no previous warning form you, or this stranger, that such a thing was in contemplation."

"If I grant it you, my Isabella, I must be obeyed."

"You shall be obeyed, father," said Isabella, with an effort, "if it cost me my life, and it will be near it; but let me keep my room until that period is up, and then do with me what you will."

"Be it so, Isabella; though it will look ungracious to our guest, yet I will endeavor to excuse you with the best grace I can."

The Lady Isabella was deathly pale, and, as she rose, she staggered, and could scarce support herself out of the apartment.

Chapter CLXV

THE WEDDING MORNING. — THE NEW ARRIVAL. — THE
DISAPPEARANCE OF THE VAMPYRE BRIDEGROOM.

*T*he signora retired to her own chamber, and remained there for many hours; but during that time two messengers had left the mansion secretly, and then all was still. The lovely and beautiful Isabella, however, was not to be seen in her usual walks, or at her father's board, as was her wont. She was only seen within the precincts of her own apartments, pallid, sad, and sorrowful.

"Your daughter, count," said the stranger, one morning, "does not appear as usual. I trust she is quite well?"

"Yes; quite well."

"I hope I have given no cause of offence if so, I hope I may be informed of my error, that I may speedily amend it."

"There is none, chevalier; but my daughter, Isabella, has asked a week's preparation for the nuptials — which week she will pass in her own apartments secluded, and at the end of which time, she leaves them for your protection, and which will, I trust, be to her happiness."

"It shall be my business to make her happy, and, for want of good will and hearty endeavor, she shall never lack content and bliss. I have every presage of a most happy and felicitous life in the future. I am sure she will be happy."

"It is my great hope, chevalier; it is the one object of my life. I would it were settled, and the affair over. I should die unhappy if I thought poor Isabella in the hands of any one who would not use her as she deserved to be. She is of herself a treasure."

"She is — she is."

"And when she is once a wife, she will not look for a father's protection, neither will she need it. My death, when it does happen, will be a great and heavy blow; but it will be less when she has the comfort and consolation of a husband to console her for what would otherwise be irreparable."

"Yes, it would have the effect of deadening the blow, and of shortening the duration of its intensity, though it will be by no means prevented."

"I cannot say I should desire it."

"No, certainly not; and Signora Isabella never could forget such a parent."

"I have done my duty, I hope."

"And many congratulate yourself, count; but then, with regard to Isabella, she will meet me as usual here on the day of the ceremonial"

"Most assuredly."

"And I am to be denied her company till then?"

"Yes; she will meet you on the morning at the altar."

"Be it so — but I could have been happy in her society. At any rate I must be so, by reflecting that I shall soon be the favored, happy husband of Isabella, for with her my happiness will be complete."

"And my happiness will be complete, in knowing hers is so."

"I could have wished that some of those who have known me in France had been here to see my happiness; but that cannot be."

"Could you not send to them?"

"There would not be time for their return. And, moreover, if there had been, I question whether I ought to hold any communication with them, lest I bring them under the ban of the government, and I may not do that."

"Truly, you have the same feelings as I used to have; but I have long since ceased to feel any of that kind of interest."

"Time cures that."

"It does; and you will find it will heal all those wounds which such a separation from your country causes you."

"I hope so. My offences there they will never forgive."

*T*hus conversed the stranger and the count, and thus six days passed, during which time the Signora Isabella was seen by none save her attendants, who were few, and most of her time was spent in tears and prayers.

She had a heart full of grief, but he dared not disobey her father, he whom she loved so well, and whom she had never thought for one moment as being opposed to her own ideas of propriety and her own wishes. She had always been taught to suppress her own, and submit to his.

Thus it was now, at the eleventh hour, she had no means of fortifying herself in any preconceived liking she may have had.

Submission was all she had learned — a blind and willing submission to a fond and doting parent. She knew no other course of action.

Her heart, however, had other yearnings. She had loved another; but she knew not how to act. She dared not even entertain the thought of throwing herself at her father's feet, and imploring him to save her from perpetual sorrow — much less did she think of opposing him; but she had done this much.

In the first moment of her terror and anguish, she had written off to her brother, informing him of her danger; but, at the same time, she had advised nothing, and expressed no wish — only told him the fact and her fears.

*T*he wedding morning arrived, and the house of the count gave indications of the festivity; and, with the day, came guests richly dressed, and the bells rang a merry peal upon the occasion, and the count was in high spirits; but the bride was not seen.

"How is Signora Isabella, your daughter?" inquired one of the guests.

"She is as well as maiden modesty will permit."

"I have not seen her."

"Nor I."

"Nor you!" replied the guest, astonished.

"No; she has secluded herself, but will appear presently, when the bell rings for the service. The fact is, she cannot leave her father, even for the arms of a husband, without feeling a grief for the change."

"I hope she will be happy."

"I have no doubt of it; the man is worthy of her."

"And capable of making her happy, I hope."

"I have no doubt of that."

"Hark! the bell sounds; is that the signal?"

"Yes; follow on. I will bring my daughter forth;" and, as he spoke, he left the guests, who hurried to the chapel, and found the stranger awaiting his bride with some impatience.

He acknowledged the courtesy of those who came to him, and looked towards a small door, which presently opened, and the count and his daughter appeared. She was of marble paleness, and no signs of happiness were seen in her face. She trembled, and her whole soul seemed to be intent on something afar from her presence.

She lifted her eyes and gazed upon the throng; but apparently saw none — or not those whom she wished. Her father spoke to her; she heaved a deep sigh, and appeared to be resigned to her fate.

*T*he ceremony commenced, and Isabella stood; but her eyes occasionally sought the chapel door; and in a few moments more, before the important part was concluded, a bustle took place near the door, and, immediately afterwards, some officers, in the Venetian uniform, entered the chapel, among whom was the young count, Isabella's brother, and with him a young officer, into whose arms she instantly threw herself, and fainted.

"Father," said the young count — "father, this must not be."

"Why not, my son?" said the count.

"Because my sister loves another, and yon man is a monster."

"What mean you, sir?" said the chevalier. "If you were other than what you are, your words would beget a different answer."

"You are a vampyre," replied a young Neapolitan, who stepped forward. "I knew you before. Know you not the holy father whom you murdered?"

"'Tis false. I'll bring one to prove it."

As the chevalier spoke, he crossed the chapel, and left the place; but he did not appear again; and, upon inquiry, he had quitted the palace in a gondola, and never reappeared.

Chapter *CLXVI*

THE TWO HIGHWAYMEN. – THE MURDER AT THE GIBBET'S
FOOT. – THE RIDE TO THE GOLDEN PIPPIN.

*T*he evening set in a stormy mood; sudden, gusty showers rattled
against the traveler; whilst the wind swept over the country, bending
the tall trees, and whistling round the peasant's cot, and making the
chimneys appear as if they were the residences of imprisoned spirits,
which moaned and groaned most dismally to hear.

The clouds came rapidly across the sky; now darkening the earth, and
now they had fled past, leaving the moonbeams pouring a flood of light
upon the fields and roadways; but this was soon followed by another
darkness, a cold rain, and rushing wind, the night being inclement and
very boisterous – not to say a night too bad to permit traveling.

It was late on such a night, when down a lone cross-road a single
horseman might be seen to ride slowly and carefully. He was wrapped
up in a large cloak, and rode a powerful horse, and appeared to be
somewhat tired.

There was much difficulty in traveling over a bad road, that was loose
and shifty, with here and there a slough of some magnitude.

In a very wild and desolate spot stood a mound of stones that had
been heaped at the foot of a gibbet, and had been collected there in
consequence of the unpopularity of the occupant of the instrument of
punishment.

On the gibbet, swinging to and fro, was the body of a malefactor,
hung in chains – an awful and disgusting spectacle – whose death no
one regretted, inasmuch as he was the terror of the whole neighborhood.

It was the body of a highwayman, or of a robber, who had committed
all kinds of depredations, and several murders. He was the son of a
person of property, but addicted to vicious courses, and, to support
them, he had recourse to robbery and murder.

Several of his former friends were robbed, and at length his own father fell by his hands, when he refused to give up his purse in the road at this spot. His own son shot him through the heart.

This was the last crime he ever committed; for he was taken and tried, when enough was proved that would have hung a hundred men; and there was not one man who could, or who would, speak one word in his favor. He was executed; and so detested was he by all, that every one who came by this spot threw a stone, until it grew, by these means, a goodly heap, which remained a memento of their hate.

It was this spot the stranger was nearing, and to which he appeared to look up with some degree of either curiosity, or interest; but, before he got there, there was another horseman riding along the country lane, and who would arrive there about the same time as the first; but when he came there, it was easy to perceive that he was not alone, but another horseman was in waiting beneath some trees, and hidden from the traveler.

In a few moments more, the traveler reached the spot, and, looking up at the dead body that was swinging to and fro in the night air, the other horseman rode up; upon which the traveler was about to push his horse forward at an increased speed, when he found that there was not space enough.

"Which side do you take?" he inquired of the stranger.

"Stand and deliver!" was the reply.

"That is uncivil," replied the stranger, "and a request that I do not feel at all disposed to consent to."

"Deliver your money and a pocket-book, or you are a dead man."

"Nay," said the stranger; "I have means of defense, too."

And, as he spoke, he pulled out a bright, double-barreled pistol, which he leveled and cocked, saying, as he very leisurely did so, —

"Beware! you are playing with a determined man. I am not disposed to play. Get out of my way, or you are a dead man!"

"Ha, ha, ha!" laughed the other, and made way at the same moment, thus bringing himself alongside the traveler, leaving him room to go on. "You are not to be frightened — well, well, go on."

The traveler put his spurs to his horse, but at the same moment received a bullet from the treacherous highwayman.

"Ha!" cried the traveler, putting his hand to his side, and in a moment more he staggered and fell over the side of the horse on to the ground.

"Ha, ha, ha!" said the highwayman, who immediately dismounted; but before he could search the body, the other horseman came up at a gallop.

"Well, Fred, have you quieted him?"

"I have."

"Resisted, then?"

"Yes. Have you got your lantern?"

"Yes; but it is not yet lighted. But that is soon done."

"Then let us have it as quick as you can; for he has fallen down here in a slough, and I should like to get the money without more mire than I am obliged to put up with."

"Here it is," said the other, handing the lantern — a small one, which he had lighted by means of some chemical matches.

The highwayman took the lantern, and, after some examination, he secured the pocketbook and the purse, and having done this, he examined the fingers, but saw no rings and no watch, and he said to his companion, —

"Just come here. Did you ever see such a set of features as these? They are truly strange and singular; I could never forget them."

"Indeed! I must have a look at them," said his companion, dismounting and bending over the body; and when he looked at them, he said, —

"I saw that man today where I dined, and thought he took the other road, and there waited for him."

"Did you, though?"

"Yes, till I was tired; and then I came across the country in search of you, but did not expect you to have any quarry."

"Did you ever see such a countenance? it is most strange and ghastly."

"Yes, it is; but he has died a violent death, you see, and therefore there is much to be done by way of allowance."

"Yes, yes, I know all that; but the nose, mouth, and teeth——"

"They are not the most agreeable in the world, certainly. Well, well, it don't matter; you have done all your business with him, have you not?"

"I have got all, I believe," said the other. "He has no watch or chain — not even a ring has he got on his finger."

Perhaps you'll find enough in his purse and pocket-book to console you; though I must say, Ned, that he dined very sparingly. But no matter the amount; ride on, for you know it is not a good plan to stand longer here than necessary; for we may have other riders down upon us."

"Not very likely, on this road, and as this hour; but 'tis bad. I'm off, and he will remain behind till found by some frightened peasant or other, who will go to the nearest market town, with a frightful account."

"Ride away; I hear horses' feet, I think."

"I am ready; forward! ho!"

The two highwaymen rode off at a rapid rate, conversing as they went; but yet it was in suppressed tones for some distance; and after some riding, one of them pulled up his horse, partially, saying, —

"Well, I don't think it wise we should thus wear our steeds out; there is no need of our riding for life; our horses never ought to be put to their mettle, unless there be plenty of occasion, which there is not."

"No – all is right, tonight."

"Have you done much lately, Ned?"

"No; I have been rather upon the seek than find; I have been looking out brightly, but have not been successful."

"I have myself only done moderately; but I have done better than I should have done, because I was fortunate enough to come across a fat grazier who had more money than any three or four persons I have met lately."

"Your fortune is somewhat like mine."

"You have met with little good then, Ned."

"Indeed, I have not; but it is a long lane that has no turning,"

"Yes; indeed, it is."

"However, I hope this queer-looking customer will reward one for one's pains; if you can but keep the game a going, you are sure to succeed in the end; 'tis only two years or better since I first began to ride."

"That is, put a period to other people's rising."

"Exactly."

"Well, then, where do you intend to put up for the night? for I suppose you do not intend to stay out all night any more than myself."

"No; I think of going on until I come to 'The Golden Pippin,' where I intend to stay for the night. The landlord can wink hard at his friends, and not know they are in the house, or he can tell them a thing if they want to know anything at all to their interest."

"He's the sort of man; I know him. I was thinking of going there; I don't know better or snugger quarters than are to be had at his hostel."

"Then we'll have a good supper and a bottle at 'The Golden Pippin.'"

"With all my heart; but you don't think there'll be any danger of our being pursued for this matter."

"Oh, dear, no; the direct road lies another way, and we shall be quite fifteen miles from the spot where the body lies."

"So far."

"Yes; we have come over the ground very rapidly, and have gone more than two-thirds of that distance. When we get there we shall be safe, easy, and comfortable; and right good wines are there to be had at 'The Golden Pippin.'"

Chapter *CLXVII*

THE HORRORS OF THE NIGHT. – THE DISCOVERY IN THE
ROAD. – CONTENTION BETWEEN MAN AND HORSE. –
COMFORTABLE QUARTERS IN THE GOLDEN PIPPIN.

*T*he malefactor's body swung to and fro on the gibbet, and the
chains squeaked and groaned as the wind impelled the body's motions.
The wind itself whistled heedlessly by, and the transient, but heavy
shower passed on, heedless of the deed of blood that had been perpe-
trated beneath its monitory shadow.

Now and then there was a little light, and then the body might be
seen heaped up, and lying in the mud and mire, which was all discolored
with the blood of the fallen man – he was motionless. The rain fell on
him, but it mattered not – the body felt it not. The wind blew the cloak
about, but the body remained quiet, and nothing appeared to spare the
body.

There was no one nigh; that was a lonely spot, and that was tenanted
by two dismal gypsies. The body of the malefactor swung to and fro
while the body of the murdered traveler lay quit enough.

The clouds traveled across the face of the moon, and intercepted her
light from the earth; but yet it was light enough at intervals to enable
the traveler to see his way on foot, or on horseback.

About two hours after that in which the traveler had been stopped
and murdered, there came another individual riding towards the scene.

This was a countryman – a grazier, who was well-mounted, and came
along at a rapid rate, having a stout trotting nag under him.

When he neared the spot where the murder had been committed, he
gave a look up at the disagreeable object – the gibbet, and when he had
done so, he put the spur to his horse's side, with the intention of going
by at a quickened pace, exclaiming as he did so, –

"This is no pleasant place at nine o'clock at night. I wish I were at the Golden Pippin, instead of here."

As he spoke, he pushed his horse, as he manifested a design to stop; but the animal, instead of going past, reared up.

"Hilloa! brute. What art after now, eh?"

The spur was again applied, but the animal only became more and more unmanageable, and the rider near losing his seat; but he was, nevertheless, the more anxious to get onward, for the neighborhood was not pleasant; added to which, it was a wet and dismal night, and late for a cross-road.

"Curse you!" muttered the grazier; "what the deuce is the matter with you? — did you never see the gibbet before? If thee hadn't, I should not have been surprised at thee shying at the man swinging on the gibbet; but thee hast done so, and now thee art frightened. Whoa! D——n thee."

He made another attempt to force the horse by, but it was fruitless, and he was at length unseated into the mire.

"D——n!" muttered the man; "the first time I have been thrown these ten years, drunk or sober, and now I am sober."

This was apparently the first reflection that came to his mind after the first effect of the concussion; he then scratched his head, adjusted his hat, and was getting up, when for a moment his eyes rested on something dark lying in the middle of the road, and at which his horse had in reality shied.

"Oh!" he exclaimed, with a visible alteration in his demeanor; "that's what Peg shied at, eh? What the devil is it?"

As he muttered these words, his hair began to stand on end; and the more he looked, the greater his apprehension; for he began to think what he wished was further from the fact, though his notions were far from being definite, and he did all he could to dispel the rising terror.

"Why — it ain't — no, it can't be — and yet it must be! What makes 'un lay there — he must be dead, surely!"

Thrice he scrambled to his feet, and then walked a little towards the object against which his horse stood smelling and snorting with evident signs of fear.

"Whoa, brute! What's the matter with thee? — confound thee! But I suppose thee wast frightened."

As the man spoke, he walked up to the animal, and, taking the bridle, he passed it over his arms, and then approached the body.

"Aye, sure enough, he's insensible — if not dead, poor fellow! What can be done — there's no one near at hand to lend assistance?"

He paused to consider what was to be done, when it occurred to him as being the most likely thing that could be done was to probe the unfortunate man; he could not say whether he was dead or alive, from his position in the middle of the road.

"If 'un ain't dead," he argued, "he would come to no harm; for it wasn't every horse that cared as much for a man as Peg did; they might get run over, or cause some desperate accident."

Having made up his mind what to do, he secured Peg, and turned his attention to the body of the stranger, which had been left on its back, with its face upwards, but the wind had blown the cloak over it, and it was not seen by the grazier, who now essayed to move the body.

After some trouble, he succeeded in dragging him there, and propping him up against the bank, upon which grew a stunted hedge, and, when there, he opened the cloak, and looked upon the features of the dead man.

"Well," he muttered; "I never yet saw such a face! I am sure I can never forget that. Of all the ill-looking thieves, he is the worst! but much, I suppose, must be set off on the fact that he is a dead man, and a murdered one, to boot."

There was a strange markedness in the style of features in the dead man, that gave no pleasing impression to the mind; it was one that could not easily be forgotten, especially accompanied by all the horrors of their place and circumstances.

"He has been shot, no doubt," he muttered. "This must be all blood. Aye! In the breast, or thereabouts. Oh! he is dead. Well, I'll ride to the Golden Pippin, and then I'll give them notice of it."

He was just about to turn and mount his horse, when the clouds parted, and the moonbeams, for a few moments, came upon the body, without any hindrance, and the grazier thought he saw a movement.

"It must have been gammon," he muttered. "I'll be off — I'm quite cold and shivery here. I'll go to the Golden Pippin, and get some good cheer, for I'm terribly shaken. Eh! what was that? The devil!"

The latter exclamations were uttered in consequence of the figure turning towards the moon's rays, and then opening its eyes, which had such an effect upon the unfortunate man, that he staggered back terrified.

"Lord have mercy!" he ejaculated. "What's — what's that? He — he's coming too — hilloa, friend! — how are you?"

The figure turned his large motionless eyes upon the terrified man, and they had such an effect upon him, that, despite all he could do to rally himself, he sprang involuntarily to his horse's back, and galloped off furiously.

*I*t was scarce an hour before this occurred, when the two highwayman rode up to the Golden Pippin.

"Hilloa! hilloa! ostler — here!" shouted one of them, and in a few moments more the ostler came out, willing enough.

"Hilloa, Jem! you are sharp tonight. How is it you are not asleep?"

"I was just going to roost, master; but I shall have a job instead, I can see."

"You will; but not an empty handed affair, this time; take care of the nags, and there's a crown for you."

"Thank you, master — you are always generous."

"When I can, Jem; but what company have you in the house?"

"Little to speak of," said the ostler; "about three or four people, as lives about here; but nobody that I know — anybody or anything — only people that have to earn their own living; they are in the kitchen."

"Good fire?"

"Yes."

"Then we will go there, too," said the highwayman; "it's a raw cold night, and one in which a good super and a good fire will do one good."

The two highwaymen then entered the house, and walked into the kitchen, which was a large room, with beams across the top, and a variety of utensils proper to the place; but the grand feature was the large fire-place, in which burned brightly some good logs, and threw a glowing warmth and bright light over the whole apartment, in which, however, was one candle, as if to be mocked by the light of the fire. The use of this solitary wick was to enable the smokers to light their pipes without stirring, and also to be taken away at a moment's notice for any purpose that might be needed.

The three guests turned their attention to the new comers, without, however, exchanging one word, and the landlord himself arose.

"Oh, landlord," said one of the highwaymen, "I'm glad you have a good fire; 'tis one of the best things, after a cold ride, a man can have met with."

"Except a good hot supper, and a cup afterwards," said his companion.

"All these are very good things in their way, gentlemen," said the landlord, emptying the ashes of his pipe out into the fireplace by tapping the pipe on the toe of his shoe, and thus dropped the ashes out of danger.

"You are right, landlord," said the other.

"But I always, think, gentlemen," said the landlord gravely, "that they are always a great deal better when they can be had together — they are better for their company's sake — the one helps the other."

"So they do."

"Well, then, let us have them all, old cock, as soon as you please, for we are both cold, tired, and hungry."

"And they are the best accompaniments you can have as a preparatory for all that is to follow."

"Amen! and about it," said the highwayman.

The two new guests sat themselves down in one quarter of the kitchen, and near to a table facing the fire, where they could enjoy its genial warmth, which they appeared to do with much gusto.

Having opened their coats, and taken off their shawls, removed their hats, and sat down in a comfortable manner, they began to look about them.

"Well, Ned, we have made a good exchange."

"How do you mean?"

"Why, we have exchanged the road to comfortable quarters, which, you will, at least, admit, is all the better."

"Yes, much better; though I have ridden many a long and weary a night before now, with the runners at my heels."

"Ay — ay, so have I; but hush — say no more of that there. I have no idea of letting these blacks suspect anything; they are what you call honest men, and men who would give a clue in a moment, if they thought it was wanted."

"I dare say it is so, Ned; but what are you going to have for supper?"

"I don't know. Landlord, what can we have for supper — anything hot?"

"Why," said the landlord, "I can kill a couple of chickens and brander them, or there is some chicken pie, and a cold ham."

"Well, what do you say, Ned?"

"Can't you make the chicken pie warm?"

"It is warm now," said the landlord. "I can't make it quite hot without doing too much; 'tis uncommon good, and has not long been put by from supper; it was made for supper, but there's a good half left."

"Eh? What do you say to chicken pie, Ned?"

"With all my heart; chicken pie let it be, then," replied Ned.

"Well, then, landlord, put the chicken pie on, flanked by the ham — some of your foaming October, you know."

"Ay — ay, sir; some with a head on, that would take a blacksmith's bellows to blow off, it is so strong."

"Ha — ha — ha! that's the strike for us."

The landlord now arose, and set about getting the necessary articles, and spreading them upon a table before the two guests, who were nothing loath to see the expedition that he had made to please them.

"I think," said the landlord, "you will say you never eat such chickens; they are my hatching, and have been well fed; they have been well killed, cooked, and I hope, will be well eaten."

"That is our part of the business, landlord; and if they are such as you speak of, why, you may depend upon our doing our duty by them."

"And the ham is my own breeding and curing."

"Better and better, — and the October?"

"Why, I am just going to get that. What say you to a tankard?"

"Yes, a foaming tankard."

"Yes, gentlemen, I will obtain what you want; it is in beautiful condition, and when chilled, will give you a cream as thick as new cheese; and as mild as new milk,

Chapter CLXVIII

THE GRAZIER'S RELATION, AND HIS FIRST TERRORS. – THE EFFECTS OF GOOD CHEER AND THE SUDDEN INTERRUPTION TO A PLEASANT PARTY.

*T*he landlord was not long gone for the October; he came back with a placid smile and a smacking of his lips, when he shut the door behind him, and then deliberately placing the candlestick down, he said, handing them the tankard, –

"There, gentlemen, if you find any better brewed than that in the three adjoining counties, why, you may take measure for my coffin, for I won't live after I am told there is any so good anywhere else."

"We will not take your word, landlord," said one of the highwaymen, putting the tankard to his lips, which act produced an approving nod from the jolly landlord, who said, with much encouragement, –

"That's right; never trust nobody; that's my motto, and I chalks it up over the fire-place, and acts upon it – try for yourself, and then you won't be deceived. What's your opinion upon that now, sir?"

"Never drank its equal, ever here."

"I thought you'd say so; it comes out of a particular cask – one as I puts by for myself; but you have ridden hard, and I thought a brew of an extra strike would be an acceptable drink."

"You are right. It is cold and very wet. I'm as tired as if I had ridden far – the wind has blown me about so."

"Ah, don't you hear how it roars in the chimney?"

"So it does. What do you think of the brew, Ned – ain't it first rate?"

"Indeed it is: I never had any equal to it. I tell you what, landlord, it will make an excellent night-cap, for a man who has taken a glass or two of this, would not be better able to keep his saddle."

"No; it's lucky we intend putting up for the night here; you have beds."

"Yes, good, and well aired."

"That is capital. Well, your chicken-pie is good, landlord, your ham good, and the October excellent; and now — what's that?"

At that moment there was a sound of horses' feet galloping furiously towards the houses; and they had not listened long before they came close to the door, and then there was evidently a sudden pull up.

"Hilloa! what is that?" said his companion.

"I think it is somebody pulled up at the door," said the landlord; "whoever they are they have come in haste."

The two highwaymen half rose, but a look at each other caused them to resume their seats, and in another moment there was a loud shouting, and a call for the ostler; but there was no one at hand.

"Where is that Jim got to — I must go and see after him, at all events — he won't come if I don't."

So saying, he walked away whilst the guests remained silent watching the actions of the two highwaymen.

"It is but a single horseman," said the first.

"No," said the other; "but still he may be mischievous; and yet I can hardly think he would venture here at such a time; besides, it can't be known; we are much better here than anywhere else."

"I think so; we have nothing to fear."

"Nothing."

At that moment the landlord retired; and, at the same time, the door was suddenly opened, and the grazier entered the kitchen. He glanced around him, much confused. The fire and light, no doubt, had some share in that; but he stared, and appeared terrified, and all splashed over.

"Where's the ostler?" he cried out.

"Here I be," said the worthy behind.

"Look after my horse; he is very hardly ridden. See to him, that's a good fellow," said the grazier."

"Yes; I'll see to 'un," said Jem, who departed with the animal.

"Landlord — landlord!"

"Yes; here I am, Master Green — here am I!"

"Give me something strong; I'm half dead. I'm cold, and I'm frightened, and that is the truth. Where's the fire?"

"Why, Master Green, I never saw you in this state before. Give me your hand, Master Green. I'll show you the fire," said the landlord, holding out his hand to Green. "Why, you are cold — what has happened?"

"You shall hear — you shall hear," said the half-terrified Green. "Only give me a toss of brandy, and get me a supper, and then I shall be able to tell you more about it. At present I can say nothing."

"Well, that is pretty well for a man that can't speak," said the landlord. "You are getting better, Mr. Green."

"I hope I shall; the fire is comfortable."

"Here's some good brandy; take a gill, man. It won't hurt you on such an occasion as this. I have seen you do as much before; but, as for supper, why I can't say much. These two gentlemen have had the only thing I had in the house, and, save the ham, I doubt much if there will be any left."

"If the gentlemen will join us, he is welcome to take a share of what we have," said one of the highwaymen. "Here will be enough for us all, I dare say, sir, if you do not object to our company."

"Thank you — thank you," said Green. "I will accept of your offer gladly; for I have had a long ride, and have had much that is uncomfortable to put up with, to see and to fear. Lord have mercy on me say I!"

"Well, what is the matter, Mr. Green?"

"Why," said Mr. Green, as he, between his words, poked in large mouthfuls of food, and now and then washed it down by the aid of the October. "You all of you know the highwayman's corner, about fifteen miles from here?"

"Yes," said the landlord, "I know it well; there's a chap hanging up in chairs there, now, at this present day, that is, if nobody hasn't run away with it, or it hasn't been blown down."

"Exactly. Well, that's the spot; there's been another dreadful murder been done there. Oh! it was dreadful."

"Well, did you see it?"

"Yes; I did."

"What! the murder!" said both highwaymen at once.

"No; the body — I only saw the body."

"Where was it lying?"

"Stop, stop a bit — not so fast," said Mr. Green, who was eating very fast indeed, but paused a moment. "You must not ask too many questions at once, because I have one way of telling a tale, and you'll spoil it."

"Well, go on your own way."

"Well, then, listen. I was coming along at a rattling pace, I can tell you, for I was late, and tired, as it was. When I had reached the gallows, I looked up at the body swinging in the wind, and creaking and screaming on its rusty swivels; but I had scarcely done so, when my horse shied, and very nearly landed me in the mud, but I contrived to keep my seat, though not without trouble."

"What! at the dead man?" inquired one of the highwaymen.

"Aye," replied his companion. "I am sure they ought not to put men up there like scarecrows, to frighten horses with; for my part, I never pass it but my horse snorts and bolts, and I am obliged to be wary."

"I don't know much about that. I have come by without my nag being any the worse. At all events, I thought there was something in his shying at the gallows, and I tried to push him by, but he would not go."

"What did you do?"

"Why, I was obliged to get down," said the grazier.

"Thrown?"

"No, no."

"Forced to get down, you mean," said the highwayman.

"Why, in some sort of way I did feel myself compelled to get down, because the brute wouldn't go a-head, and I saw something on the ground as the clouds cleared away a little, and showed me that there was something suspicious in the middle of the road, very much like a bundle of clothes."

"Indeed!" said the landlord, "what was it?"

"I'll tell you, in course. Now, you see, I saw the animal would not move, so I got off to see what was the matter."

"Forced off," adde the highwayman.

"D—n it, man, what can it matter; then I got off," said the grazier, getting into a passion, and then, after a pause, which he employed in taking a long pull at the October, and then wiping his lips, he continued, —

"What is the matter now?" thought I; "so I went to the object, and found it was a man rolled up in a cloak in the middle of the road, dead."

"Dead?"

"Aye, dead as a door nail."

"Lor!" said the highwayman. "Why, then he must have been murdered, I suppose?"

"You may take your davy of that," said the grazier; "but I tried to wake him up, but he was not to be disturbed, so I dragged him to the bank, where I left him."

"Where was he hurt?"

"Shot right in the side, or stabbed, I don't know which, but that's where the blood came from, so I was sure he was dead; but when I removed the cloak from his face, I saw he had as ugly a set of features as a man can desire — a long, peculiar face, large, but thin nose, an awkward set of teeth, with one or two projecting in front, and oh! such eyes, that is when he opened them."

"Opened them," said the highwayman; "both?"

"Opened them," repeated the landlord; "why, did you not tell me he was dead?"

"Aye; but when the moonlight came upon him, he opened his eyes. Oh! what eyes — why, they were like a pair of enormous great fish eyes — cod's eyes, that had become suddenly lighted up, or the moonlight reflected back from the bottom of a new tin saucepan, and then you have 'em."

"The devil," said the highwayman; "and what did you do?"

"Why, I came away as fast as I could. I wasn't to be done by a dead man. I didn't wait to see more than that. He turned round and stared at me. He was so horrible, that I got upon my horse the best way I could, and came on here as fast as the animal would come."

"The body, I dare say, rolled over, and you thought it moved of itself."

"I know better; besides, it opened its eyes."

"The moon shone on them, and you thought he looked at you. You were terror-stricken, and that is the truth of it."

"Then I know better," said the grazier, doggedly; "it ain't anything of the kind. I know it ain't a matter that happens every day, and that's why you don't believe it, and don't understand it, but I know I'm right."

"House, here, house! ostler!" shouted a loud, authoritative voice without the door of the inn, which caused them all to start and listen for a repetition of the same sounds to prove that they were not illusory.

Chapter CLXIX

THE MYSTERIOUS STRANGER'S ARRIVAL. — THE
CONSTERNATION OF THE GUESTS. — THE GRAZIER'S
TERRORS, AND POWERS OF IDENTITY. — THE LANDLORD'S
DAUGHTER.

"Hilloa! house! house! shouted the strange voice on the outside, but in a tone that seemed unearthly; whether it were merely a fancy, or reality, yet it had its effect, and the landlord sat staring vacantly with his two hands resting on either knee, leaning forward as if he was staring some imaginary object out of countenance.

"Well," said one of the highwaymen, "ain't anybody going to the door."

No one answered, but Jem the ostler was hastening by another passage to the door, and then they heard some confused speaking, as if the stranger was giving some directions for the care of his horse.

The grazier was fixed in his attention to what was going on, and appeared petrified, and held a morsel on the end of his fork, halfway between his mouth and the plate, with his eyes directed towards the door.

In a few moments more they heard the steps of some one approaching the door, and one of the highwaymen said to his companion, —

"Ned, there are people late on the roads tonight."

"Yes; it appears so, but it is very uncomfortable traveling; the night is bad, and the roads no better. Who's this, I wonder?"

"We shall now see," said the other, but their backs were turned towards the door, and they could not see who entered the door so well as the grazier, who sat in the same attitude, without a motion or movement, even to wink his eye, when the door opened, and in walked a tall man, wrapped in a horseman's cloak.

The expression of horror in the grazier's face, and the swelling of his eyes almost out of his head, at once showed them there was something extraordinary, and they both mutually turned round, and to their extreme terror they perceived the very man, or his double, they had left dead upon the spot where the grazier had seen him.

Neither were they alone surprised, for all present were able at once to recognize the same man without any difficulty.

"It's the same man — I'm d——d!" said the grazier, as if he had made an effort to speak, and when he had so, he couldn't help himself. Oh, Lord! — who would have thought it? — it's — it's the — the — what do ye call it?"

"The devil," suggested the landlord.

"No," said the stranger, "no. I am merely a traveler, somewhat weary and tired — do not disturb yourselves. I am cold — very cold — the fire will do me good; it is a very cold night — the roads are bad very unsafe."

"Very," said one of the highwaymen, involuntarily.

"Did you speak?" inquired the stranger, suddenly turning to the highwayman who had spoken with a look of such a peculiar character, that he caused the bold roadster involuntarily to start; but he suddenly recovered himself, and said, —

"I did."

"What did you say, sir?"

"The same as you," replied the highwayman.

The stranger made no reply to the highwayman, whose natural

effrontery, and the necessity he always had or presence of mind in circumstances of peril, gave him a greater superiority than most men possessed under such circumstances.

"I'm not well," said the stranger.

"Perhaps you've ridden far."

"I have," replied the stranger. "Landlord, will you have the goodness to let me have some supper; I am weary."

"I have only the remains of the chicken-pie and some ham," said the landlord, looking back at the already referred-to chicken-pie, which, thanks to its being made of great size, had already supped three hungry men, — "and there is but little of that."

"It is not much that I want — a small matter will suffice — a little ham, and something warm, and then I will to-bed — 'tis late."

"Very well, sir," said the landlord; "here's some good October; will you like that? or is there anything else? I have French spirits."

"Then let me have some brandy."

"Yes, sir, I'll fetch my daughter down stairs," said the landlord; "she's young, and her hand is steadier than mine. I shall upset the bottle; my — my hand, you see, is always unsteady after I've drawn the October; somehow or other I always get out of order."

"What is the reason of that?" inquired the highwayman.

"Why, it's so strong; I believe it's nothing else whatever."

As the landlord turned to go, he give another look at the guest, and appeared greatly disturbed, and certainly thought him a strange and unaccountable man; for he believed that he was in truth the very man spoken of, who had been left for dead on the bank, near the foot of the gallows.

"Mary," said the landlord, when he had ascended half a dozen stairs, which led out of the kitchen, "Mary."

"Yes, father," was the ready answer, in a clear, pleasing voice.

"I want you, my dear. Bring the brandy down — the French — the sealed bottle; the other's out; I took the last this morning before breakfast."

"Ho! ho!" said the highwayman; "hark at our landlord, how early he must begin — no wonder his hand shakes."

"Ah!" said the landlord, as he came back with a wink; "when you have been a father and an innkeeper as long as I have, you'll do many things you don't now dream of; but, no matter, I ain't as young as I used to be."

At that moment a very pretty and genteel girl, about eighteen, descended the stairs with a spirit bottle in her hand, and advanced to the table.

"How will you take it, sir?" inquired the landlord.

"Mixed."

"Make a glass, my dear," said the landlord.

"Is that your daughter?" inquired the stranger, fixing his eyes upon her, — and they were such leaden eyes, that the girl shrank from him in dismay.

"Yes," said the landlord.

"Any more?"

"None," replied the landlord, and then there was a pause of some moments, during which the stranger watched the young girl's motions with a greedy jealousy, as if he feared to lose one movement, and in a manner that especially annoyed the old landlord, who, however, could say nothing, he having been quite cowed by the stranger's superiority in station and demeanor; besides which, there was something very strange and peculiar, not to say superhuman, about him that gave weight, and caused a kind of awe to pervade all present, and they looked upon him as something fearful or terrible.

It was not long before the stranger ate his supper — it was soon done; he ate but little, and, when that was done, he turned to the brandy and water; but there appeared an air of compulsion, upon his part, as if everything he took was taken under the feeling that it was absolutely necessary to take something, which did not escape the discerning eyes of all present, especially the landlord, who felt it a slight upon himself and his cheer.

"If I had known you were coming here," said the landlord, "I would have got something ready for you, but, as it was, I had nothing but 'pot-luck' for you."

"What is that?" inquired the stranger. — "What is that? — I never heard of such a dish before. I am a stranger in these parts."

"Oh, it only means you could have anything what is in the house."

"It will do," said the stranger, quietly.

"Will you have anything more that we have in the house?"

"Nothing. I came by the gibbet, not far from this place; and I met with an accident there that has left me but little stomach.

"By gosh, I should think not," muttered the grazier; "it would have settled my stomach altogether, and anybody else's."

"Well," muttered one of the highwaymen, "It would have left me no stomach, save what would be in a fair way to become food for the worms."

"What kind of accident was it, sir?"

"A terrible blow in the side; it seemed to go through me."

"Well, well, I imagine there would be but little comfort in a man's bowels after he had anything go through his side."

"It depends upon the constitution," said the stranger, quietly.

"The what?" inquired one of the highwaymen, incredulously.

"The constitution," replied the stranger, quietly.

There was a pause for some minutes, during which the strangers exchanged glances at each other, when one of the highwaymen said, —

"Perhaps a bullet put in your side might be no hindrance to your animal economy, and would in the course of nature become digested."

"Why, I dare say it would not hurt me so much as many; but it would take me some little while to recover the shock, which would be great; but I am unwell, and perhaps had better retire. Will the young female, your daughter, act as my chambermaid and show me my room?"

"Yes," said the landlord, mechanically; "here, Mary, show the gentleman into No. 6, and leave the light."

"Good night," said the stranger, rising, and walking away erect, but slowly, from the group, who gazed after him with amazement.

"Good night, sir," said the landlord, which was echoed by those present; and, when the stranger was gone, there was a general release in their conversation from the constraint which the presence of the last comer occasioned.

"Well, what do you think of him, Mr. Green?" inquired the landlord.

"The very same man I saw on the bank at the gallows corner."

"Are you sure?"

"Quite."

There was a general pause, as if there was something for them all to think over; and their thoughts appeared to be so unsatisfactory, that those who lived close at hand left the house, and those that remained there went to their respective beds, and in half an hour the house was quite silent.

Chapter *CLXX*

THE MIDNIGHT CRY OF ALARM. – THE VAMPYRE'S MEAL. –
THE CHASE ACROSS THE FIELDS. – THE DEATH OF THE
LANDLORD'S DAUGHTER.

*T*he old inn was in a state of repose; its various parts were no longer
vexed by the busy tramp of men, the noisy voice of the toper, or the
untiring hands of the housewife, who does not spare any part of its
edifice from her ablutions. The brush and the broom are sad intruders
and disturbers, and yet they are in perpetual requisition. However, the
inhabitants were all steeped in slumber.

Among those who lay in that house, there was not one, except one,
indeed, who did not lie down to rest, and fall into a deep sleep; but that
one exception was the stranger, who appeared to have other views.

He threw himself into a chair, and there appeared to meditate upon
the clouds which passed across the sky, in endless variety of shape and
form. He sat motionless, and still his large, lusterless eyes were fully
opened, and he was gazing earnestly for nearly an hour without motion.

At length, as if his attention was of itself wearying to continue so
long, he moved, then sighed deeply, or rather groaned.

"How long is this hated life to last?" he muttered. "When shall I cease
to be the loathsome creature I am?"

There was some reflection in this that was very bitter to him. He
shuddered, and buried his face in his hands, and remained in that state
for some minutes; but then he lifted his head up again, and turned
towards the moon's rays, muttering, –

"But I am faint; I feel the want of my natural slumbers. Blood alone
will restore me my strength. There is no resisting the dreadful appetite
that goads me on. I must – I must – I will satisfy it."

He arose suddenly, and drew himself up to his full height, and threw
aloft his arms, as he growled out these words with frantic energy; but in

a few seconds he became more calm, and said, –

"I saw the maiden enter the room next to mine. I can enter it by the same door, for I have the key, and that will place her at my mercy. Good fortune for once avail me, and then my wants will be satisfied."

He walked softly to his own door, and undid it stealthily, and listened for some minutes.

"They are all asleep," he said – "all, save one. I alone walk through the place. All are in peaceful slumbers, while I, like the creatures of prey, seek those whom I may devour. I must on."

He crept into the passage, and advanced to the door of the young girl, who lay soundly sleeping in innocence and peace, little dreaming of the fate that awaited her – much less did she think that the destroyer was so close at hand.

She might, indeed, have dreamed that there was some one in the house who was scarcely of her nature – one that was loathsome and dreadful – one who, in fact, lived upon the blood of the innocent and fairest.

"She sleeps," he muttered – "she sleeps!"

He listened again, and then he gently put the key into the door, and found that it was not locked, and then, turning the handle, he found there was some impediment to its opening; but of what character he could not tell.

"'Tis unlucky; but this must be moved."

He place his hand and foot close to the door, and pressed it gradually and hardly against it, and he found that it gradually gave way, and that the impediment gave by degrees, and that, too, with hardly any noise.

"Fortune favors me," he muttered; "she does not hear me. I shall win the chamber, and shall, before she can wake up, seize upon the dear life-stream that is no less precious to me than to herself."

He now had succeeded in effecting an entrance into the room, and found that it was only an easy chair that had been placed against the door, because there was no other means of securing it, the key having unaccountably disappeared, and left her without any other means of securing her door.

"I will lock it," he muttered; "if I be disturbed, I shall be better able to escape, and I shall be safe. My meal will be undisturbed; at least not before so much has been taken as will revive my strength."

He now approached the bed, and with eager eyes devoured the fair form of the youthful and innocent sleeper.

"How calm, and how unsuspicious she lies," he muttered; "'twere a pity, but I must, I must – there is no help."

He leaned over her. He bent his head till his ear almost touched the lips of the sleeper, as though he were listening to the breathing of the young girl.

Something caused her to start. She opened her eyes, and endeavored to rise up, but she was immediately thrust back, and the vampire seized her fair flesh with his fanged teeth, and having fleshed them, he was drawing that life current from her which ensanguined them both.

Horror and fright for a moment deprived her of strength, or the power of uttering a sound of any kind; but when she did do so, it was one wild unearthly shriek, that was heard throughout the whole house, and awakened every human being within it in a moment.

"Help! murder, murder!" she shrieked out, as soon as the first scream subsided, and she regained breath.

These cries she uttered rapidly, as well as attempting a desperate resistance to her persecutor; but she was growing gradually more and more faint.

*T*he landlord had just got out of an uncomfortable dream about some strange adventure he was having with some excisemen when he was young, when the heart-piercing shriek of Mary came upon him.

"God bless me," he muttered, "what's that? I never heard anything so horrible in all my life. What can it be?"

He sat up in bed, and pulled his nightcap off, while he listened, when he heard the cries of help issuing from his daughter's room.

"Good God! it's Mary," he muttered, "What can be the matter?"

He did not pause a moment, but huddled on his clothes, and then rushed out of his room with a light, to his daughter's bedroom.

"What is the matter?" inquired one of the highwaymen, who had been disturbed by the dreadful shriek.

"I don't know; but — but help me."

"Help you to what?"

"To burst open this door; 'tis my daughter's room, and the noise comes from that place. Hark!"

"Help, help!" said a faint voice.

"Damnation!" said the highwayman, "something's wrong there; somebody's sucking; surely the stranger is not there?"

"Burst the door open."

"Then lend a hand; it must give," said Ned; and they all three made a rush at the door, and in it went, for their weight carried it all before them, and they all three went into the apartment without any hindrance, for the frail lock gave immediately, and the other impediment only served to add to the noise.

Though they went in easily, yet they did not do so quickly enough, for they all rolled over each other, and before they could rise they distinctly saw the figure of the stranger start up and rush out of the room with Mary in his arms.

"Help! help! mercy!" she shrieked out.

"'Tis she," said the landlord.

"Mary—"

"Yes, after her boys — after her; for Heaven's sake, after her."

"We will not leave her," said the highwaymen in concert, and at the same moment all three rushed after her.

"The stranger has made his way down into the kitchen, and I think he has her with him," said the landlord.

"I will after him," said Ned; "I saw her in his arms. She was all over blood. Good Heavens! what can he mean? does he want to murder her?"

"Help! help! murder!" shouted the girl, and at that moment they heard the stranger attempting the kitchen door below. In a moment they all three ran down stairs as fast as they could, to seize the villain before he could escape; but they had hardly got into the kitchen before they saw the door swing to after him.

"He's gone," said the landlord; "he's gone."

"We'll after them; come on, never mind a chase; she's in white, and the moon's up, so we shall have them in sight."

"Away after them, lads; save my girl — save my Mary!"

Away they went with great speed, but the stranger somehow or other kept ahead of them; his great height gave him an advantage in length of stride; but then he bore the landlord's daughter in his arms, which was more than enough to balance their powers; for though she was not heavy, comparatively speaking, yet she was heavy to be borne along in this manner; but the stranger appeared to possess superhuman strength, and moved along safely until they lost sight of him among some hay-stacks, for which they made.

"There, he's gone into Jackson's rick-yard," said the landlord; "get up; push on; we may be yet in time to prevent mischief."

The highwaymen ran hard; they had been out of breath for some time, and cold hardly move their feet, but they made a sudden effort, or spirit, and away they ran, and, in less than a minute, came up to the rick-yard.

They rushed into the yard, and then beheld the stranger seated upon some partially cut hay with the helpless maiden on his lap, but his fanged teeth were fleshed in her fair neck, and he was exerting himself in drawing the life stream from her veins.

As soon as he saw the highwaymen he arose, and the unfortunate girl rolled to the earth, and he started up and fled, the highwaymen firing a parting shot after him, with pretty good aim, yet it took no effect. The landlord's daughter was picked up warm, but lifeless. Whether it was in consequence of her wound and loss of blood, which was doubted, or from sheer fright, is not known, but the latter was considered most probable.

Chapter *CLXXI*

THE HOTEL. – THE FASHIONABLE ARRIVAL. – THE YOUNG HEIRESS.

*C*an it be true, and if so, how horribly strange, that a being half belonging to a world of spirits, should thus wander beneath the cold moon and the earth, bringing dismay to the hearts of all upon whom his strange malign influence is cast!

How frightful an existence is that of Varney the Vampyre!

There were some good points about the – man, we were going to say – and yet we can hardly feel justified in bestowing upon him that title, – considering the strange gift of renewable existence which was his. If it were, as, indeed, it seemed to be the case, that bodily decay in him was not the result of death, and that the rays "of the cold chaste moon" were sufficient to revivify him, who shall say when that process is to end? and who shall say that, walking the streets of giant London at this day, there may not be some such existences? Horrible thought that, perhaps seduced by the polished exterior of one who seems a citizen of the world in the most extended signification of the words, we should bring into our domestic circle a vampyre!

But yet it might be so. We have seen, however, that Varney was a man of dignified courtesy and polished manners; that he had the rare and beautiful gift of eloquence; and that, probably, gathering such vast experience from his long intercourse with society – an intercourse which had extended over so many years, he was able to adapt himself to the tastes and the feelings of all persons, and so exercise over them that charm of mind which caused him to have so dangerous a power.

At times, too, it would seem as if he regretted that fatal gift of immortality, as if he would gladly have been more human, and lived and died as those lived and died whom he saw around him. But being compelled to fulfill the order of his being, he never had the courage absolutely to take measures for his own destruction, a destruction which should be final in consequence of depriving himself of all opportunity of resuscitation.

Certainly the ingenuity of such a man might have devised some means of putting such an end to his life, that, in the perishable fragments of his body there should linger not one spark of that vitality which had been so often again and again fanned into existence.

Probably some effort of that kind may yet be his end, and we shall see that Varney the Vampyre will not, like the common run of the world's inhabitants, be changed into that dust of which is all humanity, but will undergo some violent disruption, and be for ever blotted out from the muster-roll of the living creatures that inhabit the great world.

But to cease speculating on such things, and to come to actual facts, we will now turn over another leaf in the strange eventful history of Varney the Vampyre.

*O*ne stormy, inclement evening in November, a traveling carriage, draggled with mud, and dripping with moisture, was driven up to the door of the London Hotel, which was an establishment not of the very first fashion, but of great respectability, situated then in Burlington-street, close to Old Bond-street, then the parade of fashion, and, as some thought, elegance; although we of the present day would look with risibility upon the costumes that were the vogue, although the period were but fifty years ago; but fifty years effect strange mutations and revolutions in dress, manners, and even in modes of thought.

The equipage, if not of the most dashing character, was still of sufficiently aristocratic pretensions to produce a considerable bustle in the hotel; and the landlord, after seeing that there was a coronet upon of the panels of the carriage door, thought it worth his while personally to welcome the guests who had done him the honor of selecting his house.

These guests consisted of an oldish man and woman, a young man of frivolous and foppish exterior, of about twenty-two years of age, and a young lady, who was so covered up in a multitude of shawls, that but little of her face could be seen; but that little was sufficient to stamp her at once as most beautiful.

The whole party evidently paid great court to this young lady, but whether they did so from affection, or from some more interested motive, it would not be proper just now to say, as those facts will come out before we have proceeded far in this little episode.

"Mind how you step, Annette," said the old gentleman, as the young lady descended the carriage. "Mind how you step, my dear."

"Oh! yes, yes," said the old lady, who was not so very old either, although entering upon the shady side of fifty. "Yes. Oh! mind my dear, how you get out."

The young lady made no reply to all these kind injunctions, but pushing aside the proffered arm of the younger gentleman, she tripped into the hotel unaided.

The old lady instantly followed her.

"Now, Francis," said the old gentleman to the servant, who got down from the rumble of the traveling carriage. "Now, Francis, you perfectly recollect, I hope, what my brother, Lord Lake, said to you?"

"Yes, sir," said Francis, but there was not the most respectful intonation in the world in the voice with which he returned the affirmative.

"You remember," continued the old gentleman; "you remember, Francis, that my brother told you, you were to wait upon us just the same as upon himself, with the carriage."

"Oh, yes."

"Oh, yes! what do you mean by saying 'oh, yes!' to me?"

"Do you want me to say, 'oh, no?'"

"Francis, this won't do. You are discharged."

"That for you, and the discharge, too," said Francis, as he snapped his fingers in the face of the old gentleman. "I never meant to serve you, Mister Lake; I'm Lord Lake's groom, but I ain't a going to be turned over to a canting fellow like you, so you have only took the words out of my mouth, for I meant to discharge myself, and so will George. I say, George."

"Yes," replied the coachman; "what is it?"

"Are we going to be at the beck and call of Jonathan Lake?"

"See him d——d first," was the laconic reply of the coachman.

"Now, Mister Lake," added Francis, "you knows what we thinks of you. You is a humbug. We only came so far, because we wouldn't put Miss Annette, our young lady, to the inconvenience of a post-chaise, while my lord, her father's carriage here, was so much more comfortable. We shall take that to the coach maker's, where my lord's other carriages are standing, till he comes to England, and then you won't see us no more."

"You rascals!"

"Oh, go on. You're a humbug; ain't he, George?"

"Oh, a *riglar* one — a *numbug* he is," aid the coachman; "and what's more, we don't believe a word of all what's been a going on. Lady Annette is Lady Annette, bless her sweet eyes. Come on, Francis, I'm wet."

"And I'm damp," said Francis, as he shook himself, and made as much splashing round him as a great Newfoundland dog, who has just had a bath. "I'm ready now, mister, and you knows our minds, and we ain't the sort of folks to alter 'em. We serves our master; but we doesn't serve a humbug."

Some of the waiters at the hotel had come to the door to hear this rather curious colloquy, and not a little surprised were they at it. At all events, whatever other effect it had upon them, it did not increase their respect for the new arrivals, and one of them, named Slop, ran after the carriage, and called out to Francis, —

"I say — I say!"

"Well, what?"

"I say, young fellow, just tell me where you will be staying, and I'll come and see you, and stand a glass."

Francis leant over the roof of the carriage, and said, —

"George — George!"

"Here ye *air,*" said George.

"Here's one o' the waiters at the hotel wants to make an acquaintance. It won't be a bad thing to know him, as you see he can tell us all about Lady Annette, and what the ladies are doing. What do you say to it, George?"

"A good idea, Francis."

"Very well. Hilloa! what's your name, old fellow?"

"Slop — Solomon Slop, they calls me."

"Well, if you come any evening to the King's Head, in Welbeck-street, you'll find either me or George; and we always likes good company, and shall be very glad to see you whenever you like. Suppose you say tomorrow?"

"I will, — I will; tomorrow I can come easily at eight o'clock, so you may expect me. Good night."

"Good night, Slop. Pleasant evening, ain't it? Drive on, George; I shall be in a ague presently; drive on, good luck to you, and let's get a change of things, whatever you do I never was so wet, I do think, in all my life."

"Nor me, nor me," said George, who it will be perceived was not very particular about his grammar; but that didn't matter much. He was paid for a knowledge of horses, not of moods, tenses, and cases.

Leaving the servants, then, of Lord Lake, as they had announced themselves to be, let us return to the hotel, where the family party had by this time got into comfortable enough quarters.

As far as the landlord of that establishment was concerned, Mr. Lake had won him over completely, by ordering the best rooms, a supper, as good as the house could afford, regardless of the price; the best wines, and altogether showed a right royal disposition as regarded expenditure.

But the waiters, who had often found by experience that the most extravagant people were not the most liberal to them, did not forget what had passed at the door, and many a whispered surmise passed from one to the other regarding the circumstances that had induced the coachman and groom to treat the family so very cavalierly, and so obstinately to decline serving them.

When Slop returned, he got some of his companions round him in the hall.

"I shall know all about it," he said; "I'm to go and take a glass with them tomorrow night, at the King's Head, in Welbeck-street, and you see if they don't tell me what it's all about. I wouldn't miss knowing for a trifle."

"Nor me — nor me."

"Well, I'll of course tell you all when I come back. You may depend upon it it's something worth knowing. Have you seen the young lady any of you. I caught just a look of one eye, and the end of her nose, and I should say she's a out-and-outer, and no mistake."

Chapter *CLXII*

THE SECOND ARRIVAL AT THE LONDON HOTEL. – THE MYSTERIOUS GUEST.

Scarcely had the bustle of the arrival we have noticed subsided at the London Hotel, when another traveling chariot dashed up to the door, and the landlord made a rush out to welcome his new arrival, considering himself quite in luck to have two such customers in one evening.

A gentleman, on whose head was a fur traveling cap, was at one of the windows of this carriage, and he called to the landlord, saying, —

"Are your best rooms occupied?"

"Not the best, sir," was the reply, "for we have several suites of apartments in all respects equal to each other; but we have a family just arrived in one suite. The Lake family, sir."

"Well, it don't matter to me who you have; I will get out if you can accommodate me."

"Oh, certainly, sir; you will find here accommodation of the very first character, I can assure you, sir. Pray, sir, alight. Allow me, sir, to hold an umbrella over you. It's a bad night, sir; I'm afraid the winter is setting in very strangely, sir, and prophetically of—"

"Silence. I don't want your opinion of the matter. If there's one thing I dislike more than another, it's a chattering man."

This rebuff silenced the landlord, who said not another word, although probably he thought the more; and those thoughts were not of a very kindly character as regarded the stranger, who had so very unceremoniously stopped his amiable remarks.

Indeed, when he got into the hall, he consigned the new comer to the care of the head waiter, and retired to his own apartment in great dudgeon.

"I hope everything is quiet here," said the stranger to the head waiter.

"Oh, dear, yes, sir; the house is as quiet as a lamb, sir, I can assure you. We have only three inmates at present, sir. There's the Lakes, — highly respectable people, sir. A brother of Lord Lakes, sir, I believe, and the—"

"I don't want to hear who you have. What the devil is it to me? If there's anything I dislike more than another, it's a d—d magpie of a waiter."

The head waiter was terribly offended, and said not another word, so that the gentleman was left in the sole occupation of his apartments, and then to fling himself upon a couch.

"Ah, ah! God knows how it will all end. Well, well, we shall see, we shall see. They have arrived, and that's one comfort; I am now, then, I think so well made up, that they will not readily know me. Oh, no, no, I should hardly know myself, now, shaven clean as I am, after being accustomed on the continent, to wear beard and moustache. Well, well, we shall see, how it will all end. Thank the fates, they have not gone somewhere where I could not find them." He rung the bell.

"Waiter, let me have the best the house affords, will you? and remember my name is Blue."

"Sir! Bl — Blue, sir?"

"Yes, Diggory Blue."

"Yes, sir, — yes sir. Certainly. What an odd name," soliloquized the waiter, as he went down stairs to tell his master. "I say sir, the gent in No. 10 and 11 says his name is Diggory Blue."

"Blue, Blue." said the landlord, "it is an odd name for a Christian."

"Perhaps he ain't a Christian," said the very identical Mr. Blue himself, popping his head over the bar in which the little discourse was going on, between the landlord and the waiter. "How do you know he's a Christian?"

"I beg your pardon, sir, really I – I – a-hem! a thousand pardons sir."

"Pshaw!"

The strange gentleman went to the door, and gave some directions to the servants belonging to his carriage, which sent them away, and then Mr. Blue started up into his rooms again, without saying another word to the landlord, who was terribly annoyed at being caught canvassing the name of one of his guests, with one of his waiters.

"Confound him," he muttered, "he has no business to have such a name as Blue and good God! if his surname was Blue, what the devil made his godfathers and godmothers call him Diggory? Sam, Sam!"

"Yes, sir."

"Put down in the book, Diggory Blue."

"Yes, sir."

"Bless us! why there's somebody else as I'm a sinner." The landlord could not have sworn by a better oath.

He ran to the door, and there beheld another traveling carriage, out of which stepped a gentlemanly looking man enveloped in a rich traveling cloak lined with fur.

"Can you accommodate us?" he said.

"Yes, sir, with pleasure."

"Who have you here, landlord?"

"A family named Lake, sir, and a Mr. – a – Blue, sir."

"Quiet people I dare say, I shall most likely remain with you a week or two. Let me have the best apartments you have unoccupied at present."

"Yes, sir. This way if you please, sir – this way."

The last arrival seemed to be in bad health, for he walked very slowly, like a man suffering from great bodily exhaustion, and more than once he paused as he followed the landlord up the principal staircase of the hotel, as if it were absolutely necessary he should do so to recover breath, and moreover the landlord heard him sigh deeply, but whether that was from mental or physical distress he had no means of knowing. His curiosity, however, was much excited by the gentleman, and his sympathies likewise, for he was the reverse of Mr. Blue, and listened with a refined and gentlemanly courtesy to whatever was said to him by any one apparently, although it was evidently an effort to speak, so weak and ill did he seem to be.

"I am sorry, sir," said the landlord, when he had shewn the gentleman into his rooms, "I am sorry sir, you don't seem well."

"I am rather an invalid, but I dare say I shall soon be better, thank you – thank you. One candle only, I dislike too much light: charge for as many as you please, but never let me have but one, landlord."

"As you please, sir, as you please; I hope you will make yourself comfortable here, and I can assure you, sir, that nothing shall be wanting on my part to make you so."

"I am sure of that, landlord; you are very good, thank you."

"What name shall I say, sir, in case any gentleman should call to see you, sir?"

"Black."

"Black, sir!" — "Black." — "Oh, Mr. Black! — Yes, sir, certainly, why not? Oh, of course. I — only thought it a little odd, you see, sir, because we have a gentleman already in the house called Blue. That was all, sir. Mr. Black, thank you, sir."

The landlord bowed himself out, and Mr. Black inclined his head with the look of a condescending emperor, so that when the landlord got down stairs, he said to his wife, —

"Now that *is* a gentleman. he listens to all you have got to say, like a gentleman, and don't snap you up as that Mr. Blue did. Mr. Black, it is quite clear to me, is a man of the world, and a perfect gentleman. Hilloa, what's that? Eh? What! why it's Mr. Black's bell, and he must have almost broken the wire. Sam, Sam! run up to 8, and see what's wanted."

Sam did run up to 8, and when he got there, he found Mr. Black lying upon the floor in a fainting fit, and wholly insensible.

The alarmed waiter ran down stairs to his master with the news, and the nearest medical man was sent for, but with as little parade as possible, for the hotel-keeper did not wish to alarm all his other guests with the news of the fact that there was a sick person in the house, which he knew was not plesing to many persons, and might induce them to change their quarters.

When the medical man came, he was shown up stairs at once, when Mr. Black had been lifted on to a sofa, where he lay without any signs of consciousness at all, much to the horror of the landlord, who began to think he was dead, and that there would be all the disagreeableness of having a corpse in his house.

The surgeon felt the pulse and the heart, and then he said, —

"He is in a swoon, but he must be in a desperately weak state."

"He looks it, don't he, sir?"

"He does indeed. How dreadfully emaciated he is!"

By dint of great exertion and the use of stimulants, the surgeon succeeded in restoring Mr. Black to consciousness, and when he was so restored, he looked around him with that strange vacant expression which a man wears who has newly come out of a trance and whose memory is in a state of abeyance.

"Well, sir, how are you now?" said the surgeon.

He made no reply.

"I should advise that he be put to bed, landlord," added the medical man, "and something of a warm nourishing quality given to him. I will send him some medicine."

Mr. Black now made an effort to speak, and his memory seemed to have come back to him as he said,

"I fear I have been a deal of trouble, but the fatigue of traveling fast – it is that has unnerved me – I shall be much better tomorrow. Thank you all."

"I will call tomorrow" said the surgeon, "and see how you get on, if you please."

"I shall be much obliged; I feel myself quite strong enough to retire for the night without assistance, thank you."

He made no opposition to the landlord sending him up by Sam some spiced wine, and when it came, he said, –

"I hope no one sleeps near me who will come in late and disturb me, as I require a full and clear night's repose."

"Oh no, sir," said Sam, "it's a young lady sir, as belongs to the Lake family sleeps in the next room but one to you, that is to say, No. 9. The very next room ain't occupied at all, sir, to night, so you will be as quiet as if you was in a church, sir."

"Thank you, thank you, good night, Samuel."

Chapter CLXIII

THE NIGHT ALARM – A SCENE OF CONFUSION. – MR. BLUE SUSPECTED.

*I*t is midnight, and the landlord of the hotel suddenly springs out of bed on to the floor as if he had been galvanized, carrying with him all the bed-clothes and leaving his wife shivering.

"Good gracious! what was that?" he cried.

And well he might, for the repose of the whole house was broken in upon by two loud shrieks, such as had never before sounded within those walls, and then all was still as the grave.

"Murder! murder!" shouted the landlady, "somebody has stolen all the bed-clothes."

"Bother the bed-clothes" cried the landlord, as he hurried on his apparel by the dim light of a night lamp that was burning on the dressing table. "There's something wrong in the house, or else I have had one of the strangest dreams that ever anybody had, and one of the most likely reality too. Did you hear them?"

"Oh, those horrid screams!"

"It's not a dream then, for two people don't dream the same thing at the same moment of time that's quite clear. Hark — hark! what's that, what a banging of doors to be sure. Who's there? Who's there? Wait a bit."

The landlord lifted the night bolt of his bed room, and then there dashed into the room in only one garment, which fluttered in the breeze, no other than the young man who had come with the ladies. He made but one spring into the landlord's bed, crying, —

"Oh! take care of me. Oh, save me! There's thieves or something and I shall be hurt. Oh, save me, save me, I can't fight, I never did, spare my life, oh, spare my life."

"Oh, the wretch!" shrieked the landlady, and the landlord, justly enough enraged at that intrusion, seized upon the intruder and shot him out of the room *vi et armis*, and that with such force too that he rolled all the way down the stairs, upsetting Sam who was rushing up with a lantern, it having been his turn to sit up all night, as one of the establishment always did, in case of fire or anything happening which might make it necessary to arouse the inmates of the house.

The landlord, however, had completed enough of his toilette to enable him to make a decent appearance; so out he sallied, having lit a candle, and the first person he met upon the landing was Mr. Blue, fully dressed and with a pistol in his hand.

"Good God, sir," cried the landlord, "what is it all about, what has happened sir?"

"I cannot tell you, and am as anxious as you can be to know. This way, this way. It was the young lady who screamed. For God's sake, lend me a light!"

The landlord resigned his light mechanically, and he saw to his surprise, that there was a black patch now over one of Mr. Blue's eyes, and he thought his face was painted. At all events, he was so much disguised that it was only by his voice that the landlord knew him.

Before however, they either of them got across the corridor to the door of the young lady's room, Mr. and Mrs. Lake half-dressed, made their appearance, both eagerly inquiring what was the matter.

"I don't know," said the landlord, "I only heard a scream."

"Which came from the apartment of that young lady," said Mr. Blue.

"What young lady?" said Mr. Lake sharply. "It's rather odd that you, a stranger, should know so precisely which was the apartment of that young lady. Mrs. Lake go in and see if anything be the matter with Annetta; I hope to Heaven, nothing is amiss with her."

Mr. Lake looked suspiciously at Mr. Blue, and so did the landlord, for when Mr. Blue had spoken in the presence of the Lakes, his voice was completely altered, so that the landlord no longer could have recognized him by it, and he was more puzzled than ever.

"Oh! come in, come in, Mr. Lake," cried Mrs. Lake, appearing at the door of Annetta's room, "she is dead."

"Dead!" cried Mr. Blue with a shout, "Oh! no, no, no!"

He dashed past Mr. Lake, the landlord, and Mrs. Lake, and was in the room in a moment. They went after him as soon as they had recovered sufficiently from their surprise to do so, and they saw him with his hands clasped, and bending over the form of the beautiful young girl as she lay in bed.

"No, no, no," he said, "she is not dead. She has fainted. God knows what the cause may be, but she is not dead. Thank Heaven!"

He turned from the bedside, and without saying another word to the parties present, he walked away to his own room, and left them staring at each other in surprise. The young lady now opened her eyes, and looked wildly about her for a few moments, and then she spoke quickly,

"Oh, help! help! help! away, away. Oh, horror — horror — horror!"

"Annetta, my dear Annetta," said Mrs. Lake, "what is this? Pray, sir, retire," to the landlord. "My dear Annetta, what has alarmed you? My dear, go away, Mr. Lake. I will let you know all about it. It's a mystery to me at present. Go away, I'll be back soon."

Mr. Lake left the room, and in the corridor he found the landlord, who was looking as bewildered as any mortal man could well look, for he could make neither head nor tail of the whole affair.

"Landlord," said Mr. Lake, "who is that party who behaved so strangely just now?"

"His name is Blue, sir."

"Blue — Blue. An odd name, and an odd man. Where can I have seen him before. Just as he cried out, and went into the room, I thought there was a something in his voice that came familiarly to my ears, and yet I don't know him; I suspect landlord, that he has had more to do with this midnight disturbance than he would care to own."

"Well, sir, I don't know," said the landlord, whose interest it was not to disoblige, or throw suspicion upon any of his guests. "It really ain't very likely, sir. I should say the young lady has had a bad dream, sir, and that's almost all that can be said about it."

"It may be so."

"You may depend that's what it will turn out to be, sir."

"I hope so, I hope so. These things are not at all pleasant, and if anything of the kind should happen again we should have to quit directly, you know, but I can say nothing now about it until I have heard from Mrs. Lake what account Annetta gives of the affair. That alone must guide us in the whole business. In the morning we will talk about it, sir."

There was a great deal of austerity in the manner of Mr. Lake; indeed he might well enough be excused for not being over pleased at what had taken place, and as for Mr. Blue there certainly was sufficient in his behavior to induce a large amount of suspicion, that he was in some way connected with the affair. Moreover the efforts he evidently made in the way of disguise were extremely suspicious in themselves. He evidently had a something to conceal, and when the landlord was now left alone in the corridor, he was strongly induced to make one of his first acts in the morning a notice to Mr. Blue, that he would much prefer his room to his company at the London Hotel.

And then it all of a sudden came into the landlord's head, how poor Mr. Black must have been distressed at what had taken place; for Sam had told him what Mr. Black had said about wishing to sleep quietly, so that he felt quite a pang at the idea of so civil a gentleman having been so awfully disturbed, as he must have been, and he had no doubt but that in the morning he would go away.

"I wonder if he is awake?" thought the landlord; "if I could but make some sort of apology to him tonight, and soothe him, all might be well. I'll first go and listen at his door; it may be that he really wants something, and if so perhaps it would look attentive to knock and see him; I think I will. It's quite out of the question that he should have slept in the middle of all this riot."

He approached Mr. Black's door, and listened.

All was still as the very grave.

"What a horrid thing it would be if the shock, in his weak state, has been the death of him!" thought the landlord, and the very idea made him quake again.

After a few moments passed in this state of painful thought, he found that it would be quite out of the question for him to go to his own room again, without ascertaining how Mr. Black was, and accordingly he knocked at the door, first gently and then louder, and then louder still, but received no answer.

"Oh, this won't do, I must get in somehow," thought the landlord.

He tried the handle, and found in a moment that the door was not fast; a light was burning on the side of the table which was close to the bed, and there lay Mr. Black fast asleep, and looking so calm and serene, although he was an ugly man, that the landlord was truly astonished to see him.

"Well," he said, "that's what I call sound sleeping, at all events. It's a mercy however." Oh lor! he' going to awake."

Mr. Black opened his eyes, and looked up.

"I beg your pardon, sir," said the landlord, "I earnestly beg your pardon, but as there had been a little noise in the house I came to see, first, if you had been disturbed, an then if you wanted anything, sir."

"No, no, thank you. Has there been a noise, do you say."

"A — a little, sir."

"Well, I was fast asleep and did not hear it. However, I do sleep so sound that I think a cannon going off at my ear would hardly awaken me. I am much obliged however for your attention, landlord."

"Can't I get you anything, sir?"

"Nothing until the morning, thank you."

"Thank you sir, good night sir, good night." — "Well," said the landlord, as, finding all quiet, he took his way now back to his own room, "well, he is a gentleman, every inch of him, that he is. How very mild and polite. — He hasn't been disturbed, well that's a comfort."

Chapter CLXIV

THE WAITER TELLS THE STORY OF THE LAKES' DISTURBANCE TO GEORGE AND FRANCIS.

Nothing further occurred during the night to cause any alarm to the inmates of the London Hotel, but we may as well give Miss Annetta's account of the night's transaction; and account which she gave to Mrs. Lake at the time, and which soon spread all over the hotel, with, no doubt, many additions and embellishments as it was carried.

She said, that having retired to rest, she, being fatigued by her journey, soon dropped off asleep. That she, to the best of her belief, fastened her room door, although she certainly could not absolutely swear to having done so, she was so very weary. She did not know how long she had slept, but she had a frightful dream, in which she thought she was pursued by wolves who ran after her through a large tract of country until she took shelter in a wood, and then all the wolves left her and abandoned the pursuit, except one, and that one caught her and fastened his fangs in her throat just as she sunk down exhausted upon a great heap of dried leaves that came in her way in the forest.

She then went on to say that in the agony of her dream she actually awoke at that moment, and saw a human face close to her, and that *a man had his mouth close to her neck, and was sucking her blood.*

It was then that she uttered the two screams which had so alarmed the whole house; and then she stated that the vampire, for such she named the apparition, left her and she fainted away.

Now this story so far as it went, might all be very well accounted for by being called a dream, and the change from a wolf to a man might be but one of those fantastic changes that our sleeping visions so frequently undergo, but — and in this case this was a serious but — but *she showed upon her neck the marks of two teeth,* and there was a small wound on which even in the morning was a little portion of coagulated blood.

This staggered everybody, as well it might, and the whole hotel was in a state of confusion. Mr. Blue kept his room. Mr. Black got up and declared that he was much better than the day before, attributing his indisposition to bodily fatigue; and the Lakes were in a state of consternation difficult to describe.

The landlord, too, was nearly out of his senses at the idea of a vampire being in his house, and a grand consultation was held in the bar parlor between him, Mr. and Mrs. Lake, and Mr. Black, who was asked if he would step down and give his opinion, which compliment was paid to him on account of his being such a gentlemanly and quiet man.

They took it in turns to speak, and the landlord had the first say.

"Gentlemen," he said, "and you madam, you can easily conceive how grieved I am about what has taken place, and I can only say that anything in the world that I can do to find out all about it, I will do with the greatest possible pleasure. Command me in any way, but — but if I have a suspicion of anybody in this house, it is of that Mr. Blue."

"And I too," said Mrs. Lake.

"I don't know what to say further," remarked Mr. Lake, "than that my suspicions of some foul play on the part of Mr. Blue, are so strong, that if he is not turned out of the Hotel, we will leave tonight."

"That's conclusive," said the landlord. "But if you Mr. Black, would favor us with your opinion, I'm sure, sir, we should be all much obliged."

"I am afraid," said Mr. Black in his quiet, gentlemanly way, "that my opinion will be of very little importance, as I know nothing of the whole affair, but just what I have heard from one and another; I slept all the while it appears. But there is one circumstance that certainly to me is an unpleasant and a suspicious one, and that is that Mr. Blue, as he calls himself, was up and dressed, and that, with the exception of your night-watchman, he was the only person in the hotel who was so."

"That's a fact," said the landlord, "I met him."

"Then that settles the business," said Mr. Lake, "send him away. God knows if there be such things as vampires or not, but al all events, the suspicion is horrid, so you had better get rid of him at once."

"I will — I will."

"Stop," said Mr. Black. "Before you do so, is it not worth while to make some effort to come at the precise truth, and that in my opinion, would be very desirable indeed."

"It would — it would," said Mr. Lake, "you must understand, sir, that the young lady is especially under my care, and in fact I esteem her greatly — very greatly I may say, for a variety of reasons, and therefore anything that I can do, which may have the effect of securing her peace of mind and happiness will be to me a sacred purpose."

"Then I should recommend," said Mr. Black, "that this lady and your wife, landlord, keep watch in the young lady's chamber tonight."

"Oh, I couldn't — I couldn't," said the landlady.

"Nor I," replied Mrs. Lake, "nor I, I'm sure, I cannot think of such a thing, I could not do it, I should faint away from terror.

"And so should I," cried the landlady. "I feel quite ill even now at the thought of the thing."

"Then I can say no more, ladies. Of course, gentlemen cannot very well, unless they are very near relatives, undertake such a job. I tell you what we can do, though; suppose we watch in the corridor, you and I, Mr. Lake, and leaving the door of the young lady's chamber just closed we shall hear if there be any alarm given from within and effectually secure her from intrusion without. What say you to this, as a plan of proceedings? There is your son too, might keep watch with us."

"I'm afraid he is too nervous."

"Yes," said the landlord, "and he might pop into my bed again, as he did last night in his fright. Oh don't have him gentlemen, I beg of you. I would go myself, but I am so sleepy always, that I never can keep my eyes open after twelve o'clock. Not that I am at all afraid of anything, but its downright sleepiness you see, gentlemen. I am on my feet all day, and — and so you see I'd rather not on the whole."

"I am willing," said Mr. Black.

"Sir," said Mr. Lake, "I am quite ashamed of giving you so much trouble, but I can only say that I shall be very much obliged indeed, by your company, and I do hope that we shall have the pleasure of catching Mr. Blue if he be guilty."

"Or acquitting him if innocent," added Mr. Black. "Let us be just even in the midst of our suspicions. It would be a terrible thing to stigmatize this gentleman as a vampire, when perhaps he may have as great a horror of such gentry as we possibly can."

At this moment young Lake made his appearance. He looked rather pale as he apologized to the landlord for his unintentional intrusion into his room over night.

"The fact is," said he, "I am as constitutionally brave as a lion, and so whenever anything occurs I run away."

"Indeed, sir, an odd way of showing courage," said Mr. Black. "Why do you run away?"

"For fear, sir, of doing something rash."

"Well, I certainly never heard a better excuse for an undignified retreat in one's shirt, before in my life. But you will not be called upon to do anything tonight. You had better shut yourself up, and let you hear what you will, you need not come out of your room, you know."

"Well, do you know, sir, I think that it would be the best way, for if I came out I might do something rash, such as kill somebody, which I should afterwards be sorry for, you know."

"Certainly."

"Then that's understood, father, that let what will happen I won't come out. I have been speaking to Annetta, but I can't somehow or another get her to be pleasant."

"Hush!" said old Lake, and he bent his brows upon his son reprovingly, as if he fancied that he was letting out more of the family secrets than he ought to have done. The young man was silent accordingly, for he seemed to be in great dread of his father, who certainly if not a better man, was a man of much more intellect and courage than the son, who was but a very few degrees removed from absolute silliness. He was fool enough to be wicked, and the father was cunning enough to be so. How strange that vice should usually belong to the two extremes of intellect, that folly and talent should lead to similar results, a disregard of the ordinary moral obligations; but it is so.

We may pass over the rest of the day, and we do so the more willingly, because we are anxious that the reader should be possessed of some particulars which George and Francis, the servants of Lord Lake communicated without any reserve at all to Slop, the waiter.

Indeed, far from having anything like a wish to conceal anything, they seemed to glory in saying as much as they could with respect to those matters that were uppermost in their mind.

This was just the frame of mind that Slop would have wished in his prayers, had he prayed at all upon the subject, to find them in; for although Slop was quite remarkable for neglecting his own affairs, he never neglected anybody else's and curiosity had been the bane of his existence.

Upon arriving at the King's Head, in Chiswell-street, he found that the servants of Lord Lake were there, according as they had said they should be, and glasses of something uncommonly hot and strong having been ordered, they and Slop soon grew quite happy and familiar together.

First, though, before they would commence a history of anything they had to tell of the Lake family, they resolved upon hearing form Slop all that had passed at the London Hotel, and you may be quite sure, that it lost nothing in the telling, but was duly made as much of as the circumstances would permit. No doubt the fumes of the something hot materially assisted Mr. Slop's invention and general talents upon the interesting occasion.

Chapter CLXV

THE COMMUNICATION OF THE SERVANTS RESPECTING THE LAKE FAMILY.

*T*he coachman and groom, evidently listened with great interest to what Slop had to relate. For a wonder, they were completely silent while he spoke; and when he had concluded, they looked at each other, and nodded, as much to say, — Ah! we can draw some conclusion from all that, that you Mr. Slop, really know nothing at all about.

"Is that all?" said George.

"Yes," said the waiter, "and sufficient I think."

"More, a good deal," remarked Francis. "But howsomdever, as you seem a proper sort of fellow, we don't mind telling you what we think of the matter."

"No, no," interposed George, "not exactly that."

"And why not?"

"Because you see, Francis, we have never known yet, my boy, what to think about it."

"Well there's some truth in that at all events. But we will tell Mr. Slop what happened once before that wasn't much unlike what has taken place at the London Hotel."

"Well, but tell him first who she is," said George. "Then he'll understand all the rest better, as well as taking more interest in it."

"Very good. Then listen, Mr. Slop."

"With all my ears," said Slop.

At this moment a bell rung sharply, and Slop on the impulse of the moment, sprung up, —

"Coming — coming — coming."

Both George and Francis burst into a great laugh, and Slop was quite disconcerted.

"Really, gentlemen," he said, "I'm sorry, very sorry, but I'm so used to cry, coming, when a bell rings, that, for the moment, I forgot there was no sort of occasion to do so here. I begs you won't think no more of it, but tell me all as you have got to tell."

"Don't mention it," said Francis, and then after taking another draught of the something strong, and settling himself in his seat, commenced.

"Lord Lake, you know, is our master, and a very good sort of a man he is, only he's a — a — a; what did the doctor call him George?"

"Oh, I know, a — a — a, what was it Frank?"

"Well, I asked you. It was a *wallytoddyhairyhun,* I think."

"Something like it. Odd wasn't it?"

"Wery."

"I beg your pardon, gentlemen," said a gentlemanly looking man who was seated in an obscure corner of the room, and who was desperately ugly — at least so much as could be seen of his face, for it was much muffled up. "I beg your pardon, but the word you mean I suppose is valetudinarian."

"That's it, that's it! I knows it when I hears it. That's it; well they say that in consequence of being that ere he was rather cross-grained a little when there wasn't no sort of occasion for it, and barring that, which, poor man, I suppose he could not help, he was about as decent a master as ever stepped in shoe leather, wasn't he, George?"

"I believe you, my boy."

"Well, the Countess of Bhackbighte was his mother-in-law, you see, a wicious old woman as ever lived, and when Lady Lake died it was she as brought the news to Lord Lake that his wife was dead, and the wirtuous baby as she had just brought into the world was dead too, wasn't that it, George?"

"I believe you my boy, rather."

"Well, Lord Lake was *inconsolotable* as they says, for ever so long, and he made friends with his brother who would come next into the property; they all went abroad together."

"All who?" said Slop.

"Wery good, I'll tell you, Lord Lake, his brother, his brother's wife and son. Them as is now at the London Hotel. Now you knows, don't you?"

"Go on, I knows."

"Well they hadn't been there above a matter o' fourteen years when the old Countess of Bhackbighte dies, and then there comes a letter to my lord as says that the precious baby as his wife had brought into the world just afore she went out of it herself, wasn't dead at all, but had been smuggled away by the old Countess, nobody knows what for, and that she was alive and kicking then, and ready to come to her papa whenever he said the word, and so come she did, you see, and that's our young lady Annetta, you see, as is at the London Hotel."

"Well, but I don't understand," said Slop.

"Of course you don't"

"Oh."

"But you will if you goes on a listening; you can't expect to understand all at once you know. Just attend to the remainder and you'll soon know all about it; but George is the man to tell you, that he is."

"Oh, no, no," said George.

"Why, you heard it, and told it to me. Come, don't be foolish, but tell it at once, old fellow."

"Well, if I must, I must," said George, "so here goes; though when I has to tell anything, I always feels as if I was being *druv* with a curb half-a-dozen links too tight. But here goes."

"I am very much amused," said Slop, "and should certainly like to hear it all. Pray go on?"

"Well, you must know we was at an old tumble down place in Italy, as they call's Rome. Horridly out o' repair, but that's neither here nor there. In course we had stables and riding out; and there was a nice sort o' terrace where Lord Lake used to walk sometimes, as well as his brother, while the carriage was being got out, so that I could hear what they said if I chose to do so.

"Well, one day the brother, Mr. Lake, or the Honorable Dick Lake as he was sometimes called, was walking there alone, and I seed as he was all of a tremble like, you understand! but I could not have any idea of what it was about. Once or twice I heard him say, — 'It will do — and it will do'"

"Presently, then out comes Lord Lake, and he says, giving the other a letter, 'Good God, read that!' Give us a trifle more sugar?"

"What?"

"Why, what do you mean," said Francis. "Is that the way to tell a story, to run into what people says what you happens to want yourself? Here's the sugar, and now go on."

"Well, the brother reads it, and then he says; 'Gracious Providence,' says he 'this here says as the Lady Annetta, ain't your daughter, but a *himposter.'*

"'Yes,' says Lord Lake, 'oh, what will become of me now?'

"'Calm yourself,' says the brother, 'and leave this affair to me. Let her go with me to England, and we will clear up the mystery. I love her as I would a child of my own; but still this here letter' says he, 'seems to contain such a statement;' says he——"

"Well? Well?"

"That's all! After that, they walked off the terrace and I didn't hear no more at all. After that, in a day or two Lord Lakes comes to me; and says, 'George, my brother and his family, with Lady Annetta, are going to England. I wish you and Francis to accompany them and to attend upon them, just the same as you would on myself,' says he, and in course I didn't like to say anything; so we came, but as our idea of the brother is that he's a humbug, we wouldn't have no more to do with him, after we got to London, you see; and so off we went as you heard."

"Well, but," said Slop; "there was a something else you was to tell me;"

"So there was," said Francis "and this was it. While we were staying at a place called Florence, and sleeping all of us in an old palace, there was an alarm in the middle of the night, and we found it came from the chamber of the Lady Annetta; who said that a man had got in by the window, and she just woke in time to see him; and when she screamed out away he went again, but nothing could be seen of him; the oddest thing was that the window was so high from the ground, that it seemed to be quite out of the question that he could have got at it without a ladder; yet the deuce of a ladder was there to be seen."

"And who was it?"

"Nobody ever knew, but the night after it was said that a vampire had visited a cottage near at hand, and fastened on the throat of a little girl of about seven, and sucked half the blood out of her, so that she was lying at the point of death; and the description the child gave of him was so like what the Lady Annetta said of the man that had got in at the window of her bedroom, that my lord got very uneasy about it, and moved away from Florence as quick as he could, and no wonder, either, you will say."

"It was odd."

"It was, and what you have told me of last night, put me in mind of it, you see."

"No doubt; Lord, I'm all of a twitter myself."

"Why, what need you care? those who know about vampires say that there are two sorts, one sort always attacks its own relations as was, and nobody else, and the other always selects the most charming young girls, and nobody else, and if they can't get either, they starve to death, waste away and die, for they take no food or drink of any sort, unless they are downright forced."

"But who told you?"

"Oh, an old Italian priest, who spoke English."

Chapter CLXVI

THE MYSTERIOUS STRANGER. – THE NIGHT WATCH.

At this moment, the stranger who had put the coachman and groom right about the word valetudinarian, rose from the seat he had occupied in the corner of the room, and uttering a deep, hollow groan, walked towards the door.

The party looked at him with awe and astonishment. He was of great height but frightfully thin, and the slight glance they could get of his face, showed how perfectly ugly he was. In another moment he had left the place, and there was a silence of several minutes duration after he had done so, but it was at length broken by the coachman, who said, –

"I say, Frank, my boy."

"Here you is," said Francis.

"Don't you think if you never seed anybody as looked like a vampire before, you have seed one now."

"The devil," said Francis, "you don't mean that?"

"Yes, I do though, and it strikes me wonderful as we have been a telling all we had to tell afore the very indiwidual, of all others, as we oughtn't to a told it to, that's a vampire. If a *hoss* is a *hoss*, that's a vampire, Frank! I knows it – I feels it."

Frank looked aghast.

"Why, why," then he said, "we have just told him where to find the

Lady Lake if he wants her. Lor — what — suppose it's the same one as got in at the window at Florence! I'll have him, he can't have got far, I should say, by this time, and hang me if I don't stop him and know what he is, afore he goes any further. I shan't sleep if I don't."

Without waiting for any reply, although the coachman, and Mr. Slop both seemed to be upon the point of saying something, out rushed the valorous Francis into the street. But in about three minutes he came back, and sat down with a disappointed look.

"He's off," he said.

"In course," said the coachman, "through the air like a sky rocket, you might a know'd that; but arter all, Frank, he mayden't be a vampire. Do vampires come into public houses, eh? Answer me that will you; I rather think that's a settler, Frank."

"Do you" said Frank. "It might be, old fellow, if you could prove it. It would be an odd thing for a vampire to come into a public house and drink, but I don't see, if he has anything again by it, anything to prevent him coming and ordering and paying for something, and then leaving it. Look there!"

Frank pointed to the brimming glass of something which was on the table just where the mysterious man had sat, and this to the coachman and to Slop was such proof positive that they both looked at each other with the most rueful expression of their countenances.

"I think you are convinced now, you old ump," added Frank.

"Rather, rather."

"I'm all over of a cold *inspiration,*" said Slop.

"Well," added Frank, "it's not never of no use, you know, putting yourself out of the way about it, and that's the fact, and all I've got to say is that I've got nothing to say."

"Wery good, wery good."

"But if you, Mr. Slop, will give us a call tomorrow and let us know if anything wrong has took place at the London Hotel, we shall be very much obliged to you; for it's natural for us that we feel an interest in what's going on there on account of our young lady, who we won't and don't think is anything else but our young lady, and if she was not, she ought to be; and I tell you what, just keep an eye on the spooney, young Lake."

"I will."

"He wants to be quite sweet with the Lady Annetta, but she can't abide him. But you tell us if he tries to pitch it too strong, and we shall perhaps hit on some scheme of operations."

All this Slop promised faithfully, and with his own nerves rather startled at the idea of having been in the same room for the better part of an hour with a vampire, he walked back to the hotel, and as he had not been enjoined to any secrecy he gave the landlord a full and particular account of all that had taken place.

This was listened to with no small degree of interest, but as mine host of the London Hotel could make nothing of it, he could do nothing with it.

"Slop," he said, "I don't like the state of things at all, I assure you, Slop, and I rather shake than otherwise about what's to occur tonight. You know there's to be a watch kept in the corridor by the young lady's room, or else poor thing no doubt she wouldn't get a wink of sleep, and I'm quite sure that I shan't at all events, let what will happen or what won't; I'm all in a twitter now as it is, I've broke nine wine glasses already; and all I can say is, I wish they would all go away."

The landlord did not like to give good guests notice to quit his house, but he had a consultation with Mr. Black, whom he considered to be quite his sheet-anchor in this affair, for if that gentleman had not offered to sit up and watch for the vampire, he, the landlord, certainly would, despite all profitable considerations, have requested guests who brought with them such questionable connections to leave.

The night had now come on, and as hour after hour passed away, the anxiety of all concerned in the affairs that were taking place at the London hotel increased. But we need not occupy the time and attention of the reader with surmises and reflections while facts of an interesting and strange nature remain to be detailed.

Suffice it that at eleven o'clock the Lady Annetta retired to rest.

Two chairs, and a table on which burnt two candles, were placed in the corridor just outside the room in which the fair girl who had the previous night had such a visitor reposed, and there sat Mr. Black and Mr. Lake, both determined to do their utmost to discover the mystery of the vampire's appearance, and to capture him should he again show himself.

During the first half hour's watch, Mr. Lake related to his companion the particulars of the affair at Florence, which as it has already been told by Francis, we need not again recapitulate, suffice it to say that the narration was listened to by Mr. Black with great interest.

"And did you," he said, "make no discovery of who this midnight visitor was?"

"None whatever."

"'Tis awfully strange."

"It is, and has given her abundance of uneasiness."

"And well it may, sir, I shall be very happy if through my means any elucidation of these mysteries and truly terrific visitations should take place."

"You are very good sir. What is that?"

"Twelve o'clock, I think, striking by some neighboring church timekeeper. Hush! is it not so? Yes, twelve."

"It is. How still the house is. I was told this was a very quiet hotel, and so indeed I find it, but yet, I suppose upon this occasion there is more stillness than usual."

"Doubtless. Hush, hush! what was that? I thought I heard something like a window opening slowly and cautiously. Hark! There again. Do you not hear it. Hush, hush. Listen now."

"On my life I can hear nothing."

"Indeed your sense of hearing then is not so sharp as mine. Look there."

He pointed as he spoke to the door of Mr. Blue' chamber, which was opened a very short distance, not above a couple of inches, and then he added in a whisper, "What do you think of that?"

"By heaven! I suspected him before."

"And I — and — be still, whatever you do. But yet perhaps it would be better. Go down stairs and bring up the hall porter, we may as well be in force you know. The door at the head of the stairs is open. You can depend upon my keeping a good watch while you are gone. Now, now, quick, or we may be pounced upon and murdered before we are aware."

Thus urged Mr. Lake ran down stairs for the purpose of rousing up the night-porter, and he found that that individual did indeed require rousing up.

"Hilloa, my man," he said, "get up!"

"Eh? eh? what? fire!"

"No, no, they want you up stairs, that's all. You are a pretty fellow to consider yourself a night-watch here and to be fast asleep. Why, with the exception that you have your clothes on you, you are no more ready than anybody else in the house."

"I beg your pardon sir, I always sleeps with one eye open."

"Well well, come up stairs!"

A loud scream at this moment came upon their ears, and the night-porter staggered back again into his great leathern chair, from whence he had just risen, and looked aghast! while Mr. Lake turned pale and trembled fearfully.

"Good God!" he said, "what's that?"

A bell was run furiously, and then ceased, with a sudden jar, as if the wire had broken, which was indeed the fact. Then Mr. Lake, mustering all the courage he possessed, ran up stairs again, leaving the night-porter to follow him, or not as he felt inclined; but when he reached the door at the top of the staircase, he found that it was fast, nor could he with all his strength force it open.

"Help! help! help!" he heard a voice cry.

Chapter *CLXVII*

THE VAMPIRE'S FEAST. – THE ALARM AND THE PURSUIT.

A general ringing of bells now ensued in the hotel, from all the bedrooms that were occupied, and the din in the house was quite terrific.

Mr. Lake hammered away at the door leading to the corridor, and he was soon joined by the hall-porter, who having now recovered from the first shock which the scream had given him, showed more courage and determination than any one would have given him credit for. He was rather a bulky man, and without any more ado, he flung himself bodily against the door with such force that he dashed it open and rolled into the corridor.

All was darkness.

"Lights! lights! lights!" shouted Mr. Lake. "Lights! – Mr. Black, where are you? Mr. Black! Mr. Black!"

A door, it was that of Mr. Blue, was now dashed open, and that gentleman appeared with a candle in his hand, and a pistol firmly grasped in the other. It was very strange but he wore an artificial masquerade nose of an enormous size, and had on a red wig.

"Who locked my door?" he cried, "who locked my room door on the outside and forced me to break it open – who did it?"

"Where is the vampire?" said Mr. Lake.

"Lights! lights! Lights!" shouted the night-watchman, and in another minute the landlord and several waiters, half-dressed but carrying lights, and each armed with the first weapon of offence he could lay his hands on at the moment, made their appearance on the scene of action.

"What is it? What is it?" cried the landlord. "Oh what is it?"

"God knows," cried Mr. Lake, and he darted into the apartment of the young lady. In another moment he emerged, and tottered towards one of the seats.

"She is covered with blood," he said.

Mr. Blue and the landlady of the Hotel both made a rush then into the room, and the former came out in a minute, and going to his own apartment shut the door. They thought that they then heard him fall at full length upon the floor. All was mystery.

"I'm bewildered," said the landlord, "What *is* it all about?"

"And where is Mr. Black?" asked Mr. Lake.

"Here," cried a waiter as he pointed to an insensible form lying so close to the table, that nobody had as yet noticed it. "Here he is. He looks as if he was dead."

Poor Mr. Black was lifted up, his eyes were closed as well as his mouth, and he seemed to breathe with difficulty. He was placed in a chair, and then held, while water was dashed in his face to recover him, and after a time, just as one of the waiters who had been sent for the surgeon again who had before attended the young lady, made his appearance with that gentleman, he slowly opened his eyes.

"Oh! mercy, mercy! Where am I now?"

"What is all this about?" inquired the medical man.

"Nobody knows sir," said the landlord, "that's the beauty of it. But the young lady is very bad again; will you, wife, show the doctor into her room. Good God, I shall go out of my wits, and my hotel that has a character forming one of the quietest in all London — yes, the quietest I may say. I'm a ruined man."

"Mr. Black," said Mr. Lake, "I implore you if you can to tell the meaning of all this."

"All — all I know," said Mr. Black faintly. "All I know, —"

Everybody gathered round him to listen, and with looks of fright and apprehension, and a trembling voice, he said: —

"I — I was sitting here waiting for Mr. Lake to come back with the night porter, for we had some cause to wish for further help, when somebody came suddenly up to me, and struck me down. The blow was on the top of my head, and so severe, that I fell as if shot."

"And then? and then?"

"Nothing. I don't know anything else till you recovered me, and then, I seemed as if all the place was scouring round me; and then —"

"But, Mr. Black, cannot you tell us who struck you? What was he like? Could you identify him again?"

"I fear not. Indeed I hardly saw more of him than that he was tall."

"Well," cried Mr. Lake, "all I can say is that I have had my suspicions since last night, and now I am certain, that is to say circumstantially certain. What say you, landlord? Is there not one person in the house who may not fairly enough be suspected."

He looked towards the door of Mr. Blue's room, as he spoke, and indeed all eyes were turned in that direction, and the landlord mustering up courage advanced to the door and said, as he did so, "We will have him out. He shall not stay another hour on my premises. We will have him out, I say. This sort of thing won't do, and it shall not do. We will have him out. I say gentlemen we will have him out."

One thing was quite clear, and that was that the landlord wanted somebody to come forward, and assist him in having out Mr. Blue; but when he found that nobody stirred he turned round at the door, and looked rather foolish.

Under any other circumstances, perhaps, this conduct might have excited the risible faculties of all who were present; but the affair, take it all in all, was of too mysterious and serious a character to indulge in any laughter about.

"I," said Mr. Lake, advancing, "will have him out, if nobody else will!"

It would appear as if Mr. Blue had been listening to what was going on; for on the instant, he flung open his door, and said, —

"Who will have me out, and what for?"

"Vampire, vampire," cried a chorus of voices.

"Idiots!" said Mr. Blue.

"Detain him!" sad Mr. Lake; "detain him, we shall never be satisfied until this affair is thoroughly and judicially enquired into. Detain him I say."

"Let him who sets no value on his life," said Mr. Blue, "lay but a hand upon me, and he shall have to admire the consequences of his rashness. I am not one to be trifled with; it is my fancy to leave this hotel this moment let any one dare to stand in my way."

"Your name is not Blue," said the landlord, "you are not what you seem."

"Granted."

"Ah! you admit it," said Lake. "Lay hold of him, I will give ten pounds for him dead or alive; I have often heard of vampires, and by Heaven, I now believe in them. Seize him, I say, seize him."

He dashed forward himself, as he spoke, and was on the point of seizing hold of Mr. Blue, when one well-directed blow from that individual sent him sprawling. After this nobody showed any very marked disposition to attack him, but he was allowed to walk calmly and slowly down the staircase of the hotel; while Lake gathered himself up, looking rather confused at the tumble he had had. But his passion was not subdued, for he made a rush still after the supposed vampire, but he was too late. The hotel door was closed with a bang, that reverberated through the house, and Mr. Blue was gone, vampire, or no vampire.

"Landlord, I shall leave your house," said Lake.

"I'm ruined," said the landlord. "This affair will get into some Sunday paper. Mr. Black, what is to be done?"

"Really, the top of my head is so hurt," replied Mr. Black, "that I can think of nothing else."

"A plague upon the top of your head," muttered the landlord.

The Lakes now, that is Mr. and Mrs. Lake found their way to the young lady's chamber, when they found her in a state of great alarm. The story she told amounted to this: —

She was asleep, she said, having perfect confidence that no harm could come to her, while the door of her room was watched in the way it was. She had a light burning in her room, but it was one that gave a very faint light, as she had usually an objection to sleeping otherwise than in profound darkness; but she had no notion of how long she had been asleep, when she was awakened by a hand being placed over her mouth, which prevented her from breathing.

She struggled to free herself but it was in vain. The monster attacked her on the neck with his teeth, and all she remembered was getting sufficiently free to utter one scream, and then she fainted away.

"My dear," said Mrs. Lake, "I must have some serious talk with you upon a subject which I have before urged. Go away, Lake."

Lake left the room, and then, Mrs. Lake continued.

"This is a very dreadful affair, Annetta. You know that it is fancied you are not the child of Lord Lake, and that we have the care of you. Now we so much love and admire you, —"

"Stop madam, stop," said the young lady, "I know what you are about to say, you are going to urge me again to marry your son, which I will never do, for I have the greatest aversion to him."

"You will not? who will protect you from a vampire better than a husband."

"Probably no one, but at least I reserve to myself the right to choose to whom I give that task, I am ill now and weak, I pray you not to weary me further upon a subject concerning which it is quite impossible we can ever agree. I only wish I were dead."

"And that you may very well soon be if your blood is all sucked away by a vampire."

"So be it. Heaven help me!"

"Pshaw! you may die as soon as you like."

Chapter *CXVIII*

THE MEETING IN ST. JAMES'S PARK.

*A*nother day passed over at the London Hotel, and as Mr. Blue had been kind enough to take his departure, and that departure seemed to be final, for he did not show himself again, Mr. Lake rescinded the resolution he had made to leave.

Probably it was much more convenient for him to stay, although he pretended that he did so out of consideration for the landlord, who ought not to be punished for innocently harboring so suspicious a character as Mr. Blue, whether he were a vampire, or not.

But the day, as we say, has passed away, and it is about half-past eight o'clock in the evening, and quite dark, for the moon did not rise for an hour afterwards, when Mr. Lake might have been seen making his way towards Saint James's Park.

He entered it by the narrow mode of ingress by Spring Gardens, and made his way towards the palace of Saint James, that is to say, the wall of its private gardens that look upon the park; and then, under some shady trees, he paused and looked inquiringly about him.

"He was to have been here a little before nine," he muttered. "Hush!"

The Horse Guards clock chimed three-quarters past eight.

Mr. Lake draw back, as two men came at a slow pace towards where he stood, and then he muttered, —

"It is Miller, but confound him, who is that he has brought with him? Hang the fellow! I did not give him leave to make a confident in this ticklish piece of business."

One of the men only now advanced, leaving the other about twelve paces from him.

"Mr. L — , I think," he said.

"Yes, Miller, it is I; but who in the name of all that's infernal have you brought with you? Are you mad to trust to anybody but yourself?"

"Oh, don't trouble yourself about that, sir. The fact is, he has been with me for a number of years; he is my managing clerk, and as great a rogue as you would wish him to be. I cannot keep anything wholly from him, so the best way, I find, is to make a confident of him at once."

"I don't half like it."

"You may thoroughly depend upon Lee, that is his name, and you never knew such a rogue as he is, sir; besides, somebody, you know, must have been trusted to personate the father, and he will do that, and then, you know likewise, sir, that—"

"Hush, hush! speak lower! will you? bring this accomplished rogue this way, since I must do business, it seems, with him! Call him here, Miller, and we will talk as we walk on, that is always safer than holding a conference in one spot, near which any one may hide; but it is a much more difficult thing for a spy to follow and overhear you at the same time."

"You have a genius, Mr. Lake."

"Bah! I don't want any compliments from you, Miller; we want downright business."

By this time, Mr. Miller had made a sign to his clerk, Lee, to come up, which that individual did, and at once saluted Mr. Lake, and made some trivial remark about the weather, in an off-hand way.

Mr. Lake made rather a distant reply and then he said, —

"I presume, sir, that Mr. Miller has made you acquainted with the affair in which, it seems, I am to purchase your kind co-operation?"

"Oh no," said Miller, "I have certainly given him a brief outline, but I always prefer that the principal himself should give all the directions possible to every one, and tell his own story."

"Well, sir, I think you might as well have told him, and not given me the trouble. But, however, if I must, I must; so pray attend to me sir."

"I will," said Lee.

"My brother then, is Lord Lake. It's a new title rather, as our father was the first who had it, and he left large estates to my brother, and to his son if he had one, or his daughter, if he had one. The title descending to heir males, I must have the title by outliving my brother, if I do, but hang it all, he has a daughter, and she will have the estates."

"I comprehend."

"The old countess of Bhackbighte smuggled the child away at its birth, and took care of it for a consideration that used up two-thirds of my income, but the old cat on her death confessed that the child was Lord Lake's, but luckily, you see, without criminating me. Now Mr. Miller was her solicitor, and so between us we have forged a letter supposed to be found among the old countess's papers, in which she states that she intends to palm off a child as the Lord Lakes when she is dying, but that his child really did die, you see."

"Oh yes."

"Now this has had an effect upon Lord Lake, who to some extent had repudiated the girl, and what I want is to clinch the matter, by providing some one who will actually own her."

"I understand." said Lee, "but it will be an awkward affair if found out."

"I want to provide against any consequences of a disagreeable nature, by getting her to marry my son, but I don't think she will. Absolute distress to which I am determined to bring her, if I can, may move her to that step, and then all's right. The secret is in my hands to play with, as I think proper."

"A very good plan."

"You see, there's a lover of hers too, a young officer in the Guards, but he will be off as soon as he finds that she's the daughter of a lawyer's clerk instead of a lord — ha! ha! ha!"

"Likely enough. I'll father her."

"Thank you; and now about money matters. Miller gets a thousand pounds — what do you want? Be moderate."

"I ought to have five hundred pounds to pay me."

"The deuce! Well, I don't want to stint you. But you will bear in mind that that is very good pay; and now we must get up a first rate story, so complete in all its parts that there shall be no sort of doubt about it, you see — a story that will stand the test of examination and criticism."

"That can be better done in my chambers," said the attorney; "I think now we understand each other perfectly well, and that we need hardly say any more just at present. Money matters are settled, and as Mr. Lee has once undertaken the business, I am quite satisfied, for one, that it will be well done."

"I am glad to hear you say that, Miller, and I am quite reconciled, which I must own I was not at first, to Mr. Lee having a finger in the pie."

"Thank you," said Lee, "thank you; we shall manage it all right, no doubt. Indeed now that you have fully explained it to me, it seems quite an easy and straightforward affair."

"You think so."

"I certainly do think so."

"Then you take off my mind a load of anxiety for thought it would be a difficult thing to arrange, and require no end of chicanery and trouble, but you quite reassure — you quite reassure me, Mr. Lee."

"Oh, these things are done every day, my dear sir."

They had walked to and fro as they spoke till now, by the time they had settled their affairs thus far, they stood by the center of the principal mall. The park was very quiet, and had quite a deserted aspect. Indeed, it was near the time when there would be more difficulty in traversing it in consequence of the extra vigilance of the night sentinels.

The moon faded gradually away, or seemed to fade away as the light fleecy clouds swept over it's face, and the parties who had held this interesting dialogue separated. Mr. Lake walked hurriedly towards his hotel, and the attorney and his accomplice stood for a few moments conversing in whispers. They then turned towards the Green Park, and as they did so, they were crossed by a tall, spectral-looking figure wrapped up in an immense cloak, but who did not seem to observe them, for his eyes were fixed upon the moon, which at that moment again began to emerge from the clouds.

He stretched forth his arms as if he would have held the beautiful satellite to his heart.

"An odd fish," whispered the attorney.

"Very," said his companion. "I should like now to know who he is."

The attorney shrugged his shoulders, as he said, "Some harmless lunatic most likely. They say that such often wander all night about the parks."

"That's strange; only look at him now. he seems to be worshipping the moon, and now how he strides along; and see, there is another man meets him, and they both hold up their arms in that strange way to the moon. What on earth can be the meaning of it?"

"I really don't know."

"Some religious fanatics, perhaps."

"Ah! that's as likely as not. We have all sorts of them, jumpers and screamers and tearers, and why not a few who may call themselves Lunarians. For my part I would rather worship the moon than I would, as most church and chapel going women do, worship some canting evangelical thief of a parson, who has — oh dear! such elegant hands, and such whiskers, and speaks so soft and impressive. Of all the rogues on earth, I do detest those in surplices!"

Chapter *CLXIX*

THE CHURCHYARD AT HAMPSTEAD. – THE RESUSCITATION
OF A VAMPIRE.

*I*t wants half an hour to midnight. The sky is still cloudy, but glimpses of the moon can be got as occasionally the clouds slip on before her disc, and then what a glorious flood of silver light spread itself over the landscape.

And a landscape in every respect more calculated to look beautiful and romantic under the chaste moon's ray, than that to which we would now invite attention, certainly could not have been found elsewhere, within many a mile of London. It is Hampstead Heath, that favored spot where upon a small scale are collected some of the rarest landscape beauties that the most romantic mountainous counties of England can present to the gratified eye of the tourist.

Those who are familiar with London and its environs, of course, are well acquainted with every nook, glade, tree, and dell in that beautiful heath, where, at all and every time and season, there is much to recommend that semi-wild spot to notice. Indeed, if it were, as it ought to be, divested of its donkey-drivers and laundresses, a more delightful place of residence could scarcely be found than some one of those suburban villas, that are dotted round the margin of this picturesque waste.

But it is midnight, nearly. That time is forthcoming, at which popular superstition trembles – that time, at which the voice of ignorance and of cant lowers to whispers, and when the poor of heart and timid of spirit imagine worlds of unknown terrors. On this occasion, though, it will be seen that there would have been some excuses if even the most bold had shrunk back appalled at what was taking place.

But we will not anticipate for truly in this instance might we say sufficient for the time are the horrors thereof.

If any one had stood on that portion of the high road which leads right over the heath and so on to Hendon or to Highgate, according as the left hand or the right hand route is taken, and after reaching the Castle Tavern, had looked across the wide expanse of heath to the west, they would have seen nothing for a while but the clustering bushes of heath blossom, and the picturesque fir trees, that there are to be beheld in great luxuriance. But, after a time, something of a more noticeable character would have presented itself.

At a quarter to twelve there rose up from a tangled mass of brushwood, which had partially concealed a deep cavernous place where sand had been dug, a human form, and there it stood in the calm still hour of night so motionless that it scarcely seemed to possess life, but presently another rose at a short distance.

And then there was a third, so that these three strange-looking beings stood like landmarks against the sky, and when the moon shone out from some clouds which had for a short time obscured her rays, they looked strange and tall, and superhuman.

One spoke.

"'Tis time," he said, in a deep, hollow voice, that sounded as if it came from the tomb.

"Yes, time," said another.

"Time has come," said the third.

Then they moved, and by the gestures they used, it seemed as if an animated discussion was taking place among them, after which they moved along in perfect silence, and in a most stately manner, towards the village of Hampstead.

Before reaching it, however, they turned down some narrow shaded walks among garden walls, and the backs of stables, until they emerged close to the old churchyard, which stands on high ground, and which was not then — at least, the western portion of it — overlooked by any buildings. Those villas which now skirt it, are of recent elevation.

A dense mass of clouds has now been brought up by a south wind, and had swept over the face of the moon, so that at this juncture, and as twelve o'clock might be expected every moment to strike, the night was darker than it had yet been since sunset. The circumstance was probably considered by the mysterious beings who sought the churchyard as favorable to them, and they got without difficulty within those sacred precincts devoted to the dead.

Scarcely had they found the way a dozen feet among the old tombstones, when from behind a large square monument, there appeared two more persons; and if the attorney, Mr. Miller, had been there, he would probably have thought they bore such a strong resemblance to those whom he had seen in the park, he would have had but little hesitation in declaring that they were the same.

These two persons joined the other three, who manifested no surprise at seeing them, and then the whole five stood close to the wall of the church, so that they were quite secure from observation, and one of them spoke.

"Brothers," he said, "you who prey upon human nature by the law of your being, we have work to do tonight — that work which we never leave undone, and which we dare not neglect when we know that it is to do. One of our fraternity lies here."

"Yes," said the others, with the exception of one, and he spoke passionately.

"Why," he said, "when there were enough, and more than enough, to do the work, summon me?"

"Not more than enough, there are but five."

"And why should you not be summoned," said another, "you are one of us. You ought to do your part with us in setting a brother free from the clay that presses on his breast."

"I was engaged in my vocation. If the moon shine out in all her luster again, you will see that I am wan and wasted, and have need of —"

"Blood," said one.

"Blood, blood, blood," repeated the others. And then the first speaker said, to him who complained, —

"You are one whom we are glad to have with us on a service of danger. You are strong and bold, your deeds are known, you have lived long, and are not yet crushed."

"I do not know our brother's name," said one of the others with an air of curiosity.

"I go by many."

"So do we all. But by what name may we know you best."

"Slieghton, I was named in the reign of the third Edward. But many have known me as Varney, the Vampyre!"

There was a visible sensation among those wretched beings as these words were uttered, and one was about to say something, when Varney interrupted him.

"Come," he said, "I have been summoned here, and I have come to assist in the exhumation of a brother. It is one of the conditions of our being that we do so. Let the work be proceeded with then, at once, I have no time to spare. Let it be done with. Where lies the vampyre? Who was he?"

"A man of good repute, Varney," said the first speaker. "A smooth, fair-spoken man, a religious man, so far as cant went, a proud, cowardly, haughty, worldly follower of religion. Ha, ha, ha!"

"And what made him one of us?"

"He dipped his hands in blood. There was a poor boy, a brother's only child, 'twas left an orphan. He slew the boy, and he is one of us."

"With a weapon."

"Yes, and a sharp one; the weapon of unkindness. The child was young and gentle, and harsh words, blows, and revilings placed him in his grave. he is in heaven, while the man will be a vampyre."

"'Tis well — dig him up."

They each produced from under the dark cloaks they wore, a short double-edged, broad, flat-bladed weapon, not unlike the swords worn by the Romans, and he who assumed the office of guide, led the way to a newly-made grave, and diligently, and with amazing rapidity and power, they commenced removing the earth.

It was something amazing to see the systematic manner in which they worked, and in ten minutes one of them struck the blade of his weapon upon the lid of a coffin, and said,

"It is here."

The lid was then partially raised in the direction of the moon, which, although now hidden, they could see would in a very short time show itself in some gaps of the clouds, that were rapidly approaching at great speed across the heavens.

They then desisted from their labor, and stood around the grave in silence for a time, until, as the moon was longer showing her fair face, they began to discourse in whispers.

"What shall become of him," said one, pointing to the grave. "Shall we aid him."

"No," said Varney, "I have heard that of him which shall not induce me to lift hand or voice in his behalf. Let him fly, shrieking like a frightened ghost where he lists."

"Did you not once know some people named Bannerworth."

"I did. You came to see me, I think, at an inn. They are all dead."

"Hush," said another, "look, the moon will soon be free from the vapors that sail between it and the green earth. Behold, she shines out fresh once more; there will be life in the coffin soon, and our work will be done."

It was so. The dark clouds passed over the face of the moon, and with a sudden burst of splendor, it shone out again as before.

Chapter *CLXX.*

THE VAMPYRE. – THE FLIGHT. – THE WATCHMAN IN THE
VALE OF HEALTH.

A death-like stillness now was over the whole scene, and those who
had partially exhumed the body stood as still as statues, waiting the
event which they looked forward to as certain to ensue.

The clear beauty and intensity of the moonbeams increased each
moment, and the whole surrounding landscape was lit up with a perfect
flood of soft, silvery light. The old church stood out in fine relief, and
every tree, and every wild flower, and every blade of grass in the
churchyard, could be seen in its finest and most delicate proportions
and construction.

The lid of the coffin was wrenched up on one side to about six inches
in height, and that side faced the moon, so that some rays, it was quite
clearly to be seen, found their way into that sad receptacle for the dead.
A quarter of an hour, however, passed away, and nothing happened.

"Are you certain he is one of us?" whispered Varney.

"Quite, I have known it years past. He had the mark upon him."

"Enough. Behold."

A deep and dreadful groan came from the grave, and yet it could
hardly be called a groan; it was more like a howl, and the lid which was
partially open, was visibly agitated.

"He comes," whispered one.

"Hush," said another, "hush; our duty will be done when he stands
upon the level ground. Hush, let him hear nothing, let him know
nothing, since we will not aid him. Behold, behold."

They all looked down into the grave, but they betrayed no signs of
emotion, and the sight they saw there was such as one would have
supposed would have created emotion in the breast of any one at all
capable of feeling. But then we must not reason upon these strange

frightful existences as we reason upon human nature such as we usually know it.

The coffin lid was each moment more and more agitated. The deep frightful groans increased in number and sound, and then the corpse stretched out one ghastly hand from the open crevice and grasped despairingly and frantically at the damp earth that was around.

There was still towards one side of the coffin sufficient weight of mould that it would require some strength to turn it off, but as the dead man struggled within his narrow house it kept falling aside in lumps, so that his task of exhumation became each moment an easier one.

At length he uttered a strange wailing shriek, and by a great effort succeeded in throwing the coffin lid quite open, and then he sat up, looking so horrible and ghastly in the grave clothes, that even the vampyres that were around that grave recoiled a little.

"Is it done?" said Varney.

"Not yet," said he who had summoned the to the fearful rite, and so assumed a sort of direction over them, "not yet; we will not assist him, but we may not leave him before telling him who and what he is."

"Do so now."

The corpse stood up in the coffin, and the moonlight fell full upon him.

"Vampyre arise," said he who had just spoken to Varney. "Vampyre arise, and do your work in the world until your doom shall be accomplished. Vampyre arise — arise. Pursue your victims in the mansion and in the cottage. Be a terror and a desolation, go you where you may, and if the hand of death strike you down, the cold beams of the moon shall restore you to new life. Vampyre arise, arise!"

"I come, I come!" shrieked the corpse.

In another moment the five vampyres who had dug him from the grave were gone.

Moaning, shrieking, and groaning he made some further attempts to get out of the deep grave. He clutched at it in vain, the earth crumbled beneath him, and it was only at last by dint of reaching up and dragging in the displaced material that lay in a heap at the sides, so that in a few minutes it formed a mound for him to stand upon in the grave, and he was at length able to get out.

Then, although he sighed, and now and then uttered a wailing shriek as he went about his work, he with a strange kind of instinct, began to carefully fill up the grave from which he had but just emerged, nor did he cease from his occupation until he had finished it, and so carefully shaped the mound of mould and turf over it that no one would have thought it had been disturbed.

When this work was done a kind of madness seemed to seize him, and he walked to the gate of the grave yard, which opens upon Churchstreet, and placing his hands upon the sides of his mouth he produced such an appalling shriek that it must have awakened everybody in Hampstead.

Then, turning, he fled like a hunted hare in the other direction, and taking the first turning to the right ran up a lane called Frognal-lane, and which is parallel to the town, for a town Hampstead may be fairly called now, although it was not then.

By pursuing this lane, he got upon the outskirts of the heath, and then turning to the right again, for, with a strange pertinacity he always kept, as far as he could, his face towards the light of the moon, he rushed down a deep hollow, where there was a cluster of little cottages, enjoying such repose that one would have thought the flutter of an awakened bird upon the wing would have been heard.

It was quite clear that the new vampyre had as yet no notion of what he was about, or where he was going, and that he was with mere frantic haste speeding along, from the first impulse of his frightful nature.

The place into which he had now plunged, is called the Vale of Health: now a place of very favorite resort, but then a mere collection of white faced cottages, with a couple of places that might be called villas. A watchman went his nightly rounds in that place. And it so happened that the guardian of the Vale had just roused himself up at this juncture, and made up his mind to make his walk of observation, when he saw the terrific figure of a man attired in grave clothes coming along with dreadful speed towards him, as if to take the Vale of Health by storm.

The watchman was so paralyzed by fear that he could not find strength enough to spring his rattle, although he made the attempt, and held it out at arm's length, while his eyes glared with perfect ferocity, and his mouth was wide enough open to nourish the idea, that after all he had a hope of being able to swallow the specter.

But, nothing heeding him, the vampyre came wildly on.

Fain now would the petrified watchman have got out of the way, but he could not, and in another moment he was dashed down to the earth, and trodden on by the horrible existence that knew not what it did.

A cloud came over the moon, and the vampyre sunk down, exhausted, by a garden-wall, and there lay as if dead, while the watchman, who had fairly fainted away, lay in a picturesque attitude on his back, not very far off.

Half an hour passed, and a slight mist-like rain began to fall.

The vampyre slowly rose to his feet, and commenced wringing his hands and moaning, but his former violence of demeanor had passed away. That was but the first flush of new life, and now he seemed to be more fully aware of who and what he was.

He shivered as he tottered slowly on, until he came to where the watchman lay, and then he divested that guardian of the Vale of his greatcoat, his hat, and some other portions of his apparel, all of which he put on himself, still slightly moaning as he did so, and ever and anon stopping to make a gesture of despair.

When this operation was completed, he slunk off into a narrow path which led on to the heath again, and there he seemed to waver a little, whether he would go towards London, or the country. At length it seemed that he decided upon the former course, and he walked on at a rapid pace right through Hampstead, and down the hill towards London, the lights of which would be seen gleaming in the distance.

When the watchman did recover himself, the first thing he did was, to be kind enough to rouse every body up from their sleep in the Vale of Health, by springing his rattle at a prodigious rate, and by the time he had roused up the whole neighborhood, he felt almost ready to faint again at the bare recollection of the terrible apparition that had knocked him down.

The story in the morning was told all over the place, with many additions to it of course, and it was long afterwards before the inhabitants of the Vale could induce another watchman, for that one gave up the post, to run the risk of such a visitation.

And the oddest thing of all was, that the watchman declared that he caught a glance at the countenance, and that it was like that of a Mr. Brooks, who had only been buried the day previous, that if he had not known that gentleman to be dead and buried, he should have thought it was he himself gone mad.

But there was the grave of Mr. Brooks, with its circular mound of earth, all right enough; and then Mr. B. was known to have been such a respectable man. He went to the city every day, and used to do so just for the purpose of granting audiences to ladies and gentlemen who might be laboring under any little pecuniary difficulties, and accommodating them. Kind Mr. Brooks. He only took one hundred pounds per cent. Why should he be a Vampyre? Bless him! Too severe, really!

There were people who called him a bloodsucker while he lived, and now he was one practically, and yet he had his own pew at the church, and subscribed a whole guinea a year to a hospital — he did, although people did say it was in order that he might pack off any of his servants at once to it in case of illness. But then the world is so censorious.

To this day the watchman's story of the apparition that visited the Vale of Health is talked of by the old women who make what they call tea for Sunday parties at nine pence a head. But it is time now that we go back to London, and see what is taking place at the hotel where the Lakes are staying, and how the villainy of the uncle thrives — that villainy of which he actually had the face to give such an exposition to Mr. Lee the clerk of the attorney.

Let us hope that the right will still overcome the injustice that is armed against it, and that Lord Lake and his beautiful child may not fall victims to the machinations that are brought into play against them, by those who ought to have been their best friends.

Chapter CLXXI.

MISS LAKE PASSES A FEARFUL NIGHT. – THE IMPOSTOR PUNISHED

*T*he landlord of the London Hotel made every possible exertion to keep a profound secret the events of the night, but people will talk when even they have not anything particular to say, so that we cannot wonder at their doing so when they have.

In fact the story of the vampyre at the London Hotel got known pretty well half over London in the course of the day succeeding that second attempt upon the life blood of the young lady, who had become the object of attack from the monster.

Mr. Lake was in a strange frame of mind as regarded the whole affair. He did not yet know whether to really believe it or not – whether to ascribe it, after all, to a dream, or, as Mrs. Lake hinted, for she was a woman fond of scheming herself, so always ready to suggest its existence in others – a mere plan upon the part of the young girl to get rid of the projected alliance with young Master Lake, and possibly evoke the sympathy of all who heard her story.

This view of the matter however, although it did not make much impression upon Mr. Lake, suggested a something to him, that he thought would chime in well with his other plans and projects.

"If," he said "I could but instill a little courage into my son he might now, at all events make a favorable impression upon his cousin."

Full of this idea, he summoned the young gentleman to a conference with him, and having carefully closed the door, he said in a low confidential tone, –

"Of course you have heard all about this — this vampyre business?"

"Yes, governor, to be sure I have. Who could fail of hearing all about it? Why, nobody in the house will talk about anything else. I'm afraid to go to bed, I can tell you; that is to say, for fear I should do anything rash, you know, that's all."

"I understand you, and it's no use blinking the fact to me, that you are a coward."

"I am a coward, I — oh, you are very much mistaken. I'm a long way off that. I'm only always desirous of getting out of the way when anything happens, for fear of doing a rash act; it's excess of courage you know — that's what alarms me."

"Well, there are cases in which there would be no harm resulting, were you ever so rash."

"Ah! only show me one, and then you'll see."

"Very well, your cousin, you know — and you know she is you cousin — won't have you. Now, unless you are married to her, all our nicely got up plans are liable to be blasted by any accident, or by any breath of treachery that may come across them. But if you were the husband of your cousin, policy, habit, and, indeed, everything would combine to induce Lord Lake and her to smother up the affair. You comprehend."

"But what am I to do, if she won't have me?"

"I will tell you. You must awaken her gratitude by rescuing her from all these foolish terrors about vampyres, and when once a woman feels and knows that a man has done a brave act in her behalf, the principal entrance to her heart is open to him."

"Oh, but — I — I — the vampyre; that's rather unpleasant."

"Come, now, you are not such a fool, as really to believe that it's, after all, anything but a mere dream. Don't tell me. Vampyres, indeed! At all events you can vapor as much as you like upon that subject without any danger occurring."

"Yes, yes — you may think so."

"I know so. Listen to me."

The son did listen, and the father added:

"You must volunteer to watch alone by your cousin's door for this vampyre, and of course nothing will think of coming. It's too ridiculous altogether, that it is; so, you see, you run no risk at all. You comprehend that?"

"Well, but if I run no risk, I don't see what's the use of doing it, you know; for if all is quite, how can she be grateful to me for having rescued her from nothing at all?"

"Very well put, very well indeed. But as there will be nothing really to rescue her from, suppose we make something that will just suit our own purposes."

"What do you mean?"

"Why, you know my great grey traveling cloak — what is to hinder you having that with you, and whenever you are quite certain that your cousin is fast asleep, you can put that on over your face partially, and go into the room, and pretend to be the vampyre, and when she is in a paroxysm of terror do you dash out the light, and then in your natural voice, cry out, 'Ah, wretch, I have you, I have you. How dare you invade the sanctity of this chamber?' and all that sort of thing, you know, and you can knock about the chairs as much as you like, so as to induce the belief that you are engaged in a deadly struggle, and then you call for lights, and you are there, and the vampyre gone."

"Well, I rather like that, and if I were quite sure —"

"Of what?"

"That there was no real vampyre, you know, why I wouldn't mind it."

"Pshaw!"

"Well, well, I'll do it, I'll do it, I tell you. I see all the importance of getting her for my wife. Ahem! and if I do," he added to himself aside, "I'll take deuced good care you don't get hold of the money, for after we are married, I shall just tell Lord Lake all about it."

During the day Mr. Lake had sought an opportunity of speaking to Mr. Black.

"My dear sir," he said to him, you don't seem well at all, and I shall insist that you do not trouble yourself to watch tonight by the door of the young lady, who has had so disagreeable a visitor."

"I am certainly not quite well," said Mr. Black. "The fact is, my health will not bear anything like a shock; a family occurrence has so shattered my nerves."

"My dear sir, say no more; you shall have no more trouble about us. My son who loves his cousin, and is quite jealous of anybody defending her but himself, will watch alone by her door. He has great courage when once his spirit is up, and it is now."

"I'm glad to hear it: it takes some time to get it up!"

"Why, a — a — yes, sometimes."

"I must be on the look out myself tonight, or the cowardly fellow will spoil all," thought Mr. Lake; "any unusual noise in the house, I suppose, will be almost sufficient to induce him to faint away. Confound his cowardice, it mars all."

Mr. Lake was not by any means so clear in his own mind as he pretended to be of the fact of the vampyre being only a delusion and a creation of the brain of his niece; so when the evening came, he did all that was in his power to keep the courage of his son to the mark.

He even took care that he should have a glass of something strong and hot, for he knew by personal experience that while they lasted, the fumes of hot alcohol did something for a weak heart.

But what pleased Mr. Lake most of all was the ease with which he had thus managed matters with Mr. Miller and his clerk, who he had no doubt, would fabricate such a story as would convince the single minded Annetta of his claims to be her father.

"Then," thought the old Lake, "we can surely among us badger her into marrying my son. Oh, it will be all right. Let no plot henceforward hope to succeed if this one does not. It must, and it shall; it shall, and it must."

It's all very well of any one to say that a scheme shall succeed;
"But how light a breath of air will chase away,
The darkly woven fancies of a thousand plots."

Mr. Lake stood upon a precipice which he little saw, or the terrific height of it would have driven him distracted.

Miss Lake was in a great state of mental depression; if anything, more than another was calculated to thoroughly break down the spirits of a young and innocent girl, it certainly would be such circumstances as those which now surrounded her, and deprived too, as she was, of that aid and sympathy she would have received at the hands of a father or a mother, it was only a wonder that she did not sink under the affliction most completely.

She made no objection to young Lake watching by the outside of her door. Indeed, she was weeping and depressed, so that she could scarcely know what proposal was made to her.

"I shall not sleep," she said. "God knows what will become of me."

"Do not despair, all may be well; it was a very sad thing that my brother Lord Lake ever found out that you were not his daughter. I'm sure I would have given freely all I possessed to have averted any such news, for it has attacked both his happiness and yours."

The young girl made no reply to this, but the look she gave him was quite sufficient to show him how much she doubted the sincerity of the professions of friendship and affection for her that fell from his lips. There was a something in his hollow, heartless character which, young and innocent and unknowing in the ways of the world even as that young girl was, she saw through, and he felt that she did so.

This was the most provoking thing of all that his heartlessness and selfishness should be transparent to one so young as she was.

But the night came at last, and with it the fidgety fears of young Lake increased mightily. He was all of a shake, as Slop the waiter said, like a lot of jelly.

It was only by repeated doses of brandy-and-water that he kept himself from declaring off the adventure altogether, so that by eleven o'clock at night he was in a terrible state between fear and intoxication; and as any two impulses will each do its best to defeat the other, he was prevented from getting entirely drunk by his fears, and from getting entirely afraid by the liquor.

But at last he did actually take his place by the door of the chamber occupied by his cousin, and then with a table before him on which were lights, brandy-and-water, and cigars, he prepared to go through what to him was a terrible ordeal.

"You — you — really think," he whispered to his father, who came to promise him that he would not undress himself, but remain in his own room within call, "you really think there is no vampyre?"

"Tut, tut."

"Well, but really now, really —"

"Have I not told you before? Come, come, nonsense, there's the old grey traveling cloak, put it under the table, and now I shall leave you; its about half-past eleven, and you have nothing in the world to do but just to enjoy yourself, you know. Good night."

Chapter CLXXII.

THE VAMPYRE DISCOVERED. — THE ESCAPE ON THE THAMES.

"*E*njoy myself!" muttered the young Lake, "enjoy myself! That may be his idea of staying here vampyre-catching, but it ain't mine. What a fool I was to consent to come here, to be sure, and all alone too. Eh, what was that? Oh! I'm all of a shake. I though I heard somebody, but I suppose it was nothing. Oh dear, what a disagreeable affair this is; what an infernal fool I am, to be sure. Eh? eh?"

The hair on his head nearly stood up as he heard, or fancied he heard, a low grown. He shook so while he arose from his seat that he was glad to sit down again as quickly as he possibly could, for he found his strength evaporating along with the Dutch courage, or rather as it should be called, French courage, that had been instilled into him by the brandy.

"What shall I do," he gasped, "what shall I do? Oh, what will become of me? I'm in for a row, I'm in for it to a certainty; I — I think I'll call the old man."

He did not, however, call his father, whom he designated the old man, more familiarly than respectfully, but as all continued now quiet, he thought he would wait until the next alarm, at all events, before he made a piece of work and thoroughly exhibited his own pusillanimity.

"It may be nothing" he said, "after all, perhaps only the wind coming through some chink in a door or window. Lord bless us, I've read of such things in romances till my blood had turned to curds and whey. There was the Bloody Specter of the Tub of Blood, or the Smashed Gore. Eh? eh? I thought somebody spoke. No, no — oh, it's all what do they call it, imagination, that's what it is, and the sooner I get the job over the better, so I'll just pop on the cloak, and do the business."

With trembling hands Mr. Lake junior drew the cloak from under the table and put it on, bringing the collar of it right up to the top of his head, so that but a small portion of his head was at all visible when he was thus equipped, and he certainly might look like a vampyre, for he did not look like anything human by any means.

"Now, I wonder if she's asleep," he muttered as he laid his hand gently on the lock of the door, "if she ain't, it would be a pity; but still I can say, I only wanted to know how she was, so I'll just make the trial at all events. Here goes."

He opened the door of the bedroom a very short distance, and said, —

"Hist! hist! are you awake, eh? eh? What did you say? — nothing, oh, she's asleep, and now here goes — upon my life when one comes to think of it, ain't by any means a bad plan. But just before I begin, I'll have another drink."

About two-thirds of a glass of brandy-and-water were in the tumbler on the table, and that he tossed down at once, and feeling very much fortified by laying in such a stratum of courage, he drew up the cloak to its proper vampyre-like position, as he considered it, and advanced two steps within the chamber of the sleeping girl.

She was sleeping, and slightly moaning in her sleep. It was a great satisfaction to young master Lake, to hear her so moaning, for it convinced him that such were the sounds which he previously heard, and which had gone near to terrifying him out of his project.

He had no compunction whatever regarding the amount of alarm which this dastardly project was likely to give to Miss Lake. No, all he looked to and thought of was himself. A light was burning in the chamber, and that according to the directions of his father he blew out, and then groping his ways towards the bed, he laid his hands upon the young girl's face, and said, —

"The vampyre! the vampyre has come! — blood, blood, blood! — the vampyre!"

She awoke with a cry of terror as usual, and then master Lake moved off to the door, and said in his natural voice,

"I'll protect you — I'm coming — I'll soon clear the room of the vampyre. Come on, you wretch! Oh, I'll do for him. Take that — and that — and that."

Then he commenced kicking about the chairs, and nearly upset the washing-stand, all by way of making the necessary disturbance, and convincing his cousin what a sanguinary conflict he was having with the vampyre. In the midst of this something laid hold of him by the ears and whiskers on each side of his head, and the door swinging open, his own light that was upon the table in the corridor shone upon a hideous countenance within half an inch of his own. The long fang-like teeth of which, with the lips retracted from them, were horrible to look upon, and a voice like the growl of an enraged hyena said, —

"What want you with the vampyre, rash fool? He is here."

Master Lake was absolutely petrified with horror and astonishment. The hair bristled up upon his head. His eyes opened the width of saucers, and when in a low voice the vampyre said again, — "What want you, reptile, with the vampyre?" he let his feet slide from under him, and had he not been upheld by the horrible being who grasped him, he would have fallen.

Bang went a pistol out of the corridor, and the vampyre uttered a cry and let go his hold of Lake, who then fell, and being out of the way, showed his father standing on the threshold of his own door, with a pistol in his hand recently discharged, and another apparently ready.

In another moment the vampyre kicked the insensible form of young Lake out of the way, and shut himself in the girl's bedroom. The father heard him lock the door, and although he instantly sent another pistol shot through the paneling, he heard no sound indicating its having done any execution.

"Help, help, help," he cried, "help here. The vampyre, the vampyre, the vampyre!"

All this had not taken above two or three minutes, and the whole house was now alarmed by the sound of fire-arms, and as nobody had completely undressed themselves to go to bed since the first alarm of the vampyre, the landlord and several of the waiters, and the night watchman ran with all speed to the spot, looking full of consternation, and all asking questions together.

"Force the door, force the door," cried Mr. Lake, "a hammer, a hatchet, anything, so that we may get the door forced; the vampyre is inside."

"Oh lor!" cried one of the waiters who had gone close to the door, but who now made a precipitate retreat, treading upon the stomach of young Lake as he did so.

"If you'll pay for the door, Sir," said the landlord, "I'll soon have it open."

"Damn it, I'll pay for twenty doors."

The landlord took a short run at the door, probably he knew its weakness, and burst it open at once. There was the pause of about a moment, and then Mr. Lake, snatching up the candle, the light of which had first revealed the hideous features of the vampyre to his son, rushed into the room.

In these cases all that is wanted is a leader, so he was promptly enough followed. The state of affairs was evident at a glance. The young lady had fainted, and the window was wide open, indicating the mode of retreat of the vampire.

"I thought you told us," said Mr. Lake "that this window was too far from the ground to anticipate any danger from——"

"Yes, so I did, sir. But don't you see he could easy enough jump off the sill on to those leads there. Nobody could get in by the window, but anybody that wasn't afraid could get out. But we have him, sir, we have him now as sure as a gun."

"Have him. How?"

"Why don't you see sir, there's nothing but high walls. He must be among our stables, and he can't get out, for I have the keys of the outer doors myself, we shall not lose him now, sir, I'm not a little thankful for it. Come on, everybody, round to the stables, and nothing now can prevent us catching him if he is flesh and blood. Come on, come on."

By this time Mrs. Lake had reached the scene of action, and although the first thing she did was to tumble, sprawling, over her hopeful son, who lay in the doorway of his cousin's chamber, she gathered herself up again, and remained in charge of Annetta and the chamber, while Mr. Lake accompanied the landlord and the waiters to the stables of the hotel, which were surrounded by high walls and only to be approached by a pair of large gates, which were quite satisfactorily fastened, and there was not a chink large enough for a cat to get through.

The landlord had the keys, and he opened a small wicket in one of the large gates.

"Now be careful," he said, "for fear he bounces out."

At this everybody but Mr. Lake, who to do him but justice, had certainly the quality of courage, looked as alarmed as possible, but he said, —

"I have re-loaded my pistols, and he shall not escape me."

The wicket was opened, and in an instant out walked Mr. Black! He appeared at first somewhat agitated, but speedily recovered his self-possession, and looking at the group, he said, —

"Have you caught him? I have been upon the look out, notwithstanding my indisposition, and jumped out of the bedroom window after him; I cannot see him anywhere. Have you caught him."

"Yes," cried Mr. Lake, "I saw you in the room when I fired at you — *you* are the vampyre!"

He made a rush forward as he spoke, but Mr. Black got dexterously out of the way, and seizing the landlord by the hair of the head he cast him so fairly in Mr. Lake's way that they both fell down together; with amazing rapidity the vampyre then fled from the spot.

"After him, after him," cried Mr. Lake, as he scrambled to his feet, "don't let him escape, after him, whatever you do; alarm the whole city, rather than let the monster elude you. This way — this way, I see him. Follow me, a vampyre, a vampyre; help — help, seize him, a vampyre!"

"Fire," cried the landlord, and he too ran.

But all the running was in vain, the vampyre had fairly got the start of them, and he took good care to keep it, for with the most wonderful fleetness he ran on, until, to his great relief, he found his pursuers were distanced.

He made his way to the Strand, and diving down one of the narrow streets terminated by the river, and at the end of which was a landing place, he called aloud, —

"Boat, boat!"

An old waterman answered the hail.

"Where to, your honor?"

"Up the river, I will tell you where to land me, row quick, and row well, and you may name your own fare, without a chance of its being questioned."

"That's the customer for me," said the waterman.

Chapter *CLXXIII.*

THE PLOT DISCOVERED. – THE LETTER LEFT AT THE HOTEL BY THE VAMPYRE.

*T*he further pursuit of the vampyre was very soon given up by those who had commenced it with, as they had vainly imagined such an assurance of success.

Probably with the exception of Mr. Lake himself none were really very eager in it at all, and they were not sorry for a good excuse to drop it.

There sat upon the countenance of Mr. Lake an appearance of great anger, and when they got back to the hotel, he said to the landlord,

"This is a very disagreeable affair, and I cannot think of remaining here over tomorrow."

"But sir, the vampyre has gone now!"

"Yes, and may come again, for all I know."

"Oh, dear me, surely not now, sir. After what has happened, I should be inclined to say that you will find this the quietest hotel in London."

Mr. Lake would not be moved from his determination, however, and briefly again announced that he would on the morrow remove.

"How very vexatious," thought the landlord, but he could do nothing in the matter. His only hope, and that was a very slight one indeed, was, by the morning the exasperated feelings of Mr. Lake would be somewhat assuaged, and therefore, he thought it would be, at all events, a prudent thing to say no more to him just then, when he was in such a mood.

When Mr. Lake retired to his own apartment he was in anything but a pleasant frame of mind, for he found that things were not exactly turning out as he wished, and he much feared that all his schemes would turn out abortive, in which case they would recoil upon his own head in their consequences.

It was quite by accident, that happening to cast his eyes upon the dressing-table, he saw a sealed letter lying there, and upon looking at the superscription he was surprised to find that Annetta was the person for whom it was intended.

It was not, as the reader may suppose from what he knows of Mr. Lake, from any honorables scruples that he hesitated at once to open the letter addressed to his niece, but he was for a time considering whether he might not, by doing so, be getting himself into some scrape from which he might find it very difficult to extricate himself.

"Who the deuce can it come from?" he said.

He turned the epistle about in all directions, but such an inquiry did not assist him, and finally he made up his mind that come what might, he would break the seal and look at the contents.

He soon, after coming to the determination, carried it into effect, and to his surprise he found that the letter contained the following statement. —

"To the lady Annetta Lake.

"Fear nothing, lady. He who disturbed your repose will disturb it no longer. Be happy, and do not let the dread of such another visitation ever disturb your pure imaginings. Your father will rescue you from your present unhappy circumstances, and you will, likewise, soon see one who ere this would have been with you, had he known of your being in London.

"This comes from
"VARNEY THE VAMPYRE.

"If Mr. Lake, your bad uncle, upon whose dressing table this note is placed, delivers it not to you, woe be to him, for I will make his nights hideous with realities, and his days horrible with recollection and anticipation."

Mr. Lake was superstitious. Are not the unprincipled always so?

He read the postscript to the note with a shudder; and he felt that he could no more muster courage enough to destroy the letter, than he could to lay violent hands upon himself. There he was with an epistle that he would fain have kept from Annetta, and yet he dared not do so.

"Confound my unlucky destiny," he said, "for bringing me to this hotel. Perhaps if I had gone elsewhere, all this would not have happened. Oh, if I could but have suspected what this Mr. Black really was, I would have tried some means for his extermination."

He paced his chamber in an agitated manner until Mrs. Lake made her appearance from the chamber of the lady Annetta, where she had been staying, and to her then he at once communicated the letter that gave him so much uneasiness.

"I don't know what to do," he said, "or what to think."

"Indeed!"

"Yes, indeed. Perhaps you can suggest something?"

"And can you allow yourself to be made a slave of such fears. There is but one course to pursue, and that is, tomorrow to put the affair altogether in a different shape, by overwhelming Annetta with the seeming evidence that she is the daughter of an attorney's clerk, instead of her real father, Lord Lake. I know of no other way; and then when she finds such, as she will think, to be the case, it's my opinion that she will no longer hesitate to marry our son."

"You thing so?"

"Indeed do I, The girl is not an absolute fool surely."

"Well, of course, I should be very glad if that darling project could be, after all, brought about, but what is to be done with this letter?"

"Can you ask?"

"I do, when I consider the threat that is in it. That threat, recollect, is to me, and you can afford to think lightly of it."

"I will take the consequences. It is hardly likely that you will be punished for what you can't help. I will take good care that this letter never reaches Annetta, and as you have it not, why of course you cannot deliver it, and so cannot be blamed."

"But I might have it."

"No such thing," said the lady snatching it up. "You know me rather too well, I should think, to hope that I would give it up to you, and as for your taking it by force, I should think you knew me too well likewise to make such a ridiculous attempt."

"Well, then I wash my hands of it."

"Ah! you may as well. I don't know what has come over you of late, you are as mean spirited as you can be, and formerly you used to be able to cope with anything."

"We never played for such a stake as we have now upon the board, and I confess that I am rather nervous for the consequences."

"Pshaw! I see that I must guide you, or all will be lost. Tomorrow let the whole affair be settled. Let this attorney Miller, as you call him, come here, and bring with him the person who is to claim Annetta as his own daughter. Let him have all the evidence that you tell me he has been so ingenious in getting up, ready, in order that he may be in a position to answer any questions."

"Yes, yes."

"And then, when all is settled, our son must come forward, and make a speech, saying, he don't care a bit, who or what she is, that he loves her and will make her his wife, although she has not a penny piece in the world."

"I see, I see."

"I think, from what I know of her, that such a course of proceeding will have a great effect upon her."

"Well, I hope so."

"You hope so! How despondingly you talk."

"Why the honest truth —"

"Good God! what do you mean by making use of such words, I never told the honest truth in all my life; you may depend that won't do in this world, on any consideration. Never let me hear you say such a thing again, I beg of you."

"I was merely going to remark that this vampyre's business had really so completely unsettled my whole nervous system, that I could not act with all the tact and the determination that used to characterize my proceedings, and for which you were ever disposed to give me so much credit."

"Really."

"Yes. But I cannot regret such a state of things so much as I should otherwise do, because I see that you are unmoved and as energetic as ever."

"Well, well, say no more."

"I am done."

"I will prepare our boy for the part he is to act tomorrow; and mind, I shall rely upon you to see your associates and get all the affair in train. Let it be all over by twelve in the morning, so that if you like you can send to Lord Lake where he is staying, at Florence still I presume, an account of the matter by post that same night; only let me see the letter before you send it."

"I will, I will; you are my guardian angel."

"Pho, pho; you are getting quite romantic and foolish; we have both made up our minds to get money, and we have likewise known so much the want of it, in abundance that is to say, that we have resolved to get it in any way we can."

"Yes, that I rather thing is our principle of action."

"And has it not succeeded hitherto. Have we not lived well without troubling ourselves to earn the means by which we have done so. Earn, indeed! I leave that to a parcel of sleepy drones of people who have not the wit to live upon others as we have; so now got to bed and sleep off some of the unmanly fears that seem of late to be continually pressing upon you. It is well you have me to look after you as I do."

Chapter *CLXXIV.*

THE MEETING IN THE MORNING AT THE HOTEL – THE PREPARATIONS OF THE ATTORNEY.

*I*t is no less than strange, the difference that takes place in people's feelings with regard to precisely the same circumstances in the morning, from what they really felt and thought in the evening, and when the shadows of night were upon them.

This mental phenomenon was not wanting in the case of Mr. Lake.

He felt as he rose the next day, and the sun was shining in at the window of his bedroom, most thoroughly ashamed of his fears and his nervous tremors of the preceding night.

His wife saw with a smile the change in his feelings.

"You are no longer," she said, "afraid of the vampyre."

"Oh, say no more about it," was his reply. "I shall go immediately after breakfast and see Mr. Miller, and with him make such arrangements as will bring the affair upon which we have set our hearts to a crisis, and while I am gone you can instruct our son in what he has to do."

"I will."

The breakfast passed over in rather a constrained manner. Mrs. Lake had made an attempt to persuade Annetta that she was really too unwell to get up for an hour or two, but that Annetta would not submit to, as she felt herself, notwithstanding all her sufferings and all her fright, really capable of rising.

The consequence was, that she appeared at the breakfast table, and stopped most effectually anything in the shape of a confidential discourse taking place among the Lakes.

The meal therefore passed off rather silently, and there were only a few remarks made, incidentally, about the preceding night's alarm.

Annetta was evidently in a state of great nervousness, as well she might be, for the idea that she would be again subjected to the frightful visits

of the vampyre, was ever present to her, and she was denied the consolation which the letter of Varney might, and most probably would have
given her.

After the morning meal, Mr. Lake gave his wife a significant look to
intimate that he was then going to Mr. Miller's, and that in his absence
she was to play her part.

She perfectly understood him, and nodded in return, and thus this
worthy pair separated.

We will follow Mr. Lake.

The attorney did not live in one of the most respectable haunts of
the profession, but he was a man of his word, and by the time Mr. Lake
reached his chambers he was there, it being then not much above ten
o'clock.

There was some delay in admitting Mr. Lake to the private room of
the attorney, and he thought that the clerk who was in the outer office
looked a little confused.

"Is anybody with Mr. Miller?" asked Lake.

"Yes — that is to say — I mean no."

"A strange answer. Yes, and you mean no."

"Why, Sir, I only meant that Mr. Miller was rather busy, and we are
so much in the habit when that is the case, of saying that he has some
one with him that it slipped out unawares, only as we would not deceive
you, sir, for the world, you understand that that was why, you perceive,
sir, that in a manner of speaking, I corrected myself."

This explanation was rather more wordy than satisfactory to Mr. Lake,
however, for want of a better, he was compelled to put up with it, and
he said nothing, but waited with the most exemplary patience, until Mr.
Miller's bell rang.

The clerk answered it, and in a few moments returned to say that Mr.
Miller had got through a legal document he had been engaged upon,
and the he much regretted having kept Mr. Lake waiting, but was then
quite at his disposal.

Now Lake could have sworn that he had heard the sound of a voice
from the private room of the attorney, and he consequently did not feel
quite easy.

When he went in he found Mr. Miller with a number of letters before
him.

"Ah, my dear sir," cried the lawyer, "sit down."

"Thank you. I thought somebody was with you?"

"Oh, dear no, not at all. I was going through a lease, you see, and
from long experience in such matters, I have found that I have a better
and clearer understanding of the matter, if I read it aloud to myself, but
perhaps that is only a peculiarity of mine."

"Then it was your voice I heard just now?"

Mr. Lake's suspicions were about half removed, certainly not more than half, but he could say no more about it, although he cast now and then suspicious glances round the room; yet if he had been asked what he was suspicious of, he would hardly have been able to give a clear and understandable answer to the question.

It is one of the curses of conscious guilt ever to live in an atmosphere of doubt and dread, and to the full did Mr. Lake feel that curse.

"Well, Mr. Miller," he said, after a pause, "I have called upon you to say that I hope it will suit your convenience to settle a little affair today at twelve o'clock at the hotel."

"Twelve — let me see — twelve. Not at the hotel my dear sir, I am compelled to be in chambers in case of a letter coming on very particular business, but if you will bring her here, I can manage it very nicely; if she don't leave this place with a conviction that she has a father in London, I'll eat my boots."

"Well, I don't see why we should not come here, as you give me great satisfaction Mr. Miller by avowing yourself to be so confident of the result."

"I am as confident as that I sit on this three legged stool."

"Good — then you may depend upon our coming here at twelve o'clock precisely. There will be myself, Mrs. Lake, my son and the young lady. Mind she is no fool, she must be perfectly overwhelmed with proofs of what we wish to make her believe."

"Exactly, that she is not the daughter of Lord Lake, but a mere changeling imposed upon him as his own child — the said own child being dead."

"Precisely."

"Agreed, sir, agreed. With respect to my reward, I have been thinking that I should like, you know, to have some acknowledgment. You tell me you have no money now, but that this obstacle once removed you will come in for all the Lake estates, and that Lord Lake cannot live long."

"That's the state of the case."

"Then sir, will you give me a note for #2000 pounds, payable on demand."

"On demand?"

"Yes; of course it would be needless folly of me to present it until you have money you know."

"True, true."

We need not pursue the conversation further, but satisfy the reader by stating the result, which was, that the attorney got the note for #2000 pounds form Lake, likewise a paper signed, which admitted the debt more fully still, and effectually barred Lake from objecting to any proceedings on account of want of consideration for the promissory note, or that it had not been fairly obtained of him, pleas which might have inconvenienced Mr. Miller if he chose to pursue Lake for the amount.

In the meantime Mrs. Lake had not been idle, but had spoken to her booby and cowardly son, making him aware of what he had to do in the business, namely, to shew his great disinterestedness in taking for his wife Annetta after she was supposed to be proved not the daughter of Lord Lake, but quite a different personage, and altogether destitute of pecuniary resources.

He managed pretty well always to understand any villainy, and so entered life and soul into the scheme of his mother.

"Ah! I like that a monstrous deal better than keeping watch for a vampyre, which is a sort of job that don't at all suit such a constitution as mine, do you see?"

Mrs. Lake not being aware of the alteration of arrangements by which they were all to proceed to the lawyer's chambers, instead of coming to the hotel, took no trouble with Annetta, conceiving that it would perhaps be better at twelve o'clock, when the parties were assembled, to take her by surprise, than to say anything to her beforehand, which might have the effect of preparing her for what was to come, and so getting up a spirit of resistance and of inquiry which it might be difficult to resist or satisfactorily to meet.

When Mr. Lake came home from Gray's Inn, she was made aware of the alteration, and consultations ensued as to how Annetta was to be got there at all. At length after several modes of managing the matter had been discussed, Mrs. Lake said,

"You two can walk there, and then I can say to Annetta that I am going for a drive and to make a few purchases, so that she will have no objection to go with me for an airing, and I will take good care to be with you at the hour of twelve."

"That will do prime," said the son. "Leave mother alone for managing things."

"Well," said Mr. Lake, "it shall be so, I don't see any objection to the scheme, nor can I suggest a better one, so we will look upon that as settled. All you have to do," turning to his son, "is to play your part well."

"Oh! never fear me, I like the girl and I like money."

Chapter *CLXXV.*

THE VAMPYRE'S VISIT TO THE BARRACKS AT KINGSTON. — THE YOUNG OFFICER.

We do not wish altogether to lose sight of Varney in these proceedings, and it so happens that he is sufficiently mixed up in what further occurred to make it desirable that we should now again refer to him.

It was not the least singular fact in the character of that mysterious being, to notice how he always endeavored to make some sort of amends or reparation to those whom he had so much terrified by his visitations.

We have seen in the case of the family of the Bannerworths how eventually he was most anxious to do them a service, as a recompense for the really serious injury he had inflicted upon them, and how it was really and eventually through him that they emerged from the circumstances of difficulty and danger in which they had been pecuniarily engaged.

We shall now see if Varney, who really in his way is a very respectable sort of a personage, is about good or evil.

We left him on the river, after promising in his usual liberal spirit, a handsome reward to the waterman whom he employed to row the boat in which he embarked.

After going some distance, the waterman, finding his fare was silent, thought it would be as well again to ask him where he was going.

Accordingly, with a preparatory hem, he began by saying,

"About as nice a tide, sir, as we could have for going up the stream."

"Very likely," was the brief reply.

"Do you land near hand, sir?"

"I want to go to Kingston; take me to some Quay on the river as near as you can, for the purpose of my walking there."

"Kingston?" said the waterman, with a look rather of surprise. "It's a long pull to Kingston, and if your honor could get a conveyance, your best way would be to get out at Putney."

"Wherefore?"

"Why after that, the river takes such a plaguey lot of windings and turnings that you have to go treble the actual distance before you reach Teddington."

"I said Kingston."

"Well that's close by Teddington; but I'll row your honor if you like, only it will take us some hours to get there that's all."

"Go on."

"Very good, pull away, pull a — way."

Having now, as he knew, a long job before him, the waterman husbanded his strength, he did not row near so fast, but to a low kind of tune he muttered to himself he worked away at his sculls, slowly and surely, and got through the water at a moderate easy rate, while rather a quick jerking one would soon have exhausted him.

The boat went slowly onward, and many an interesting sight was passed upon the banks of the river, but none appeared in the least to attract the attention of the man who sat in the boat, apparently deeply absorbed in his own meditations.

The boatman began much to wonder who he had got a fare, and to think that it would be but a dull and wearisome job to row all the way to Teddington without any amusing gossip by the way, so he made yet another attempt to break the stillness that reigned around.

"The river up this way, sir," he said, "is quiet enough at night; it's different below bridge though, for there there is always some bustle going on."

"Ah!" said Varney.

"But here, somehow, it is dull to my mind."

"Ah!"

"Though the gentry and those as is book-learned find a deal of pleasure in looking at the old places on the banks, where things have been done and said by folks many a long year since, whose heads don't ache now, sir."

"Ah!"

There was no getting on at this rate, so, after two or three more remarks and getting nothing by "Ah!" as a reply, the waterman gave it up as a bad job altogether, and pulled away, chanting in a low tone his song again, without making another attempt to disturb the taciturnity of his fare, who sat as still as a statue in the boat, and looking as if he did not breathe, so rigid and strange were his attitude, and the lifeless-like appearance he had.

The waterman was really a little alarmed by the time they reached Teddington, for he thought that it might be possible his fare was dead, and the horrid idea that he had stiffened in that attitude as he sat, began to find a place in the boatman's imagination.

When, however, he boat's keel grated on the landing-place, he cried, – "Here we are, your honor."

The vampyre rose and stepped on shore. He held out his hand and dropped a guinea into the extended palm of the waterman, and then stalked off.

After he had walked some distance he spoke to a watchman whom he met, saying, –

"Are there not military barracks somewhere hereabout?"

"Oh, yes."

"Thank you. Can you direct me?"

"Certainly. You have only to go on, and take the second turning to your left, and you will see the gate; it's horse soldiers that's there now – the 4th Light Dragoons."

By keeping to the directions which the watchman had given, Varney soon reached the gate of the barracks, and then it was three o'clock in the morning. A sentinel was pacing to and fro at the gate. To him Varney at once went, and with a lofty kind of courtesy, that made the man at once respectful to him, he said, –

"Is Lieutenant Rankin in barracks?"

"Yes, sir, – on duty."

"Indeed! Is he on guard tonight?"

"Yes, sir, to four o'clock. He will be relieved then."

"That's fortunate, I want to see him. It is on business of the very first importance, or of course I would not trouble him or myself. You must send to him somehow."

The sentinel hesitated.

"I hardly know," he said, "how the lieutenant will take it – he is on duty."

"But I suppose he is human for all that, and is liable to all the accidents and alternations of human affairs, which may make it absolutely necessary he should be communicated with, even at such an hour as this. I will hold you harmless."

This was so reasonable, and there was such an air of quiet gentlemanly authority about Varney, that the soldier began to think he should run less risk of offending somebody of importance if he consented to disturb the lieutenant than if he refused. Accordingly he stepped a pace or two within the gate and called out.

"Guard!"

A soldier from the guard-room answered the summons.

"Ay," he said, "what is it? – a strange cat I suppose."

"No, none of your nonsense. Here is a gentleman, I think a general officer, by Jove, wants to see Lieutenant Rankin. Go and tell him."

"And give him this," said Varney, as he handed the soldier a card, on which was written, —

"A friend to a friend of Lieutenant Ranking, whose initials are A. L."

"I know that this young soldier loves the Lady Annetta," muttered the vampyre to himself, "and he shall be given the opportunity of flying to her rescue from her villainous relations. So far, I will make reparation to her."

In less than three minutes, Lieutenant Rankin came hurriedly to the gate.

"Where is the gentleman?" he said.

"Here sir," said Varney, "step aside with me."

The young officer did so, and then Varney said to him, —

"It matters not how I became acquainted with the fact, but I know that you love the Lady Annetta Lake, and that you are far from being indifferently regarded by her. She is in London at the London Hotel. A vile plot is formed to marry her to her cousin, the gist of which is to make her both her and her father believe that she is a changeling and not the daughter of Lord Lake. You love her, young man. Go and rescue her."

"Annetta in London!"

"Yes, what I tell you you may rely upon, as if it were a voice from heaven that spoke to you. Go and snatch her whom you love from the base hands of those who, under the mask of pretended friendship, would betray her."

"And you," cried the young soldier; "who are you, and how can I repay you for bringing me this intelligence of her whom I —"

"Enough," said the vampyre. "I have performed my mission. It is for you, young sir, to take a due advantage of that which I have told to you."

In another moment he was gone.

Chapter *CLXXVI.*

AN ECLAIRCISSEMENT. – THE INNOCENT TRIUMPHANT.

*I*t is eleven o'clock, Mr. and Mrs. Lake are standing by one of the windows at the hotel conversing in whispers, while the hopeful son is brushing his hat.

"It is time, you think?" said Mrs. Lake.

"Yes," was the reply. "and I will be off now at once, and depend upon you following with Annetta to Mr. Miller's."

"That you may be sure of. She has had a refreshing night's rest, and this morning she eagerly enough caught at the proposal to take a drive round the principal thoroughfares in the carriage we have hired so that is no longer a difficulty."

"What is to be done if she rejects?"

Mr. Lake gave a jerk with his head in the direction of his son, to signify that it was of him he talked.

"It can't be helped if she does. Then I should say all we have to do, is to persevere in making her out no child of Lord Lake, and wait for his decease. We must be careful what we are about, though, or he may take it into his head to make some ample provision for her, to the decrease of his personal means, which I hope to see all ours."

The only way to stop that will be getting Miller and the pretended father to make it as a complete part of the plan that Annetta herself should seem latterly to have been a party to palming herself off upon him as his daughter when she knew the contrary quite well."

"Ah, if that could be done."

"It must and shall; Miller's ingenuity in such matters is immense. He will accomplish anything in the world – aye seeming impossibilities – for money."

"He is just the man for us, so now be off with you at once, and expect me in good time."

In a few moments afterwards, Mr. Lake set off with this booby son to the lawyer's, enjoining him all the way as they went, to be especially careful how he maintained the character of a disinterested suitor, which had been marked out for him in the program of the family proceedings.

"Oh, never fear me, father."

"Well, I hope that you will do and say the right things, and what is as important, I hope you will do and say them at the right time, otherwise you will spoil all."

Thus armed at all points, as they thought, for conquest, old Lake and young Lake, than whom all London could not have produced two more unprincipled persons, arrived at Gray's Inn, and were received in the outer room of Mr. Miller's chambers with every demonstration of respect.

"Walk in, gentlemen, walk in to the clients' private-room if you please," said the clerk. "Mr. Miller left directions with me that when you came, you should be shown in at once."

All this was very gratifying indeed, and the solicitor was there, seated in his easy chair, looking as full of serenity as possible, and as if the least affair in the world was on *tapis.*

Scarcely had the usual salutations passed, when the clerk announced Mrs. Lake and a young lady.

"My wife with Annetta!" exclaimed Lake; and in a moment his words were verified by the appearance of the parties he had named.

"Tell me at once," said Annetta, "why I am brought here?"

"My dear young lady," said Mr. Miller, "if you will condescend to take a seat, I will explain."

"Be brief, sir."

The party was seated, and then Mr. Miller, clearing his throat said, —

"Ahem! You are of course aware, miss, that great doubt arose in the mind of Lord Lake with regard to your proper identity, and he sent you over to this country from Italy with his brother and family, to have those doubts resolved — ahem! They are resolved, and you are found to be the daughter of a gentleman now in London."

"The proofs, sir," said Annetta, with a dignity and a calmness that surprised the whole party.

"Ah, ah — the proofs. Let me see, oh yes; there are the papers. No. 1, copy of a confession made by —"

"Stop, sir," said young Lake, "stop. This is — it must be painful to the feelings of this young lady, and very, very painful is it to my feelings, for I have been long fervently attached to her, and let her be whose daughter she may, she is to me all perfection. I love her and would gladly make her my wife, let her be named whatever she may."

"But she is destitute, — quite destitute," said Miller.

"It don't matter to me," cried young Lake — he was playing his part famously — "it don't matter to me; I love her, and will work for her — she shall never want while I have life-blood in my veins."

"If this now were sincere," said Annetta, "I should begin for the first time to respect you. But you will excuse me for doubting it very much. I likewise doubt much the pretended evidence that you bring forward regarding my birth."

A tremendous knock at the outer door of the chambers now disturbed the party. An altercation was heard with the clerk — then a shout for police, and a heavy fall as if somebody had been knocked down, and in another moment the door of Mr. Miller's private room was dashed open, and Lieutenant Rankin, in his undress military uniform, stood upon the threshold.

"Annetta!" he cried.

"Rankin — oh, George, George!" shrieked Annetta, and in another moment she was in his arms.

"Here's a go," cried young Lake; "I say, young fellow, this won't do."

"Oh, George, George!" said Annetta, "they will have it that I am not my own father's child, that I am some nameless, houseless thing."

"They lie, Annetta who say so," replied the young soldier; "you shall be mine, and the proudest that ever stepped shall treat you with becoming respect, or shall rue the consequences."

"Well, I think it's time!" cried Mr. Miller in a marked manner, and throwing open the door of an inner room, he added, "my Lord Lake, come forth; no doubt you have heard all." Lord Lake himself — the Mr. Blue of the London Hotel, the sham confidential clerk of Miller — made his appearance, to the utter confusion of the Lakes.

"My father," said Annetta, "my dear father!"

"Hold," said Lord Lake, gravely, "I suspected, Annetta, from the first that your birth was impugned by my brother from the most interested motives, and I followed you from Italy — Mr. Miller disclosed all to me, and the infamous plot is discovered."

"Then I am your child?"

"Confusion," muttered Lake, "death and the devil, what a *contre temps.*"

"Stop," added Lord Lake, "the strangest thing of all has yet to be told. This plot to make out that you are not my child is but a plot, but it is not baseless as to the fact. You are not my daughter. I have by mere chance found out that lately, and I cannot provide for you, as the resources I have must go to him who will inherit my title. What say you, Master Lake, this girl with all her beauty is destitute, her name is Smith — will you have her?"

"Not I in faith, thank you for nothing."

"Will you, young soldier, knowing what she is?"

"Ay, will I with all my heart! she is the highest, brightest treasure this world can offer me. Any name or no name — poor or rich — noble or commoner — she is still my own dear girl, and her resting place shall be my heart, the whole world shall not tear her from it."

"God's blessings on you," cried Lord Lake, grasping his hands; "I did but this to give yon shrinking coward a chance of creeping into favor with me, because he boasted so of his disinterested affection a while ago. She is my child, the Lady Annetta Lake — I never doubted it, and she is yours — George Rankin, and you shall be the dear son of my adoption."

"I say, father," said young Lake, "I — I think we had better go."

"Curse you all," cried Lake, "and doubly curse you, lawyer Miller, you have betrayed me; but I'll be revenged."

"Through the bars of a prison," said the lawyer. "An officer is down stairs to arrest you for two thousand pounds. Ha, ha, ha!"

*T*hus then was it that this episode in the life of Varney the Vampyre terminated. But still he lived, and still there existed all the strange and fearful mixture of good and evil that was in his disposition. There he was yet upon the earth's surface, looking like one of the great world, and yet possessing so few feelings in common with its inhabitants.

Surely to him there must have been periods of acute suffering, of intense misery, such as would have sufficed to drive any ordinary mind to distraction, and yet he lived, although one cannot, upon reviewing his career, and considering what he was, consider that death would have been other than a grateful release to him from intense suffering.

Perhaps, of all the suffering that, in consequence of his most awful and singular existence, was inflicted upon human nature, he suffered the most, for that he was a man of good intellect no one who has followed us thus far can doubt, and one cannot help giving in almost at times to as strange and fanciful theory of his own, namely that this world was to him the place of perdition for crimes done in some other sphere.

"It must be so!" he would say, "but as the Almighty Master of all things is all merciful, as he is all powerful, the period of my redemption will surely come at last."

This was the most consolate thought that Varney could have, and it showed that even yet there was a something akin to humanity lingering at his hears. bears? heart?

This showed that despite the dreadful power he had — a power, as well as an awful propensity — he had some yearnings after a better state.

What had he been? How did he become a vampyre? Did the voice of fond affection ever thrill in his ears? Had little children ever climbed the knee of that wretched man? Fearful questions, if he could have answered them the affirmative – if he bore about with him, deep in his memory, a remembrance of such joys gone by.

=

Chapter CLXXVIII.

THE VAMPYRE HAS SERIOUS THOUGHTS. – THE DREAM. –
THE RESOLUTION.

*T*he next day after the events that we have detailed, Varney found himself in a hotel in London. He did not even make the effort to inquire how the affair connected with the Lady Annetta, in which towards the last he had played a generous part, prospered.

He was too spirit-broken himself to do so.

For nearly the whole day he remained in a room by himself, and although to avoid uncomfortable and ungracious remarks being made by the people of the house, he ordered from time to time food and wine, he, in accordance with his horrible nature, which forbade him any nourishment but human blood, touched neither.

During that day he seemed to be suffering acutely, for now and then as the waiters of the hotel passed the door of the private room he occupied, they heard deep agonizing groans, and when once or twice they went in, fancying that he must be very ill or dying, they found him seated at a table on which his head was resting.

He would start up on these occasions, and sternly question them for interrupting him, so at last they left him alone.

Let us look at him in his solitude.

It is getting towards the dim and dusky hours of late twilight, and he can only barely be described as he sits bolt upright in a high-backed arm-chair, looking at vacancy, while his lips move, and he appears to be conversing with the spirits of another world, that in their dim intangibility are not visible to mortal eyes.

Now and then he would strike his breast, and utter a dull groan as if some sudden recollection of the dreadful past had come over him, with such a full tide of horror that it could not be resisted.

It was not until a considerable time had elapsed, and the darkness had greatly increased, that he at length spoke.

"And I was once happy," he said mournfully, "once happy, because I was innocent. Oh! gracious Heaven, how long am I to suffer?"

A spasmodic kind of movement of his whole features ensued, that was quite dreadful to look upon, and would have terrified any one who could have seen them. Then he spoke again.

"I was happy one hundred and eighty years ago," he said, "for that has been the awful duration my life as yet; yes, a hundred and eighty years have, with their sunshine of summer, and their winter storms, passed over my head; and I had a wife and children, who, with innocent and gladsome prattle, would climb my knee and nestle in my bosom. Oh! where are they all now?"

He wrung his hands, but he did not weep the fount of tears had dried up for a hundred years in his bosom.

"Yes, yes! the grave holds them — holds them? said I. No, no, long since have they crumbled into dust, and nothing of them remains as a faint indication even of who once was human. I, I it was who listened to the councils of a fiend, and destroyed he her? who had give up home, kindred, associations, all for me."

He rose up from the chair, and seemed to think that he would find some relief in pacing the room to and fro, but he soon threw himself again into the seat.

"No, no," he said, "no peace for me; and I cannot sleep, I have never slept what mortals call sleep, the sleep of rest and freedom from care, for many a long year. When I do seen seem? to repose, then what dreadful images awake to my senses. Better, far better than my glaring eyeballs should crack with weariness, than that I should taste such repose."

The sympathetic shudder with which he uttered these words was quite proof sufficient of his deep and earnest sincerity. He must indeed have suffered much before he could have give such a sentiment such an utterance. We pity thee, Varney!

"And when, oh, when will my weary pilgrimage be over," he ejaculated; "Oh when will the crime of murder be cleansed from my soul. I killed her. Yes, I killed her who loved me. A fiend, I know it was a fiend, whispered suspicion in my ear, suspicion of her who was as pure as the first ray of sunlight that from heaven shows itself to chase away the night, but I listened and then created from my own fevered brain the circumstances that gave suspicion strength and horrible consistency — and I killed her."

After the utterance of these words he was silent for a time, and then in heart-rending accents he again repeated them.

"I killed her — I killed her, and she was innocent. Then I became what I am. There was a period of madness, I think, but I became a vampyre; I have died many deaths, but recovered from them all; for ever, by some strange accident or combination of circumstances, the cold moonbeams have had access to my lifeless form, and I have recovered."

By this time the landlord of the hotel in which Varney was staying, had got in a fearful fidget, for he began to think that he had a madman in his house, and that it would turn out that his guest had made his escape from some lunatic asylum.

"I wonder now," he thought, "if a little soothing civility would do any good; I will try it. It can't surely do any harm."

With this intent the landlord went up stairs to the room in which Varney the Vampyre was, and he tapped gently at the door.

There was no reply, and after a few moments' consideration, the landlord opened the door and peeped in, when he saw his customer sitting in an arm-chair, in the manner in which we have described him to sit.

"If you please, sir," said the landlord, "would you not like——"

"Blood!" said Varney, rising.

The landlord did not wait for any more, but bustled down stairs again with all the promptitude in his power.

It was a bed-room and sitting-room that Varney occupied at the hotel, the one adjoining the other, and now although he groaned and sighed at the idea of repose, he flung himself upon the bed, full dressed, as he was, and there he lay as still as death itself.

One of those strange fitful kind of slumbers, such as he had himself described as being so full of dread, came over him.

For a time he was still, as we have said, but then as various images of agony began to chase each other through his brain, he tossed about his arms, and more than once the word "mercy" came from his lips in accents of the most soul-harrowing nature.

This state of things continued for some considerable time, and then in his sleep a great change came over him, and he fancied he was walking in a garden replete with all the varied beauties of a southern clime, and through the center of which meandered a stream, the crystal music of which was delightfully calming and soothing to his senses.

All around seemed to speak of the peace and loveliness of an Eden.

As he wandered on, he fancied that some form was walking by his side, and that he heard the gentle fall of its feet, and the flutter of garments.

"Varney," it said, "you have suffered much."

"I have. Oh, God knows I have."

"You would die, Varney, if the moonbeams could be prevented from reaching you."

"Yes, yes. But how — how?"

"The ocean. The deep, deep sea hides many a worse secret than the corpse of a vampyre."

It might have been that, after all, his sleep was to some extent refreshing to him, or that the dream he had, had instilled a hope into him of a release from what, in his case, might truly be called the bondage of existence; but he certainly arose more calm, cool, and collected, than he had been for some time past.

"Yes," he said, "the deep sea holds a secret well, and if I could but be washed into some of its caverns, I might lie there and rot until the great world itself had run its course."

This idea took great possession of him. He thought over various modes of carrying it out. At one time he thought that if he bought a boat on the sea coast, and went out alone, sailing away as far from land as he could, he might be able to accomplish his object. But then he might not be able to get far enough.

At length he thought of a more feasible and a better plan than that, and it was to take his passage in some ship for any port, and watch his opportunity, some night when far from land, to steal up upon the deck and plunge in the waves.

The more he considered of this plan the better he liked it, and the more it wore an appearance of probability and an aspect of success, so at length the thought grew into a resolution.

"Yes, yes," he muttered, "who knows but that some friendly spirit — for the mid air that floats 'twixt earth and heaven is peopled with such, may have whispered such counsel in my ears. It shall be done; I will no longer hesitate, but make this attempt to shake off the dreadful weight which mere existence is to me."

Chapter CLXXIX.

THE SCOTCH PACKET SHIP. – THE SUICIDE.

*I*t was in pursuance of this resolution, so strangely and suddenly formed, that the unhappy Varney rose on the following morning and went to that region of pitch, slop clothing, red herrings, and dirt – the docks.

But yet, somehow, although the docks may not be the cleanest or them most refined part of the vast city of London, the coarseness and the litter there – for after all it is more litter than dirt – are by no means so repulsive as those bad addenda to other localities.

There is a kind of rough freshness induced by the proximity of the water which has a physical and moral effect, we are inclined to think, upon the place and the people, and which takes off much of what would otherwise wear the aspect of what is called low life.

But this is all by the way, and we will at once proceed to follow the fortunes of Varney, in carrying out his plan of self annihilation.

The hour was an early one, and many a curious glance was cast at him, for although he had humanized and modernized his apparel to a great extent, he could not get rid of the strange, unworld-like (if we may use the phrase) look of his face. He was very pale too, and jaded looking, for the thoughts that had recently occupied him were not such as to do good to the looks of any one.

He cared little in what vessel he embarked. He had but one object in embarking at all, and that was to get out to sea, so that the ultimate destination of the ship that should receive so very odd and equivocal a passenger was a matter of no moment.

Stopping a personage who had about him a sea-faring look, Varney, pointing to a bustling place of embarkation, said, –

"Does any vessel start from there today?"

"Yes, there's one going now, or as soon as the tide serves her. She is for Leith?"

"On the coast of Scotland, I think?"

"Yes, to be sure."

Varney walked on until he came to a kind of counting-house, where sat a man with books before him, and, not to take up more valuable space, he secured what was called a berth on board the "Ocean," a dirty, small, ill-convenient ship bound for the port near the Scotch metropolis of Edinburgh.

Not wishing to be himself much noticed, and having no desire to notice anybody, Varney went down below, and seated himself in a dark corner of the generally dingy cabin, and there, amid all the noise, bawling, abuse, and bustle contingent upon getting the ill-conditioned bark under weigh, he never moved or uttered a word to any one, although the cabin was frequently visited.

But Varney had no idea of the amount of annoyance to which he was likely, in the course of the evening, to be subjected.

The vessel was got under weigh, and as both wind and tide happened to be favorable, she dropped down the river rapidly, and soon was clear of the Nore-light, and holding on her course northward.

The cabin now began to fill with the passengers, and extraordinary as the fact may appear, there were many Scotchmen actually going back again. They were, however, only going to pay visits, for it is one of the popular delusions that Scotchmen try to keep up in this country, that they have left something dear and delightful behind them in Scotland, and that, take it altogether, it is one of the most desirable spots in the whole world. It becomes, therefore, quite necessary for them to go back now and then, in order to keep up that delusion.

Personal vanity, too, is one of the great characteristics of the nation; and many a Scotchman goes back to Edinburgh, for example, to make an appearance among his old friends and family connections, totally incompatible with his real position in London.

By about nine o'clock at night, when the shore to the west could only be discovered as a dim, grey line on the horizon, the cabin of the "Ocean" packet was crammed.

Whisky was produced, and a drink that the Scotch call "bottled yell," meaning ale; and as these two heady liquids began to take effect "Auld Lang syne" was chanted in the vernacular by the whole party. At length a feeling of annoyance began to grow up from the fact of the isolated aspect of Varney, and the quiet, unobtrusive manner in which he looked on at the proceedings, appearing not in the smallest degree enthusiastic, even when the most uproarious Scotch songs, in the most unintelligible of all jargons, were sung, for strange to say, the authors of that nation take a pride in slaughtering the English language.

At length a Scotchman approached Varney and said, —

"Ye'll take a glass to auld Reekie mon?"

Edinburgh is called Reekie in consequence of the absence of drainage, giving it a horrible fetid smell, a reeky atmosphere, in a manner of speaking; which may be illustrated by the Scotchman, who was returning to that place from England, on the top of a stage coach, when within about fifty miles he began sniffing and working his nose in an extraordinary manner.

"What are you doing that for?" said an Englishman. "Eh! mon, I can smell the gude auld toon."

"I do not understand your language," said Varney, and he walked from the cabin to the deck of the vessel. He recoiled an instant, for the moon was rising.

"Ever thus, even thus," he said, "how strange it is that I never dream of ridding myself of the suffering of living, but the moon is shining brightly. Can its rays penetrate the ocean?"

The deck was very still and silent indeed. The man at the helm, and one other pacing to and fro, were all that occupied it, save Varney himself, and he stood by the side gazing in the direction, where he had last seen the dim grey speck of land.

"A pleasant run, sir, we shall have of it," said the man who had been pacing the deck, "if this kindly wind continues."

"It blows from the west."

"Yes, nearly due-west; but that suits us. We keep her head a few points in shore, and do well with such a wind, although a south-west by south is our choice."

"How far are we from land?"

"It's the coast of Suffolk that is to our left, but we are I hope a good thirty miles or more from it."

"You hope?"

"Yes, sir. Perhaps you are not sufficient of a sailor to know that we never hug the shore if we can possibly help it."

"I understand. And there?"

"Oh, there lies the German Ocean."

"How deep now should you say the sea was here?"

"Can't say, sir, but it's blue water."

This was not much information to Varney, but he bowed his head and walked forward, as much as to say that he had had enough of the information and conversation of the man, who was the mate of the vessel, and quite disposed to be communicative. Perhaps in the very dim light he did not see exactly what a strange-looking personage he was talking to.

"Thirty miles from land," thought Varney, "surely that is far enough, and I need have no dread of floating to the shore through such a mass of water as that thirty miles. The distance is very great; I can tonight in another hour make the attempt."

To his great joy some heavy clouds climbed up the sky along with the moon, and congregating around the beautiful satellite, effectually obscured the greater number of its beams. There was in fact, no absolute moonlight, but a soft reflected kind of twilight coming through the clouds, and dispersed far and wide.

"This will do," muttered Varney. "All I have to fear are the direct moonbeams. It is they that have the effect of revivifying such as I am."

The man who had been pacing the deck finally sat down, and appeared to drop off to sleep, so that all was still, and as Varney kept to the head of the vessel, the man at the wheel could see nothing of him, there being many intervening obstacles. He was perfectly alone.

Now and then, with a loud roaring about, he heard some boisterous drinking chorus come from the cabin, and then a rattle of glasses as fists were thumped upon the tables in token of boisterous approbation, and then all would be still again.

Varney looked up to the sky and his lips moved, but he uttered no sound. He went closer to the vessel's side and gazed upon the water as it lazily rippled past. How calm and peaceful, he thought, he ought to be, far beneath that tide.

A sudden plunge into the sea would have made a splash that would have been heard, and that he wished of all things to avoid. He clambered slowly over the side, and only held on by his hands for a moment.

The cool night air tossed about his long elfin locks, and in another moment he was gone.

Chapter CLXXX.

THE OLD MANOR HOUSE. – THE RESCUE. – VARNEY'S
DESPAIR.

*A*t about ten o'clock on that same night on which Varney the

Vampyre plunged into the sea with hopes of getting rid of the world of troubles that oppressed him, a small fishing boat might have been seen a distance of about twenty-five miles from the Suffolk coast, trying to make for land, and baffled continually by the wind that blew off shore.

In this boat were two young men, and from their appearance they evidently belonged to the wealthier class of society. They were brothers.

From their conversation we shall gather the circumstances that threw them into such situation, not by any means divested of peril as it was.

"Well, Edwin," said one, "here we have been beating about for five hours, trying to get in shore, and all our little bark permits us to do is I think not materially to increase our distance from home."

"That is about the truth, Charles," said the other, "and it was my fault."

"Come, Edwin, don't talk in that way. There is no fault in the matter; how could you know that the wind would stiffen into such a breeze as it has, so that we cannot fight out against it; or if there be fault, of course it's as much mine as yours, for am not I here, and do I not know full well what an amount of consternation there will be at the Grange?"

"There will indeed!"

"Well, their joy when we get back will be all the greater."

"Shall we get back?"

"Can you ask? Look at our little boat, is she not sea-worthy? Does she not dance on the waves merrily? It is only the wind after all that baffles us, if it would drop a little, we could, I think make head against it with the oars.

The brothers were silent now for a few moments, for they were each looking at the weather. At length Edwin spoke, saying, —

"We shall have the moon up, and that may make a change."

"Very likely — very likely. There is not, I think, quite so much sea as there was; suppose we try the oars again?"

The other assented, and the two young men exerted themselves very much to decrease their distance from the Suffolk coast by pulling away right manfully, but it was quite evident to them that they did no good, and that they had just as well dropped westward as they had been doing, by keeping the sail set, and steering as near as possible to the wind.

"Why, if this goes on, Charles, where shall we get to by the morning?"

"To Northumberland, perhaps."

"Or further."

"Well, if we go far enough, what say you to attempting the *vexata questio* of the north-west passage?"

"Nay, I cannot jest — it's a sad thing this — more sad a good deal for those who are at home, than for us. Tomorrow is Clara's wedding day, and what a damper it will be upon all to suppose that we have perished at sea."

"They will never suppose that we would do anything so ridiculous. Why, at the worst, you know, we could go before the wind and run on to Holland."

"Yes, if no storm arises or such a gale as might founder our boat. There, there is the moon."

"Yes, and she will soon be overtaken by yon bank of clouds that seem to be scudding after her in the blue heavens. Ha! a sail, by Jove!"

"Where? where?"

"Not I think above four miles there to the east, by our little compass which it is a thousand mercies we have with us. Look, you may see her sails against that light cloud – there."

"I see her. Think you she will see us?"

"There is every chance, for her swell of canvass will be all the other way. Fire your fowling-piece and the sound may reach her, the wind is good for carrying it."

Charles took a fowling-piece from the bottom of the boat. The brothers had merely gone out at sunset or a little before it, to shoot gulls, and he tried to discharge the piece, but several seas that they had shipped, while they were thinking of other things than keeping the gun dry, had, for the time being, most effectively prevented it from being discharged.

"Ah!" said Edwin as he heard the click of the lock, "that hope is lost."

"It is indeed, and to my thinking the ship is distancing us rapidly. You see our mast and sail, will, at even this distance, lie so low in the horizon that they will hardly see us unless they are sweeping the sky with a night glass."

"And that is not likely."

"Certainly not, so we have nothing for it but to hold on our way. I am getting hungry if you are not."

"I certainly am not getting hungry, for I have felt half famished these last two hours; but I suppose we may hold out against the fiend hunger some hours yet. What are you looking at so earnestly, eh?"

"I hardly know."

"You hardly know? Let me see – why – why what is it?"

"There seems to me to be something now and that much darker than the waves, tiding on their tops; there, do you not see it? There it is again. There!"

"Yes, yes."

"What on earth can it be?"

"A dead body."

"Indeed! ah! it drifts towards us. There is some current hereabouts, for you see it comes to us against the wind."

"Don't deceive yourself, brother. It is we who are going with the wind towards it, and now you can see there is no doubt about what it is. Some poor fellow, who has been drowned. Get out the boat-hook, get it out."

"Why, you would not take in such a cargo, Edwin."

"God forbid! but I feel some curiosity to see who and what sort of a personage it is. Here we have him. What a length he is to be sure."

The body was nearly alongside the boat, and one of the brothers detained it with a boat-hook, while they both looked earnestly at it.

It was the body of a man, remarkably well dressed, and had no appearance of having been under the water long. The features, as far as they could see them, were calm and composed. The hands were clenched, and some costly looking rings glittered on the fingers through the salt spray that foamed and curled around the insensible form.

"Charles," said Edwin; "what we shall do?"

Edwin shook his head.

"I — I don't like."

"Like what?"

"I don't like to cast it adrift again, and not take it ashore, where it can rest in an honest man's grown if he be one. Fancy it being one of us, would it not be a consolation to those who love us to know that we rested in peace among our ancestors, in preference to rotting in the sea, tossed and mangled by every storm that blows. I do not like to cast the body adrift again."

"It's a ghastly passenger."

"It is, but that ghastliness is only an idea, and we should remember that we ourselves——"

"Stop, brother, stop. Do not fancy that I oppose your wish to convey this body to the shore, and place it in some sanctified spot. What I expressed concerning it was merely the natural feeling that must arise on such an occasion, nothing more."

"Then you are willing?"

"I am."

The two brothers now, without further doubts or remarks upon the subject, got the body into the boat, and laid it carefully down. Then Edwin folded and tied a handkerchief over the face, for as he truly enough said, —

"There is no occasion to have to encounter that dead face each moment that one turns one's eyes in that direction; it is sufficient that we have, by taking the body in at all done, all that humanity can dictate to us."

To this Charles agreed, and it was remarked by them both as a strange thing that from the moment of their taking in the dead body to the boat, the wind dropped, and finally there was almost a calm, after which there came soft gentle air from the south-east, which enabled them with scarcely any exertion on their own parts to make great progress towards their own home, from which they found they had not by any means been driven so far northward as they had at first thought.

The brothers looked at each other, and it was Edwin who broke the silence, and put into words what both thought, by saying, —

"Charles, there is something more in this whole affair than what lies just upon its surface."

"Yes, it seems as if we were driven out to sea by some special providence to do this piece of work, and that having done it, the winds and the waves obeyed the hand of their mighty Master, and allowed of our return."

"It does seem so," said the other.

Chapter *CLXXXI.*

A FAMILY SCENE. – THE SISTERS. – THE HORRIBLE ALARM.

*I*n the course of two hours more, the young men were so close in shore that they could see the lights flashing along the coast, and they even fancied they could catch a glimpse of human forms moving along with torches; and if such were the case, they doubted not but that these people were sent to serve as a guide to them should they with their little bark be hovering near the coast.

"Look, Edwin," said Charles, "we are expected, are we not?"

"Yes, yes."

"I am certain that those lights are meant as guides for us."

"They may spare themselves the trouble, for do you not see that the clouds are wearing away, and that in a few minutes more we shall have the undimmed luster of a full moon looking down upon us."

"It will be so."

The boat had now got so far within a large natural inlet of the ocean that but very little wind caught its gently flapping sail, so that the brothers bent manfully to their oars, and got the boat through the water at a rapid rate.

Oh, how very different their sensations were now to what they had been when they were beating about at the mercy of the winds and waves, but a few short hours since, and when it certainly was but an even chance with death whether they would ever see their home again.

If a gale had sprung up, accompanied by anything in the shape of a very heavy sea, they must have been lost.

Soon they saw that their boat was descried, and at a particular portion of the coast there stood a complete cluster of men with torches, inviting them there to land, and they knew that such landing place was upon their father's property, and that in a few minutes they would be safe on shore.

Neither of them spoke, but reflection was busy in the hearts of both.

There was a loud and thoroughly English shout, as the boat grated upon the sandy beach, and Edwin and Charles jumped on shore. They were in another moment pressed in their father's arms.

"Why, why, boys," he said, "what a fright you have given us all; there's Clara and Emma have been forced — I say forced, for nothing but force would do it — to go home, and the whole country has been in an uproar. You were blown out to sea, I suppose?"

"Yes, father, but we have not been in any danger."

"Not in any danger with such a cockleshell of a boat fairly out into the German Ocean. But we will say no more about it, lads. Not another word, come home at once, and make all hearts glad at the old Grange-house."

"There's something in the boat," cried one of the men who held a light.

"Good God, yes!" exclaimed Charles.

"We had forgotten," said Edwin, "we met with a little adventure at sea, and picked up a dead body."

"A dead body?"

"Yes, father, we could not find it in our hearts to let it be, so we brought it on shore that it might have the rites of Christian burial in the village church-yard. Somebody who loved the man may yet thank us for it, and feel a consolation to know that such had been done."

"You are right boys, you are right," said the father, "you have done in that matter just as I would wish you; I will give orders for the body to be taken to the dead house by Will Stephens, and tomorrow it shall be decently interred."

This being settled, the father, accompanied by his two sons, who were not a little pleased to be safe upon *terra firma* again, walked together up a sloping pathway, which led to the Grange-house, as it was called.

The joy that the return of the brothers caused in the family, our readers may well imagine. The sisters Clara and Emma wept abundantly, and the mother, who had let her fears go further than any one else, was deeply affected.

But it is time that we should inform the reader who these people were, whom we have introduced upon the scene of our eventful history.

Sir George Crofton, for such was the name of the father of Edwin and Charles, was a wealthy warm-hearted country gentleman, and constantly resided upon his own estate all the year round, being a good landlord to his tenantry, and a good father to his four children, who have already been to some extent presented to the reader.

The mother was a kind-hearted, but rather weak woman, with an evangelical bias that at times was rather annoying to the family.

This, however, was perhaps the good lady's only fault, for with that one exception, she was fond of her children to excess, notwithstanding, as Sir George sometimes jestingly said he verily believed, she in her heart considered they were all on the high road to a nameless abode.

The night was so far advanced when the young men got home that, of course, not much was said or done, and among other things that were put off until the following morning, was the story of the finding of the body.

"There is no occasion," whispered Sir George, "to say anything to your mother about it."

"Certainly not, father."

"At least not till tomorrow, for if you do, I shall not get a wink of sleep for her reflections on the subject."

The two young men knew very well that this was no exaggeration, and that their mother would, like any divine, eagerly seize the opportunity of what is called "improving the occasion" by indulging in a long discourse upon the most dismal of all subjects that the mind of any human being can conceive, namely, the probability of everybody going to eternal perdition unless they believe in a particular set of doctrines that to her seem orthodox.

The consequence of this was that the dead body was quietly taken out of the boat by men who did not possess the most refined feelings in the world, and carried to the bone house.

"He seems a decent sort of chap," said one, as he looked at the very respectable habiliments of the corpse.

"Ah! look at the gould rings."

"Yes, you may, look, Abel, but eyes on, hands off."

"Why?"

"Why, you gowk, do you think as young Master Charles and Edwin don't know of 'em, and more besides, who would touch dead man's gold off of his fingers?"

"Is it unlucky?"

"Horrid!"

"Then I'll have naught to do with un."

The body was placed on the ground, for there was no coffin of any sort to put it in, and the door was shut upon it in the dead house, and then the party who had brought it there thought it a part of their duty to wake up Will Stephens the sexton, to tell him that there was such a thing as a dead body placed in his custody, as it were, by being put into the dead house, which was not above a hundred yards from the cottage occupied by Will.

They hammered away rather furiously at his door, and no wonder that he felt a little, or perhaps not a little, alarmed upon the occasion.

In a few moments a casement was opened and out popped a head.

"Hilloa! you ragamuffins, what do you mean by hammering away at an honest man's door at this rate, eh? Am I to have any sleep?"

"Ragamuffin yourself," cried one; "there's a dead body of a drowned man in the bonehouse. All you have got to do is to look after it, and there's a lot of gold rings on its fingers with diamonds in them, for all we know, worth God knows how much. You may make the most of it now that you know it."

"A dead man! Who is he?"

"Ah, that's more than we can tell. Good night, or rather good morning, old crusty."

"Stop! stop! – tell me——"

The men only laughted, for they had no desire to protract a conversation with the sexton, and he called in vain after them to give him some further information upon the subject of this rather mysterious information.

"A drowned man," he pondered to himself, "a drowned man, and with fingers loaded with gems, and brought to the bonehouse! Oh, pho! pho! It's a hoax, that's what it is, and I won't believe it. It's done to get me up in the cold, that's all, and then there will be some trick played off upon me safe, and I shall be only laughed at for my pains."

Full of this idea, the sexton turned into his bed again, and hoped that by speedily going to sleep, he should get the laugh of his tormentors, instead of they getting it of him, as well as lose the shivering that had come on him through standing at the open window, exposed to the night air so very indifferently clad.

Chapter *CLXXXII.*

THE SEXTON'S AVARICE. – THE DEAD AND THE LIVING. – THE RING.

*I*t was all very well for the sexton to wish, and to try to got to sleep, but actually to succeed in procuring

"Nature's sweet oblivion" was quite another matter.

In vain he tossed and turned about, there was no rest for him of any kind or description, dreamless or dreamful, and still he kept repeating to himself, –

"A dead body, with gold and diamond rings in the bone-house."

These were the magic words which, like a spell that he was compelled by some malign influence continually to repeat, kept Will Stephens awake, until at last he seemed to lose entirely his first perception of the fact that he might be only hoaxed, and all his imagination became concentrated on the idea of how came the dead body in the bone-house, and how was it that gold and diamond rings were left on its fingers in such a place?

These were mental ruminations, the result of which was transparent from the first, for that result in the natural order of things was sure to be that the passion of curiosity would get the better of all other considerations, and he, Will Stephens, would rise to ascertain if such were really the state of things.

"It ain't far off morning, now," he reasoned with himself, "so I may as well get up at once as lie here tossing and tumbling about, and certainly unable to get another wink of sleep, and besides after all I may be wrong in thinking this a hoax. There may really be such a dead body as those fellows mentioned in the bone-house and if there be, I ought certainly to go and look after it."

We easily reason ourselves into what is our pleasure, and so while these cogitatory remarks were uttered by the sexton, he rose.

He found that if he drew back the blind from before his window, the moon which was now sailing through a nearly cloudless sky, would give him amply sufficient light to enable him to go through the process of dressing, so he at once began that operation.

"Yes," he said, "I ought to go, it's my positive duty to do so, after getting the information I have, and if that information be untrue, let it recoil on the heads of those who invented the falsehood. I shall go, that's settled. What a sweet moonlight."

It was a sweet moonlight indeed. The floods of soft silvery light fell with an uncommon radiance upon all objects, and the minutest thing could have been seen upon the ground, with the same clearness and distinctness as at mid-day.

The only difference was that a soft preternatural looking atmosphere seemed to be around everything, and a kind of marble like look was imparted to all objects far and near on which those soft silvery rays rested in beauty and sublimity.

The sexton was full dressed, and although the moonlight guided him well, he thought that he might in the bone-house require another mode of illumination, and he lighted and took with him a small lantern which had a darkening shade to it.

Thus prepared, he walked at a rapid pace from his own house towards the small shedlike building which served as a receptacle for the unowned dead, and for such human remains as were from time to time cast ashore by the waves, or flung up from new graves by the spade and the mattock.

Familiar as he was and had been for many a year with that bone-house, and often in contact with the dead, he yet on this occasion felt as if a strange fear was creeping over him, and then a flutter of his heart and the fiery feel that was in his brain were circumstances quite novel to him.

"Well, this is odd," he said, "and I suppose it is what they call being nervous I can't make it out to be anything else, I'm sure."

Thus reasoning with himself upon his own unwonted timidity, he reached the bone-house.

The door of the dilapidated building which was known by that name, was only secured by a latch, for it was not considered that the contents of the place were sufficiently interesting for any one's cupidity to be excited by it.

The sexton paused a moment before he lifted the latch, and glanced around him. Even then he half expected to hear a loud laugh expressive of the triumph of those who had combined to play him the trick, if it were one, of getting him out of his bed on a bootless errand. But all was still around him — still as the very grave itself, and muttering then in a hurried tone, "it is true, there is no trick," he hastily opened the door, and went into the bone-house.

All was darkness save one broad beam of moonlight that came in at the door-way, but the sexton closed the entrance, and applied to his lantern for a light.

He slid the darkening piece of metal from before the magnifying glass, and then a rather sickly ray of light fell for a moment upon the corpse that lay then upon its back — a ray only sufficiently strong and sufficiently enduring to enable the sexton to make quite sure that there was a body before him, and then his lantern went out.

"Confound the lantern!" he said, "I ought to have looked to it before I started, instead of lighting it on the mere hazard of its going on comfortably. What's to be done? Ah, I have it, I remember."

What the sexton remembered was that on the same wall in which the door was situated, there was a large square aperture only covered by a kind of shutter of wood, the withdrawal of a bolt from which would cause it to fall in a moment on its hinges.

The sexton knew the place well, and drawing back the somewhat rusty bolt, down went the shutter, and a broad flood of moonlight fell at once upon the corpse.

"Ah," said Will Stephens, "there it is sure enough. What a long odd-looking fellow to be sure, and what a face — how thin and careworn looking. I do very much wonder now who he really is?"

As he continued to gaze upon the dead body, his eyes wandered to the hands, and then sure enough he saw the bright and glittering gems the men had spoken of, and which the salt water had not been able to tarnish into dimness. Perceiving that the setting was gold and the stones real, —

"Ahem!" said Stephens, softly; "they will not bury the corpse with those rings on his fingers. Why, he must have half a dozen on at least; they will be somebody's perquisite of course, and that somebody won't be me. The idea of leaving such property unprotected in a bone-house!"

Will Stephens remained now silent for a short time, moving his head about in different directions, so that he caught the bright colors of the jewels that adorned the dead man's hands, and then he spoke again.

"What's more easy," said he, "than for some of the very fellows who brought him here, to slip back quietly, and take away every one of those rings?"

After this much, he went to the door of the bone-house and listened, but all was perfectly still; and then his cogitations assumed another shape.

"Who saw me come from my house?" he said. — "Nobody. Who will see me go back to it? — Nobody. Then what is to hinder me from taking the rings, and — and letting the blame lie on some one else's shoulders, I should like to know? Nothing will be easier than for me to say in the morning that owing to the strange and insolent manner in which the information was given me of the arrival of the dead body in the bone-house, I did not believe it and therefore did not rise, and so — so I think I may as well eh?"

He thought he heard something like a faint sigh, and the teeth chattered in his head, and he shook in every limb as he bent all his energies to the task of listening if there were really any one in or at hand, playing the spy upon him.

All was as before profoundly still, and with a long breath of relief, he cast off his terror.

"What a fool I am to be sure," he said; "it was but the wind after all, no doubt, making its way through some one of the numerous chinks and crevices in this shed; it did sound like a sigh from some human lips, but it wasn't."

The propriety of making short work of the affair, if he wished to do it at all, now came forcibly to the mind of the sexton, and arming himself with all the courage he could just then summon to his aid, he advanced close to the corpse.

Kneeling on one knee he took up one of the hands from which he wished to take the rings, and when he saw them closer, he felt convinced that they did not belie their appearance, but were in reality what they seemed to be — jewels of rarity and price.

The hand was cold and clammy and damp to the touch, and the knuckles were swollen, so that there was great difficulty in getting the rings over them, and the sexton was full five minutes getting one of them off.

When he had done so, he wiped the perspiration of fear and excitement from his brow, as he muttered, —

"That's always the case with your drowned folks, they are so swelled when first they come out of the water, and so I shall have quite a job, I suppose."

The sexton's cupidity was, however, now sufficiently awakened, to make him persevere, despite any such obstacles, in what he was about, and accordingly, kneeling on both knees he clasped the wrist of the dead man in one hand, and with the other strove to coax off, by twisting the hoop of gold round and round, a ring that had one diamond, apparently of great value, set in it, and which the robber of the dead thought was a prize worth some trouble in the obtaining.

In an instant, the dead hand clasped him tight.

Chapter *CLXXXIII.*

THE RECOVERY. – THE SEXTON'S FRIGHT. – THE COMPACT.

W̲hat pen shall describe the abject fright of Master Will Stephens, the sexton, as the cold clammy fingers of the supposed corpse closed upon his hand.

The blood seemed to curdle at his very heart — a film spread itself before his eyes — he tried to scream, but his tongue clove to the roof of his mouth, and he could utter no sound.

In good truth he was within an ace of fainting, and it was rather a wonder that he did not go clean off.

Power to withdraw his hand from the horrible grasp he had not, and there he knelt, shivering and shaking, and with his mouth wide open, and the hair literally bristling upon his head.

How long he and the dead man remained in this way together in silence, he knew not, but he was aroused from the state of almost frenzy in which he was, by a deep sepulchral voice — the voice of the apparently dead.

"What has happened?" it said, "what has happened? Is this the world which was to come?"

"M-m-mer-cy — help," stammered the sexton. "I — I — I — am a poor man — I — I don't want your rings, good Mr. — Mr. Ghost. Oh — oh — oh — have mercy upon me I — I — implore you."

The only reply was a frightful groan.

The perspiration rolled down the sexton's face.

"Oh, don't — oh, pray don't — hold — hold me so — so tight."

"Now," said the dead man, "I know all. The die is cast; my fate has again spoken. Steel shall not slay me, the bullet shall kill me not, fire shall not burn me, and water will not drown while yon bright satellite sails on 'twixt earth and heaven."

"Yes — yes, sir."

"The fiat has gone forth, and I am wretched, oh, Heaven so unutterably wretched!"

"Perhaps, good Mr. Ghost, you — you will let me go now. Here's your ring, I don't want to keep it. Here's the only one I took off your worshipful fingers, good Mr. Ghost."

A very thin filmy sort of cloud had been going over the moon's disc, but now had passed completely away, and such a flood of unchecked untempered brilliancy poured in at the open window, if it might be so called of the dead-house that it became quite radiant with the silvery beams.

The drowned man rose with a wild howling cry of rage, and springing at the throat of the sexton, bore him down to the earth in an instant, and placed his knee upon his chest.

"Villain," he groaned out between his clenched teeth, "you shall die, although you have made me live. There shall be one victim to the fell destroyer."

The sexton thought his hour was come.

"Wretch!" pursued the revived corpse, "wretch, what devil prompted you to do this most damnable deed? Speak — speak, I say, who are you?"

"What — what deed?" gasped the sexton.

"The deed of restoring me to life — of dragging me from the ocean, and forcing me to live again."

"I — I — oh dear."

"Speak. Go on."

"I didn't do anything of the sort. The truth is, I only came to — to — to—"

"To what?"

"To borrow a ring of you, that's all, and the greatest calamity that ever happened to me is your coming to life."

"How came I here?"

"That I can't tell your worship. I am the sexton of this place, it's called Culburn, and is in Suffolk, and they picked your worship up at sea, and brought you here. That's all I know about it, as I hope for mercy. It can't do you any good to kill a poor fellow like me. I don't think you are a ghost now, but some ugly — no I mean handsome fellow — supposed only to be drowned."

"Do you tell me truth?"

"As I live, and hope your worship will let me live I do. And here's the ring, I came to borrow of you, sir, as a proof."

"Of what?"

"Of — of — of — I hardly know what to say to you, sir."

"If you are not the great enemy to me that I thought you — you are a mere thief. You came to steal the jewels I had upon my fingers. Is not that the truth?"

"I — I rather think it is, sir."

"You may save your wretched life if you like. If you promise me that you will keep all that has happened a secret, except so much of it as I shall empower you to reveal, I will spare you; but if after having so promised, you break faith with me, and let your tongue wag further than I wish it, you will not live twenty-four hours afterwards, be assured, for I will find you out, and twist your head from your shoulders."

"Anything, sir, I will promise anything, I will swear if you like."

"I heed no oaths. Consideration for your own safety will keep you silent. Rise."

He took his knee off the chest of the sexton and his hand off his throat, and then Will Stephens tremblingly rose to his feet. The idea did cross him for a moment of measuring his strength with the resuscitated man, but when he beheld the tall, bony, gaunt figure before him, he saw he had not the shadow of a chance in a personal struggle.

Moreover he had a lively remembrance of a most vice-like pressure upon his throat, which seemed to say that the ugly stranger was by no means in an exhausted state.

Upon the whole, then, the sexton was glad to have escaped so well.

"You have only to say, sir, what you would have me do," he said.

"Answer me first. Have you always lived here? Is this your native place?"

"Oh, no, sir, I came from London; but then it's years ago."

"Very well. You must say that you remember me in London, as a gentleman of good repute, and you must add that you came to the bone-house here, and found me reviving, and that you took measures to complete my recovery."

"Yes, sir. And here is your ring."

"Keep it as a memento of this affair."

"Many thanks, sir. Will it please you to tell me your name and condition?"

"John Smith, a foreign merchant; and now tell me, minutely, how I was rescued from the ocean, or did the waves themselves give up their dead?"

The sexton who was now assured in his own mind that it was no ghost he was speaking to, entered as far as he knew into the story of the finding the body, and bringing it to the bone-house, but as that information was not great, he volunteered, if Mr. Smith would go with him to his cottage, to get him all the particulars.

To this the other consented, and they both left the bone-house together.

On the short bit of road, the sexton began to think that his companion must be some madman, for ever and anon when the moon was brightest, he saw him lift up both his arms to it, as if he were worshipping it, and at those times too, he heard him mutter some words in a language that he did not comprehend. At length the singular being spoke in English.

"Henceforth," he cried, as if quite forgetful of the presence of another, "henceforth, begone remorse, begone despair. The great sea has rejected me, and not again will I seek destruction; I will live, and I will live to be the bane and curse of the beautiful."

"Sir," said the sexton, "here is my house, sir; if you will step in, I will soon dish you up a little something in the way of refreshment. You see, sir, I live alone, that is to say, an old woman who keeps my cottage in order and waits upon me goes away at night, and comes again in the morning, but as it is not her time yet, I will get you anything you like to eat or to drink."

"I never eat nor drink."

"Not eat! – nor – drink! Never, sir?"

"Never. I shall cost you nothing to entertain me. I want some rest, and while I am taking it, do you go and get me such information as you can regarding me. Make no concealment that I am alive, but go at once, and return with what expedition you may, and remember that your fate is in my hands."

"I will, sir."

The sexton was quite terrified enough to do what he was bidden, and perhaps, the consciousness that the strange and mysterious man whom he had for a guest might accuse him of the projected robbery of the jewelry he had about his person influenced him more than the rather obscure threat of personal vengeance by the promised screwing his head off.

But the matter, take it for all in all, was anything but an agreeable one for Master Will Stephens, and most heartily did he wish he had remained in his bed and left the stranger to recover, if was to recover, by himself. Will did not attribute that recovery to the moonlight he had himself let in.

Chapter *CLXXXIV.*

THE NIGHT ALARM. – THE VAMPYRE'S ATTACK UPON THE BRIDE.

*T*he particulars concerning the bringing in of the body that had been picked up at sea by the brothers Edwin and Charles Crofton, were to be learnt from many mouths so soon as the sexton evinced a disposition to know them, and in a very short time, and as the daylight was making the fainter and more spiritual light of the moon fade away, he again reached his own abode, where he had left a guest of whom the reader knows much, but of whom Will Stephens knew but little.

He found the self-christened Mr. Smith waiting for him rather impatiently.

"Well," he cried, "your news? your news?"

"May be told, sir, in a few words," replied the sexton, and then he made his new fried acquainted with the whole story, just as he had heard it of the fishermen on the coast.

Mr. Smith, or as we may as well call him at once the vampyre, hesitated for a few moments as if he had not exactly and accurately made up his mind what to do, and then he said, –

"You will go to the Grange-house and tell the story that I have before informed you I would have told. Be sure that you expatiate upon my gentility and respectability, for I want to be upon good terms with the Crofton family."

"Well, but sir, I'm a tenant of Sir George Crofton's and so you see –"

"What," said the vampyre, his eyes flashing with indignation as he spoke "dare you dispute my positive commands?"

"No, sir, I – I only——"

"Peace caitiff, and know that I hold thy life in my hands for your attempted robbery of me."

The sexton trembled. That was indeed the weak point now of all his defenses against whatever commands might be put upon him by his master, as we may now call the vampyre, although after all it was but the usual dominion of a strong mind over a weak one, for there was not so much in reality for the sexton to be afraid of as his own guilty conscience dictated to him.

It were easy enough for the vampyre to charge him with robbery, but not at all so easy for him to prove such a charge, and at the same time to substantiate, as by some inquisitive counsel he might be called upon to do, his own position in society.

But it is most true

"Conscience doth make cowards of us all." And feeling that his intention regarding the rings of the supposed drowned man had been of a dishonest character, he could not summon courage sufficient to defy him now.

"I will go," he said, "I am going."

"'Tis well."

In far from the pleasantest train of thought the sexton went to the Grange, and asked to see Mr. Charles Crofton, and to him he related the version of the resuscitating of the supposed drowned man. It was heard with, as might be expected, the most profound astonishment, and the sexton soon found himself confronted with the whole assembled family, and force to repeat the wonderful facts over again.

It seemed, as indeed it might well do, a something quite beyond belief.

"Why, Edwin," said Charles, "he must have been in the water far beyond the length of time that it mostly takes to drown any one before we saw him."

"I think so too."

"It must be so, for this reason, that he was a considerable distance from land, and there was no vessel near enough for him to have come from."

"Hold!" said Sir George Crofton, "my dear boys, you are forgetting the most important fact of all."

"Are we, father?"

"Yes, and that is that the gentleman is alive. You cannot get over that, you know, and as I have often heard that whatever is is natural, why there's no use in disputing any more about it; and besides how do we know but that he was in some boat which was swamped a few minutes before you saw him."

"That is a most rational supposition," said Edwin.

"And that we can say nothing against," added Charles; "what is to be done father?"

"Why, do not let us do good by inches, we know that this is the only decent house within a considerable distance for a gentleman to remain in, if he have the habits of comfort about him. So Master Stephens, if you will go and give our compliments to the stranger, and ask him to come here, I shall be much obliged to you."

"I will, Sir George."

"And you can tell him that we are plain folks, but assure him of a hearty welcome."

Will Stephens made his bow and exit.

"Well," said Edwin, "it's very odd, although of course, it must be all right, and I am the last person who would wish to make anything out of a common-place event, but to all appearances dead he was when we took him into the boat, and I never before heard of a spontaneous recovery like this from such a state."

"Then you have added to your stock of experience," said his father, laughing, "and I must own, for my own part, that I am rather curious to see this person, who was a curiosity in appearance, according to your accounts when he was dead or supposed to be dead."

"He was so," remarked Charles, "for I am certain you might travel the world over without meeting a more singular looking man than he was; in the first place, he looked particularly tall, but that might have arisen from the fact that we only saw him in a horizontal position, and then there was a something about the expression of his face which was perfectly indescribable, and yet at the same time filled you with feelings of curiosity and dread."

The sisters heard this account of the mysterious stranger with feelings of great interest.

"Why," said Emma, "we have all of us often complained of being dull here, but such an animal as this will be quite an acquisition."

"And just as Clara is going, too, what a pity," laughed Edwin.

"I shall endeavor to survive the horrid disappointment," said Clara, for she was to be married on that day, to one who had been the chosen companion of her heart for many a day, and was to leave the home of her childhood to proceed far away to his house in Wales, where she was to be the light of joy to another admiring and loving circle.

"Ah, well, I pity you," said Emma.

"Then you had better at once," remarked Clara, forbid the occasional visits here of a certain young officer who, I'm afraid, has some audacious intentions."

The ready color flushed to the cheek of the younger sister, who had scarcely expected such a retort, although she had fairly provoked it.

"Come, girls," said the father, "we will have no more lance breaking between you about your lovers."

"Certainly not, father," said Clara, "but then, you know, unless Emma is made to see that she is vulnerable, she will go on tormenting me."

"In other words, Emma," said Edwin, "you see that people who live in glass houses should not throw stones — a most useful maxim."

"I don't care for any of you," said Emma, half crying, as she ran out of the room.

Clara followed here, for there was really the very best understanding and the kindest feeling between the two young girls, although occasionally a smart repartee would be uttered upon some such occasion as the present, but all that was soon forgotten.

The sexton who was getting each moment more and more uneasy about the share he had in the affair of the resuscitated man of the bone-house, went back to the cottage, and there informed the self-named Mr. Smith of the success of his mission to the Grange-house.

"You think they will welcome me," said the vampyre.

"I am sure of it, sir. They are the frankest, freest family I ever knew, and they would not have asked you to got to the Grange if they did not mean to use you well."

"And there are two daughters?"

"Yes, sir."

"And young and fair, you tell me."

"They are two as handsome girls as you will find in this part of the country, sir. They have always been much admired. One of them, as I before mentioned, is going to be married and taken away, but the other stays at home."

"'Tis well, not you will not fail to remember the awkward situation in which you are. Keep the ring which you took from my finger, and with it keep your own counsel, for any babbling upon your part will most assuredly lead to your destruction."

"Yes, sir, I know."

"And although that destruction might not be immediate, you would lead a life of trembling terror until your doom was accomplished, and that doom should be a dreadful one in its manner. Now farewell! farewell! and remember me."

"I shall never forget you the longest day I have got to live," said the sexton, with a shudder, as he saw the tall, angular, gaunt-looking form of his most mysterious new acquaintance leave his cottage, and make his way towards the Grange.

Chapter CLXXXV.

THE DEFILE IN THE ROCKS. – THE HORSEMAN AND THE ACCIDENT.

*T*he Grange-house was visible from the cottage of the sexton, and so the vampyre had declined the offer of Will Stephens to be his guide.

As it happened, though, it would have been better regarded his reaching the Grange quickly that he should have taken the sexton with him, for the cliffs that were close at hand concealed to the eye many deep gullies and frightful precipices that had to be coasted round, before any one could reach the Grange-house by that route.

If he could have gone directly onward, about half a mile's walking would have sufficed to enable him to reach the place, but before he had proceeded a quarter of that distance, he came upon a deep ravine or splitting in the cliff, too wide to jump across, and with all the appearance of extending inland a considerable distance without narrowing.

"I had indeed better have brought a guide with me," muttered Varney.

He then paused for a few moments, as if he was debating with himself whether or not he should return back and get the sexton. But the mental hesitation did not last long, and accustomed as he was to trust to his own sagacity and his own resources more than to other people, he walked along by the side of the fissure in the cliff, muttering to himself, –

"Were all the guides in the country here, they could but do as I am doing, namely, walk on until the ravine closes."

With this idea he pursued it, but to his mortification he found that it widened instead of presenting the least symptoms of closing, and suddenly it opened to his eyes to a width of about fifty feet, and he paused again irresolute.

"How am I to proceed?" he said; "this is a perplexity."

He advanced close to the brink, and looked down. The depth was very considerable, and at the bottom there was evidently a road made of sand and chalk, which wound down somewhere from the interior of the country to the sea-beach.

As he looked, he heard the rapid sound of a horse's feet.

In another moment there dashed down the road towards the sea, a horse bearing on his back a man, who was exerting himself in every possible way to stop the maddened, headlong career of the animal, but it would not be checked.

With starting eyes and dilated nostrils, and with its flanks covered with foam, the frightened steed, which had evidently come some distance in that state, rushed on, but the broken nature of the ground made it almost impossible that it should make such great speed then as it had been making, at least with any degree of safety.

This was what occurred to the thoughts of Varney, and it was sufficiently proved to be a correct idea, by the horse stumbling the next moment, and throwing his rider heavily upon the sand and broken rock that was strewn around.

The steed, now disencumbered of its load, recovered itself in a moment, and with a snort of rage and probably of pain likewise, dashed and disappeared from the sight, round the abrupt corner of the ravine to the left hand on the beach.

"So be it," said the vampyre, calmly; "another being is snatched away from the muster roll of the living, one who perhaps would gladly have preserved his existence, while I — I remain and cannot, let me do what I will to accomplish such a purpose, shake off the cumbrous load of life that will cling to me."

Suddenly quite a whirlwind of passion seemed to come on him, and, standing on the brink of the ravine with his arms extended, he cried, —

"Since death is denied to me, I will henceforward shake off all human sympathies. Since I am compelled to be that which I am, I will not be that and likewise suffer all the pangs of doing deeds at which a better nature that was within me revolted. No, I will from this time be the bane of all that is good and great and beautiful. If I am forced to wander upon the earth, a thing to be abhorred and accursed among men, I will perform my mission to the very letter as well as the spirit, and henceforth adieu all regrets, adieu all feeling — all memory of goodness — of charity to human nature, for I will be a dread and a desolation! Since blood is to be my only sustenance, and since death is denied to me, I will have abundance of it — I will revel in it, and no spark of human pity shall find a home in this once racked and tortured bosom. Fate, I thee defy!"

He continued for some few moments after uttering this speech in the same attitude in which he had spoken the words. Then suffering his hands slowly to fall, again he looked cold, and passionless, as he had been before.

But his determination was made.

By looking carefully about him, he saw that there was a kind of footpath down the side of the ravine, which an active person might descend by, although, probably, not altogether without some risk, for the least false step might precipitate him to the bottom.

The vampire, however, had no such fears. He seemed to feel that he possessed a kind of charmed life, and that he might adventure to do what others might well shrink from.

This feeling begot a confidence which was almost certain to be his protection, even if it had been only founded upon imagination, for it fortified his nerves, and when he began the descent down the side of the ravine, it was without the smallest terror.

He found, however, that when he was fairly on the path, it was a better and a wider one than he had a first supposed it to be, and in the course of five minutes he had got completely down to the narrow road, on which, apparently dead, lay the wounded man, for he was only grievously hurt by his fall, although he was quite insensible.

The vampyre strode up to him.

"Ah," he said, "young, and what the world would call handsome. Ha! ha! Heaven takes but little care sometimes of its handiwork."

After a few moments' contemplation of the still form that lay at his feet, he knelt on one knee by its side, and placed his hand upon the region of the heart, after roughly tearing open the vest of the stranger.

"He lives — he lives. Well, shall I crush the fluttering spirit that now is hovering 'twixt life and death, or shall I let it linger while it may within its earthly prison? Let it stay. The worst turn that any one can do another in this world, is surely to preserve existence after once the pang of what would be all the agony of death is past."

The vampyre rose, and was moving away up the ravine, when a sudden thought seemed to strike him, and he turned back again.

"Gold," he said, "is always useful to me, and I think with my new thoughts and feelings it will now be more so than ever. This insensible man may have some about him."

Again he knelt by the side of the young man, and soon possessed himself of a tolerably well-stocked purse that he found upon him. Round his neck, too, by a thin chain of gold, hung a small portrait of a young and beautiful girl, upon which Varney gazed intently.

"She is fair," he said, "very fair — she would make a fit victim for me. I will take this portrait; it might stand me in some stead should I encounter the original."

He placed the portrait in his pocket, and was in the act of rising, when he heard the sound of a footstep.

"Ah, some one comes; it will be no part of my plan to have been seen by the body."

He darted forth down the narrow gorge or ravine, and was soon sufficiently hidden from the sight of those who were advancing. They proved to be some fishermen going to spread their nets upon the beach, which just below the spot where the seemingly fatal accident had taken place, was as level as a carpet, screened from the wind, and composed of the finest sand.

Of course, it was impossible to avoid seeing the body that lay in their path, and Varney had no need to be fearful that he would be seen, when an object of so much greater and more absorbing interest lay in their direct and unavoidable path.

He heard from the sudden exclamations that fell from them, that they had seen the body, and upon advancing a step or two, he found that they were collected round it in a dense throng, for there were about a dozen men in all.

"'Tis well," said Varney, "it matters not to me if he be living or dead. I can doubtless now find my way to the Grange-house by this path along the shore. I will pursue it at all events, and see whither it will lead me."

He did so, and after going about half a mile, he found another ravine, which, upon entering and ascending for a time, led him quite close to one of the entrances of the Grange-house, as it was called, and which he was so anxious to reach.

Chapter CLXXXVI.

THE DISAPPOINTMENT AT THE GRANGE. – THE NEWS OF DESPAIR. – THE FINDING THE BODY.

*I*t was a fine old place the Grange, view it from what aspect you might, and had not the mind of Varney, the vampyre, been so fearfully irritated by the circumstances of his horrible existence, he must have paused to admire it.

It was one of those ancient English edifices, which, alas, are fast disappearing from the face of once merry England. Railways have gone tearing and screaming through the old parks and shady glens. Alas, all is altered now, and for the sake of getting to some abominable place, such as Manchester, or Birmingham, in a very short space of time, many a lonely spot of nature's own creating is marred by noise and smoke.

"So," said Varney, "this then is the home of these young men who have done me such an injury as to rescue me from the sea."

He ground his teeth together as he spoke, and it was quite clear that he felt disposed to consider that a most deadly injury had been done to him by Edwin and Charles Crofton, who had only followed the proper dictates of humanity in rescuing him from the waves.

"It shall go hard with me," added Varney, "but I will teach such meddling fools to leave the great sea in charge of its dead. Oh, had I but been allowed to remain until now, which but for these officious persons might still have been the case, I should have sunk deep — deep into the yellow sands, and there rotted."

His passion as he uttered these words had in it something fearful, but in a few moments the external symptoms of it passed away, and he walked slowly and to all appearance calmly enough towards the Grange.

The distance he had to go was still as before, a deceiving one, for he had to wind round a clump of trees before he really got to the gate, which appeared to be just in sight, but at length he reached it, and paused as he saw an old man, who was a kind of warder there.

"Is this Sir George Crofton's?" he said, and he threw into his voice all that silvery softness which at times had been so fascinating to the Bannerworth family.

"It is, sir."

"Will you announce me?"

"I do not leave this gate, sir, but if you go down this avenue, you will reach the mansion, and some of the servants will attend to you."

Varney walked on.

The avenue was one formed by two stately rows of chestnuts, the spreading branches of which met over head, forming a beautiful canopy, and notwithstanding that they were so near the sea — that foe to vegetation, these trees were in good truth most luxuriantly beautiful.

"There was a time," muttered Varney, "when I should have admired such a spot as this, but all that has long since passed away. I am that which I am."

He now arrived in front of the house itself, and being perceived by one of the domestics, he was politely asked what he wanted.

"Say that Mr. Smith is here," was the message that Varney gave.

The servant had already heard that such was the name of the person who had been rescued from the sea by his young masters Edwin and Charles, he now hastened with the information to the drawing-room, where the family was assembled.

"Oh, if you please, sir, he has come."

"Who has come?"

"The drowned man, Mr. Smith."

"Admit him instantly."

The servant ran back to Varney, and then politely ushered him into the large really handsome room, in which the family sat awaiting his arrival with no small share of curiosity. What the sexton had said of him had excited much speculation, and the eagerness to see a man who was, as it were, a present from the sea, was extreme.

"Mr. Smith," announced the servant; and Varney with one of his courtly bows, and a smile that was half hideous, half charming, entered.

There was a decided effect produced by his appearance, and perhaps that effect is best described by the word awe. They all seemed as if they were in the presence of something very peculiar, if not something very superior.

Sir George Crofton broke the rather awkward silence that ensued by addressing his visitor with all the frankness that was a part of his nature.

"Sir," he said, "I am glad to see you and hope you will make yourself as much at home as if you were in a house of your own."

"Sir," said Varney, "you know how much I owe your family already, and I fear to increase the heavy debt of gratitude."

"Oh, you are welcome, most welcome. Stay here as long as you like; we are rather dull at times in this isolated house, and the arrival of an intelligent guest is always an event."

Varney bowed, and Edwin advanced.

"Mr. Smith," he said, "I suppose I may almost call myself an old acquaintance."

"And I," said Charles.

"Gentlemen, if you be those to whom I am indebted for my preservation, I owe you my warmest thanks."

"Oh, think nothing of it," said Sir George; "it was not at all likely that my two boys would see a fellow creature in such a situation, and not, dead or alive, take possession of him. Your recovery is the only remarkable thing in the whole affair."

"Very remarkable," said Varney.

They waited a moment as if he was expected to make some sort of explanation of that part of the business, but as he did not, Sir George said —

"You have no idea of how you became resuscitated."

"Not the least."

"Well, that is strange indeed."

"Perhaps the good fellow who afforded me an immediate shelter, applied before that, some means of recovering suspended vitality."

"Oh no. Will Stephens is to the full as much surprised as any one.

But, however, I dare say, to you, sir, that is not the most entertaining subject in the world, so we will say no more about it, except that we are very glad to have a living guest instead of a dead one."

"I much fear, from what I have heard," said Varney, "that I shall be intruding at a time like this into your family circle."

"Oh, you allude to the marriage today of one of my daughters, and that puts me in mind of really quite an omission on my part. Mr. Smith — my daughters, Clara and Emma."

The vampyre bowed low, and the young ladies went with established grace through the ceremony of the introduction to the remarkable personage before them.

At this moment there came upon the ears of all assembled there the sound of hurried footsteps, and a servant without any ceremony burst into the apartment, exclaiming —

"Oh, Sir George — Oh, oh, sir —"

"What is it? Speak!"

"Oh, oh. They have found him — killed in the ravine."

"Who, who?"

"Mr. Ringwood, as was to be married —"

"My daughter."

Clara uttered a cry of despair, and sank into a chair in a state of insensibility. The scene of confusion and general consternation that now ensued baffles all description, and the only person who looked calm and collected upon the occasion was Mr. Smith, although it was not the insulting calmness of seeming indifference.

In a few minutes, however, Sir George himself recovered from the first shock which the intelligence had given to him, and he said, —

"Where is he? Where is he? Let me to the spot."

"And allow me, sir, to accompany you," said Varney. "Believe me, sir, I feel deeply for the family misfortune. Let me be useful."

"Thank you, sir, thank you — Edwin, Charles, come with me and this gentleman, and we will see if this dreadful report be true. Let us hope that fear and ignorance have exaggerated a very simple affair into so seemingly dreadful a circumstance.

Leaving Clara to the care of her sister and some of the female domestics of the Grange, who were hastily summoned to attend upon her, the little party, consisting of Sir George, his two sons, Varney, and several of the men-servants, turned from the Grange in the direction of the ravine.

Their intimate acquaintance with all the neighborhood enabled them to reach the place much sooner than Varney thought it possible to do, and as they came within sight of the spot where the accident had occurred, they saw a crowd of villagers and fishermen assembled.

They quickened their pace, and forcing through the throng, Sir

George Crofton saw his intended son-in-law, to all appearance, lying dead and bleeding on the sands.

Such a sight was enough, for a moment, to paralyze every faculty, and it really had, for a time, that effect upon Sir George.

Chapter CLXXXVII.

THE SICK CHAMBER AT THE GRANGE. – THE NIGHT.

"*I*s he dead? Is he dead? cried Sir George.

"We don't know, sir," replied one of the fishermen; "some of us think he is, and some of us think he is not."

"What is to be done?"

"Have him taken at once to the Grange, father," said Charles, "and let us get medical assistance; who knows but the affair may turn out in reality very different from what it first appeared. He may be only stunned by a fall."

"I hope to Heaven it may be so. Can you, among you, my men, make anything like a litter to carry him on?"

This was soon done. Some of the loose seats from some boats close at hand, and a rough cloak or two, made a capital couch for the dead or wounded man, as the case might be. They lifted him carefully into it, and then four of them lifted the rude but easy and appropriate conveyance, and carried him towards the hall.

"How could this have happened?" said Sir George.

"Perhaps I may be able to throw some light upon it," said Varney. "As I came here to your hospitable house, a horse without a rider, but caparisoned for one, passed me furiously."

"That must have been his horse then," said Charles. "You may depend, father, he was riding on to see Clara before the hour appointed for their marriage, and has met with this accident. Come, there is some consolation in that. A fall from his horse is not likely to kill him."

"Where is Edwin?"

"Oh, he went off at once for Dr. North, and no doubt he will get to the Grange about as soon as we shall."

"That was right — that was right. I really have been taken so much by surprise that I hardly know what I am about. It was very right of Edwin."

Nothing of any importance now passed in the way of conversation, nor did any incident worth recording take place until the melancholy little procession reached the Grange, and by the advice of Varney, the young bridegroom was carried direct to a bed-chamber before he was removed from the litter on which he had been carried.

The operation was scarcely performed, and he laid upon a bed, when Dr. North came, having mounted his horse upon hearing the information from Edwin that he was wanted in a case of such great emergency at the Grange, and ridden hard all the way.

He was at once introduced to his patient, and upon a cursory examination, he said, —

"This is a concussion of the brain, but don't let that alarm you. It may be very slight, although it certainly has an awkward sound, and a little rest and blood-letting may put him all to rights."

This was to some extent cheering, and the doctor at once proceeded to bleed his patient. As the ruddy stream fell into a crystal goblet, the young man gradually opened his eyes, and looked round him with a bewildered glare.

"Darken the room," said Dr. North; "he is right enough, but he must be kept quiet for a day or two at all events."

"What has happened?" said the wounded man.

"Nothing particular," replied Dr. North, "nothing particular. You have had a fall from your horse."

"Clara!"

"Ah, I know, and now listen to me. If you remain quiet and don't speak, you will see Clara soon; but if you are willful and disobey orders, you will bring on a brain fever and you won't see her at all in this world; so now you can judge for yourself."

"You are rather harsh," said Sir George.

"Pardon me sir, I am not. There is nothing like making a patient thoroughly understand his own position; and I give this young gentleman credit for sufficient wisdom to enable him to profit by what I say to him."

Mr. Ringwood nodded.

"There, you see, all's right; now he will go to sleep, and as all will depend upon the state in which he awakens, I will, if you please wait here, unless I should be urgently sent for from home, for I have left word where I am."

"Pardon me, doctor, for finding any fault with you."

"Don't mention it; what I said did sound harsh."

Sir George went now at once to the room where his daughter Clara had been taken to, for the purpose of informing her of the hopeful state of affairs. He found her just recovered from her swoon, so that recollection had not yet sufficiently returned to give her all the agony of thinking that the news so heedlessly and so suddenly communicated by the servant might be true in its full intensity.

"My dear, you must not distress yourself," said Sir George. "Ringwood was riding over here, it seems, to see you, and his horse, getting restive, has thrown him; Dr. North says, there is nothing particular the matter, and that after a little rest he will recover."

Clara tried to speak, but she could not — she burst into tears.

"Ah!" said the old nurse, who was attending her, and who had been in her family many years, "ah, poor dear, she will be all right now. I was just wishing that she would have a good cry; it does any one a world of good, it does."

"What an agitating night and day this has been, to be sure," said Sir George. "First the terror of losing both my boys, then their return with the dead man, who, so oddly comes to life again; Then this dreadful accident to Ringwood; upon my word the incidents of a whole year have been crammed into a few hours. I only hope this is the last of it."

"And I shall see him again, father," sobbed Clara.

"Of course you will."

"You — you have sent him home very carefully?"

"Home? no. He is here under this roof and here he shall stay till he recovers, poor lad. Oh dear no, I never thought of sending him home, but I must send some one, by-the-by, with the news of what has happened. This is well thought of."

The knowledge that her lover, and her affianced husband was doing well, and that he was under the same roof with her, gave Clara the most unalloyed satisfaction, and she recovered rapidly her good and healthful looks. It was duly explained to her, that she must not go near Ringwood to disturb him, as rest was so very essential to his recovery; so she did not attempt it. The whole household was commanded to be unusually quiet, and never had the Grange before presented such a collection of creeping domestics, for they went up and down stairs like so many cats.

Clara did not omit to thank Mr. Smith for the assistance he had rendered them in this evil emergency, and Dr. North stood with the family in the dining room waiting, perhaps with greater anxiety than he chose to express, the awaking of his patient.

A servant was left in the adjoining chamber to that occupied by Ringwood, who was told to bring to the dining-room the first intimation that the wounded man was living.

About two hours elapsed when the servant came in with an air of affright.

Dr. North sprang to his feet in a moment.

"What is it, is he awake?"

"Not exactly awake, sir, but he is speaking in his sleep, and it's all about a — a—"

"A what?"

"A vampyre."

"Stuff."

"Well, sir, he's a having some horrid dream, I can tell you, sir, and he said, 'Keep off the vampyre; save her, oh, save her from the vampyre!'"

"How singular!" said Varney, "what an absurd belief that is! A vampyre! what on earth could have put such a thing in his head, I wonder?"

"I will go to him," said Dr. North, "if he should be very much disturbed, perhaps I shall think it preferable to awake him; but I can inform you all that such dreams show that there is much excitement going on in the brain."

"Then you do not consider the symptom favorable, doctor?"

"Certainly not; quite the reverse of favorable."

Dr. North rose, and as Varney offered very politely to accompany him, he made no sort of objection, and they proceeded to the chamber of the bridegroom.

During the time that the doctor had been in the society of Varney, he had been much pleased with him, for he found that he possessed a vast store of knowledge upon almost any subject that could be touched upon, besides no small amount of skill and theoretical information upon medical matters, so he let him come with him, when perhaps he would have objected to any one else.

Varney the vampyre could fascinate when he liked.

When they reached the chamber the young man was quiet, but in a few minutes he began to toss about his head, and mutter in his sleep, —

"The vampyre, the dreadful vampyre. Oh, save her! Help, help, help!"

"This won't do," said the doctor."

He went to the toilette table, and procuring a large towel he soaked it well in cold water, and then wrapped it round the head of Ringwood, and so carefully too as not to arouse him. The effect was almost instantaneous. The vexed sleeper relapsed into a much easier attitude, the breathing was more regular, and the distressing fancies that had tortured his fevered brain were chased away.

"A simple plan," said Varney.

"Yes, but a most efficacious one."

Chapter *CLXXXVIII.*

A MIDNIGHT ALARM. – THE CHASE. – THE MYSTERY.

Young Ringwood did awaken about two hours afterwards, and the state he was in, although not such as to create alarm, was not pleasing to Dr. North. That gentleman desired that he should be carefully watched and kept quiet, while he went to his own house for some medicines.

He returned as soon as he possibly could, and administered such remedies as he considered the urgency of the case required, and having, as he always made a practice of doing, left word at his own house where he was, he offered to remain at the Grange the whole of the night.

It is scarcely necessary to say, that such an offer was most gratefully accepted.

Clara was profuse in her acknowledgements of the doctor's kindness, and they all passed the evening together in the large dining room, to which Varney was first introduced.

Not, however, for a long time had so gloomy an evening been passed at the Grange as that; nobody was in spirits, and although there was a great deal of conversation, it somehow assumed always a very somber shape, let it commence on what subject it might.

Half past ten o'clock was the usual hour at which the family retired for the night, and it was quite a relief to every one, when that hour came, and Sir George ordered lights for the bed chambers.

Clara, indeed, being much oppressed, had retired some time before, and so had Emma, so that there were none but gentlemen in the dining room at half past ten.

"I have ordered a bed to be prepared for you close to your patient's," said Sir George to Dr. North.

"Oh, thank you, but I shall only lie down in my clothes, a couch would have done just as well, I am used to sitting up all night upon occasion."

"No doubt, but I hope you will not be disturbed, and that tomorrow-morning we shall have a better account of your patient."

"I hope so too; a good calm night's rest may do much."

"You speak doubtingly."

"Why in these cases it is difficult to know the extent of injury. There is no fracture of the skull, but it is as yet impossible to say what amount of shaking he has had."

"Well, we can but hope for the best. Mr. Smith, although we retire at this early hour, there is no sort of occasion for you to do so. Order what wines you please, and sit as long as you please."

"By no means, Sir George; I am a great patron of early hours myself."

Varney was shown into a bed-room which was upon the same floor with those of the family, and which formed one of a range of chambers, all opening from a corridor that ran the entire length of the house, and which in the daytime was lighted by a very large, handsome window at one end, while at the other was a broad flight of stairs ascending from the lower part of the house.

The sisters occupied contiguous chambers, and then there was an empty room, and next to that again was the bed-room in which was Ringwood, and then Dr. North's.

Exactly opposite was Varney's room, and close at hand slept the sons, while Sir George himself occupied a room at the furthest corner of the corridor.

Emma made Clara an offer to sleep with her that night, as she was in grief and anxiety, but this Clara would not permit, for she could not think of sacrificing her sister's repose to attend upon her.

"No, Emma," she said," I will hope for the best, and strive to rest."

The bade each other affectionately good night, and shortly afterwards retired to their separate apartments.

By eleven o'clock all was still in the house.

Dr. North had begged a book from the library, for he thought it likely enough that he should not be able to get much repose, and with that he sat in his room, the only one, as he thought, in all the house who was not in bed.

He continued reading for about an hour, and then, after visiting his patient, and finding him asleep, he thought it would be just as well for him to pull off his boots and his coat, and lie down on the bed to snatch a few hours' sleep.

He performed all the operations but the final one — the sleeping — for scarcely had he lain down, when he heard a soft sliding sort of noise close to the room door, he thought, and he sprung up in a sitting posture to listen to it.

"Who's there!" he cried.

There was no answer, and jumping off his bed, he took the light which he had not put out, and opened his door. All was deserted and still in the corridor.

"Imagination, or some accidental noise that I am not familiar with," said the doctor, as he closed his door again.

Down he laid himself, and he was just upon the point of getting to sleep, when he heard a scratching sound as he thought upon the very panel of the door of his room.

Up he sprang again, and this time without the delay of asking who was there; he opened his door, and looked out into the corridor, holding the light above his head so as to diffuse its rays as much as possible, but he saw no one, and all the other doors were close shut.

"A plague take it," he said, "I may keep myself at this sort of thing all night, if I am foolish enough. It's a cat, perhaps, for all I know; however it may scratch away, I won't move again."

Shutting the door, he lay down, now fully determined that he would not move, unless something very much out of the common way, indeed, should take place.

Again he started. There was a curious sound about the lock of his door, and he listened intently.

"Now, what on earth can that be?"

All was still, and he nearly dropped asleep. Twice, however, he thought he heard the sound again, but he would not move, and in a few moments more, he was enjoying a sound repose.

How long this repose lasted, he had no means of telling, for he was suddenly awakened by such a cry, that at first he lay overpowered completely by it, and unable to move. It was a loud shrieking cry, such as might come form any one in a most dreadful agony.

"Good Heaven!" he cried, "what's that?"

Now, Dr. North was not a fearful man, nor a nervous one, and he soon recovered. Besides, such a cry as that, he knew very well, must have the effect of arousing everybody in the house, so he sprung out of his bed, and rushed to the door.

It was fast.

In vain he tried the lock, and hammered at it and pushed. The door was a thick and a heavy one, and it was quite clear he was a prisoner.

This was serious, and he cried out, —

"Help! help! here, undo the door, undo the door. Who has locked me in?"

He heard the scraping of feet, the sound of voices, the ringing of bells, and all the symptoms of a suddenly disturbed and alarmed household, but nobody paid any attention to him. He dragged on his boots, in order that he might be able to keep up a constant kicking on the lower part of his door, and he did keep it up with a vengeance.

At length he heard voices close to his door, and some one cried, —
"Open the door, sir, open the door!"

"Open it yourself," said Dr. North, "you have fastened it on the outside, I suppose."

There was some further running about, and then with a crash the door was forced open with a crowbar, and upon emerging from the apartment, the doctor found assembled in the corridor, the whole family, with the exception of the two girls, and several servants half-dressed bearing lights.

"What's the matter," cried Sir George, "what's the matter?"

"Ah," said the doctor, "that's what I want to know."

"Yes, why — why you made all the disturbance."

"I beg your pardon, there was a scream came from somewhere, and when I tried to come out to find what it was, my room door was fast. That's all I know about it."

Bang — bang, bang, bang, came now a sound. Bang, bang, bang; and all eyes were turned in the direction of the chamber occupied by Mr. Smith, and they heard his voice from within shouting in loud and frightened tones.

"Help! help! is it fire! Open my door, help — help. Do you lock in your guests here? Help!"

"Why, God bless me," said Dr. North, "that gentleman is locked in likewise."

"But it can't be," said Sir George, "for the keys of all these doors are in the library in a drawer. The fact is, we none of us fasten up our bed-rooms, and the keys were all removed years ago."

"Help! help! help!" cried Mr. Smith.

"Break the door open," said Sir George, "this is inexplicable to me, I cannot make it out in the least."

The same crow-bar that had been brought by one of the servants to bear upon the door of Dr. North's room, was now applied to that of Mr. Smith, and it soon yielded to the force of the lever that was used with strength and judgment.

Mr. Smith partially dressed, and with rather a terrified look, emerged.

"Good God," he cried, "I wish you wouldn't lock one in; what has happened? I heard a shriek that awoke me up, as if the last trumpet had sounded."

"My daughters, are they safe," cried Sir George.

He flew to the door of Clara's room, it yielded to his touch.

"Clara, Clara," he called.

"I am paralyzed," said Dr. North, "and so are you, sir. Come in."

He seized a light from one of the servants, and with a presentiment that there was to be found a solution of, at all events, the mystery of the dreadful shriek that had alarmed all the house, he dashed into the chamber of the young girl, followed by the father.

Chapter *CLXXXIX.*

THE SIGHT OF TERROR. – THE DOCTOR'S SUSPICIONS. –
THE NIGHT WATCH.

*T*he sight that met the eyes of the father in his daughter's chamber, was, indeed, one calculated in every respect to strike him with horror and misery.

Emma was lying insensible at the side of the bed, and Clara seemed to be dead, for she was ghastly pale, and there was blood upon her neck.

The father staggered to a seat, but Dr. North at once rushed forward, and held the light to the eyes of Clara, at the same time, that he placed his finger on her wrist to note if there was any pulsation.

"Only a fainting fit," he said.

"But the blood – the – the blood," cried Sir George.

"That I know nothing about, just at present, but let us see what's the matter here."

He raised Emma from the floor, and found that she too had fainted, but as she appeared to be perfectly uninjured. She slightly recovered as he lifted her up, and he resigned her at once to the care of some of the female servants, who now made their appearance in the chamber, all terribly alarmed at the shriek that had awakened them.

"This is strange," said Dr. North, "here is a small puncture upon the throat of your daughter Clara, that almost looks like the mark of a tooth."

"A tooth!"

"Yes, but of course that cannot be."

"Hear me, oh, hear me," cried Emma, at this moment. "Horror – horror!"

"What would you say – speak at once, and clear up this mystery if you can. What has happened?"

"I heard a noise, and came from my own chamber to this. There was some one bending over the bed. 'Twas I who shrieked."

"You?"

"Yes, oh yes! 'Twas I. I know not what then happened, for I either fell or was struck down, and I felt that my senses left me. What has happened? I too ask; oh, Clara! What was it? what was it?"

"Imagination, most likely," said the doctor. "You had better go to your room again, Miss Emma, for you are trembling with cold and apprehension. Perhaps in the morning, all this affair will assume a different shape. At present we are all to much flurried to take proper cognizance of it. There your sister is rapidly recovering. How do you feel now, Miss Clara?"

"I — I — am mad!"

"Oh, pho! pho! nonsense!"

"Oh, God help me! How horrifying ! How more than dreadful! That awful face! Those hideous teeth! — I am mad! — I am mad!"

"Why, my dear child, you will drive me mad," cried Sir George, "if you talk in such a strain. Oh, let me beg of you not."

"Don't heed her," said Dr. North. "This will soon pass away. Come, Miss Clara, you must tell me freely, as your medical man, what has happened. Let us hear the full particulars, and then you know well, that if any human means can aid you, you shall be aided."

This calm mode of discourse had evidently a great effect upon her, and after the silence of a few moments, she spoke much more collectedly than before, saying, —

"Oh, no — no! I cannot think it a dream."

"What a dream?"

"You — you shall hear. But do not drag me from my home, and from all I love, if I am mad; I pray you do not — I implore you!"

"You are quite safe. Why, what a ridiculous girl you are, to be sure. Nobody wants to drag you from your home, and nobody will attempt such a thing, I assure you. You have only to tell us all unreservedly, and you will then be quite safe. If you refuse us you confidence how can we act for you in any way?"

This argument seemed to be effective, and to reach her understanding quite, so that after a shudder, and a glance around her of great dread and dismay, she spoke, saying in a low, faltering voice, —

"Something came; something not quite human, yet having the aspect of a man. Something that flew at me, and fastened its teeth upon my neck."

"Teeth! everybody says 'teeth!'" exclaimed the father.

"Hush!" said the doctor, with an admonitory wave of his hand; "keep that a secret from her, whatever you do. I implore you, keep quiet on that head. Well, is that all, Clara?"

"Yes — yes."

"Then it was a dream, and nothing else, I can assure you. Nothing but a dream; make yourself comfortable, and think no more of it. I dare say you will have a quiet sleep now, after this. But you had better let your sister Emma lay with you, as your nerves are a little shattered."

"Oh, yes, yes."

Emma, who truth to tell, was very little better than her sister, professed her readiness to stay, and the doctor giving Sir George a nod, as much as to say, "Let no more be said about it just now," led the way from the room at once.

When he reached the corridor, where Varney and the two sons were waiting, he said, —

"We shall none of us after this, I am certain, feel inclined to sleep; suppose we go down stairs at once and think and talk this matter over together; there is more in it, perhaps, than meets the eye; I will follow you in a moment, when I have just seen that my patient is all right."

They all proceeded down stairs to the dining-room, and in a few minutes, the doctor followed; lights were procured, and they sat down, all looking at the doctor who had taken the lead in the affair, and who evidently had some very disagreeable, if not very true, ideas upon the subject matter of the evening's disturbance.

"Well, doctor," said Sir George, "we rely upon you to give us your opinion upon this business, and some insight into its meaning."

"In the first place then," said the doctor, "I don't understand it."

"Well, that's coming to the point."

"Stop a bit; it was no dream."

"You think not."

"Certainly not a dream, two people don't dream of the same thing at the same time; I don't of course deny the possibility of such a thing, but it is too remarkable a coincidence to believe all at once; but Emma avows that she saw a somebody in her sister's room."

"Ah," said Sir George; "she did, I had in my confusion forgotten that horrible confirmation of Clara's story. She did so, and before Clara was well recovered too, so she could not have put the idea into her head. Good God! what am I to think? For the love of Heaven some of you tell me what are your opinions upon this horrible affair, which looks so romantically unreal, and yet so horrible real."

All except the doctor looked at each other in surprise.

"Well," he said, "I will tell you what the thing suggests; not what it is, mind you, for the affair to me is too out of the way of natural causes to induce me to come to a positive conclusion. Before I speak, however, I should like to have your opinion, Mr. Smith; I am convinced it will be valuable."

"Really I have formed none," replied Varney; "I am only exceedingly surprised that somebody should have fastened me in my bed-room. I know that that circumstance gave me a terrible fright, for when I heard all the outcry and confusion, I thought the house was on fire."

"Ah! the locking of us in our rooms, too," said the doctor, "there's another bit of reality. Who did that?"

"It puzzles me beyond all comprehension," said Sir George; "how the doors could be locked I cannot imagine; for as I told you the keys are in a drawer in my library."

"At all events, the doors could not lock themselves, with or without keys," said Charles; "and that circumstance shows sufficiently evidently that some one has been at work in the business whom we have still to discover."

"True," said Mr. Smith.

"Well, gentlemen," added the doctor, "I will tell you what I suggest; and that is contained in a letter, written a long while ago by a distant relation of mine, likewise a surgeon. Mind, I do not of course pledge myself at the present time, for the truth and accuracy of a man who was dead long before I was born; he might too have been a very superstitious man."

"But what did he suggest?"

"He did more than suggest; he wrote for a medical publication of that day an account, only of course suppressing names, of the appearance of a vampyre."

"A what?"

"A vampyre!"

"I have heard of such horrors," said Mr. Smith, "but really at the present day, no one can think of believing such things. Vampyres indeed! No — that is too great a claim upon one's credulity. These existences, or supposed existences, have gone the same way as the ghosts, and so on."

"One would think so, but you shall hear."

Sir George Crofton and his sons looked curious, and thought that the doctor was going to draw upon his memory in the matter to which he alluded, but he took from his pocket a memorandum book, and from it extracted some printed papers.

"The communication was so curious," he said, "that I cut it out of the old volume in which it appeared, and kept it ever since."

"Pray," said Mr. Smith, "what was the name of your distant relation, the medical man?"

"Chillingworth."

"Oh, indeed; an odd name rather, I don't recollect ever hearing of it."

"No, sir, it is not likely you should. Dr. Chillingworth has been dead many years, and no one else of his name is at present in the medical profession to my knowledge. But you shall hear, at all events, what he says about it."

The doctor then opened the folded paper, and read as follows: —

"Notwithstanding the incredulity that has been shown regarding vampyres, I am in a condition from my own knowledge to own the existence of one, I think he is dead now. His name was Varney, at least that was the name he went by, and he came strangely enough under my observation, in connection with some dear friends of mine named B——"

"Is that all?" said Mr. Smith.

"Not quite," replied Dr. North, "He goes on to say that but for touching the feeling of living persons, he could and would unfold some curious particulars respecting vampyres, and that if he lived long enough he will perhaps do so, by which I suppose he meant if he outlived the parties whose feelings he was afraid of hurting by any premature disclosures."

"And — and," faltered Sir George, "do you draw a conclusion from all that, that my daughter has been visited by one of these persons — surely not."

"May be, Sir George; I draw no conclusions at all, I merely throw out the matter for your consideration. It is always worth while considering these matters in any possible aspect. That is all."

"A most horrible aspect," said Sir George.

"Truly dreadful," said Mr. Smith.

"This shall be settled," said Charles, "Edwin and I will take upon ourselves tomorrow night to set this question completely at rest."

At this moment there was a loud cry of "Help, help, help," in the voice of Emma, and they all rushed up stairs with great speed.

"Oh, this way, this way," she cried, meeting them at the head of the stairs. "Come to Clara."

They followed her, and when they reached the room, they found to their horror and surprise that Clara was dead!

Chapter CXC.

FAMILY TROUBLES. – THE HOUSE OF MOURNING.

*I*t was too true. It was not the mere appearance of death, but the reality of the fell destroyer that the Crofton family had to mourn. She who, but a few short hours since, was in all the bloom of apparent health, and youth, and beauty was now no more.

The poor father, the sisterless sister, the astonished, indignant, and agonised brothers formed a group that was too sad to contemplate.

As they gazed upon the wreck of her whom they had all loved so fondly, they could scarcely believe that death had indeed claimed her as her own; they

"Thought her more beautiful than death," and could not, as they gazed tremblingly upon her still form, bring themselves to believe that she had indeed gone from them for ever.

Dr. North, however, soon put all doubt upon the subject to rest by an announcement that her spirit had really fled. In vain he tried all the means that his art suggested. That mysterious and mighty something which we call life, which we miss and yet see no loss, which is so great, yet so evanescent and impalpable, was gone.

"Come away," he said, "we can do no good here now. Come away, all of you!"

"Oh, no, no," cried Sir George. "Why should we leave my child?"

"That," said the doctor, as he pointed to the corpse, "that is not your child."

The old man shuddered, and with an aspect upon his face, as if ten years of added age had at least passed over him in those few moments, he suffered them to lead him from the room. They all passed down stairs again, leaving Emma in her own chamber along with the female servants, so hastily again called up to remain with her.

When the dining-room was reached once more, Mr. Smith, who bore all the appearance of being quite thunder-struck by what had passed, spoke in the most feeling manner, saying, —

"This is truly one of the most affecting circumstances I ever remember. It is dreadful; a young girl to be at once snatched from a circle of admiring and loving friends in this manner, is too sad a picture for any one with a heart to feel for the distresses of others to contemplate. What, sir, is your opinion," to Dr. North, "of the actual cause of death?"

"The shock to the nervous system I suspect has induced some sudden action of the heart that has been too much for vitality."

"Dreadful!"

"Alas, alas!" sobbed Sir George. "What have I done, that Heaven should thus launch against me the bolts of its bitterest vengeance? Why should I be robbed of my child? Surely there were angels enough in Heaven without taking mine from me."

"Hush, hush," said Dr. North; "you are in grief, sir, and know not what you say. These were not else the words that would fall from the lips of such a man as you are."

The bereaved father was silent, and the sons looked at him with countenances in which dismay was most strongly pictured. They seemed as if as yet they had not become fully alive to the loss they had sustained, or of what had really happened within the once happy domestic circle, of which the fairest portion was now so ruthlessly dragged from them.

"It is like a dream," said Edwin, addressing his brother Charles in a whisper. "It is much more like a dream than aught else in the world."

"It is, it is. Oh, tell me that this is not real."

"It is too real," said the doctor, "you must bow with what amount of resignation you can call to your aid to that stroke of destiny which you cannot control; you should consider that as regards her who has gone from you, that she is now no object of pity. Death is an evil to you in your loss, but it is the end of all evil and pain to her; and then again, she has but gone a few years, after all, earlier than usual, for how long shall we — ay, the best and strongest of us — be behind her?"

This was consolation of the right sort, and was sure to have its effect upon persons in the habit of conversing coolly and calmly upon general subjects, so that in a short time, the father even felt much better, and although the sons were quite convinced of their loss they no longer looked at each other with such bewildered aspects, but exhibited the rational grief of men.

Charles spoke after a time with great energy, saying, —

"It is true that we may call our reason to our aid, and contrive to rid ourselves of our grief in a great measure; but there is another duty we have to perform, and that is, to diligently inquire why and how it was, that our sister got this horrible fright, that has had the effect of hurrying her into eternity."

"Yes, brother," said Edwin, "you are right! our sister's memory shall be vindicated, and woe be to him who has brought this desolation and grief upon us.

Sir George looked from one of his sons to the other, but said nothing; he appeared to be prostrated too much by his feelings, and the doctor strongly urging him to retire to rest, he shortly did so, where we will leave him for a time, hoping that he will find the oblivion of sleep creep over him, and

"Knit up the raveled sleeve of care."

"Now," said Dr. North, "here we are four men with cool heads, and active enough judgments. For God's sake, let us try to come to some sort of conclusion about this dreadful affair. What do you say, Charles?"

"In the first place, I should recommend that the house be searched diligently, in order that we may see if any stranger is in it, or discover any means by which an entrance to the premises has been effected. We don't know but that after all some robbery may be the aim, and that the fright of our sister which has had so fatal an effect, may be the consequence merely of the appearance of a thief in her room."

"Agreed," said Edwin, "let the search of the house be our first step."

Two of the new servants were summoned with lights, and the party of four proceeded to an examination of the house, which on account of its size was not a very short process, for there was so many staircases and rooms opening the one into the other, that the hiding places were numerous enough.

At length, however, they were not only satisfied that no one was concealed on the premises, but likewise that all the fastenings were quite secure, and had been made so before the servants retired to rest. The mystery therefore was rather increased.

Had there not been the collateral evidence of Emma and the singular fact of the fastening up of the doors of the doctor's and Mr. Smith's bed-chambers, no doubt the whole affair would have rested where it was, and have been put down as a remarkable death arising from the influence of a dream.

But that was out of the question — somebody had been seen, and whether that somebody was really not an inhabitant of this world was the question.

In the midst of all this, the day began to dawn.

Sir George had had no sleep, but he had done himself some good in the solitude of his own chamber. He had prayed long and earnestly, and his prayers had had the effect which they almost invariably have upon all imaginative persons, namely, of bringing him an amount of mental calmness, peace, and resignation, highly desirable in his circumstances.

The breakfast table was laid in silence by the servants, and when Sir George met his sons and his guests, he spoke calmly enough, saying to them, —

"You will no more hear from me the accents of grief or of despair. I accept what consolation I can find, but as a man, and a father I will have justice; my child has been terrified to death, and I will find who has done the deed, for let him be whom he may, he is as much her murderer as though he had plunged a dagger in her heart."

"It is so," said Mr. Smith.

"Being so, then let him beware."

Varney thought that as the father uttered these last words, he glanced in a peculiar manner at him, but he was not quite sure that such was the case. Had he been sure, perhaps, he would have taken other steps than he did.

Little more passed during the breakfast, but when the meal was over, Sir George said, —

"Edwin, we are but dull and poor company to Mr. Smith; it will amuse him, perhaps, if you take him through the grounds, and show him the estate."

Edwin made no objection, and as the thing was put in the shape of an amusement to him, Varney could only say some civil things, and rise to go.

"I regret," he said, "to be of so much trouble."

"Not at all," said Edwin, "no trouble, sir; my own mind, God knows, wants something to distract it from too close a contemplation of its own thoughts. If you will accompany me in a walk over the estate, it will, perhaps, put me into better spirits."

They left the room, and when they were gone, Sir George Crofton rose and shut the door, fastening it on the inside carefully, rather to the surprise of the doctor and his son Charles, who looked at him in silence.

"Charles," he then said, "and you, doctor, I have something particular to say to you."

"What is it? What is it?"

"God forgive me if I am wrong, but I suspect our guest? !"

"Mr. Smith?"

"Yes, I don't like his looks at all; now we know nothing of him but from his own report; we have searched the house right through, or at least you have, you tell me, and found nothing. He is the only stranger within our doors. Perhaps it is uncharitable to suspect him, but I cannot help it, the thought came too strongly upon me last night, as I was alone in my chamber, for me to overcome it. I have now spoken to you both frankly, and tell me what are your thoughts."

"I don't like him," said Charles.

"He is a singular man," said Dr. North.

"What — what now if he were — were —"

"Why do you hesitate, father? what would you say?"

"Go on, sir," said Dr. North, with a nod, that signified, I know very well what you are going to say. "Go on, sir."

"What, then, if it were really true, that there were such things, and he is a vampyre?"

Edwin sprang to his feet in surprise, and said, —

"Good God! you put a frightful idea into my brain that will now never leave it. A vampyre?"

"Heaven forbid," added Sir George, "that I should say such a thing heedlessly, or that I should take upon myself to assert that such is the case; I merely throw it out as a supposition — a horrible one, I grant, but yet one that perhaps deserves some consideration."

"Get rid of him," said Dr. North.

"It is difficult after telling him he was welcome to stay, to now tell him that we want him to go. I would much prefer watching him closely, and endeavoring by such means, either to confirm or to do away entirely with my suppositions. And you can take an opportunity of speaking to Edwin upon the subject, quietly and carefully."

"I will, father."

"Then we can be all upon the alert; but above all things I charge you say nothing to Emma of the really terrific idea. Only I should say that tonight it is in the direction of her chamber that I would wish to keep the closest watch."

"And that, too, without her knowing it," said the doctor. "If she is aware of anything of the sort, there is no knowing what tricks her imagination might play her, and now, Sir George, I must say that I take the greatest interest in the matter, and will with your permission remain here until I am sent for. Poor Ringwood still reminds insensible, and I take it that under the circumstances that it is really a mercy, for what a sad communication has to be made to him, when he does recover sufficiently to hear it."

"Sad, indeed."

It was now finally agreed among them that there was to be no variation whatever in their conduct towards Mr. Smith, but that after they had taken leave of him for the night, and had all gone to bed, they should each glide out of his chamber, and wait at the extreme end of the corridor in silence, to mark if anything should happen.

This was duly announced to Edwin, who with a shudder announced that he had his suspicions, too, of Mr. Smith, so he of course came into the scheme at once; and now they waited rather anxiously for the night to come again.

Chapter CXCI.

THE NIGHT WATCH. – THE SURPRISE. – THE CHASE.

*E*verything was now said and done that could induce a feeling in the mind of Varney, that he was perfectly welcome at the Grange, and to dispel the least idea of anything in the shape of supposition that he might have had, that he was suspected, although he had not himself by word or look betrayed such a feeling.

The day to all parties seemed a frightfully long one. Ringwood remained in the same state of unconsciousness as he had been in the day previous, and the only circumstance that served to break the monotony of the time, was the arrival of some of his friends to see him.

It is not essential to our story that we should take up space in detailing what they said and what they did; suffice it that all the grief was exhibited that was to be expected, and that finally they left the Grange with a conviction that the wounded man was in as kind hands as they could possibly wish him, and everything would be done, that kindness and skill could suggest, to recover him and preserve his life.

Probably the dreadful catastrophe that had happened in the family of the Croftons had in effect in reconciling the Ringwoods to the lesser calamity, for Dr. North gave them strong hopes of his ultimate recovery.

And so the time passed on, until the dim shadows of the evening began to creep over the landscape, and the distant trees imperceptibly mingled together in a chaotic mass. The song of the birds was over — the herds and flocks had sought their shelter for the night, and a solemn and beautiful stillness was upon the face of nature.

Assembled once more in the dining-room of the Grange, were the Croftons — but not Emma, she was in her chamber — the doctor, and Mr. Smith.

Varney had exerted himself much to be entertaining, and yet not obtrusively so, as under the calamitous and extraordinary circumstances in which the family was placed, that would have been bad taste; but he led the conversation into the most interesting channels, and he charmed those who listened to him, in spite of themselves.

Dr. North was peculiarly pleased with so scientific a companion, and one who had traveled so much, for Varney spoke of almost every portion of the globe as familiar to him.

In this kind of way, the evening sped on, and more than once, as Varney was giving some eloquent and comprehensive description of some natural phenomenon that he had witnessed in some other clime, not only were the suspicions entertained against him forgotten, but even the grief of the family faded away for a brief space before the charm of his discourse.

At length the time for rest came.

Sir George rose, and bowing to Varney, said, —

"Do not let our example influence you, sir. We retire now."

"I shall be glad to do so," said Varney, "likewise; last night was a disturbed as well as a melancholy one for all in this house."

"It was indeed."

In another five minutes, the dining-room was vacant, and all that could be heard in the house was the noise of putting up extra bars, and shooting into their places, long unused bolts in order that it should be quite beyond all doubt that no one could get into the premises.

After that, all was still.

The moon was in her last quarter now, but only at the commencement of it, so if the night proved not to be cloudy, it would be rather a brilliant one, which might, or might not be of service to those who were going to watch in the corridor the proceedings of Mr. Smith.

An hour elapsed before there was any movement whatever, and then it was Dr. North who first, with great care, emerged from his room.

He had drawn on his stockings over his shoes, so that his footsteps might not be heard, and he took his station in a dark corner by the large window we have before spoken of as lighting the corridor.

The moon was up, but it only shone in obliquely at the window, so that one side of the corridor was enveloped in the deepest gloom, while on the other the pale rays fell.

A few minutes more, for half-past eleven was the hour on which they had all agreed, and Sir George, with Edwin and Charles joined the doctor, who merely nodded to them, as they could faintly see him.

Sir George spoke in a very faint whisper, saying, —

"We are well armed."

"Good," replied the doctor, in a similar cautious tone, "but let me implore you to be careful how you use your arms. Do nothing hastily I beg of you; you don't know what cause of regret the imprudence of a moment may give rise to."

"Depend upon us, we will be very careful indeed."

"That is right."

"We had better not talk," said Charles, "these corridors carry sound sometimes too well; if we are to do any good, it must be by preserving the profoundest silence."

This advice was too practical and evidently good to be neglected, and consequently they were all as still as they could be, and stood like so many statues for the next half hour.

They heard a clock that hung in the hall below strike the hour of twelve, and when the reverberations of sound were over, a stillness even more profound than before seemed to pervade the whole house. The half hour they had waited in such silence appeared to them to be of four times the usual length, and they were glad to hear twelve strike.

Still they said nothing, for if silence before twelve o'clock was a thing to be desired, it was much more so after that hour, for it was then that the alarm of the preceding evening had taken place. Their watchfulness, and their anxiety momentarily increased.

The old clock in the hall chimed the quarter past twelve, and yet all was as still as the grave; not the smallest sound disturbed the repose of the house.

The moon had shifted round a little, so that the gloom of the corridor was not so complete as it had been, and Dr. North was aware that in another hour the spot where they all stood would be visited by some rays which would render their concealment out of the question.

But as yet all was right, and there was no need to shift their position in the least.

Suddenly Sir George Crofton laid his hand upon the arm of the doctor, and an exclamation involuntarily escaped him, but not in a loud tone.

"Hush, for God's sake," whispered the doctor.

They had all heard a slight noise, like the cautious opening of a door. They looked eagerly in the direction from whence it came, and to their surprise they found it proceed from the chamber of the dead!

Yes, the door of the room in which lay the corpse of Clara slowly opened.

"God of Heaven!" said Sir George.

"Hush — hush," again whispered the doctor, and he held him by the arm compulsively.

All was still. The door creaked upon its hinges a little, that was all.

A quarter of an hour passed, and then Sir George was about to say something, when he started as if a shock of electricity had been applied to him, for the door of Varney's room was swung wide open, and he appeared, full dressed.

All the doors opening from the corridor creaked unless they were flung open smartly and quickly, and there could be no doubt but that Varney knew this, and hence the apparent precipitancy of his appearance.

There he stood in the moonlight, close by the threshold of his room, gazing about him. He bent himself into an attitude of intense listening, and remained in it for some time, and then he with slow sliding steps made his way towards the door of Emma's room.

His hand was actually upon the lock, when Sir George, who could stand the scene no longer, leveled a pistol he had taken from his pocket, and without giving any intimation to those who were with him of what he was going to do, he pulled the trigger.

The pistol only flashed without being fully discharged.

"How imprudent," said the doctor. "You have done it now! Follow me!"

He rushed forward, but he was too late, Varney had taken the alarm, and in a moment he regained his own room and fastened it securely on the inside.

"We must have him," cried Charles. "He cannot escape from that room. There is no other door, and the window is a good thirty feet from the garden below. Alarm the servants, we will soon open his door. It can't be very secure, for the lock was broken last night."

As he spoke, Charles made a vigorous effort to open the door, but it resisted as if it had been a part of the solid wall, while within the chamber all was perfectly still, as if Mr. Smith had quite satisfied himself by shutting out his assailants, and meant to take no further notice of them.

"This is strange," said the doctor, "but we shall soon find out what he means by it. The door must be forced as quickly as possible."

Edwin ran down stairs by his father's orders to arouse some of the men servants, besides getting some weapon or tool by the assistance of which the door might be forced, and he soon returned with several of the men, and one armed with the identical crow-bar that had been used with such effect on the preceding evening. They brought lights with them too, so that the capture of Mr. Smith appeared to be no longer a matter of doubt with such a force opposed to him.

"Now," cried Sir George, "do not mind what mischief you do, my men, so that you break open the door of that room, and quickly too."

People somehow are always glad to be engaged in anything that has a destructive look about it, and when the servants heard that they might break away at the door as much as they liked, they set about it with a vengeance that promised soon to succeed in the object.

The door yielded with a crash.

"Come on, come on. Yield yourself," cried Sir George, and he rushed into the room followed by his sons and by Dr. North.

There was no Mr. Smith there.

"Escaped," said Dr. North.

"Impossible, — impossible! and yet this open window. He must be lying dashed to pieces below, for no one could with safety drop or jump such a height. Run round to the garden some of you, at once."

"Stop," said Charles. "There is no occasion. He has had ample time to escape. Look here."

Charles pointed out the end of a thick rope, firmly fastened to the ledge of the window, and by which it was quite clear any one could safely descend into the garden, it only requiring a little nerve to do so with perfect ease.

"This has all been prepared," said Dr. North.

"Still," cried Sir George, "I will not give the affair up. Mind I offer a reward of twenty guineas to any one of my household who succeeds in catching Mr. Smith."

"Lor, sir! what has he done?" said a groom.

"Never you mind what he has done. Bring him in, and you shall have the reward."

"Very good, sir. Come on, Dick, and you Harry; let's all go, and you know it will be all the pleasanter to share the reward among us. Come on."

Thus stimulated by their companion, the servants ran out of the house into the moonlit park in search of Varney the Vampyre.

Chapter CXCII.

THE FUNERAL. — A STRANGE INCIDENT.

*I*t was all very well for Sir George Crofton to offer his twenty guineas for the taking of Mr. Smith, and nothing could be more legitimate than his servants making active exertions to endeavor to earn that amount of money, but the really succeeding in doing so was quite another thing.

To be sure they went out into the park, and did the best to catch him, and being well acquainted with every turn and every pathway within it, they considered they had a fair chance of succeeding, but after their pains they were at length obliged to give up the affair as a bad job, after an hour or two's most active search.

While they were away though, there was something that occurred at the Grange which gave a great additional shock to Sir George and his sons.

It will not fail to be remembered that the first door they saw move while they were keeping watch and ward in the moonlit gallery was the door of the chamber in which lay the corpse of Clara, who had met with so melancholy an end.

This circumstance recurred to them all with fearful force when they felt convinced that the now more suspected Mr. Smith had really and truly made his escape.

Upon proceeding to that room of the dead, Dr. North being first, they found some difficulty in opening the door, but upon using force they succeeded, when to their absolute horror they saw that the dead body was lying upon the floor close to the door, and that it had been the obstruction to moving it.

Dr. North would fain have spared the feelings of Sir George this affecting sight, but the baronet was so close behind him that he could not do so.

"Oh, God!" cried the father, "my child, my child."

"Take your father away, boys, for heaven's sake," said Dr. North to the two young men; "this is no sight for him to see."

It appeared too as if it was no sight for any one to see unmoved, for both Charles and Edwin stood like statues gazing at it, and for a time incapable of motion.

"My sister — is it indeed my sister?" said Charles.

The doctor fairly closed the door upon them all, and turned them so out of the room. Then he having professionally lost all dread of the dead, lifted the body upon the bed again, and disposed of it properly, after which, without saying a word, he walked down to the dining-room.

"Tell me, tell me," said Sir George "what does all this mean?"

"Do not ask me," replied Dr. North, "I cannot tell you; I confess I do not know what advice to give you, or indeed what to say to you."

The old man rested his head upon his hands, and wept bitterly, while his two sons sat looking at each other perfectly aghast, and unable to think anything of a rational import concerning the most mysterious proceedings that had taken place.

*L*et our readers then suppose that a week has passed away, and that the morning has arrived when the body of Clara is to be placed in a vault appropriated as the resting place of the Croftons, beneath the church that was close at hand.

During that time nothing whatever had been heard of Mr. Smith. He seemed to have completely disappeared from the neighborhood as well as from the Grange-house.

Fortunately, although Sir George had offered twenty guineas for the apprehension of Mr. Smith to his servants, he had said nothing of the cause why he offered such a reward, and the neighborhood was left to its own conjectures upon the subject.

Those conjectures were of course sufficiently numerous, but it was quite agreed between Sir George, Doctor North, and the two sons that nothing more should be said upon the subject.

They of course did not wish

"To fill the ear of idle curiosity" with such a tale as they might tell, but had a thousand reasons, each good and substantial of its kind, for withholding.

Young Ringwood was sufficiently recovered to be about, and to have told him the story that widowed his heart. He fell into a profound melancholy which nothing could alleviate, and as his recovery went on, he asked permission to remain at the Grange.

Sir George, and indeed all the Crofton family, gladly pressed him to remain with them as long as he would do so, for it was some alleviation of their own distress to have him about them.

He begged permission to be present at the funeral, and it is of that funeral we have now to speak, for it took place on that day week on which the vampyre had first taken up his dreadful residence at the old Grange-house, where all before had been so happy.

The church, as we have remarked, was not very distant, and a mournful procession it was, consisting of the funeral equipages, followed by Sir George Crofton's carriage, that at twelve o'clock in the day started to place the youngest and the fairest of the name of Crofton that had ever reposed in the family vault.

The whole neighborhood was in a state of commotion, and by the time the funeral cortege reached the churchyard, there was not a person capable of being out, for some miles around, that was not congregated about the spot.

The old church bell tolled a melancholy welcome to the procession, and the clergyman met the corpse a the entrance of the graveyard, and preceded it to the church, where it was placed by the altar while he made an impressive prayer.

This brief ceremony over, the coffin was carried to the part of one of the aisles, where upon the removal of a large stone slab, the resting-place of the Croftons was visible.

"I have not looked upon these stone steps," said Sir George, "since my poor wife went down there in the sleep of death."

"Compose yourself," whispered Dr. North, who was present. "You ought not, sir, to have been present at such a scene as this."

"Nay, it surely was my duty to follow my own child to her last resting-place."

The body was lowered into the vault, and the funeral service was read impressively over the cold and still remains of Clara.

"All is over," said the doctor.

"Yes," faltered Sir George; "all is over. Farewell, my dear child, but not a long farewell to thee; this blow has nearly stricken me into the grave."

"Leaning on the arm of his son Charles, who as well as Edwin was deeply affected, the old man now allowed himself to be led from the church. He met at the door Will Stephens, the sexton, who seemed desirous of speaking to him.

"What is it, Will?"

"Will your honor have some fresh sawdust put down in the vault. It wants it, Sir George; there ain't been any put in for many a long day."

"Very well. It will be ready for me when I go. It won't be long before the vault is again opened."

"Oh, do not say that, father," said Edwin. "Do not leave us; think that if you have lost one child who loved you, you have others who ought to be as dear to you."

"That's right, Edwin," said the doctor.

Sir George made no distinct reply to this, but he pressed the hand of his son, and looked kindly upon him, to signify that he felt the full justice of what he had just said, so they had hopes that time would soon produce its usual effects upon that feeling which of all others is, while it lasts, the most poignant, at the same time that it is the most evanescent – grief for the dead.

And well it is that it should be so, otherwise we should be a world of weepers and mourners, for who is there that has not felt the pang of losing some fond heart in which we have garnered up the best affections of human nature.

Emma since her sister's death had been terribly broken down in spirit, and when they all got home to the Grange, they found her looking so ill, that the old baronet took Dr. North on one side, and said to him in tones expressive of the deepest anguish, –

"Am I to lose both my girls?"

"Oh no – no; certainly not," was the decided reply. "Why, my old friend, you used to be a man of great moral courage. Where has it all gone to now?"

"It is in the grave of my child."

"Come, come, you must for your own sake, as well as for the sake of others, who are near and dear to you, rouse yourself from this state of mental torpor, as I may call it. You can do so, and it is worthy of you to make the effort. Only think what would have been your situation if you had had but one child, and that had been snatched away from you; but you have yet three to comfort you, and yet you talk despairingly, as if every tie that bound you to the world had been suddenly burst asunder."

After this Sir George Crofton was almost ashamed to make such an exhibition of his grief, and whatever his thoughts were he kept them to himself, as well as exercising a much greater control over his voice, and the external expression of the feelings, which were still busy at his heart.

The despondency of Ringwood was great. He could not help fancy that if he had not met with the unlucky accident in the ravine, Clara would have been saved, and in some obscure way to his mind, the circumstances seemed to be connected together. He could not account either for the loss of her miniature, which he had been in the habit of wearing but which he missed upon his convalescence, so that he was irresistibly led to the conclusion that some unfriendly hands had been about him during his insensibility.

So highly did he prize the miniature, that he offered a sum of money, exceeding its intrinsic value by twenty times, for its recovery and pledged himself to make no inquiry as to how it came into the possession of the party who should restore it to him; but for all that it was not forthcoming.

The reader of this narrative knows very well in whose possession it was. Varney the Vampyre had possessed himself of it in the ravine, when he saw the young bridegroom lying insensible at his feet, and he kept it, although why he did so does not as yet appear, for surely the sight of it could only remind him of one of his victims; but then Varney had other thoughts and feelings than he used to have.

Alas, what a thousand pities it was that the ocean had presented him to the two brothers? Why did he not sink — why did not some wave hide him from their observation? What misery would have been spared to them, and to all dear to them. And what misery would have been spared to the wretched Varney himself!

It is true that he had given expression to sentiments, and declared intentions which would go far to prove that he had for ever given up and got rid of all human feelings and influences, but has he really so got rid of such feelings? It is a question which time alone can answer.

We shall soon see in his now very short career whether he is most to suffer or to inflict suffering, and what will be the result of his new principles of action — those principles which he had in the despair and the agony of his heart painted to himself as the main springs of a

combined existence, he had with such vain and such fruitless perseverance strove to rid himself of. It was sad — very sad, indeed, that such a
being could not die when he chose, the poor privilege of all.

Chapter CXCIII.

THE STRANGE VISITOR TO THE OLD CHURCH AT NIGHT.

*T*he request of Will Stephens to be allowed to put some sawdust in
the vault of the Croftons, was one of those regular things that he always
propounded to any one who had a vault opened beneath the old church,
and he generally made a very good thing of it.

People were always too much taken up with thinking of the loss of
the relation who had just been placed in that dismal repository, to think
much of a guinea to Will for a shilling's worth of sawdust, and if they
did ever intimate that they thought it rather too much, he always had
his answer ready at the tip of his tongue.

"How should you like, sir, or madam, as the case may be, to go into
a vault among the dead, to lay the sawdust for 'em."

That argument was generally conclusive, and Will would get his
guinea.

With Sir George Crofton he was quite sure and safe, so he had no
scruples upon the subject, and the little bit of sawdust he meant to carry
in when he had time, was more for the say of the thing, than for any
utility it was at all likely to be of, but then as he said, —

"Where's the odds, the dead 'uns can't see it, and living 'uns won't
go to see it, so it does very well, and I pockets my guinea, which does
better still, for after all a sexton's ain't the most agreeable life in the
world, and he ought to be paid well; not that I care much about it, being
used to it, but there was a time when I had my qualms, and I've had to
get over 'em the best way I could, somehow, if I am now all right."

These were Will's arguments and reflections to himself before night, when he meant to go and place the little bag of saw-dust in the Croftons' family vault.

But, before we follow Will Stephens on his saw-dust expedition, as we intend to do, we wish first to draw the attention of the reader to another circumstance, the relation of which to Will Stephen's proceedings will very shortly appear indeed.

As the night came on there was some appearance of stormy weather. The wind blew in a strange, gusty and uncertain manner, shifting about from point to point of the compass in an odd way, as though it had not made up its mind from whence to blow. The most weather-wise personages of the neighborhood were puzzled, for just as they prognosticated one species of weather from the particular direction whence the wind came, it shifted and came from some other quarter very nearly directly opposite.

This was extremely provoking, but at all events it was generally agreed that the moon would not on that night, shed its soft light upon the earth.

How far they were mistaken in this surmise we shall presently see.

Will Stephens had an opinion, from certain admonitory symptoms arising from his corns, that it would rain; so he delayed going to the church until he should see what sort of weather it was going to be, inwardly deciding that it would be a capital excuse not to go at all that night if the rain should come down pretty sharply.

This period of indecision he passed at a public house, known as the Blue Lion, the charms of the excellent ale of that establishment materially assisting him in coming to the conclusion that if it should rain ever so little it would be better to put off his job until the morning.

Now it was not that Will was afraid that he hesitated. He was too used to death to feel now any terrors of fear. It was nothing but the ale. Why then was the hurry? Simply that the flat stone which was over the vault of the Croftons was left unfastened until the aforesaid saw-dust was placed within the receptacle of the dead, and the next day was Sunday, so that the job must be finished before the service should commence.

At night, therefore, or very early the following morning, Will must seem to earn his guinea by going to the vault. He did not like to venture saying he had been and yet neglect going, for he knew there were too many gossips about the village to make that safe.

While he is however regaling himself at the ale house, another person totally, to all appearance, heedless of wind and threatening rain, is abroad in the neighborhood of the church.

A tall figure enveloped in a large murky looking cloak, is moving slowly past the few cottages in the immediate vicinage of the church, and so noiselessly that it looks like a spirit of the dead rather than a living person.

It was unseen by any one, for it was a time of the night — half-past eleven — now at which few persons in that little quiet place were abroad, and as we have said, Will Stephens, perhaps the only inhabitant who had any real business to be abroad at such an hour, was still solacing himself at the Blue Lion with the ale that seemed to get better every glass he took.

The figure moved on at a slow and steady pace among the old tomb stones that lay so thick around in the circuit of the church-yard, until it reached the church itself, and then it walked slowly around the sacred edifice, looking with a curious eye at the windows that presented themselves to observation, and apparently scanning the height from the ground.

Finally he paused at a rugged-looking part of the wall, and commenced, with great muscular power and most wonderful agility, climbing up to one of the windows.

To look at that wall it would have seemed that nothing human could possibly have succeeded in ascending it, and yet this stranger, catching at asperities which scarcely seemed to be such, did, with a wonderful power and strength, drag himself up until he grasped an iron bar, close to the window immediately above him, and then he had a firm hold.

After this his progress was easy, assuming that his object was merely to get up to the window of the old church, for he stood upon the narrow ledge without in a few moments.

There was a slight noise, it was of the breaking of a pane of glass, and then the stranger introduced his hand into the church, and succeeded in removing a rude primitive looking fastening which held the window in its place.

In another moment he disappeared from external observation within the sacred building.

What could he want there at such an hour, and who was he? Did he contemplate disturbing the repose of the dead with some unhallowed purpose? Was robbery his aim?

Let us be patient, and probably we shall soon enough perceive that some affairs are in progress that require the closest attention, and which in the vaults are calculated to fill the reflecting mind with the most painful images, and awake sensations of horror at the idea that such things can really be, and are permitted tacitly by Heaven to take place on the beautiful earth destined for the dwelling place of man.

Chapter CXCIV.

WILL STEPHEN'S VISIT TO THE FAMILY VAULT WITH THE SAW-DUST, AND WHAT HE SAW THERE.

Will Stephens waited at the ale-house much longer than he intended. To be sure the rain cleared off, but what of that? It was not a circumstance that made the ale anything worse, and so he waited to drink it with a gusto that improved each glass amazingly, and then some of those who were present — jolly topers like himself — began to laugh and to say, —

"Ah, Will, you may as well poke that bag of saw-dust into some corner; you won't do anything with it tonight, old fellow, we know."

Now, some people get good tempered and complying when they have had the drop too much, and others again, get particularly obstinate and contradictory. Will of the two, certainly had more pretensions to belong to the latter class than the former, so when he heard such a prophecy concerning his movements and knew it was all an assumption based upon the ale he had drank, he felt indignant.

"Not go!" he cried. "Not go. You may fancy if you please that I will not go, but you will find yourselves mistaken, I will go."

"What, so late."

"What's the odds to me. Any of you now would be frightened out of your lives to set foot in the old church at such a time as this, I know; but I'm none of the timid sort, I'm afraid of nobody living, and it ain't likely that I am now going to be afraid of anybody dead."

"Then you really will go."

The only reply that he made to this was to finish off the glass of ale that was before him, shouldering the bag of saw-dust, and sally out into the open air. Will Stephens felt highly indignant and touchy about his honor, and as he had said he would go and then somebody chose to imply a doubt still, he was grievously offended.

When he got out, he found that the night was anything but an inviting one. He was still sober enough to see that, and to feel that although the heavy rain had ceased, there was a little disagreeable misty sort of vapor in the air.

He staggered at the first turning he came to, for rather an uncomfortable gust of wind blew in his face, carrying along with it such a shower of small cold rain that he was, or fancied himself to be, wet through in a moment.

"Pleasant, this," thought Will, "but I won't go back to be laughed at."

As for the saw-dust he was carrying, its weight was by no means any great consideration for it was just as light as it could be.

"No, I won't go back — back indeed, not I; they would make me stand a pot of ale to a certainly if I were to go back, and besides it would be all over the parish tomorrow that Will Stephens after he got half way to the church was afraid to go any further. Confound the small rain, it pricks like pins and needles."

Nothing is more sobering than rain, and as he, Will, gradually got saturated with the small aqueous particles, the effect of the strong ale as gradually wore off, until by the time the dim, dusky outline of the church rose before him he was almost as sober as need be.

"Ah," he said, "here I am at last at any rate. I do hate this sort of rain, you can hardly make up your mind that it is raining at all, and yet somehow you get soaked before you know where you are. It's just like going through a damp cloud, that it is, and yet somehow or another, I don't much mind it; I'm earning a guinea easy enough. Ha, ha!"

This was by no means an unpleasant reflection.

"Yes," he added, "I am earning a guinea easily enough that's quite clear, but then it's not everybody who would, for a guinea, go into anybody's family vault at such a time. By-the-by, I wonder now what the time is exactly."

Scarcely had Will spoken those words when the old church-clock struck twelve.

It was a very serious, deliberate sort of clock that, and it took a long time to strike twelve, and Will listened with the greatest attention with the hope of persuading himself that it was only eleven, but there could be no mistake, twelve it was.

"Really," he said, "is it so late, well, I didn't think —"

Will stood within the porch of the church door, and he gave a sort of shiver, and then, with the bag of sawdust in his hand, he stopped to listen attentively, for he thought he heard a slight sound.

"What was that, eh? what — I though, nay, I am sure I heard something; it's very odd — very odd indeed."

As if then to afford Will an excuse for resolving the sound to something else, the wind at this moment came in such a sudden gale round the ancient edifice, that quite congratulated himself he was within the porch and protected from its fury, and besides it to his mind was a sufficing explanation of the noise he had heard.

"Some of the old doors," he muttered, "rattled by the wind, that's all. Now I suppose we shall have a clear night after all the rain. Such a gale will soon blow off the damp clouds."

Will was right. The gale, for a gale it was, blew from the north, and away went the rain clouds as if a curtain had been drawn aside by some invisible hand.

After some rummaging Will found in his pocket the key of the church; it was not the key of the principal door, but of a smaller side entrance, at which the officials, who required at all times free ingress and egress, made application. The little arched door creaked upon its hinges and then Will stood in a sort of vestibule, for another door that was never fast had to be opened before he could be fairly said to be within the church.

This second door was covered with green baize, and could be opened and shut very noiselessly, indeed.

Will Stephens stood in the vestibule until he had got a small lantern out of one pocket, and some matches from another. Then, in a few moments he had a light, and once again shouldering the bag of sawdust, he pushed open the inner door, and stood in the church.

It might have been fancy — nay, he felt certain, it could be nothing else — but he thought as he opened the door that a faint sort of sigh came upon his ears.

Fancy or not, though, it was an uncomfortable thing at such an hour, and in such a place too, and he had never before heard anything of the sort upon his visits to the church, and he had visited it at all hours, many and many a time.

"It's odd," he said, "it's uncommonly odd, I never felt so uncomfortable in the church before. I — I never used to mind coming to it in the middle of the night. But now, I — eh? — what was that?"

Again an odd sort of noise came upon his ears, and he dropped the bag of sawdust.

All was still again, save the regular roar of wind, as it swept round the sacred building, and although Will Stephens stood for nearly ten minutes in an attitude of listening, he heard nothing to augment his terrors. But let an impulse once be given to fear, and it will go on accumulating material from every trivial circumstance. The courage of the sexton was broken down, and there was no knowing, now, what tricks his awakened imagination might play him.

He began to wish he had not come, and from that wish, to think that he might as well go back, only shame forbade him, for it would be easily known on the morrow, that he had not placed the sawdust in the vault, and lastly, he began to think that some one might be playing him a trick.

This last supposition, probably, had more effect in raising his courage than any preceding one. Indignation took possession of him, and he no longer thought of retreating. He went forward at once, and fell over the bag of sawdust.

"Murder!" shouted Will.

The moment he did so, he recollected what it was that had occasioned his fall, and being ashamed of himself he called out impulsively, as if somebody was there to hear him, —

"No — no, it's only the sawdust. No — no."

He rose to his feet again, heartily ashamed of his own fears. Luckily, his lantern had not been broken or extinguished in his fall, and now, without another word, he prepared himself to execute the work he came to do, and leave the church to its repose as quickly as possible.

At one end of the church, the southern end, there was a large window, which might be said to light the whole of the interior, for the little windows at the sides were more ornamental than useful, being nothing but lattices; and across this window was drawn a heavy cloth curtain, so that when the sun shone too brightly upon the congregation on a summer's day, it could be wholly or partially excluded upon a sign from the clergyman.

The curtain was drawn close on the window now, at night, and Will just glanced up to it, as he walked on towards the aisle where the opening to the family vault of the Crofton's was situated.

"All's right," he said, "what a fool I have been, to be sure." Upon my word I might have saved frightening myself all night, and some people would too, but that's not my way of doing business. So here we are, all right. The door on one side, so that I have just room enough to go down into the vault. Oh! when one comes to think of it, it was rather a melancholy thing, the death of such a young girl as she was, going to be married too. Well, that's the way the world goes."

The stone steps leading down to the vault were rather steep, and Will threw down the bag of sawdust first, in preference to carrying it, and then with his lantern in his hand, he commenced his own descent.

"That'll do," said Will, when he felt his feet upon the soft old sawdust that was on the floor of the vault. "That'll do — now for it, I shall soon have this job settled, and then I'll get home no faster than I can."

Somehow, or another, he felt very much inclined to talk; the sound of his own voice, conversing, as he might be said to be, with himself, gave him a sort of courage, and made the place not appear to be altogether so desperately lonely as it really was.

That, no doubt, was the feeling that brought forth so many indifferent remarks from Will Stephens. He held up his light to look round him, and turned gradually upon his heels as he did so.

The light shook in his hand. The hair almost stood on end on his head — his teeth chattered, and he tried to speak in vain, as he saw lying at his feet, a coffin lid.

It was new. The nails that held the blue cloth upon it, were bright, and fast — the ate plate? shone like silver. Yes, it was the lid of the coffin of Miss Clara Crofton; but how came it off — unsecured, and lying upon the floor of the vault, while the coffin was in its proper niche?

"Gracious goodness!" gasped Will at length. "What does this mean?"

The question was easy to ask, but most difficult to answer, and he stood trembling and turning over in his mind all the most frightful explanations of what he saw, that could occur to any one.

"Has she been buried alive? Have the body snatchers been after her? How is it — what — what has happened?"

Then it occurred to Will, that it would be just as well to look into the coffin, and see if it was tenantless or not. If it were, and thought — he should know what to think — if the dead body was there, then he could only conclude that she had been buried alive, and had had just strength enough to force open the coffin, and cast the lid of it on the floor of the vault, and then to die in that horrible place.

It required almost more courage than Will could muster, to go and look into the coffin, for now that his usual indifference was completely broken down, he was as timid as any stranger to graves and vaults would have been. But curiosity is, after all, a most exciting passion, and that lent him power.

"Yes," he said, "I — I will look in the coffin, I shall have but a poor tale to tell to Sir George Crofton, if I do not look in the coffin. I — I — have nothing to be afraid of."

He advanced with trembling steps, the light shaking in his hands as he did so. He reached the coffin, and with eyes unusually wide he looked in: it was empty.

Chapter *CXCV.*

THE APPARITION IN THE CHURCH. – WILL STEPHENS' SWOON. – THE MORNING.

*F*or some minutes, Will Stephens continued to gaze in the empty coffin, as if there was something peculiarly fascinating in it, and most attractive, and yet nothing was in it, no vestige even of the vestments of the dead. If Clara Crofton had herself risen, and left the vault, it was quite clear she had taken with her the apparel of the grave.

Will had thought that if he found the coffin empty, all his fears would vanish, and that he should be able to come at once to the conclusion, that she had become the prey of resurrectionists. But new ideas, as he gazed at that abandoned receptacle of the dead, began to creep across him.

"I – I – don't know," he muttered, "but she may in a ghost-like kind of way be going about. I don't know whether ghosts is corpses or not. I – I wish I was out of this."

The idea of spreading the sawdust in the vault now completely left him; all he thought of was to get away, and the dread that Clara Crofton was, perhaps, hiding somewhere, and might come suddenly out upon him with a yell, got so firm a hold of him, that several times he thought he should faint with excess of terror.

That would be too horrible," he said, "I am sure I should go mad – mad – mad."

He retreated backward to the stairs, for the coffin, empty though it was, held his gaze with a strange kind of fascinating power. He thought that if he turned round something would be sure to lay hold of him. It was a most horrifying and distressing idea that, and yet he could not conquer it.

Of course, he must turn round, it would be an awkward thing to attempt ascending the staircase short as it was, backward, so he felt the necessity of turning his back upon the vault.

"I — I will do so," he thought, "and then make such a rush up the steps, that I shall be in the church in a moment, I — I can surely do that, and — and after all it's nothing really to be afraid of — it's only a matter of imagination, after all! oh, yes, that's all, I — I will do that."

He put this notable scheme into execution by turning suddenly round and making a dash at the stairs, but as people generally do things badly when they do them in a hurry, he stumbled when about half-way and felt himself at the mercy of the whole of the supernatural world.

"Have mercy on me," he cried, "I am going. Have mercy on me."

He had struck the lantern so hard against the stone stairs that he had broken it into fragments, and now all was intense darkness around him.

He gave himself up for lost.

He lay, expecting each moment to feel some dead bony fingers clutching him, and he only groaned, thinking that surely now his last hour was come; and it is a wonder that his fancy, excited as it was, did not conjure up to him the very effect he dreaded, but it did not do so, strange to say, and he lay for full five minutes without anything occurring to add to his terrors.

Then he began gradually to recover.

"If — if," he gasped, "I could but reach the church, I — I think I should be safe. Yes, I should surely be safe in the body of the church. Have mercy on me, good ghosts; I never harmed any of you, I — I respect you very much, indeed I do. Let me go, and — I'll never say a light word of any of you again, no, never, if I were to live for a thousand years."

As he uttered these words, he crawled up the remaining stairs, and to his great satisfaction, made his way fairly into the church.

But then a new surprise, if it was not exactly a new fright, perhaps it was something of both, awaited him.

The curtain that had been, as he had observed when he was walking down the aisle, closely drawn across the large south window was now drawn on one side, so that a large portion of that window was exposed, and the north wind having chased away by this time entirely the damp clouds, the moon was sailing in a cloudless sky, and sending into the old church a glorious flood of light.

"What a change," said Will Stephens.

It was indeed a change; the church was as light as day, save in some places where shadows fell, and they, in contrast to the silvery lightness of the moonbeams, were of a jetty blackness.

But still, let the moon shine ever so brightly, there is not that distinctness and freshness of outline produced as in the direct daylight. A strange kind of hazy vapor seems to float between the eye and all objects — an indistinctness and mysteriousness of aspect, which belongs not to the sun's unreflected rays. Thus it was, that although the church was illuminated by the moon, it had a singular aspect, and would scarcely have been recognized by any one who had only seen it by the mild searching light of day.

But of course Will Stephens the sexton knew it well, and as he wiped the perspiration from his face, he said, —

"What a relief to get out of that vault and find now that the night has turned out so fair and beautiful. I — I begin to think I have frightened myself more than I need have done — but it was that coffin-lid that did the business; I wasn't my own man after that. But now that I have got out of the vault, I feel quite different — oh, quite another thing."

Suddenly, then, it occurred to him, that the curtain had been close on the window, when he came into the church, and following upon that thought came another, namely, that it could not very well remove itself from before the casement, and that consequently some hands, mortal or ghostly, must have done that part of the business.

Here there was ample food again for all his fears, and Will Stephens almost on the instant relapsed into his former trembling and nerveless state.

"What shall I do?" he said; "it ain't all over yet. What will become of me? There's something horrid going to happen, I feel certain, and that curtain has only been drawn aside to let the moonlight come in for me to see it."

With a painful expectation of his eyes being blasted by some horrible sight, he glared round him, but he saw nothing, although the dense little mass of pews before him might have hidden many a horror.

His next movement was to turn his eyes to the gallery, and all round it he carried them until he came to the window again, but he saw nothing.

"Who knows," he muttered, "who knows after all, but that the wind, in some odd sort of way, may have blown the curtain on one side. I — I wish I had the courage to go up to the gallery, and see, but I — I don't think I should like to do that."

He hesitated. He knew that it would sound well on the morrow for him to be able to say that he went up, and yet it was rather a fearful thing.

"A — hem!" he said at length, "is any one here?"

As he made this inquiry, he took care to keep himself ready to make a dart out at the door into the churchyard, but as there was no response to it, he was a little encouraged. The gallery staircase was close to where he stood, and after the not unnatural hesitation of a few moments more, he approached them, and began slowly to ascend.

Nothing interrupted him, all was profoundly still, and at length he did reach the south window, and he found that the curtain was most deliberately drawn on one side, and that the window was fast, so that no vagary of the wind could have accomplished the purpose.

"Now I'll go — I'll go at once," he said, "I can't stand this any longer! I'll go and alarm the village — I'll — I'll make a disturbance of some sort."

"Awake!" said a deep, hollow voice.

Will sunk upon his knees with a groan, and mechanically his eyes wandered to the direction from whence the sound came, and he saw in a pew just beneath him, and on which the moonlight now fell brightly, a human form.

It was lying in a strange huddled up position in the pew, and a glance showed the experienced eyes of the sexton that it was arrayed in the vestments of the dead.

He tried to speak — he tried to scream — he tried to pray, but all was in vain. Intense terror froze up every faculty of his body, and he could only kneel there with his face resting upon the front of the gallery, and glare with aching eyes, that would not close for a moment, upon the scene below.

"Awake!" said a deep, strange voice again, "awake."

It was quite clear that that voice did not come from the figure in the pew, but from some one close at hand. The sexton soon saw another form.

In the adjoining pew, standing upright as a statue, with one hand pointing upwards to the window, where came in the moonlight, was a tall figure, enveloped in a cloak. It was from the lips of that figure, that the sound came, so deeply, and so solemnly.

"Sister," it said, "be one of us — let the cold chaste moonbeams endow thee with your new, and strange, and horrible existence. Be one of us. Be one of us! Hours must yet elapse, ere the faint flash of morning will kill the moonbeams. There is time, sister. Awake, be one of us."

There was a passing cloud that swept for an instant over the face of the moon obscuring its radiance, and the figure let its arm fall to its side. But when the silvery beams streamed into the church, it again pointed to the window.

"'Tis done. She moves," he said. "I have fulfilled my mission. Ha! ha! ha!"

The laugh was so terrific and unmirthful that it froze the very blood in the veins of Will, and he thought he was surely at that moment going mad.

But still he did not close his eyes, still he moved not from the position which he had first assumed when the horrible noise met his ears.

"'Tis done," said the figure, and the arm that had been outstretched was let fall to his side.

Will Stephens looked in the pew, where he had seen what appeared to be a corpse. It had altered its position. He saw it move and waive its arms about strangely and deep sighs came from its lips. It was a dreadful sight to see, but at length it rose up in the grave clothes, and moved to the door of the pew.

The figure in the adjoining pew opened the door and stood on one side, and the revivified corpse passed out.

Slowly and solemnly it passed down the aisle. It reached the door at which Will Stephens had entered, and then it passed away from his sight. The tall figure followed closely, and Will Stephens was alone in the church.

What could he do? How could he give a sufficient alarm? Would the two horrible personages return or not? Alas! poor Will Stephens, never was an unhappy mortal sexton in such frightful tribulation before. He knelt and shook like an aspen. At length a lucky thought entered his head.

"The bell. The bell," he cried, all at once finding his voice. "To the bell."

He sprung to his feet, for what he was now about to do, did not involve the necessity of going down again into the body of the church. There was a narrow staircase at the corner of the gallery, leading to the belfry. It was up that staircase that Will now struggled and tore.

Chapter CCX.

THE ALARM FROM THE BELFRY. – THE BEADLE IN A QUANDARY.

"*T*he belfry," cried Will Stephens. "Oh! if I could but reach the belfry."

He went stumbling on, now falling, then gathering himself up again to renewed exertions, for the stairs were steep and narrow, and although the little church tower was by no means very high yet the place where the bell hung was not to be reached in a moment.

Perseverance, however, will do wonders, and it was reached at last. Yes, he stood panting in a little square building in the very center of which hung a thick rope. It was the means of tolling the bell. To seize it was the work of a moment. The bell swung round and its iron tongue gave forth a loud and stunning sound. Again and again – bang – bang – bang! went the bell, and then feeling that at all events he had given an alarm, Will Stephens turned to retrace his steps."

He was half stupefied by his previous fears. The noise of the bell, so close as he had been to it, had been stunning and bewildering, and Will Stephens reeled like a drunken man. The ale too might have a little to do with that, but certainly he made a false step, and down he went head foremost from top to bottom of those old steep, narrow belfry stairs.

Will Stephens was right when he considered that the tolling of the bell would give an alarm. Most persons in the neighborhood were awakened by it, and they listened to the seven or eight pealing sounds in surprise. What could they mean? Who was doing it? It could not be fire. Oh dear no. The alarm would not leave off if it were. Somebody dead – ah, yes, it was some great person in the state dead, and the news had been brought there, and so the bell was tolled, and we shall hear all about it in the morning. And so those who had been awakened went to sleep again, and the unhappy sexton was left to his fate at the foot of the little stairs leading up to the belfry, where he had gone with so much trouble, and produced so little effect.

The long weary hours of the night crept on, and at last the faint dawn of early morning showed itself upon the ocean, and in faint streaks of light in the glowing east.

The fishermen began to ply their hazardous and hardy trade. The birds in the gardens, and in the old lime and yew trees that shaded the church-yard, shook off their slumbers. Gradually the light advanced, and a new day began.

But there lay poor Stephens, the victim of what he had seen and heard in the old church, and he was doomed to lie some time longer yet.

There was a Mr. Anthony Dorey, who was parish beadle, and he had awakened, and heard the sound of the tolling of the well-known bell.

"I say, mother Dorey," he had said to better half, "what's that?"

"How should I know, idiot," was the polite rejoinder.

"Oh, very good."

"You had better get up and see."

"Oh dear no. It's no business of mine; Master Wiggins is bell-ringer; I dare say it's something though."

This was a wise conclusion for the beadle to come to, and he turned to go to sleep again, which was wise likewise, only more easy in the conception than in the execution, for his mind was more disturbed than he had though it possible anything could disturb it, by the tolling of the bell.

Whenever he found himself just going off to sleep, he jumped awake again quite wide, crying, —

"Eh! eh! Was that the bell?"

This sort of thing, varied by a great number of punches in the ribs from Mrs. Dorey, went on until the morning had sufficiently advanced to make it quite light enough to see objects with ordinary distinctness, and then, fancying that all his attempts to sleep would be futile, the vexed beadle rose.

"I can't sleep, that's a clear case," he said, "so I will go and see what the bell was tolled for at such an odd time of the night. The more I think of it, the more I don't know what to think."

Full of this resolution, he went post haste to Mr. Wiggins's and knocked loudly at his cottage door.

"Hillo! hillo! Wiggins."

"Well," said Wiggins, looking out of his bed-room window with his head picturesquely adorned by a red night-cap, "Well what's the matter now?"

"That's what I want to know. Why did you toll the bell in the middle of the night?"

"I toll the bell!"

"Yes, to be sure, I heard it."

"Yes, and I heard it too, but it was none of my tolling, and if I had not been rather indisposed, Mr. Dorey, I should have got up myself and seen what it was all about. As it is you find me cleaning myself rather early."

"I'll wait for you, then," said Dorey.

Wiggins soon made his appearance, and he and Dorey walked off together to the church, much pondering as they went, upon the mysterious circumstance that took them there, for if neither had rung the bell they could not think who had, for although the name of Will Stephens certainly occurred to them both, they thought it about one of the most unlikely things in the world that he would take the trouble to perform upon the great bell in the middle of the night, when it was none of his business to do so under any circumstances whatever.

"Nonsense," said the beadle; "I hardly ever knew him do a very civil thing."

"Nor I either, so you may depend, neighbor Dorey, it's not him."

"It's a great mystery, neighbor Wiggins. That's what it is, and nothing else."

"I hope it don't bode none of us no harm, that's all. Times are quite bad enough, without anything happening to make 'em worse."

This sentiment, as any grumbling one always is, was acceded to by the beadle, and so they went on conversing until they reached the church door; and then the surprise of finding the smaller entrance open struck them, and they stood staring at each other for some moments in profound silence.

"There's somebody here," said Wiggins at last.

"In course."

"What shall we do, Mr. Dorey? Do you think it's our duty to – to go in and see who it is, or – or run away? You know I ain't a constable, but you are, so perhaps it alters the case so far as you are concerned, you see."

"Not at all; you are a strong man, Mr. Wiggins, a very strong man; but suppose we try to make some one answer us. Here goes."

The beadle advanced close to the threshold of the door, and in as loud a tone of voice as he could command, he said, –

"Ahem! – ahem! – Hilloa, hilloa! – What are you at there? – Come, come, I'm down upon you."

"What do they say?" inquired Wiggins.

"Nothing at all."

"Then, perhaps, it's nobody."

"Well, do you know, if I thought that, I'd go in at once, like a roaring lion – I would – and show 'em who I was – ah!"

"So would I – so would I."

After listening for some short time longer, most intently, and hearing nothing, they came to the conclusion, that although some one had evidently been there, there was no one there now; so it would be quite safe to go into the church, always taking care to leave the door open, so that, in the event of any alarm, they could run away again, with all the precipitation in the world.

It certainly was not one of the most hazardous exploits in the whole history of chivalrous proceedings to enter a church in day-light, as it then was, in search of some one, who it was very doubtful was there. But to have seen the beadle and Mr. Wiggins, anybody would have thought them bound upon an enterprise of life or death, and the latter the most likely of the two, by a great deal.

"Ahem!" cried Mr. Dorey again; "we are two strong, bold fellows, and we have left our six companions – all six feet high, at the door – ahem!"

No effect was produced by this speech, which Mr. Dorey fully intended should strike terror into somebody, and after a few minutes search, they both felt convinced that there was no one hidden in the lower part of the church, and there was only the gallery to search.

And yet that was a ticklish job, for the nearer they approached the belfry, of course the nearer they approached the spot from whence the alarm had been given. It was therefore with rather a backwardness in going forward, that they both slowly proceeded up the staircase, and finally reached the gallery, where they saw no one; and much to their relief the want of any discovery was.

"It's all right," said the beadle. "There's nobody here. Oh, how I do wish the rascals had only stayed, that's all. I'd a shewn them what a beadle was — I'd a took 'em up in a twinkling — I would. Lord bless you, Mr. Wiggins, you don't know what a desperate man I am, when I'm put to it, that you don't."

"Perhaps not, but there don't seem to be any danger."

"Not the least. Eh? eh? — oh, the Lord have mercy upon us! I give in — what's that? — take my everything, but, oh! spare my life — oh! oh! oh!"

This panic of the beadle's was all owing to hearing somebody give a horrible groan — such a groan that it was really dreadful to hear it. Mr. Wiggins, too, was much alarmed, and leant upon the front rail of the gallery, looking dreadfully pale and wan. The beadle's face looked quite of a purple hue, and he shook in every limb.

"I — I thought I saw a groan," he said.

"So — so — did — I — oh, look — then don't you hear a horrible bundle up in that corner. Oh, mercy! I begin to think we are as good as dead men — that we are — oh, that we are. What will become of us? — what will become of us?"

By this time, Will Stephens, who, the reader is aware, was there to make the groan, had got up from the foot of the belfry-stairs, and he began to drag his bruised and stiffened frame towards the beadle and Mr. Wiggins, which they no sooner perceived than they set off as hard as they could scamper from the place, crying out for help, as if they had been pursued by a thousand devils.

In vain Stephens called after them; they did not hear his voice, nor did they stop in their headlong flight until they reached the door of the clergyman, concerning whose power to banish all evil spirits into the Red Sea, they had a strong belief, and as the reverend gentleman was at breakfast, the first thing they both did was to rush in, and upset the tea-tray which the servant had just brought in.

Chapter CXCVII.

THE CLERGYMAN'S VISIT TO THE VAULT. – RESCUE OF THE
SEXTON.

"*W*hat the devil! sounds!"

Yes; that was what the parson said. With all due respect for his cloth, we cannot help recording the fact that the words at the commencement of this chapter were precisely those that came from the lips of the reverend gentleman upon the occasion of the sudden and rather alarming irruption of the beadle and the bell-ringer into his breakfast parlor at the parsonage.

"We beg your pardon, sir," said the beadle, "but—"

"Yes, sir, we beg your pardon," add the bell-ringer, "but—"

"What?" cried the parson, as he looked at the remains of his breakfast lying upon the hearth-rug in most admired disorder at his feet.

"The bell, sir – the church – the gallery – a groan – a ghost – a lot of ghosts."

Such were the incoherent words that came, thick as hail, from the beadle and the bell-ringer. In vain the clergyman strove to get to the rights of the story. He was compelled to wait until they were both very nearly tired out, and then he said, –

"Very well, I don't understand, so you may both go away again."

"But, sir—"

"But, sir—"

"If one of you will speak while the other listens I will attend, and not otherwise. This is Sunday morning, and I neither can, nor will waste any more time upon you."

Nothing is so terrible to a professed story teller, and the beadle was something of that class, as to tell him you won't listen to him, so Mr. Dorey at once begged that Wiggins would either allow him to tell what had happened, or tell it properly himself. Mr. Wiggins gave way, and the beadle as diffusely as possible told the tale of the bell tolling, and the visit to the church, with the awful adventure that there occurred.

"What do you think of it, sir?" he concluded by asking.

"I have no opinion formed as yet," replied the clergyman, "but I will step down to the church now, and see."

"You'll take plenty o' people with you, sir."

"Oh dear no, I shall go alone. I don't gather from what you have said that there is any danger. Your own fears, too, I am inclined to think, have much exaggerated the whole affair. I dare say it will turn out, as most of such alarms usually do, some very simple affair indeed."

The parson took his hat, and walked away to the church as coolly as possible, leaving Mr. Dorey and Mr. Wiggins to stare at each other, and to wonder at a temerity they could not have thought it possible for any human being to have practiced.

But the clergyman was supported by a power of which they knew little — the power of knowledge, which enabled him at once in his own mind to divide the probable from the impossible, and therefore was it that he walked down to the church fully prepared to hear from somebody a very natural explanation of the mysterious bell-ringing in the night, which was the only circumstance that made him think that there was anything to explain, for he had heard that himself.

When he reached the sacred building, he found the door open, as the beadle and the bell-ringer had left it, and the moment he got into the body of the church, he heard a voice say, —

"Help! help! will nobody help me?"

"Yes," he replied, "of course, I will."

"Oh! thank Heaven!"

"Where are you." ?

"Here, sir, I think that's your voice, Mr. Bevan."

"Ah, and I think that's your voice, Will Stephens; I thought this would turn out some very ordinary piece of business, so you are up stairs; and did you ring the bell in the night?"

"I did, sir."

"Just so — come down then."

"I'm afraid I can't, sir, without some help. I have had a very bad fall, and although, thank God, no bones are broken, I am sadly shaken and bruised, so that it is with great pain, sir, I can crawl along, and as for getting down the stairs, why — I — I rather think I couldn't by myself, if there was a hundred pound note waiting for me below, just for the trouble of fetching, sir."

"Very well, I'm coming, don't move."

Mr. Bevan ascended the staircase, and without "a bit of pride," as Will Stephens said afterwards, in telling the story, helped the bruised sexton down the gallery steps to the body of the church, and then he made him sit down on one of the forms, and tell him all that had happened, which Will did from first to last, quite faithfully, not even omitting how he had stayed rather late at the ale-house, and how terrified he had been by the curious events that took place while he was in the church, ending by his fall from the stairs leading up to the belfry.

"Will, Will," said Mr. Bevan, "the ringing of the bell is good proof that you have been in the belfry, but you will scarcely expect me to believe the remainder of your dream."

"Dream, sir?"

"Yes, to be sure. You surely don't think now, in broad daylight, that it is anything else, do you?"

"I — I don't know, sir; of course, sir, if you say its a dream — why — why —"

"There, that will do. I will convince you that it was nothing more, or else you will go disturbing the whole neighborhood with this story, that it is quite a mercy, I have first heard."

"Convince me, sir?"

"Yes; come with me to the vault."

Will Stephens shrunk from this proposal and his fear was so manifest, that Mr. Bevan was, at all events, convinced that he had told him nothing but what he himself believed, and accordingly he felt still more anxious to rid Will of his nervous terror.

"You surely," he said, "cannot be timid, while I am with you. Come at once, and if you do not find that the late Miss Crofton, poor girl, is quiet enough in her coffin, I promise you upon my sacred word, that I will never cease investigating this affair, and bringing it to some conclusion. Come at once, before any curious persons arrive at the church."

So urgent a request from the clergyman of the parish to Will Stephens, the sexton of the parish, almost might be said to amount to a command, so Will did not see how he could get out of it, without confessing an amount of rank cowardice that even he shrunk from.

"Well, sir," he said, "of course with you I can have no objection."

"That's right. Come along; there are means of getting a light into the vestry; wait here a moment."

Will would not wait; he stuck close by Mr. Bevan, who went into the vestry, and soon procured a candle, lighted from materials he kept there under lock and key; and they went together to the vault, the stone of which was just as it had been left when Will emerged with so much fright.

"I will go first," said Mr. Bevan.

"Thank you, sir."

The clergyman descended, and Will Stephens followed, trembling, about two stairs behind him. Little did he expect when he emerged from that vault previous to his adventures in the church, that he should revisit it again so quickly. Indeed he had made a mental resolve that nothing should induce him to go down those stairs again, and yet there he was actually descending them.

So weak are the resolutions of mortals!

"Needs must," thought Will, "when the — parson, I mean, drives!"

"Come on, Will," said Mr. Bevan.

Will looked about him, but no coffin-lid was visible. There was Miss Crofton's coffin in its proper niche, with the lid on, and looking as calm and undisturbed as any respectable coffin could look. Will was amazed. He looked at the coffin, and he looked at the parson, and then he looked uncommonly foolish.

"Never mind it, Will," said Mr. Bevan, "never mind it, I say. The story need go no further. You can keep your own counsel if you like. You have come here under the influence of strong ale, and you have gone to sleep most likely in this very vault, and in your sleep, having a very vivid dream, you have walked up into the gallery, and thence into the belfry, where no doubt you did ring the bell under the influence of your dream; and then you fell down the belfry stairs, I believe, as you say you did."

"Ah!" said Will, "bless you, sir. It may be so, but —"

"You are not convinced."

"Not quite, sir,"

"Well, Will, you are quite right never to pretend to be convinced when you are not. I do not blame you for that, but in a short time, when the effect of the affair has worn off, you will entertain my opinion."

"I hope, sir, I may."

"That will do. Now the stone must be put over this vault."

"Sir, if you wouldn't mind, sir."

"What, Will?"

"Staying a moment or two, while I empty the bag of sawdust on the floor, sir, I shan't be a minute, no — not half a minute, and then I shall have done with the vault altogether I hope, sir."

"Very well."

Will set to work, and although at any other time he would have been rather ashamed of letting Mr. Bevan see what a wonderfully small quantity of sawdust made up a guinea's worth, superior considerations now prevailed, and he would not have spared the clergyman's company on any account.

"Now I've done, sir."

"Very well, follow me."

Will did not like to ask the clergyman to follow him, so in that difficulty, for as to his remaining behind it was out of the question, he made a rush and reached the church before Mr. Bevan could ascend two of the steps. When that gentleman did reach the church he made no remark about the precipitancy, and apparent disrespect of Will, for he put it down to its right cause, but he left the church in order to make the usual preparations for the morning service, which would now commence in an hour-and-a-half.

Will walked home with his empty bag, for the little exercise he had had sufficed to convince him that he was not so much hurt as he thought, and that the stiffness of his limbs would soon pass away.

"It's all very well," he said to himself, "for Mr. Bevan to talk about dreams, but if that was one, nothing real, has ever, happened to me yet, that's all."

Chapter CXCVIII.

THE YOUNG LOVER'S MIDNIGHT WATCH.

*D*id the clergyman really think what he said? Had he no suspicions, that after all there was a something more even than he was quite willing to admit in the story told by Will Stephens?

We shall see in good time, but at all events one thing is evident, that the parson thought it good sound policy, and it was, to endeavor to nip the thing in the head, and by ascribing it to a dream, put it down as a subject of speculation in the place.

He knew that nothing could be more dangerous than allowing any such story to pass current as a wonderful fact, and well he knew that in a short time, if such were the case, it would receive so many additions and so many embellishments, that the mischief it might produce upon the mind of an ignorant population might be extreme, and of a most regretful character indeed.

All this he felt hourly, ? and therefore Will Stephens' story was to be put down as a dream.

Now Mr. Bevan, it will be recollected, had urged Will to keep his own counsel, and to say nothing of the affair to any one, but he had faint hopes only that Will would do that, very faint hopes indeed, for after all he, Will, was the hero of the story, and there would be a something extremely gratifying in telling it, and in stating what he would have done, had not his foot slipped as he came down the narrow stairs from the old belfry, and so completely stunned him by the fall. Mr. Bevan therefore had very few if any compunctions in adopting the course he did, which was, in the evening, when there was no service at the church, to call at the Grange, to see Sir George Crofton upon the subject.

Mr. Bevan was always a welcome guest at the Grange, and he was on those intimate and good terms with the family, that he could always call whenever he pleased, so that a mere announcement of his presence by no means had the effect of preparing Sir George for any communication.

"Ah, Mr. Bevan," he said, when the clergyman entered the room, "I am glad to see you."

"And I to see you, Sir George."

"You come to a house of mourning, sir. But that will be the case here for a long, long time. Time may and will, no doubt, do much to assuage our grief, but the blow is as yet too recent."

Tears started to the eyes of Sir George Crofton, as he made this allusion to his daughter, and he turned his head aside to hide such evidences of emotion from the parson, from whom, however, he need have expected nothing but the most friendly sympathy that one human being could bestow upon another. Mr. Bevan was a man of refinement and consideration, and he let grief aways have its way, seldom doing more than merely throw out, in the form of a suggestion for consideration as it were, that death was not the great evil it was thought to be.

In such a way he generally succeeded in bring persons smarting under the infliction of the loss of dear friends and relations much sooner to proper sense of the subject, than if he had indulged in all the canting religious exhortations that some divines think applicable to such occasions.

Sir George Crofton was alone, for his two sons had gone for a stroll in the grounds. Ringwood who still remained with the family, was in the library, where now he passed most of his time, in trying by reading to withdraw his mind from a too painful and fixed contemplation of his loss.

He was still weak, but might be considered now quite convalescent.

"Pray be seated, Mr. Bevan," said Sir George. "Believe me, I take it very kindly of you to come so often."

"Pray dear sir, don't say another word about it — I — I am very sorry to feel myself obliged to allude to anything of an uncomfortable nature."

"Think nothing of doing so, my friend. Think nothing of it, I have a master grief which drowns all others."

"But it is concerning that master grief, sir, that I come to speak."

"Indeed!"

"Yes, sir, will you kindly hear me?"

"Certainly, certainly."

"You told me on the day following the melancholy death of your daughter, as a friend, the peculiar circumstances attendant upon that death. Now I do not mean to say that what I am going to relate to you has any connection at all with those circumstances, nor would I tell you what I come to tell at all, were I not fearful that the same story with some of the usual exaggerations of ignorance would reach you from other quarters, for it is not a matter consigned to my bosom only, or there it should remain."

"You alarm me."

"That I feared, but deeply regret. Listen to me, and remember always as you do so, that I think the whole affair is a mere dream — a disturbed slumberer's vision — nothing more."

Sir George Crofton did listen with breathless eagerness, and Mr. Bevan, without detracting anything or adding anything to the narrative of Will Stephens, told him the whole story just as Will had told it to him, concluding by saying, —

"That is all my dear sir, and I felt that my duty powerfully called upon me to be your informant upon the subject, simply that we might be forewarned against any coarse version of the story."

Sir George drew a long breath.

"More horrors! More horrors!"

"Nay, why should you say that?"

"Is it not so?"

"Nay I have already given my opinion, by saying, that I look upon the whole affair as but the phantasma of dream."

"Oh! Mr. Bevan, do not trifle with me. Is that really and truly your opinion, sir, or only said from kindness to me."

"It is the best opinion that I can come to."

"I thank you, sir; I thank you. Clara, Clara, my child, my child!"

The old man was overcome with grief, and at the interesting moment, Ringwood entered the room, with a book in his hand. He was astonished, as well he might be to see such a fearful relapse of grief on the part of Sir George Crofton, and he looked from him to Mr. Bevan, and from Mr. Bevan to him, for some few moments in silence, and then he said, —

"Surely all here have suffered enough, and there is no new calamity come upon this house."

"Tell him all," cried Sir George; "tell him all. It is fit that he should know; he is one of us now, he loved my child, and loves her memory still. I pray you, Mr. Bevan, to tell all to Ringwood, for I have not the heart to do so."

"I wonder," said Ringwood, calmly, "to hear you speak thus. I wonder to see that any new grief can come so near to that which we have already suffered. The image of my lost one fills up each crevice of my heart. I shall listen to you Mr. Bevan with respect, but my grief, I fear is selfish, and cannot feel more than its own miseries."

Ringwood seemed to imagine that what the parson had to say referred to something with which Clara had nothing to do; but when, as the story proceeded, he found how intimately connected she was with the affair, his cheek flushed for a moment, and then grew of a death-like paleness, and he sat trembling and looking in the face of Mr. Bevan, as he proceeded with his most strange relation.

When he had concluded Ringwood gave a deep groan.

"You are much affected, sir," said Mr. Bevan.

"Crushed! crushed!" was the reply. "Oh God!"

"Nay now this is not manly, sir, you feel this thing too much; if you are so crushed how can any one expect that from you is to proceed the necessary exertion to prove that the story in all its particulars is but a falsehood?"

Ringwood caught at this idea in a moment.

"Exertion from me?" he said. "What exertions would I not make to prove such a horror to be but a creation of the fancy? What would I not do! What would I not suffer? You have warned me, sir. Yes, I have a duty to do — a duty to Clara's memory; a duty to you Sir George, and a duty to myself, for did I not love her, and does not her gentle image still sit in my inmost heart enshrined? I will prove that this most monstrous story is a delusion. Bear with me, gentlemen, I must think. Tomorrow you shall know more, but not until tomorrow."

He rose, and left the room.

"What does he mean," said Sir George, vacantly.

"I cannot tell you, sir; but wait until tomorrow. Perhaps by then he may have proposed some plan of action, that you or I may not think of. You will use your own discretion, about communicating the strange affair to your sons or not, sir. Upon such a point as family confidence, I never venture an opinion. Allow me to call upon you tomorrow morning, sir, when I hope to find you in better spirits."

The clergyman would not have been in such haste to leave Sir George; but as he saw Ringwood leave the room; that young man made a sign to him, that he wished to see him before he left, and accordingly Mr. Bevan was anxious to know what it was he had to say to him.

When he left Sir George, he asked a servant where Mr. Ringwood was, and being told he was in the library, Mr. Bevan, being quite familiar with the house, followed him there at once, and found him pacing that apartment in great agitation, and with disordered steps.

"Thank heaven you have come, sir," cried Ringwood, "tell me, oh, tell me, what would you advise me to do, Mr. Bevan."

"I think," replied the clergyman, "you have already half decided upon a course."

"I have, I have."

"Then follow it, if it be such a one as in its result will produce a conviction of the truth. Do not, Mr. Ringwood, allow anything to turn you aside from a course which you feel to be right; you will always find strength enough to persevere if you have that strong conviction upon your What is your plan?"

"It is this night to watch in the church?"

"Be it so; I will, if you like, keep watch with you."

"Oh, no, no! let me be alone. All I ask of you, sir, is to provide me with the means of getting into the sacred edifice at midnight."

"That I will do. You shall have a private key that I have for my own use; you can let yourself in without any one knowing of your presence. But do you think you have nerve enough to go alone? if you have the smallest doubt or hesitation, let me accompany you."

"No, no — I thank you, but let me go alone, and say nothing of this to Sir George. I had it in my mind when I told him I would speak to him tomorrow about what you had communicated. I would fain, if these horrors be really true, keep him in ignorance that I have verified them. But if I keep my night watch quite undisturbed, then he shall have the satisfaction of knowing that it has been so kept.

"You are right in that; I will send the key to you in the course of another hour and remember I am at your service if you should alter your mind, and wish for company. Do not hesitate about disturbing my rest."

Chapter *CXCIX*.

THE HORRORS OF THE GRAVE. – A FRIGHTFUL ADVENTURE.

*O*ne would have thought that young Ringwood might with effect and with discretion have disclosed his plan of watching in the old church to one of the brothers of Clara, but he shrunk from doing that.

In the first place he thought he should be put down as a visionary, and as one who was disposed to insult the memory of Clara by imagining that the story of the sexton could be true, and in the second place, if anything did happen, he was afraid that the feelings of the brother might clash with his.

"No," he said, "I will go alone – I will not rest again until I have thoroughly satisfied myself that this tale is but a fabrication of the fancy. Oh, Clara! can it be possible – no, no. The thought is by far too – too horrible."

It may really be considered a fortunate thing that the communication of the clergyman was made in the evening, for had it been earlier in the day, the hours of frightful anxiety which Ringwood would have endured until the night came must have been most painful.

As it was, however, the hours that would elapse ere he could venture to go to the church on his strange and melancholy errand were not many, and they passed the more quickly, that during some of them, he was making up his mind as to what he should do.

"Yes, Clara, my best beloved Clara," he said, "I will rescue your sweet memory from this horrible doubt that is cast upon it, or I will join you in the tomb. Welcome, a thousand times welcome death, rather than that I should live to think that you are – God, no – no! I cannot pronounce the dreadful word. Oh, what evil times are these, and what a world of agony do I endure. But courage, courage; let fancy sleep, I must not allow my imagination to become sufficiently excited to play me any pranks tonight. Be still my heart, and let me go upon this expedition as a spectator merely. Time enough will it be to become an actor, when I know more, if indeed there be more to know."

The clergyman sent the key, according to his promise, by a confidential servant, who had orders to ask for Mr. Ringwood and to give it into his own hands, so that the young man was fully prepared to go, when the proper time should arrive for him to start upon his expedition.

He purposely kept very much out of the way of Sir George Crofton and his two sons during the remainder of the evening, for such was the ingenuous nature of young Ringwood, and so unused was he to place any curb upon his speech, that he dreaded letting slip some information regarding his intention to keep watch in the old church that night; in such a case it would have been difficult to refuse company.

Sir George took the advice of the clergyman and said nothing to any one of the dreadful communication that had been made to him. But he could not conceal from the family and his servants, that some unusual grief was preying upon him, beyond even the sadness that had remained after the death of his daughter. He retired to rest unusually early, that he might escape their curious and inquiring glances.

The clock struck eleven.

"It is time," said Ringwood, as he sprung from his seat in his bed-room. "It is time. For the love of thee, my Clara, I go to brave this adventure, Mine are you in death as in life. My heart is widowed, and can know no other love."

He armed himself with a pair of loaded pistols, for he made up his mind that if any trickery was at the bottom of the proceeding, the authors of such a jest should pay dearly for their temerity, and then cautiously descending from his bed-room, he crossed the dining-room, and passing through a conservatory, easily made his way out of the house, and into a flower-garden that was beyond.

He thought that if he went out of the grounds by the way of the porter's lodge, it might excite some remark, his not returning again, so he went to a part of the wall which he knew was low and rugged.

"There," he said, "I can easily climb over, and by getting into the meadows make my way into the road."

This, to a young man, was not by any means a difficult matter, and he in a few minutes more found himself quite free of the house and grounds, and making his way very rapidly towards the church, the tower of which, he could just see.

The night was again a cloudy one; although nothing had as yet fallen, the wind was uncertain, and no one could with any safety have ventured to predict whether it would be fair, or rain. Of the two, certainly, Ringwood would have preferred moonlight, for he wished in the church to be able to see well about him, without thinking of the necessity of a light.

"No," he said, as he pursued his way, "I must have no light; that would ruin all."

By the time he reached the church, he had a better opinion of the weather, and from a faint sort of halo that was in the sky, he was led to believe that the moon's light would soon be visible, and enable him to see everything that might take place.

The key that the parson had given him opened the same little door by which Will Stephens, the sexton, had entered, and there was no difficulty in turning the lock, for it was frequently used.

The young man paused for a moment, debating with himself, whether he should fasten the door securely on the inner side, or leave it open, and at last he thought, that considering all things, the latter was the best course to pursue."

"I do not wish," he said, "to stop any proceedings, so much as I wish to see what they are. There shall therefore be every facility for any one coming into the church, who may chance to have an intention so to do."

He still, it will be seen, clung a little to the hope that it was a trick.

When he pushed open the door that was covered with green baize, he found that in consequence of the cloth curtain being entirely drawn aside from before the south window, that there was not near the amount of darkness within the building that he had anticipated finding there.

When his eyes got a little accustomed to it, he could even see, dimly to be sure, but still, sufficiently to distinguish the several shapes of the well-known objects in the church. The pulpit, the communion table, the little rails before it, and some of the old monuments against the walls.

The stone slab that covered the opening to the vault of the Crofton family, had been before the commencement of the morning service properly secured, so that that entrance could be walked over with perfect safety, and Ringwood carefully ascertained that such was the fact.

"Surely, surely," he said, "it is as Mr. Bevan says. That man must have come here half stupefied by ale, and have gone to sleep, The only thing that gives the slightest semblance to such a tale, is the adventure of that most mysterious man who was reclaimed from the sea."

Yes, Ringwood was right. That was the circumstance, full of dread and awful mystery as it was, which sufficed to make anything else probable, and possible.

And what had become of him? Since the time when he made his escape from the Grange, nothing had been seen or heard of him unless that were he indeed, who was in the church pointing to the moonlight when the terrified Will Stephens was there.

And yet Stephens, although he might be supposed to be in a position to know him, did not recognize him, for we do not find in his account of the affair that he made any mention of him, or insinuated any opinion even, that the Mr. Smith of the bone-house, was the same person who had played so strange a part in the church.

The reader will have his own opinion.

"Where shall I bestow myself," thought Ringwood, "I ought to be somewhere from whence I can get a good view of the whole church."

After some little consideration, and looking about him as well as the semi-darkness would permit him, he thought that he could not by any possibility do better than get into the pulpit. From there he could readily turn about in any direction from whence any noise might proceed, at the same time, that it was something like a position which could not be very well attacked except with fire arms, and if such weapons were used against him, he should have the great advantage of seeing who was his assailant.

Accordingly he ascended the pulpit stairs, and soon ensconced himself in that elevated place.

There was something very awful, and solemn, and yet beautiful about the faint view he got of the old conventicle-looking church from its pulpit, and irresistible had he chosen to resist it, there came to his lips a prayer to Heaven for its aid, its protection, and its blessing upon his enterprise.

How much calmer, and happier he felt after that. How true it is, as Prospero says, that prayer,

— "Pierces so that it assaults
Mercy itself, and frees all faults."

Who is there in the wide world who has not felt the benign influence of an appeal to the great Creator of all things, under circumstances of difficulty, and of distress. Let us pity the heart, if there be such a one in existence, that is callous to such a feeling.

But there are none. A reliance upon divine mercy is one of the attributes of humanity, and may not be turned aside, by even all the wickedness and the infidelity that may be arrayed against it.

"All is still," murmured Ringwood. "The stillness of the very grave is here, Oh, my Clara; methinks without a pang of mortal fear, I could converse in such an hour as this, with thy pure and unsullied spirit!"

In the enthusiasm of the moment, no doubt, Ringwood could have done so, and it is a wonder that his most excited imagination did not conjure up some apparent semblance of the being whom he loved so devotedly, and whose image he so fondly cherished, even although she had gone from him.

"Yes, my Clara," he cried, in tones of enthusiasm. "Come to me, come to me, and you will not find that in life or in death the heart that is all your own, will shrink from you!"

This species of mental exaltation was sure soon to pass away, and it did so. The sound of his own voice convinced him of the impropriety of such speeches, when he came there as an observer.

"Hush! hush!" he said. "Be still, be still."

It was evident to him that many clouds were careering over face of the moon, for at times the church would get very dark indeed, and everything assumed a pitchy blackness, and then again a soft kind of light would steal in, and give the whole place a different aspect.

This continued for a long time, as he thought, and more than once he tried to ascertain the progress of the hours by looking at his watch, but the dim light baffled him.

"How long have I been here?" he asked himself; "I must not measure the time by my feelings, else I should call it an age."

At that moment the old church clock began to chime, and having proclaimed the four quarters past eleven, it with its deep-toned solemn bell struck the hour of twelve — Ringwood carefully counted the strokes, so that, although it was too dark to see his watch, he could not be deceived.

Chapter CC.

THE MIDNIGHT HOUR. – THE STONE SLAB. – THE VAMPIRE.

Yes, it was twelve o'clock, that mysterious hour at which it is believed by many that

"Graves give up their dead,
And many a ghost in church-yard decay,
Rise from their cold, cold bed
To make night horrible with wild vagary." Twelve, that hour when all that is human feels a sort of irksome dread, as if the spirits of those who

have gone from the great world were too near, loading the still night air with the murky vapors of the grave. A chilliness came over Ringwood and he fancied a strange kind of light was in the church, making objects more visible than in their dim and dusky outlines they had been before.

"Why do I tremble?" he said, "why do I tremble? Clouds pass away from before the moon, that is all. Soon there may be a bright light here, and lo, all is still; I hear nothing but my own breathing; I see nothing but what is common and natural. Thank heaven, all will pass away in quiet. There will be no horror to recount — no terrific sight to chill my blood. Rest Clara, rest in Heaven."

Ten minutes passed away, and there was no alarm; how wonderfully relieved was Ringwood. Tears came to his eyes, but there were the natural tears of regret, such as he had shed before for her who had gone from him to the tomb, and left no trace behind, but in the hearts of those who loved her.

"Yes," he said, mournfully "she has gone from me, but I love her still. Still does the fond remembrance of all that she was to me, linger at my heart. She is my own, my beautiful Clara, as she ever was, and as, while life remains, to me she ever will be."

At the moment that he uttered these words a slight noise met his ears.

In an instant he sprung to his feet in the pulpit, and looked anxiously around him.

"What was that?" he said. "What was that?"

All was still again, and he was upon the point of convincing himself, that the noise was either some accidental one, or the creation of his own fancy, when it came again.

He had no doubt this time. It was a perceptible, scraping, strange sort of sound, and he turned his whole attention to the direction from whence it came. With a cold creeping chill through his frame, he saw that that direction was the one where was the family vault of the Croftons, the last home of her whom he held still in remembrance, and whose memory was so dear to him.

He felt the perspiration standing upon his brow, and if the whole world had been the recompense to him for moving away from where he was he could not have done so. All he could do was to gaze with bated breath, and distended eyes upon the aisle of the church from whence the sound came.

That something of a terrific nature was now about to exhibit itself, and that the night would not go off without some terrible and signifi-cant adventure to make it remembered he felt convinced. All he dreaded was to think for a moment what it might be.

His thoughts ran on Clara, and he murmured forth in the most agonizing accents, —

"Anything — any sight but the sight of her. Oh, no, no, no!"

But it was not altogether the sight of her that he dreaded; oh no, it was the fact that the sight of her on such an occasion would bring the horrible conviction with it, that there was some truth in the dreadful apprehension that he had of the new state of things that had ensued regarding the after death condition of that fair girl.

The noise increased each moment, and finally there was a sudden crash.

"She comes! she comes!" gasped Ringwood.

He grasped the front of the pulpit with a frantic violence, and then slowly and solemnly there crossed his excited vision a figure all clothed in white. Yes, white flowing vestments, and he knew by their fashion that they were not worn by the living, and that it was some inhabitant of the tomb that he now looked upon.

He did not see the face. No, that for a time was hidden from him, but his heart told him who it was. Yes, it was his Clara.

It was no dream. It was no vision of a too excited fancy, for until those palpable sounds, and that most fearfully palpable form crossed his sight, he was rather inclined to go the other way, and to fancy what the sexton had reported was nothing but a delusion of his overwrought brain. Oh, that he could but for one brief moment have found himself deceived.

"Speak!" he gasped; "speak! speak!"

There was no reply.

"I conjure you, I pray you though the sound of your voice should hurl me to perdition — I implore you, speak."

All was silent, and the figure in white moved on slowly but surely towards the door of the church, but ere it passed out, it turned for a moment, as if for the very purpose of removing from the mind of Ringwood any lingering doubt as to its identity.

He then saw the face, oh, so well-known, but so pale. It was Clara Crofton!

"'Tis she! 'tis she!" was all he could say.

It seemed, too, as if some crevice in the clouds had opened at the moment, in order that he should with an absolute certainty see the countenance of that solemn figure, and then all was more than usually silent again. The door closed, and the figure was gone.

He rose in the pulpit, and clasped his hands. Irresolution seemed for a few moments to sway him to and fro, and then he rushed down into the body of the church.

"I'll follow it," he cried, "though it lead me to perdition. Yes, I'll follow it."

He made his way to the door, and even as he went he shouted, —
"Clara! Clara! Clara!"

He reached the threshold of the ancient church; he gazed around him

distractedly, for he thought that he had lost all sight of the figure. No
— no, even in the darkness and against the night sky, he saw it once
again in its sad-looking death raiments. He dashed forward.

The moonbeams at this instant being freed from some dense clouds
that had interposed between them and this world, burst forth with
resplendent beauty.

There was not a tree, a shrub, nor a flower, but what was made distinct
and manifest, and with the church, such was the almost unprecedented
luster of the beautiful planet, that even the inscriptions upon the old
tablets and tombs were distinctly visible.

Such a refulgence lasted not many minutes, but while it did, it was
most beautiful, and the gloom that followed it seemed doubly black.

"Stay, stay," he shouted, "yet a moment, Clara; I swear that what you
are, that will I be. Take me over to the tomb with you, say but that it is
your dwelling-place, and I will make it mine, and declare it a very palace
of the affections."

The figure glided on.

It was in vain that he tried to keep up with it. It threaded the
churchyard among the ancient tombs, with a gliding speed that soon
distanced him, impeded, as he continually was, by some obstacle or
another, owing to looking at the apparition he followed, instead of the
ground before him.

Still, on he went, heedless whether he was conveyed, for he might be
said to be dragged onward, so much were all his faculties both of mind
and body intent upon following the apparition of his beloved.

Once, and once only, the figure passed, and seemed to be aware that
it was followed for it flitted round an angle made by one of the walls
of the church, and disappeared from his eyes.

In another moment he had turned the same point.

"Clara, Clara!" he shouted. "'Tis I — you know my voice, Clara,
Clara."

She was not to be seen, and then the idea struck him that she must
have re-entered the church, and he too, turned, and crossed the threshold. He lingered there for a moment or two, and the whole building
echoed to the name of Clara, as with romantic eagerness, he called upon
her by name to come forth to him.

Those echoes were the only reply.

Maddened — rendered desperate beyond all endurance, he went some
distance into the building in search of her, and again he called.

It was in vain; she had eluded him, and with all the carefulness and
all the energy and courage he had brought to bear upon that night's
proceedings, he was foiled. Could anything be more agonizing than this
to such a man as Ringwood — he who loved her so, that he had not
shrunk from her, even in death, although she had so shrunk from him.

I will find her — I will question her," he cried. "She shall not escape me; living or dead, she shall be mine. I will wait for her, even in the tomb."

Before he carried out the intention of going actually into the vault to await her return, he thought he would take one more glance at the churchyard with the hope of seeing her there, as he could observe no indications of her presence in the church.

With this view he proceeded to the door, and emerged into the dim light. He called upon her again by name, and he thought he heard some faint sound in the church behind him. To turn and make a rush into the building was the work of a moment.

He saw something — it was black instead of white — a tall figure — it advanced towards him, and with great force, before he was aware that an attack was at all intended, it felled him to the ground.

The blow was so sudden, so unexpected, and so severe, that it struck him down in a moment before he could be aware of it. To be sure, he had arms with him, but the anxiety and agony of mind he endured that night, since seeing the apparition come from the tomb had caused him to forget them.

Chapter CCI.

THE YOUNG GIRL IN THE VILLAGE, AND THE AWFUL VISIT.

*I*t is now necessary that we draw the reader's attention to a humbler place of residence than the Grange, with its spacious chambers and lordly halls.

Situated not very far from the church, and almost close to the churchyard, upon which its little garden abutted, was a cottage, the picture of rural neatness and beauty. In the winter it was beautiful and picturesque, but in the summer time, when its porch was overrun with the woodbine and the sweet clematis, it was one of the sweetest of abodes that content and happiness could ever live in.

This cottage was inhabited by an old woman and her only child, a young girl of sixteen, beautiful as a rose, and as guileless as an angel. They contrived to live upon a small annuity that the mother had from a family in whose service she spent the best years of her life, and who, with a generosity that would be well to be abundantly and extensively imitated, would not see their old dependant want.

These two innocent and blameless persons had retired to rest at nine o'clock, their usual hour, and had slept the calm sleep of contentment until about half-past one, when the mother was awakened by a loud and piercing shriek from her daughter's chamber.

To spring from her humble couch was the work of a moment.

"Anna, Anna! my child, Anna!" she shrieked.

As she did so, she rushed across the small stair landing which separated the two, and the only two upper rooms of the cottage, and was about to enter her daughter's room, when the door of it was opened from within, and the old dame's heart died within her, as she saw a figure upon the threshold, attired in the vestments of the grave, and opposing her entrance.

Was it a dream, or did she really see such a sight?

Aghast and trembling the mother stood, unable for a moment or two to speak, and as she fell fainting upon the landing, she thought that something passed her, but she could not be quite sure, as it was at the instant her faculties were flitting from her.

How long she lay in that seeming death she knew not, and when she recovered, it was some few minutes before recollection came back to her, and she really remembered what had so completely overpowered her.

But when her reason did resume its sway, and she recollected that it was some danger to Anna, which had first alarmed her, she called her loudly by her name.

"Anna, Anna, speak to me."

"Mother, mother," replied the young girl. "Oh, come to me."

These words supplied strength to the old woman, and rising she made her way immediately into the chamber of her daughter, whom she found in an agony of fear; a light was procured, and then Anna flung herself upon her mother's neck, and wept abundantly.

"Oh, mother, tell me, convince me that it was only a dream."

"What, my child? oh what?"

The girl trembled so much that it was only by the utmost persuasion that the following account was got from her, of the cause of her fright.

She said that she had gone to sleep as usual within a very few minutes after going to bed, that she enjoyed a calm, and uninterrupted slumber, the duration of which she had no means whatever of guessing, but she was partially awakened by a noise at the window of her room.

She instantly rose and stood looking at the window, on which a sort of shadow seemed to pass without, which alarmed her exceedingly.

Still as it did not come gain, and as she certainly had not been fully awake when she sprung from her bed, she had thought it quite possible that all might be a dream, and had forborne from making any alarm upon the subject.

After some hesitation she had persuaded herself to go to bed again, and when there, although she sometimes started awake fancying she heard something, she at length yielded to sleep, and again slept, soundly for a time, until a new circumstance awakened her.

She thought she felt something touching her about the neck, and after opening her eyes, the moonlight, which at that moment happened to be very bright, disclosed to her a white figure standing by the side of her bed, the face of which figure was leaning over her, and within a very few inches of her own.

Terror at first deprived her of all power of speech or motion, but as the figure did not move, she at length gave utterance to her fears in that shriek which had come from her lips, and so much alarmed the mother.

This was all the young girl could say, with the exception that the figure when she shrieked appeared to glide away, but where to she had no means of telling, for some clouds at that moment came again over the face of the moon.

The mother was much affected and terrified, and at first she thought of calling up her neighbors, but at length as the night was considerably advanced, and the intruder gone, they agreed to let the matter rest till morning, and the mother retired to her room again.

How long it was before the shriek form her daughter's room came again she did not know, but come again it did.

Yes, again came the dreadful shriek. It was — it could be no delusion now — and the mother once more sprung from her couch to rush to the rescue of her child.

Confused and bewildered, she darted onward to the chamber, but the door was fast, nor could all her exertions suffice to open it.

"Anna, Anna!" she shouted, "speak to me. One word only, my child, my child."

All was still. The trembling mother placed her ear to the door, and she heard a strange sucking sound, as if an animal was drinking with labor and difficulty. Her head seemed to be on fire, and her senses were upon the point of leaving her, but she did manage to reach her own room. She flew to the little casement — she dashed it open.

"Help! help! help! — for the love of God, help!"

There was no reply.

Again she raised her voice in shrieking wild accents.

"Help! — murder! — help!"

"What is it?" shouted a man's voice. It was one who was going some distance to take in his fishing nets.

"Oh! thank God, some human being hears me. Come in, come in."

"How am I to get in?"

"Stay a moment, and I will come down and open the cottage door for you. For the love of mercy do not go away."

Trembling and terrified to a dreadful excess, the old woman went down stairs and let the man into the cottage, when they both proceeded up to the chamber of the daughter.

"What do you suppose is the matter?" asked the fisherman.

"Oh! I know not — I know not; but twice tonight — twice has this dreadful alarm happened. Do not leave us — oh, do not."

"I don't want;' but I should hardly think thieves would find it worth their while to come here at all for what they would get. You must have been dreaming."

"Oh, that I could think so!"

Anna's chamber was reached; and there, to the horror of the mother, she was found lying perfectly insensible on her bed, with a quantity of blood smeared about her neck.

"Why, it's a murder!" cried the fisherman; and firmly impressed with such a belief, he ran out of the house to spread an alarm.

The window of the chamber was wide open, and from that the mother now cried aloud for help; so that between her and the fisherman, such a disturbance was made all over the neighborhood, that they were soon likely to have more assistance than could be useful.

The people living the nearest were soon roused, and they roused others, while the distracted woman, who believed Anna was dead, called for justice and for vengeance.

The alarm spread from house to house — from cottage to hall — and, in the course of half-an-hour, most of the inhabitants of the village had risen to hear the old dame's account of the horrible proceeding that had taken place that night in the cottage.

Exaggeration was out of the question. The fact itself was more than sufficient to induce the greatest amount of horror in the minds of all who heard it, and there was one, and only one, whose information enabled him to give a name to the apparition that had assaulted Anna. That one was the schoolmaster of the place, and he, after hearing the story, said, —

"If one could persuade oneself at all of the existence of such horrors, one would suppose that a vampire had visited the cottage."

This was a theme that was likely to be popular. The schoolmaster foolishly gave way to the vanity, and explained what a vampire was — or was supposed and said to be; and soon the whole place was in a state of the most indescribable alarm upon the subject.

As yet the horrible news had not reached the Grange, but it was destined soon to do so; and better would it have been that any one had at once plunged a dagger in the heart of poor Sir George Crofton than that there should be thought to be such a horrible confirmation of his worst fears.

To be sure, his daughter was not named, but he received the news with a scream of anguish, and fell insensible into the arms of his son.

All was confusion. The servants ran hither and thither, not knowing what to do, and it was not until Mr. Bevan arrived that something like order was restored. He as a privileged friend assumed for the nonce a kind of dictatorship at the Grange, and gave orders, which were cheerfully and promptly obeyed. Then he desired a strictly private interview with Sir George.

It was, or course, granted to him; but the old baronet begged that Charles and Edwin might now know all. It was Emma alone from whom he wished to keep the awful truth.

Chapter CCII.

THE AWFUL SUPPOSITION – A RESOLUTION.

*I*t was with some reluctance that the clergyman spoke.

"Sir," he said to the old baronet, "and you, my young gentleman, I am afraid – very much afraid, that I am doing anything but right in countenancing a supposition so utterly at variance with all my own notions and feelings; but my abhorrence of a secret impels me to speak."

"Say on, sir – say on," cried Sir George. "Perhaps we are better prepared to hear what you have to tell, than you imagine."

After this Mr. Bevan had less reluctance to speak, he said, –

"I was aware, although you all were not, that Mr. Ringwood intended to keep watch last night in the church, in order to test the truth of what had been told by Will Stephens, the sexton. I did all I could to persuade him from making the attempt, but when I found that nothing else would satisfy him, I thought it prudent to give him the means of carrying out what had become such a fixed intention with him, that to oppose it was to do far more mischief than to grant it all the aid I had in my power to do."

Sir George gave a nod of assent.

"He went there," continued Mr. Bevan, "with a private key of my own, and took his place in the church."

"I wish, sir, you had been with him," said Edwin.

"Yes," added Charles. "If you, with your cool, calm, unbiased judgment had been there, we should have been much better able to come to a correct conclusion about what occurred; for that something did occur, or was supposed by Ringwood to do so, we can well guess."

"I wish, indeed, I had been there," said Mr. Bevan, "but he begged so earnestly to be allowed to go alone, that I had not the heart to refuse him."

"And what happened, sir?"

"I will tell you. I gave him a key which admitted him to the church, by the small private entrance, at which I usually go in myself; in fact, it was my own private key, for I at times visit the church, and wish to do so, when I am not expected by those who have the ordinary charge of it."

"We have heard as much."

"No doubt. Well, then, I say I gave him that key, but it was my sympathy with his evident distress rather than my judgment which consented to do so, and I had hardly done it, when I began to busy myself with conjectures, and to deeply regret that I had yielded to him so easily. 'What if he, in his excited and grief-stricken state of mind, should come to some serious mischief?' I said to myself, 'should not I be very much to blame? Would not all prudent persons say that I did very wrong to send a man in such a condition of mind into a church at midnight, alone?'"

"Your motives and your known character, sir, would protect you," said Charles.

"I hope so," continued Mr. Bevan. "I think it would from all other charges, but imprudence; and if any great mischance had befallen Ringwood, I should not so readily have forgiven myself, as others might have been induced to forgive me."

"I understand that feeling," said Sir George.

"Well, then, with such sensations tugging at my heart, no wonder I could not rest, and so at a little after twelve, I rose, and hastily dressing myself, I left my house as noiselessly as possible, and made my way towards the church. The moon's light was at that time obscured, but every spot was so familiar to me, that I was able to go with speed, and

I soon reached the venerable building. I walked round it, until I came to the door, the key of which I had given to Mr. Ringwood; it was open, but the moment I crossed the threshold, I stumbled on his insensible form."

"Go on! go on! He had seen something terrible," gasped Sir George; "I am nerved, I think, for the very worst; I pray you, sir, go on, and tell me all."

"I will, Sir George, because I feel convinced it is my duty to conceal nothing in this transaction, and because I think you had better more calmly and dispassionately, and without exaggeration, hear from me all that is to be told."

"That is a good reason, sir," said Edwin. "We should, of course, hear all from other sources, and probably, with all the aids that a feeling for the marvelous could append to it."

"That is my impression. When, then, I stumbled over a person lying just within the little private door of the church, I had no immediate means of knowing who it was; I tell you it was Ringwood, because I afterwards discovered as much. I had the means of getting a light; when I did so, I found Ringwood lying in a swoon, while at the same time, I could not but notice a large bruise upon his forehead.

"Of course, my first duty was to look after him, instead of troubling myself about his assailant, and having placed him in as convenient a posture as I could, I hurried home again, and roused up my servants. With their assistance I got him to my house, and placed him in bed."

"And did you search the church, sir?"

"I did. I went back and searched it thoroughly, but found nothing at all suspicious. Everything was in its right place, and I could not account for the affair at all, because of the wound that Ringwood had. I was most anxious to hear from him that he had had a fall."

"But — but," said Sir George, falteringly, "he told a different story."

"He did."

"A story which you will not keep from us."

"I do not feel myself justified, as I have said, in keeping it from you. this is it."

The clergyman then related to the family of the Croftons what is already known to the reader concerning the adventures of Ringwood in the old church, and which that morning, upon his recovery, Ringwood had told to him most circumstantially.

We need scarcely say that this recital was listened to with the most agonized feelings. Poor Sir George appeared to be most completely overcome by it. He trembled excessively, and could not command himself sufficiently to speak.

The two brothers looked at each other in dismay.

"Now, I pray you all to consider this matter more calmly," said Mr.

Bevan, "than you seem inclined to do."

"Calmly," gasped Sir George, "calmly."

"Yes — what evidence have we after all that the whole affair is anything more than a dream of Mr. Ringwood's?"

"Does he doubt it?"

"No — I am bound to tell you that he does not; but we may well do so for all that. He is the last person who is likely to give in to the opinion that it is a mere vision, so strangely impressed as it is upon his imagination. Recollect always that he went to the church prepared to see something."

"Oh, if we could but think it unreal," said Sir George, glancing at his sons, as if to gather their opinions of the matter from their countenances.

"I will cling to such a thought," said Charles, "until I am convinced otherwise through the medium of my own senses."

"And I," said Edwin.

"You are right," added Mr. Bevan, "I never in the whole course of my experience heard of anything of which people should be so slow of believing in, as this most uncomfortable affair. You now know all, and it is for yourselves, of course, to make whatever determination you think fit. If I might advise, it would be that you all take a short tour, perhaps on the continent for a time."

"Mr. Bevan," said Sir George, in a kindly tone, "I am greatly obliged to you. The suggestion I know springs from the very best and friendly motives; but it carries with it a strong presumption that you really do think there is something in all this affair which it would be as well to have settled in my absence."

The clergyman could not deny but that some such feeling was at the bottom of his advice; but still he would not admit that he was at all convinced of the reality of what was presumed to have happened, and a short pause in the conversation ensued, after which Sir George spoke with a solemn air of determination, saying to his sons, as well as to his friend and pastor, Mr. Bevan,

"When I tell you that I have made a determination from which nothing but the hand of heaven visiting me with death shall move me, I hope no one here will try to dissuade me from carrying it out."

After such an exordium it was a difficult thing to say anything to him, so he continued, —

"My child was dear — very dear to me in life, and I have no superstitious fears concerning one who held such a place in my affections. I am resolved that tonight I will watch her poor remains, and at once convince myself of a horror that may drive me mad or take a mountain of grief and apprehension off my heart."

"Father," cried Charles, "you will allow me to accompany you."

"And me," added Edwin.

"My sons, you are both deeply interested in this matter — you would be miserable while I was gone if you were not with me. Moreover, I will not trust my own imagination entirely — we will all three go, and then we cannot be deceived. This is my most solemn resolution."

"I have only one thing to say regarding it," said Mr. Bevan, "that is, to prefer an earnest request that you will allow me to be one of the party — you shall sit in a pew of the church, that shall command a view of the whole building."

"Accompany us, Mr. Bevan, if you will," said Sir George, "but I sit in no pew."

"No pew?"

"No. But my child's coffin, in the vault where repose the remains of more than one of my race who had been dear to me in life, will I take my place."

There was an earnest resolved solemnity about Sir George's manner, which showed that he was not to be turned from his purpose, and Mr. Bevan accordingly did not attempt to do so. He had done what he scarcely expected, that is, got a consent to accompany him to the night vigil, and at all events let what would happen, he as a more disinterested party than the others, would be able, probably to interfere and prevent any disastrous circumstances from arising.

"Say nothing of what has been determined on to any one," said Sir George, "keep it a profound secret, sir, and this night will put an end to the agony of doubt."

"Depend upon me. Will you come to my house at eleven o'clock, or shall I come here?"

"We will come to you; it is in the way."

Thus then the affair was settled, so far satisfactorily, that there was to be a watch actually now in the vault, so that there could be no delusion, no trick practiced. — What will be the result will be shown very shortly; in the meantime we cannot but tremble at what that attached and nearly heart-broken father may have still to go through.

The excitement too in the village was immense; for the story of the vampyre's attack upon the young girl was fresh in everybody's mouth, and it lost nothing of its real horrors by the frequency with which it was repeated, and the terror-stricken manner in which it was dilated upon.

Chapter CCIII.

THE GRAND CONSULTATION AT THE ALE-HOUSE. – THE AWFUL SUGGESTION.

Sir George Crofton and his family could form no idea, owing to not being in a position to know, of the state of excitement produced in the village by the mysterious and frightful attack which had been made upon the widow's daughter.

When people are very much absorbed with their own grief, they are apt to set a lighter value upon those of others, and thus it was that the family of the Croftons was so entirely taken up with what itself felt and had to do that there was little room for sympathy with others.

Mr. Bevan likewise, from his peculiar and respectable position, was not likely to be made the depository of gossiping secrets; the inhabitants of that little place were in the habit of approaching him with respect, so that, although, as we are aware, he had heard from Will Stephens, the sexton, a full and particular account of what had happened to him in the old church, and was likewise cognizant of the story of the midnight attack upon the widow's daughter, he was not fully aware of the startling effect which those circumstances had had upon the small population of that fishing village.

We are bound to believe that if he had had any idea of the real result of those operations or of what was contemplated as their result – he would have done his best to adopt some course to prevent any disastrous collision.

We, however, with all the data and materials of this most singular narrative before us, are enabled to detail to the reader facts and occurrences as they took place actually, without waiting the arrival of those periods at which they reached the knowledge of those actors in the gloomy drama of real life.

Our readers, then, will please to know that the excitement among the inhabitants of the place was of that violent and overbearing description, that all the occupations of the villagers were abandoned, and a spirit of idleness, sadly suggestive of mischief, began to be prevalent among them.

This feeling was increased by frequent visits to the ale-house, the liquor of which was well esteemed by Will Stephens, as may be readily imagined; and towards evening the large old-fashioned parlor of that place of entertainment became crowded with a motley assemblage, whose sole purpose in meeting together was to drink strong ale, and discuss the irritating and exciting subject of the appearance of the vampyre in the village.

This discussion, from being at first a sober, serious, and alarmed one, became noisy and violent; and at length a blacksmith, who was a great man in the politics of the place, and who of all things in the world most admired to hear his own voice, rose and addressed his compeers in something of a set speech.

"Listen to me," he said; "are we to have the blood sucked out of all our bodies by a lot of vampyres? Is our wives and daughters to be murdered in the middle of the night?"

"No, no, no," cried many voices; "certainly not."

"Is we to be made into victims, or isn't we? What's Sir George Crofton and his family to us? To be sure he's the landlord of some of us, and a very good landlord he is, too, as long as we pay our rent."

"Here, hear, hear."

"But there's no saying how long he might be so, if we didn't."

"Bravo, Dick!" cried the master of the place, handing the orator a pot; "bravo, Dick! take a pull at that, old fellow."

"Thank you, Muggins. Now, what I proposes is —"

"Stand on a chair, and let's all hear you."

"Thank you," said the blacksmith; and getting upon a chair, he was about to commence again, when some one advised him to get upon the table, but in an effort to accomplish that feat, he unfortunately trod upon what was a mere flap of the table, which had not sufficient power to support his weight, and down he came amid an assemblage of pots, jugs, and glasses, which made a most alarming crash.

This roused the fury of the landlord, who had no idea of being made such a sufferer in the transaction, and he accordingly began to declaim heavily at his loss.

A dispute arose as to how he was to be repaid, and it was finally settled that a general subscription would be the best mode of reimbursing him.

If anything was wanting to work up the feelings of the topers at the public-house to the highest pitch of aggravation, it certainly was their having to disburse for breakages a sum of money which, if liquefied, would have trickled most luxuriously down their throats. They were consequently ripe and ready for anything which promised vengeance upon anybody.

The blacksmith was not discomfited by his fall. When is a man who is fond of hearing himself talk discomfited by anything? and he soon resumed his oration in the following words: —

"Is we to be put upon in this kind of way? Why, we shan't be able to sleep in our beds. All I asks is, is we to put up with it?"

"But what are we to do?" said one.

"Ah! there's the question," said the blacksmith, "I don't know exactly."

"Let's ask old Timothy Brown," said the butcher, "he's the oldest man here."

This was assented to; and accordingly the individual mentioned was questioned as to his ideas of the way of avoiding the alarming catastrophe which seemed to be impending over them. He advised them to wait patiently till the next night, and keep awake till the unwelcome nocturnal visitor made its appearance, when whoever it might visit was boldly to assail it, without any fear of the consequences to himself, till further assistance could be procured. After Timothy Brown had delivered himself of this piece of advice, a dead silence ensued among the late boisterous company. There were many dissentients, and a few who seemed in favor of a trial of the practicability of the plan. Both parties seemed to give some consideration to the proposition, and they were by far too much engaged in thinking of the advice which had been given them, to pay much attention to the quarter from whence it had emanated; more particularly, too, as from his age and infirmities, he was incapacitated from carrying it out or from giving any active assistance to those who were disposed to do so.

A great many efforts were made to get him to say more, particularly with reference to the case under consideration, as being no common one, but the octogenarian had made his effort, and he only replied to the remonstrances of those who, alternately by coaxing and bullying, strove to get information from him, by a vacant stare.

"It's of no use," said the butcher, "you'll get nothing more now from old Timothy; he's done up now, that's quite clear, and ten to one if the excitement of tonight won't go a good way towards slaughtering him before his time."

"Well, it may be so," cried the blacksmith, "but still it's good advice, and as I said before it comes to this — is we to be afraid to lay down in our beds at night, or isn't we?"

Before any reply could be made to this interrogatory, the old clock that was in the public-house parlor struck the hour of eleven, and another peal of thunder seemed to be answering to the tinkling sounds.

"It's a rough night," said one, "I thought there would be a storm before morning by the look of the sun at setting – it went down with a strange fiery redness behind a bank of clouds. I move for going home."

"Who talks of going home," cried the blacksmith, "when vampires are abroad? hasn't old Timothy said, that a stormy night was the very one to settle the thing in."

"No," cried another, "he did not say night at all."

"I don't care whether he said night or day; I've made up my mind to do something; there's no doubt about it but that a vampyre is about the old church. Who'll come with me and ferret it out? it will be good service done to everybody's fireside."

Chapter CCIV.

THE NIGHT WATCH. – THE VAULT.

*I*t was each moment becoming a more difficult affair to carry on any conversation in the public-house parlor, for not only did the thunder each moment almost interrupt the speakers with its loud reverberations, but now and then such a tremendous gust of wind would sweep round the house that it would be quite impossible for any one to make himself heard amidst its loud howling noise.

These were circumstances however, which greatly aided no doubt, in the getting up of a superstitious feeling in the minds of the people there assembled, which made them ripe for any proposition, which perhaps in their soberer moments they would have regarded with considerable dismay; hence when the blacksmith rushed to the door, crying, –

"Who will follow me to the old church and lay hold of the vampyre?" about half-a-dozen of the boldest and most reckless, – and be it told to their honor (if there be any honor in such an enterprise, which after all, was a grossly selfish one,) they were the worst characters in the village – started to their feet to accompany him thither.

There are many persons who waver about an enterprise, who will join it when it has a show of force, and thus was it with this affair. The moment it was found that the blacksmith's proposition had some half-dozen stout adherents, he got as many more — some of whom joined him from curiosity, and some from dread of being thought to lack courage by their companions if they held off.

There was now a sufficiently large party to make a respectable demonstration, and quite elated with his success, and caring little for the land storm that was raging, the blacksmith, closely followed by the butcher, who had no objection in life to the affair, especially as he was at variance with the parson concerning the tithes of a little farm he kept, called out, —

"To the church — to the church!" and followed by the rabble, rushed forward in the direction of the sacred edifice.

*A*s the hour of eleven has struck, and as the reader is aware that at that hour Sir George Crofton and his two sons, accompanied by Mr. Bevan, had agreed to go to the church on their melancholy errand, we will leave the noisy brawlers of the alehouse for the purpose of detailing the proceedings of those whose fortunes we feel more closely interested in.

The baronet was by no means wavering in his determination, notwithstanding it had been made at a time of unusual excitement, when second thoughts might have been allowed to step in, and suggest some other course of proceeding.

Now, Mr. Bevan was not without his own private hopes that such would be the case; for what he dreaded above all other things was, the truth of the affair, and that Sir George would have the horror of discovering that there was much more in the popular superstition than, without ocular demonstration, he would have been inclined to admit.

Although a man of education and of refined abilities, the evidence that had already showed itself to him of the existence at all events of some supernatural being, with powers analogous to those of the fabled vampyre, was such that he could not wholly deny, without stultifying his intellect, that there might be such things.

It is a sad circumstance when the mind is, as it were, compelled to receive undeniable evidence of a something which the judgment has the strongest general reasons for disputing, and that was precisely the position of Mr. Bevan, and a most unenviable one it was.

That night's proceedings, however, in the vault, he felt must put an end to all doubts and perplexity upon the subject, and so with a fervent hope that, in some, at present inexplicable manner, the thing would be found to be a delusion, he waited more anxiously the arrival of the

Croftons at the parsonage.

At half past ten o'clock, instead of eleven, for as the evening advanced, Sir George Crofton had shown such an amount of nervousness that his sons had thought it would be better to bring him to the parsonage, they arrived, and Mr. Bevan perceived at once what a remarkable effect grief and anxiety had already had upon the features of the baronet.

He was a different man to what, but a few days since, he had been, and more than ever the kind clergyman felt inclined to doubt the expediency of his being present on such an occasion, and yet how to prevent him if he were really determined, was a matter of no small difficulty.

"My dear friend," said Mr. Bevan, "will you pardon me if I make an effort now to persuade you to abandon this enterprise?"

"I can pardon the effort easily," said Sir George Crofton, "because I know it is dictated by the best of motives, but I would fain be spared it, for I am determined."

"I will say no more, but only with deep sincerity hope that you may return to your dwelling, each relieved from the load of anxiety that now oppresses you."

"I hope to Heaven it may be so."

"The night looks strange and still," said Charles, who wished to draw his father's attention as much as possible from too close a contemplation of the expedition on which they were bound.

"It does," said Edwin; "I should not be surprised at a storm, for there is every indication of some disturbance of the elements.

"Let it come," said Sir George, who fancied that in all those remarks he detected nothing but a wish to withdraw him from his enterprise; "Let it come. I have a duty to perform, and I will do it, though Heaven's thunders should rock the very earth — the forked lightning is not launched at the father who goes to watch at the grave of his child."

Charles and Edwin, upon finding that Sir George was in the mood to make a misapplication of whatever was said to him, desisted from further remarks, but left Mr. Bevan quietly to converse with him, in a calm and unirritating manner.

It was the object of the clergyman to put off as much time as possible before proceeding to the church, so that the period to be spent in the family vault of the Croftons should be lessened as much as possible, for he felt assured that each minute there wasted would be one of great agony to the bereaved father, who would feel himself once again in such close approximation to that daughter on whom he had placed some of his dearest affections.

Sir George, however, defeated this intention, by promptly rising when his watch told him that the hour of eleven had arrived, and it was in vain to attempt to stultify him into a belief that he was wrong as regarded the time, for the church was sufficiently near for them to hear the hour of eleven pealed forth from its ancient steeple.

"Come," said Sir George, "the hour has arrived. I pray you do not delay. I know you are all anxious and fearful concerning me, but I have a spirit of resolution and firmness in this affair which shall yet stand me in good stead. I shall not shrink, as you imagine I shall shrink. Come, then, at once — it is suspense and delay which frets me, and not action."

These words enforced a better spirit into both his sons and Mr. Bevan, and in a few moments the party of four, surely sufficiently strong to overcome any unexpected obstacles, or to defeat any trickery that might be attempted to be passed off upon them, proceeded towards the church.

It will be recollected that it was just a little after that time that the storm commenced, and, in fact, the first clap of thunder, that seemed to shake the heavens, took place just as they reached the old grave-yard adjoining to the sacred building.

"There!" exclaimed Charles, "I thought that it would come."

"What matter?" said Sir George, "come on."

"Humor him in everything," said Mr. Bevan, "It is madness now to contradict him — he will not recede under any circumstances."

The natural senses of Sir George Crofton appeared to be preternaturally acute, for he turned sharply, and said quickly, but not unkindly, —

"No, he will not recede — come on."

After this, nothing was said until they reached the church door, and then while Mr. Bevan was searching in his pockets for the little key which opened the small private entrance, some vivid flashes of lightning lit up with extraordinary brilliancy the old gothic structure — the neighboring tombs and the melancholy yew trees that waved their branches in the night air.

Perhaps the delay which ensued before Mr. Bevan cold find the key, likewise arose from the wish to keep Sir George as short a time as possible within the vault, but he at length produced it, for any further delay could only be accounted for by saying that he had it not.

The small arched doorway was speedily cleared, and as another peal of thunder broke over head in awful grandeur of sound, they entered the church.

Mr. Bevan took the precaution this time to close the door, so that there could be no interruption from without.

"Now, Sir George," he said, "remember your promise. You are to come away freely at the first dawn of day, and if nothing by then has occurred to strengthen the frightful supposition which, I suppose I may say, we have all indulged in, I do hope that for ever this subject will be erased from your recollection."

"Be it so," said Sir George; "be it so."

Mr. Bevan then busied himself in lighting a lantern, and from beneath one of the pews, where they were hidden, he procured a couple of crowbars, with which to raise the stone that covered the entrance to the vault.

These preparations took up some little time, so that the old clock had chimed the quarter past eleven, and must have been rapidly getting on to the half-hour, before they stood in the aisle close to the vault.

"This marble slab," said Sir George, as he cast his eyes upon it, "always hitherto has been cemented in its place. Why is it not so now?"

"Is it not?" said Mr. Bevan.

"No – lend me the light."

Mr. Bevan was averse to lending him the light, but he could not very well refuse it; and when Sir George Crofton had looked more minutely at the marble slab, he saw that it had been cemented, but that the cement was torn and broken away, as if some violence had been used for the purpose of opening the vault; but whether that violence came from within or without was a matter of conjecture.

Chapter CCV.

THE MADMAN. – THE VAMPYRE.

"What does this mean?" cried Sir George Crofton, excitedly.

"Hush!" said Mr. Bevan, "I pray you be calm, sir. If you are to make any discovery that will give you peace of mind, rest assured it will not be made by violence."

"You do not answer my question."

"I cannot answer it." Remember that I know no more than you do, and that, like yourselves, I am an adventurer here in search of the truth."

Sir George said no more upon that head, but with clasped hands and downcast eyes he stood in silence, while his two sons, armed with the crowbars that Mr. Bevan had provided for the occasion, proceeded to lift up the marble slab that covered the vault where lay their sister's remains.

The work was not one of great difficulty, for the slab was not very large, and as it was not cemented down, it yield at once to the powerful leverage that was brought to play against it, and in a few minutes it was placed aside, and the yawning abyss appeared before them.

"Oh! sir," said Mr. Bevan, "even now at this late hour, and when the proceedings have commenced, I pray you to pause."

"Pause!" cried Sir George, passionately, "pause for what?"

"Disturb not the dead, and let them rest in peace. Absolve your mind from the dangerous and perhaps fatal fancies that possess it, and let us say a prayer, and close again this entrance to the tomb."

The sons hesitated, and they probably would have taken the clergyman's advice, but Sir George was firm.

"No, sir," he said, "already have I suffered much in coming thus far; I will not retreat until I have effected all my purpose. I swear it, by Heaven, whose temple we now are in. You would not, Mr. Bevan, have me break such an oath."

"I would not; but I regret you made it. Since, however, it must be so, and this rash adventure is determined upon, follow me; I will lead you the way into these calm regions, where you can sleep, I trust, in peace."

Sir George Crofton made a step forward, as if he would have arrested Mr. Bevan's progress and lead the way himself, but already the clergyman had descended several steps, so he had nothing to do but to follow him.

This they all did, Sir George going immediately after him, and his two sons, with pale anxious-looking faces, as if they had a suspicion that the adventure would end in something terrific, came last and they glanced nervously and suspiciously about them; but they said not a word, nor if they had spoken, it would have been to express great apprehension, and that was what they were ashamed to do.

Mr. Bevan carried the light, and when he felt that he was at the bottom of the stone steps, by finding that he was treading upon the sawdust that was strewn on the floor of the vault, he turned and held the lamp up at arm's length, so that his companions might see their way down the steps.

In another minute they all stood on the floor of the vault.

The light burnt with rather a faint and sickly glare, for so rapidly were noxious gases evolved in that receptacle for the dead, that notwithstanding it had been so frequently opened as it had been lately, they had again accumulated.

In a few moments, however, this was partially remedied by the air from the church above, and the light burnt more brilliantly — indeed, quite sufficiently so to enable them to look around them in the vault.

Sir George Crofton's feelings at that moment must have been of the most painful and harrowing description. He had lived long enough to be a witness of the death and the obsequies of many members of his family whom he had loved fondly, and there he stood in that chamber of death, surrounded by all the remains of those beings, the memory of whose appearance and voices came now freshly upon his mind.

Mr. Bevan could well guess the nature of the sad thoughts that transpired in the breast of the baronet, and the sons having by accident cast their eyes upon the coffin that contained the remains of their mother, regarded it in silence, while memory was busy, too, within them in conjuring up her image.

"And it has come to this," said Sir George, solemnly.

"We must all come to this," interposed Mr. Bevan; "this is indeed a place for solemn and holy thoughts — for self-examination, for self-condemnation."

"But there is peace here."

"There is — the peace that shall be eternal."

"Hark! hark!" said Charles; "what is that?"

"The wind," said Mr. Bevan; "nothing but the wind howling round and through the old belfry — you will remember that it is a boisterous night."

"Turn, turn, father."

Sir George turned and looked at Charles, who pointed in silence to the coffin which contained the corpse of his mother. The light gleamed upon the plate on which was engraved her name. Sir George's features moved convulsively as he read it, and he turned aside to hide a sudden gush of emotion that came over him.

After a few minutes, he touched Mr. Bevan on the arm, and said in a whisper, —

"Where did they place my child?"

The clergyman pointed to the narrow shelf on which was the coffin of Clara Crofton, and then Sir George, making a great effort to overcome his feelings, said, —

"Mr. Bevan, our worthy minister and friend, and you, likewise, my boys, hear me. You can guess to some extent, but not wholly — that can only be known by God — the agony that a sight of the poor remains of her who has gone from me in all the pride of her youth and beauty, must be to me; yet now that I am here I consider it to be my duty to look once again upon the face of my child — my — my lost Clara."

"Oh! father, father," said Edwin, "forego this purpose."

"You will spare us this," cried Charles.

"Repent you, sir," said Mr. Bevan, "of the wish. Let her rest in peace. The dead are sanctified."

"The dead are sanctified, — but I am her father."

"Nay, Sir George, let me implore you."

"Implore me to what, sir? Not to look upon the face of my own child? Peace — peace. It is no profanation for one who loved her as I loved her to look upon her once again. Urge me no more."

"This is in vain," said Charles.

"You are right — it is in vain."

A shriek burst from the lips of Edwin at this moment, and flinging his arms around his father, he held him back. Mr. Bevan, too, gave a cry of terror, and Charles stood with his hands clasped, as if turned to stone.

Their eyes were all bent upon Clara's coffin.

The lid moved, and a strange sound was heard from within that receptacle for the dead — the clock of the old church struck twelve — the coffin lid moved again, and then sliding on one side, it eventually fell upon the floor of the vault.

The four spectators of this scene were struck speechless for the time with terror. Then they stood gazing at the coffin as if they were so many statues.

And now the light which Mr. Bevan still for a miracle held in his trembling grasp, shone on a mass of white clothing within the coffin, and in another moment that white clothing was observed to be in motion. Slowly the dead form that was there rose up, and they all saw the pale and ghastly face. A streak of blood was issuing from the mouth, and the eyes were open.

Sir George Crofton lifted up both his hands, and struck his head, and then he burst into a wild frightful laugh. It was the laugh of insanity.

Mr. Bevan dropped the light, and all was darkness.

"Ha, ha, ha, ha, ha!" laughed Sir George Crofton. "Ha, ha, ha, ha, ha!" and the horrible laugh was taken up by many an echo in the old church, and responded to with strange and most unearthly reverberations. "Ha, ha, ha, ha!" Oh what a dreadful sound that was coming at such a time from the lips of the father.

"Fly Edwin — oh, fly," cried Charles.

Edwin screamed twice, for he was full of horror, and then he fell on the floor of the vault in a state of insensibility.

Charles had just sense left him to spring towards the steps, and make a frantic effort to reach the church; in his hurry he fell twice, but each time rising again with a shout of despair, he resumed his efforts, and all the while the horrible laugh of his maniac father sounded in his ears, a sound which he felt that he should never forget.

By a great effort he did reach the aisle of the church, and when there, he called aloud.

"Mr. Bevan, Mr. Bevan, help — oh help! For the love of God speak. Help, help, Mr. Bevan, where are you, speak, I implore you? Am I too going mad? Oh yes, I shall — I must. What mortal intellect can stand such a scene as this. Help, help — oh, help!"

The church was suddenly lit up by a flash of light, and turning in the direction from whence it proceeded, Charles saw Mr. Bevan approaching with a light, which he had procured from the chancel, and it would appear that immediately upon dropping in his horror the light in the vault, he had ran up the stairs with the intent of getting another.

"Who calls me? Who calls me?" he cried.

""I — I," said Charles. "Oh God, what a dreadful night is this."

The clergyman was trembling violently, and was very pale, but he made his way up to Charles, from whose brow the perspiration was falling in heavy drops, and then again they heard the mad Sir George laughing in the vault.

"Ha, ha, ha! ha, ha, ha! ha, ha, ha!"

"Oh God, is not that horrible?" said Charles.

"Most horrible," responded Mr. Bevan.

Bang — bang — bang! at this moment came a violent knocking at the church door, and then several voices were heard without shouting.

"The vampyre — the vampyre — the vampyre."

"What is that? What is that?" said Charles.

"Nay, I know not," replied Mr. Bevan, "I am nearly distracted already. Where is your brother? Did he not escape from the vault? Where is he? Oh, that horrible laugh. Good God! that knocking too at the church door. What can be the meaning of it? Heaven in its mercy guide us now what to do."

The reader will understand the meaning of the knocking, although those bewildered persons who heard it in the church did not. The fact is, that the party from the alehouse headed by the valiant blacksmith, and heated by their too liberal potations had just arrived at the church, and were clamoring for admission.

They had seen through one of the old pointed windows, the reflection of the light which Mr. Bevan carried, and that it was that convinced them some one was there who might if he would pay attention to the uproarious summons.

The knocking lasted with terrible effect, for the old door of the sacred edifice shook again, it seemed as if certainly it could not resist the making of such an attack.

Mr. Bevan was confounded. A horrible suspicion came across him, of what was meant by those violent demands for admission, and he shook with brutal trepidation as he conjectured what might be the effect of the proceedings of a lawless mob.

"Now Heaven help us," he said, "for we shall soon I fear be powerless."

"Good God! what mean you?" said Charles.

"I scarcely know how to explain to you all my fears. The are too dreadful to think of, but while that knocking continues, what can I think?"

"I understand!" they call for my sister."

"Oh call her not now by that name. Remember, and remember with a shudder what she now is."

Chapter CCVII.

THE HUNT OF THE VAMPYRE.

*A*ll these occurrences which have taken a considerable time in telling, occurred as simultaneously, that although it would appear Mr. Bevan and Charles Crofton, rather neglected Sir George and Edwin who were still in the vault, they had really not had time to think of them, to say nothing of making any effort to extricate them from the frightful situation in which they were placed.

Probably, after procuring a light, Mr. Bevan would have rushed to their rescue had not that incessant knocking at the church door suggested a new and more horrible danger, still, from the evil passions of an infuriated multitude.

"Oh, Mr. Charles," he said, "if we could but get your father away from the church, there is no knowing what an amount of misery he might be spared."

"Misery, sir; surely there is no more misery in store for us — have we not suffered enough — more than enough. Oh, Mr. Bevan we have fallen upon evil times, and I dread to think what will yet be the end of those most frightful transactions."

The knocking at the church door continued violently, and Charles indicated a wish to proceed there to ascertain what it was, but Mr. Bevan stopped him, saying, —

"No, Charles — no — let them be, I hardly think they will venture to break into the sacred edifice, but whether they do or not, remember that your duty and mine, yours being the duty of a son, and mine that of a friend, should take us now to your father's vault.

"That is true, sir," said Charles, "lead on I will follow you."

Mr. Bevan, who had all the intellectual courage of a man of education, and of regular habits, led the way again to the vault, with the light in his hand. It was a great relief that the insane and horrible laugh of Sir George Crofton had ceased, the best friend of any man could almost have wished him dead, ere their ears had drunk in such horrible sounds.

The shouts and cries from without now became incessant, and it seemed as if some weapon had been procured, wherewith to hammer violently upon the church door, for the strokes were regular and incessant, and it was evident that if they continued long that frail defense against the incursions of the rabble rout without must soon give way.

The only effect, however, which these sounds had upon Mr. Bevan was to make him hasten his progress towards the vault, for anything in the shape of a collision between those who wanted to take the church by storm, and Sir George Crofton, was indeed most highly to be deprecated.

The steps were not many in number, and once again the clergyman and Charles Crofton stood upon the sawdust that covered the flooring of the vault.

At first, in consequence of the flaring of the light, the state of affairs in that dismal region could not be ascertained; but as soon as they could get a view, they found Sir George lying apparently in a state of insensibility across the coffin of his daughter Clara, while Edwin was in a swoon close to his feet.

"Sir George, Sir George," cried Mr. Bevan, "arouse yourself; it is necessary that you leave this place at once."

The baronet got up and glanced at the intruders. Charles uttered a deep groan, for the most superficial observation of his father's face was sufficient to convince him that reason had fled, and that wildness had set up his wild dominion in his brain.

"Father — father," he cried, "speak to me, and dissipate a frightful thought."

"What would you have of me," said Sir George; "I am a vampyre, and this is my tomb — you should see me in the rays of the cold moon gliding 'twixt earth and heaven, and panting for a victim. I am a vampyre."

At this moment Edwin seemed to be partially recovering, for his eyes opened as he lay upon the floor, and he looked around him with a bewildered gaze, which soon settled into one of more intelligence as memory resumed her sway, and he recollected the various circumstances that had brought him into his present position.

"Rouse yourself, Edwin, rouse yourself," cried Mr. Bevan, "you must aid us to remove your father."

"Do you talk of me?" said Sir George, "know you not that I am one of those supernatural existences known as the death and despair-dealing vampyres — it's time I took my nightly prowl to look for victims. I must have blood — I must have blood."

"Gracious Heaven! he raves," said Charles.

"Heed him not," said Mr. Bevan — "heed him not, and touch him not, so that he leave the place — when we have him once clear of the church we can procure assistance, and take him to his own home.

"Edwin," whispered Charles, "what of our sister."

Edwin shook his head and shuddered. "I know nothing but that I saw her — oh, horrible sight, rising from her coffin, and then in a convulsion of terror my senses fled — a frightful ringing laugh came on my ears, and from that time till now, be the period long or short, I have been blessed by a death-like trance."

"Blessed indeed," said Mr. Bevan; "tarry one moment."

Sir George Crofton was ascending the steps of the vault, but his two sons paused for an instant at the request of Mr. Bevan, and then the latter approaching Clara's coffin slightly removed the lid, and was gratified as far as any feeling could be considered gratification under such circumstances, to find that the corpse occupied an ordinary position in its narrow resting place.

"All's right," he said, "let us persuade ourselves that this too has been but a dream, that we have been deceived, and that imagination has played us tricks it is accustomed to play to those who give it the rein at such hours as these — let us think and believe anything rather than that what we have seen tonight is real."

As he spoke these words, he ascended hastily the steps in pursuit of Sir George, who, by this time had alone reached the door.

The heavy strokes against the door of the church had ceased, but an odd sort of scraping, rattling sound at the lock convinced the clergyman that a workman of more skill than he who had wielded the hammer, was now at work, endeavoring to force an entrance.

"Oh, if we could but get out," he said, "by the small private entrance, all might be well; Charles, urge your father, I pray you."

Charles did so to the best of his ability, but the blacksmith who had originally incited the crowd to attack the church, in order to get possession of the body of the vampyre, had sent to his workshop for the tools of his craft, and soon quietly accomplished by skill what brute force would have been a long time about, namely, the opening of the church-door.

It was flung wide open, before Sir George Croton and his sons could reach the small private entrance, of which Mr. Bevan had the key.

The sight of the multitude of persons, for they looked such crowds in the church porch, materially increased the incipient sadness of the bereaved father.

Chapter CCVII.

THE FATE OF SIR GEORGE. – THE CROSS ROAD.

Sir George, when he saw the crowd of persons, seemed to have some undefined idea that they were enemies, but this would not have been productive of any serious consequences, if it had not most unfortunately happened that a most formidable weapon was within his grasp.

That weapon consisted of one of the long iron crowbars which had been successfully used by his own sons in order to force a passage to the family vault, where such horrors had been witnessed.

Suddenly, then, seizing this weapon, which, in the hands of a ferocious man was a most awful one, he swung it once round his head, and then rushed upon those he considered his foes.

He dealt but three blows, and at each of those one of the assailants fell lifeless in the church porch.

To resist, or, to attempt to contend with a man so armed, and apparently possessed of such preternatural strength, was what some of the party wished, and accordingly a free passage was left for him, and he rushed out of the church into the night air shouting for vengeance, and still at interval, accusing himself of being a vampyre, as most dangerous theme to touch upon, considering the then state of feeling in that little district.

Anxiety for the safety of Sir George induced his sons and Mr. Bevan to rush after him, regardless of all other consequences, so that the church, the vaults, and everything they contained, were left to the mercy of a mob infuriated by superstition, rendered still more desperate by the loss of three of their number in so sudden and exampled a manner.

They opposed no obstacle to the leaving of those persons, who thus for dearer considerations abandoned the old church, but they rushed with wild shouts and gesticulations into the building.

"The vampyre, the vampyre," cried the blacksmith, "death to the vampyre — death and destruction to the vampyre."

"Hurrah!" cried another, "to the vaults this way to Sir George Crofton's vault."

There seemed to be little doubt now, but that this disorderly rabble would execute summary vengeance upon the supposed nocturnal disturber of the peace of the district.

Ever and anon, too, as these shouts of discord, and of threatening vengeance, rose upon the night air, there would come the distant muttering of thunder, for the storm had not yet ceased, although its worst fury had certainly passed away.

Dark and heavy clouds were sweeping up from the horizon, and it seemed to be tolerably evident that some heavy deluge of rain would eventually settle the fury of the elements, and reconcile the discord of wind and electricity.

Several of the rioters were provided with links and matches, so that in a few moments the whole interior of the church was brilliantly illuminated, while at the same time it presented a grotesque appearance, in consequence of the unsteady and wavering flame from the links, throw myriads of dancing shadows upon the walls.

There would have been no difficulty under any ordinary circumstances in finding the entrance to the vault, where the dead of the Crofton family should have lain in peace, but now since the large flagstone that covered the entrance to that receptacle of the grave was removed, it met their observation at once.

It was strange now to perceive how, for a moment, superstition having led them on so far, the same feeling should induce them to pause, ere they ventured to make their way down these gloomy steps.

It was a critical moment, and probably if any one or two had taken a sudden panic, the whole party might have left the church with precipitation, having done a considerable amount of mischief, and yet as it is so usual with rioters, having left their principal object unaccomplished.

The blacksmith put an end to this state of indecision, for, seizing a link from the man who was nearest to him, he darted down the steps, exclaiming as he did so, —

"Whoever's afraid, need not follow me."

This was a taunt they were not exactly prepared to submit to, and the consequence was, that in a very few moments the ancient and time honored vault of the Crofton's was more full of the living than of the dead.

The blacksmith laid his hand upon Clara's coffin.

"Here it is," he said, "I know the very pattern of the cloth, and the fashion of the nails, I saw it at Grigson's the undertaker's before it was taken to the Grange."

"Is she there — is she there," cried half a dozen voices at once.

Even the blacksmith hesitated a moment ere he removed the lid from the receptacle of death, but when he did so, and his eyes fell upon the face of the presumed vampyre, he seemed rejoiced to find in the appearances then exhibited some sort of justification for the act of violence of which already he had been the instigator.

"Here you are," he said, "look at the bloom upon her lips, why her cheeks are fresher and rosier than ever they were while she was alive, a vampyre my mates, this is a vampyre, or may I never break bread again; and now what's to be done."

"Burn her, burn her," cried several.

"Well," said the blacksmith, "mind its as you like. I've brought you here, and shown you what it is, and now you can do what you like, and of course I'll lend you a hand to do it."

Any one who had been very speculative in this affair, might have detected in these last words of the blacksmith, something like an inclination to creep out of the future consequences of what might next be done, while at the same time shame deterred him from exactly leaving his companions in the lurch.

After some suggestions then, and some argumentation as to the probability or possibility of interruption — the coffin itself, was with its sad and wretched occupant, lifted from the niche where it should have remained until that awful day when the dead shall rise for judgment, and carried up the steps into the graveyard, but scarcely had they done so, when the surcharged clouds burst over their heads, and the rain came down in perfect torrents.

The deluge was of so frightful, and continuous a character, that they shrank back again beneath the shelter of the church porch, and there waited until its first fury had passed away.

Such an even down storm seldom lasts long in our climate, and the consequence was that in about ten minutes the shower had so far subsided that although a continuous rain was falling it bore but a very distant comparison to what had taken place.

"How are we to burn the body on such a night as this?"

"Aye, how indeed," said another; "you could not so much as kindle a fire, and if you did, it would not live many minutes."

"I'll tell you what to do at once," said one who had as yet borne but a quiet part in the proceedings; I'll tell you what to do at once, for I saw it done myself; a vampyre is quite as secure buried in a cross-road with a stake through its body, as if you burned it in all the fires in the world; come on, the rain won't hinder you doing that."

This was a suggestion highly approved of, and the more so as there was a cross road close at hand, so that the deed would be done quick, and the parties dispersed to their respective homes, for already the exertion they had taken, and the rain that had fallen, had had a great effect in sobering them.

And even now the perilous and disgusting operation of destroying the body, by fire or any other way, might have been abandoned, had any one of the party suggested such a course — but the dread of a future imputation of cowardice kept all silent.

Once more the coffin was raised by four of the throng, and carried through the church-yard, which was now running in many little rivulets, in consequence of the rain. The cross-road was not above a quarter of a mile from the spot, and while those who were disengaged from carrying the body, were hurrying away to get spades and mattocks, the others walked through the rain, and finally paused at the place they though suitable for that ancient superstitious rite, which it was thought would make the vampyre rest in peace.

It is hard to suppose that Sir George Crofton, his sons, and Mr. Bevan were all deceived concerning these symptoms of vitality which they had observed in the corpse of Clara; but certainly now, there was no appearance of anything of the kind, and the only suspicious circumstances appeared to be the blood upon the lips, and the very fresh-like appearance of the face.

If it were really a fact that the attack of Varney the Vampyre upon this fair young girl had converted her into one of those frightful existences, and that she had been about to leave her tomb for the purpose of seeking a repast of blood, it would appear that the intention had been checked and frustrated by the presence of Sir George and his party in the vault.

At last a dozen men now arrived well armed with spades and picks, and they commenced the work of digging a deep, rather than a capacious grave, in silence.

A gloomy and apprehensive spirit seemed to come over the whole assemblage, and the probability is that this was chiefly owing to the fact that they now encountered no opposition, and that they were permitted unimpeded to accomplish a purpose which had never yet been attempted within the memory of any of the inhabitants of the place.

The grave was dug, and about two feet depth of soil was thrown in a huge mound upon the surface; the coffin was lowered, and there lay the corpse within that receptacle of poor humanity, unimprisoned by any lid for that had been left in the vault, and awaiting the doom which they had decreed upon it, but which they now with a shuddering horror shrunk from performing.

A hedge-stake with a sharp point had been procured, and those who held it looked around them with terrified countenances, while the few links that had not been extinguished by the rain, shed a strange and lurid glare upon all objects.

"It must be done," said the blacksmith, "don't let it be said that we got thus far and then were afraid."

"Do it then yourself," said the man that held the stake, "I dare not."

"Aye, do," cried several voices; "you brought us here, why don't you do it — are you afraid after all your boasting."

"Afraid — afraid of the dead; I'm not afraid of any of you that are alive, and it's not likely I'm going to be afraid of a dead body; you're a pretty set of cowards. I've no animosity against the girl, but I want that we shall all sleep in peace, and that our wives and children should not be disturbed nocturnally in their blessed repose. I'll do it if none of you'll do it, and then you may thank me afterwards for the act, although I suppose if I get into trouble I shall have you all turn tail upon me."

"No, we won't — no, we won't."

"Well, well, here goes, whether you do or not. I — I'll do it directly."

"He shrinks," cried one.

"No," said another; "he'll do it — now for it, stand aside."

"Stand aside yourself — do you want to fall into the grave."

The blacksmith shuddered as he held the stake in an attitude to pierce the body, and even up to that moment it seemed to be a doubtful case, whether he would be able to accomplish his purpose or not; at length, when they all thought he was upon the point of abandoning his design, and casting the stake away, he thrust it with tremendous force through the body and the back of the coffin.

The eyes of the corpse opened wide — the hands were clenched, and a shrill, piercing shriek came from the lips — a shriek that was answered by as many as there were persons present, and then with pallid fear upon their countenances they rushed headlong from the spot.

Chapter CCVIII.

THE SOLITARY MAN. – VARNEY'S DESPAIR.

*T*here lay the dead, alone, in that awful grave, dabbled in blood, and the victim of the horrible experiment that had been instituted to lay a vampire. The rain still fell heavily.

On, surely, pitying Heaven sent those drops to wash out the remembrance of such a deed. The grave slowly began to be a pool of water; it rose up the sides of the coffin, and in a few minutes, more nothing of the ghastly and the terrible contents of that grave could have been seen.

Before that took place, a man of tall stature and solemn gait stepped up and stood upon the brink of the little excavation.

For a time he was as still as that sad occupant of the little space of earth that served her for a resting place, but at length in a tone of deep anguish he spoke, –

"And has it come to this?" he said, "is this my work? Oh, horror! horror unspeakable. In this some hideous dream or a reality of tragedy, so far transcending all I looked for, that if I had tears I should shed them now; but I have none. A hundred years ago that fount was dry. I thought that I had steeled my heart against all gentle impulses; that I had crushed – aye, completely crushed dove-eyed pity in my heart, but it is not so, and still sufficient of my once human feelings clings to me to make me grieve for thee, Clara Crofton, thou victim!"

We need not tell our readers now, that it was no other than Varney the Vampyre himself from whom these words came.

After thus, then, giving such fervent utterance to the sad feeling that had overcome him, he stood for a time silent, and then glancing around him as well as he could by the dim light, he found the spades, by the aid of which the grave had been dug, and which the men had in their great flight left behind them.

Seizing one, he commenced, with an energy and perseverance that was well adapted to accomplish the object, to fill up the grave.

"You shall now rest in peace," he said.

In the course of about ten minutes the grave was leveled completely, so that there were no signs or indications of any one having been there interred.

The rain was still falling, and notwithstanding that circumstance, he continued at his work, until he had stamped down the earth to a perfect level; and then, even, as if he was still further anxious to thoroughly destroy any indication of the deed that had been done, he took the loose earth that was superfluous, and scattered it about.

"This done," he said, "surely you will now know peace."

He cast down the spade with which he had been working, and lingered for a few brief moments. Suddenly he started, for he heard, or thought he heard, an approaching footstep.

His first impulse appeared to be to fly, but that he soon corrected, and folding his arms solemnly across his breast, he waited for the man that was now evidently making speed towards that spot.

In a few moments more he saw the dusky outline of the figure, and then Mr. Bevan, the clergyman, stood before him.

Mr. Bevan did not at the moment recognize in the form before him the man who had been the guest of Sir George Crofton, and from whom it was supposed had sprung all he mischief and horror that had fallen upon the family, at the Grange.

"Who are you?" he cried; "can you give me information of an outrage that has been committed hereabouts."

"Many," said Varney.

"Ah! I know the voice. Are you not he who was rescued from the sea by the two sons of Sir George Crofton."

"Well."

"Now I know you, and I am glad to have met with you."

"You will try to kill me?"

"No, no — peace is my profession."

"Ah! you are the priest of this place. Well, sir, what would you with me?"

"I would implore you to tell me if it be really true that — that —"

Mr. Bevan paused, for he disliked to show that the fear that it might be true there were such creatures as vampyres, had taken so strong a hold of him.

"Proceed," said Varney.

"I will. Are you then a vampyre?"

"A strange question for one living man to put to another! Are you?"

"You are inclined to trifle with me. But I implore you to answer me. I am perhaps the only man in all this neighborhood to whom you can give an answer in the affirmative with safety."

"And why so?"

"Because I question not the decrees of Heaven. If it seems fit to the great Ruler of Heaven and of earth that there should be ever such horrible creatures as vampyres, ought I his creature to question it?"

"You ought not — you ought not. I have heard much from priests, but from your lips I hear sound reason. I am a vampyre."

Mr. Bevan shrunk back, and shook for a moment, as he said in a low faltering tone, —

"For how long — have you —"

"You would know how long I have endured such a state of existence. I will tell you that I have a keen remembrance of being hunted through the streets of London in the reign of Henry the Fourth."

"Henry the Fourth?"

"Yes, I have seen all the celebrities of this and many other lands from that period. More than once have I endeavored to cast off this horrible existence, but it is my destiny to remain in it. I was picked up by the brothers Crofton after one of my attempts to court death. They have been repaid."

"Horribly!"

"I cannot help it — I am what I am."

There was a strange and mournful solemnity about the tones of Varney that went to the heart of Mr. Bevan, and after a few moments pause, he said, —

"You greatly, very greatly awake my interest. Do not leave me. Ask yourself if there is anything that I can do to alleviate your destiny. Have you tried prayer?"

"Prayer?"

"Yes. Oh! there is great virtue in prayer."

"I pray? What for should I pray but for that death which whenever it seems to be in my grasp has them flitted from me in mockery, leaving me still a stranded wretch upon the shores of this world. Perhaps you have at times fancied you have suffered some great amount of mental agony. Perhaps you have stood by the bed-side of dying creatures, and heard them howl their hopelessness of Heaven's mercy, but you cannot know — you cannot imagine — what I have suffered."

As he spoke, he turned away, but Mr. Bevan followed him, saying, —

"Remain — remain, I implore you,"

"Remain — and wherefore?"

"I will be your friend — it is my duty to be such; remain, and you shall if you wish it, have an asylum in my house. If you will not pray yourself, to Heaven, I will pray for you, and in time to come you will have some hope. Oh, believe me, earnest prayer is not in vain."

"My friend!"

"Yes, your friend; I am, I ought to be the friend of all who are unhappy."

"And is there really one human being who does not turn from me in horror and disgust? Oh, sir, you jest."

"No — on my soul, that which I say I mean. Come with me now, and you shall if you please, remain in secret in my house — no one shall know you are with me — from the moment that you cross the threshold you shall hope for happier days."

The vampyre paused, and it was evident that he was deeply affected by what Mr. Bevan said to him, for his whole frame shook.

Chapter CCIX.

THE STRANGE GUEST. — THE LITTLE CHAPEL. — VARNEY'S NARRATIVE.

*M*r. Bevan could not but see that he had made some impression, even upon the obdurate heart of Varney, and he was determined to follow that impression up by every means in his power.

"Always have in mind," he said, that by trusting me, you trust one who is not in the habit of condemning his fellows. You will be safe from anything like sanctified reproach, for to my thinking, religion should be a principle of love and tenderness, and not a subject upon which people who, perhaps are themselves liable and obnoxious to all sorts of reproach, should deal forth denunciations against their neighbors."

"Is that indeed your faith?"

"It is; and it is the real faith, taught by my Great Master."

"You are as one among many thousands."

"Nay, you may have been unfortunate in meeting with bad specimens of those who are devoted in the priesthood. Do not condemn hastily."

"Hastily! I have been some hundreds of years in condemning."

"You will come with me."

"I will for once again put faith in human nature."

"Tell me then, before we leave this spot, if you know aught of what has happened to, or become of the body of Clara Croton."

"I can tell you; it was left here buried, but uncovered."

"Indeed — the ground is level, and I see no trace of a grave."

"No; I have obliterated all such traces, I have placed the earth upon her — may she now rest in peace. Oh, that such a flower should have been so rudely plucked, and I the cause. Is not that enough to make Heaven's angels mutiny if I should essay to pass the golden gates."

"Say no more of that. I thank God that the body is so disposed of, and that it will not come in the way of any of the Crofton family. This affair had far better now be let sink into oblivion — alas! poor Sir George is now the most pitiable sufferer."

"Indeed!"

"Yes; madness has seized upon him. He only sits and smiles to himself, weaving in his imagination strange fancies."

"And call you that unhappy?"

"It is called, and considered so."

"Oh, fatal error — he is happy. Reason! boasted, God-like reason — what are you but the curse of poor humanity. The maniac, who will in his cell, fancy it a gorgeous hall, and of the damp straw that is his couch make up a glittering coronet, is a king indeed, and most happy."

"This is poetical," said Mr. Bevan, "if not true."

"It is true."

"Well, well; we will talk on that as well as other themes at our leisure. Come on, and I will at once take you to my home, where you will be safe, and I hope more happy."

"Are you not afraid?"

"I am not."

"You are right, confidence is safety — lead on, sir, I'll follow you, although I little thought to make any human companionship tonight."

Mr. Bevan walked only about a step in advance as they proceeded towards the parsonage house, and on the way he conversed with Varney with calmness which considering the very peculiar circumstances, few men could have brought to bear upon the occasion.

But Mr. Bevan was no common man. He looked upon nature, and all the living creatures that make up its vital portion with peculiar eyes, and if the bishop of his diocese had known one half of what Mr. Bevan thought, he would not have suffered him to remain in his religious situation.

But he kept the mass of his liberal opinions to himself, although he always acted upon them, and a man more completely free from sectarian dogmas, and illiberal fancies of superstition, which are nicknamed faith, could not be.

There was still, notwithstanding all the circumstances, a hope lingering in his mind that Varney might after all not be even what he thought himself to be, but some enthusiast who had dreamt himself into a belief of his own horrible powers.

We know that such was not the case. But it was natural enough for Mr. Bevan to hold as long as he could by such an idea.

And so those two most strangely assorted beings, the clergyman and the vampyre, walked together towards the pretty and picturesque dwelling of the former.

"The distance is short," said Mr. Bevan.

"Nay, that matters not," replied Varney.

"I spoke because I thought you seemed fatigued."

"No, my frame is of iron. My heart is bowed down with many griefs, but the physical structure knows no feeling of dejection. The life I possess is no common one. Oh! would that it were so, that I might shuffle it off as any ordinary men can do."

"Do not say that. Who knows but that after all your living accomplishes better things?"

"I cannot say that it accomplishes aught completely but one thing."

"And that?"

"That is my most exquisite misery."

"Even that may pass away. But here we are at my little garden gate. Come in, and fear nothing; for if you will seek Heaven, as I would wish you, you will find this place such a haven of peace, and such a refuge against the storms of life, as you hardly fancied existed, I dare say, in this world."

"Not for me. I did not fancy that there existed a spot on earth on which I could lie down in peace, and yet it may be here."

Chapter CXCVII.

VARNEY OPENS THE VAST STORE-HOUSE OF HIS MEMORY.

A more singular conversation than that which took place between Varney, the Vampyre, and this minister of religion, could not be conceived. If there was any one particle of goodness existing in Varney's disposition, we may suspect it would now be developed.

Perhaps the whole domestic history of the world never yet exhibited so remarkable an association as that between Mr. Bevan and Varney; and when they sat down together in the little cheerful study of the former, never had four walls enclosed two beings of the same species, and yet of such opposite pursuits.

But we can hardly call Varney, the Vampyre, human — his space of existence had been lengthened out beyond the ordinary routine of human existence, and the kind of vitality that he now enjoyed, if one might be allowed the expression, was something distinct and peculiar.

It speaks volumes, however, for the philanthropy and liberality of the minister of any religion who could hold out the hand of fellowship to so revolting and to so horrible an existence.

But Mr. Bevan was no common man. His religion was doctrinal, certainly, but it was free from bigotry; and his charity to the feelings, opinions, and prejudices of others was immense.

He was accustomed to say "may not my feelings be prejudices," and one of the sublimest precepts of the whole Scriptures was to him that which says, "Judge not, lest ye, too, should be judged."

Hence it was that he would not allow himself to revolt at Varney. It had seemed right to the great Creator of all things that there should be such a being, and therefore, he, Mr. Bevan, would neither question nor contemn it.

"Look about you," he said to Varney with a disordered gaze; "you seem to look very about you as if there was danger in the atmosphere you breathe, but be assured you are safe here; it shall be my life for your life if any harm should be attempted to be done you."

Varney looked at him for a few moments silence, and then in his deep and sepulchral voice he spoke, saying, —

"My race is run."

"What mean you by that expression?"

"I mean I shall no longer be a terror to the weak, nor a curiosity to the strong. In time past, more than once I have tried to shuffle off the evil of this frightful existence, but some accident, strange, wild, and wonderful, has brought me back to life again."

"Perhaps not an accident," said Mr. Bevan.

"You may be right, but when I have sought to rid the world of my own bad company, I have been moved to do so by some act of kindness and consideration, most contrary to my deserts; and then again when I have been cast back by the waves of fate upon the shores of existence, my heart is burdened, and I have begun to plan to work mischief and misery and woe to all."

"I can understand how your feelings have alternated, but I hope that out association will have better result."

"Yes, a better result, for with consummate art, with cool perseverance and extended knowledge, I trust I may think of some means which cannot fail of changing this living frame to that dust from which it sprung, and to which it should long since have returned."

"You believe in that, but do you not think there is a pure spirit that will yet live, independent of the groveling earth?"

"There are times when I have hoped that even that fable were true; but you have promised me rest, will you keep your word?"

"That will I most certainly; but will you keep yours? You have promised me some details of your extraordinary existence, and as a divine, and I hope in some degree as a philosopher, I look for them with some degree of anxiety."

"You shall have them — leave me pens, ink and paper, and in the solitude of this room, until tomorrow morning, and you shall have what I believe to be the origin of this most horrible career."

"Your wishes shall be consulted — but, will you not take refreshment?"

"Nothing — nothing. My refreshment is one I need not name to you, and when forced by the world's customs and considerations of my own safety, I have partaken of man's usual food, if has but ill accorded with my preternatural existence, I eat not — drink not — here. You know me as I am."

As he continued speaking, Varney evidently grew weaker, and Mr. Bevan could scarcely persuade himself that it was not through actual want of nourishment, but the Vampyre assured him that it was not so, and that rest would recruit him, to which opinion, as the experience of human nature generally afforded no index to Varney's peculiar habits, he was forced to subscribe.

There was a couch in the room, and upon that Varney laid himself, and as he seemed indisposed for further conversation, Mr. Bevan left him, promising to return to him as he himself requested in the morning, with the hope of finding that he had completed some sort of narrative to the effect mentioned.

It can scarcely be said that Mr. Bevan had thoroughly made up his mind to leave his guest for so long a period, and as there was a window that looked from the study in his little garden, he thought, that by now and then peeping in, to see that all was right, he could scarcely be considered as breaking faith with his mysterious guest.

"He will surely attempt nothing against his own life," thought Mr. Bevan, "for already he seems to be impressed with the futility of such an attempt, and to think that when he has made them he has been made the sport of circumstances that had forced him back to life again, despite all his wishes to the contrary."

Mr. Bevan reasoned thus, but he little knew what was passing in the mind of Varney the Vampire.

After about two hours more, when the night was profoundly dark, the liberal-minded but anxious clergyman went into his garden, for the purpose of peeping into his study, and he then saw, as he supposed, his visitor lying enveloped in his large brown cloak, lying upon the couch.

He was better pleased to see he was sleeping, and recovering from the great fatigue of which he complained, instead of writing, although that writing promised to be of so interesting a character, and he crept softly away for fear of awakening him.

The hour had now arrived at which Mr. Bevan usually retired to rest, but he delayed doing so, and let two hours more elapse, after which, he again stole out of his garden, and peeped into the study.

There lay the long, gaunt, slumbering figure upon the couch.

"I am satisfied," said Mr. Bevan to himself; "fatigue has completely overcome him, and he will sleep till morning now. I long much to become acquainted with his strange eventful history."

After this, Mr. Bevan retired to rest, but not until in prayer he had offered up his thanks, and stated his hopes of being able to turn aside from the wicked path he had been pursuing, the wretched man who at that moment was slumbering peacefully beneath his roof.

We should have less of opposition to churchmen, if they were all like Mr. Bevan, and not the wily, ravenous, illiberal, grasping crew they really are. There was no priestcraft in him, he was almost enough to make one in love with his doctrines, be they what they might, so that they were his.

Although we say that he retired to rest, we should more properly say he retired to try to rest; for, after all, there were feelings of excitement and anxiety about him which he could not repress wholly; and although he had every reason to believe his guest was sleeping, and calmly sleeping too, yet he found he was becoming painfully alive to the slightest sound.

He became nervously alive to the least interruption, and kept fancying that he heard the slightest indications of movements in the house, such as at any other time he would have paid no attention to.

It always happened too, provokingly, that just as he was dropping into a slight slumber, that he thought he heard one of these noises, and then he would start, awake, and sit up in his bed, and listen attentively, until tired nature forced him to repose again.

Those who have passed such a night of watchfulness need not be told how very very exciting it becomes, and hour after hour becomes more intense and acute, and the power of escaping its fell influence less and less.

Indeed, it was not until the dawn of morning that Mr. Bevan tasted the sweets of sound repose, then, as is generally usual after nights of fever and disquietude, the cool, pure, life-giving air of early morn, produced quite a different state of feeling, and his repose was calm and serene.

Chapter CCXI.

THE FLIGHT OF THE VAMPYRE. – THE MASS.

*A*s was to be expected, in consequence of the sleepless state in which he had been in the early part of the night, Mr. Bevan did not awaken at his usually early hour; and as his confidential servant had stolen into his room upon tip-toe, and seeing that he was sleeping quietly and soundly, she did not think proper to disturb him.

An autumnal sun was gleaming into his lattice window when he spontaneously awoke, and the reflection of the sunlight upon a particular portion of the wall convinced him that it was late.

For a moment or two, he lay in that dreamy state when we are just conscious of where we are, without having the smallest pretensions to another idea; and probably he would have dropped to sleep again had it not been that his servant again opened the door, the lock of which had the infirmity of giving a peculiar snap every time it was used, and that thoroughly awakened him.

"Oh, you are awake, sir?" said his old servant, "I never knew you sleep so long. Breakfast has been ready an hour and a half. It's a cool morning, sir, and what's worse, I can't get into your study to light you a bit of fire, which I thought you would want."

The interruption altogether, and the mention of the study, served completely to arouse Mr. Bevan to a remembrance of the events of the preceding evening, and he cried, —

"What's the time? What's the time?"

"It's after nine, and as for the study —"

"Never mind the study — never mind the study, I will be down directly."

Scarcely ever had Mr. Bevan dressed himself with such precipitation as he now did.

"How provoking," he thought, "that upon this particular occasion, when I should like to have been up and stirring earlier than usual, I am a good hour and a half later. It can't be helped though, and if my guest of last night is to be credited, he won't be waiting for his breakfast."

The simple toilet of the kind-hearted clergyman was soon completed, and then he ran down stairs to the lower part of his house, and finding that his servant was in the kitchen, he thought he might at once proceed to his study, to speak to the extraordinary inmate.

He had furnished Varney with the means of locking himself in for the night, and it would seem that the vampyre had fully availed himself of those means, for when Mr. Bevan tried the door, he found himself as much at fault as his servant had been, and could not by any means effect an admittance.

"He said his fatigue was great," remarked Mr. Bevan, "and so it seems it was, for surely he is yet sleeping. It is a comfort when one oversleeps oneself that the necessity for one's rising has been put off by the same means."

Unwilling to disturb Varney, and not hearing from the slightest movement from within that he had yet done so, Mr. Bevan went to his breakfast, much better satisfied than he had been a quarter of an hour since, and as the breakfast room adjoined the study, he had every opportunity if the vampyre should be stirring, of hearing and attending to him.

Not above ten minutes elapsed in this kind of way, when Mr. Bevan, although he saw nothing of his guest, heard something of the approach of a visitor, by the trampling of feet upon the gravel walk, and upon looking through the window, he saw that it was his friend Sir George Crofton from the hall.

It was rather an early hour for visitors, but still under the peculiar circumstances, Sir George might be supposed not to stand upon ceremony in calling upon the clergyman of his parish and upon his old friend, combining, as Mr. Bevan did, both these characters in one.

It was rather, though, placing the clergyman in a situation of difficulty, for while there was nothing he so much hated as mystery and concealment, he yet could not, upon the spur of the moment, decide whether he ought to inform Sir George of the presence of Varney or not.

After the frightful manner in which the baronet and his family had suffered from what might be called the machinations of the vampyre, it could scarcely be supposed that his feelings were otherwise than in a most exasperated state, and it might, for all he knew, be actually dangerous for the personal safety of that guest whom he had pledged his honor to protect, to allow Sir George Crofton to know at all that he was beneath his roof.

While he was engaged in these considerations, and before he could come to anything like a conclusion concerning them, Sir George was announced, and shown as a privileged visitor into the parlor.

We cannot but pause to make a remark upon the stupendous change that had taken place in the appearance of that unhappy man. When first we presented him to the reader, he was as good a specimen of the hale hearty English gentleman, as we could wish to see; good humor and good health beamed forth on every feature of his face; and well they might do so, for although the past had not been uncheckered by trials, the future wore to him a sunny aspect, and some of the feelings of his youth were returning to him, in the happiness of his children.

But what a change was now. Twenty years of ordinary existence, with extraordinary vicissitudes, would scarcely have produced the effect that the events of the last fortnight had upon that unhappy father.

He appeared to be absolutely sinking into the grave with grief, and not only was his countenance strangely altered, but the tones of his voice were completely changed from what they had been.

Alas! poor Sir George Crofton, never will the light of joy again illumine your face. There are griefs, inevitable griefs, which time will heal, griefs which the more we look upon them the more we find our reason array itself against them. But his sorrows were of a different complexion, and were apt to grow more gigantic from thought.

"Good morning, Mr. Bevan," he said, "I am an early visitor, sir."

"Not more early than welcome, Sir George. I pray you to be seated."

"You are very good," said the baronet, "but when one comes at an hour like this, I am of opinion that he ought to come with something like a good excuse for his intrusion."

"There is none needed, I assure you."

"But I have been thinking upon the advice which you have given me, Mr. Bevan, to leave this part of the country, and try the endeavor, by the excitement and changes of foreign travel, to lessen the weight of my calamities."

"I think your determination is a good one, Sir George."

"Probably it is the best I could adopt, but I must confess that I should set about it in better spirit, but I am haunted by apprehensions."

"Apprehensions, Sir George! is not the worst passed?"

"It may be, and I hope to Heaven it is, but I have another child, another daughter, fair and beautiful as my lost Clara; but what security have I that that dreadful being may not pursue her, and with frightful vindictiveness drive her to the grave."

Mr. Bevan was silent two or three minutes, and the idea crossed him that if he could get Sir George in the proper state of mind, it would be, perhaps, better that he should know that the vampyre was in the house, and in such a state of mind as not to renew any outrages against him or his family, than that he should go abroad with the dread clinging to him of being still followed and persecuted by that dreadful being.

"Sir George," said Mr. Bevan, in an extremely serious voice, "Sir George, did you ever reason with yourself calmly and seriously, and in a Christian spirit, about this affair."

"Calmly, Mr. Bevan! how could I reason calmly?"

"I have scarcely put my question as I ought; what I meant to ask was, what are your personal feelings towards the vampyre? We must recollect that even he, dreadful existence as he is, was fashioned by the same God that fashioned us; and who shall say but he may be the victim of a horrible and stern necessity? Who shall say but he may be tortured by remorse, and that the circumstances connected with your daughter, of which you so justly complain, may be to him sources of the bitterest reflection? What if you were to be assured that never more would that mysterious man cross your path, if man we can call him? Do you think that you could then forgive him?"

"It is hard to say, but the feeling that my other child was safe would prompt me much."

"Sir George, I could make a communication to you if I thought you would listen to it patiently; if you will swear to me to be calm."

"I swear, tell me — oh, tell me!"

"The vampyre is in this house."

Chapter CCXII.

THE MYSTERIOUS DISAPPEARANCE.

One may form some sort of judgment of the astonishment with which Sir George Crofton heard this statement. He looked indeed a few moments at Mr. Bevan, as if he had a strong suspicion that he could not possibly have heard aright, so that the good clergyman was induced to repeat his statement, which he did, by saying, —

"Sir George, I assure you, however remarkable such a circumstance may be, and however much you may feel yourself surprised at it, that in the extreme bitterness of spirit, and feeling all the compunction that you could possibly wish him to feel, Varney the Vampyre is now an inmate of this house."

Had a bomb-shell fallen at his feet, Sir George Crofton could not have felt more surprised, and he exhibited that surprise by several times repeating to himself, —

"Varney the Vampyre an inmate of this house! Varney the Vampyre here!"

"Yes," said Mr. Bevan, "here, an inmate of this house. He is within a few paces of you, slumbering in the next apartment, and from his own lips you shall have the assurance that never again will you have any trouble on his account, and that he most bitterly and most deeply regrets the suffering he had brought upon you and yours."

"Will that regret," said Sir George, excitedly, "restore the dead? Will that regret give me my child again? Will it open the portals of the grave, and restore her to me who was the life and joy of my existence? Tell me, will it do that? If not, what is his regret to me?"

"No, Sir George, no, his regret will not do that. There is such power, but it is not upon earth. Heaven delegates not such fearful responsibilities to any of its creatures, and the only reason which has induced me to make this confidence was to take from you the fearful anxiety of fancying yourself followed by that dreadful being."

"Vengeance," replied Sir George Crofton, "vengeance shall be mine. In the name of my lost child, I cry for vengeance. Shall he not perish who has made her whom I love perish? Make way, Mr. Bevan, make way."

"No, Sir George, no, this is my house. I, as a Christian minister, offered the hospitality of its roof to Varney the Vampyre, and I cannot violate my word."

"You speak, sir, to a desperate man," cried Sir George; "no roof to me is sanctified, beneath which the murderer of my child finds a shelter. Mr. Bevan, the respect that one man has for another, or ever has had for another, cannot exceed the respect I have for you; but with all that, sir, I cannot forget my own personal wrongs; the shade of my murdered Clara beckons me."

"Fly, Varney, fly," cried Mr. Bevan, "fly."

"Is it so?" said Sir George; "do you then side with my direst foe?"

"No — no, I side with Sir George Croton against his own furious unbridled passions."

Neither from profession nor practice was Mr. Bevan one who was likely to force to resist Sir George, and at the moment the baronet was about to lay hands upon him to hurl him from his path, he slipped aside.

"Rash man," he said, "the time will come when you will repent this deed."

The door of the study was still fast, but to the infuriated Sir George, that opposed but a very frail obstacle, and with the effort of a moment he forced it open, and rushed into the apartment.

"Varney, monster," he cried, "prepare to meet your doom. Your career is at an end."

Mr. Bevan was after him, and in the room with him in a moment, fully expecting that some very dreadful scene would ensue, as a consequence of the unbridled passion of Sir George Crofton.

Sir George Crofton was standing in the center of the apartment with Varney's large brown cloak in his grasp, which he had dragged from the sofa, but the vampyre himself was not to be seen.

"Escaped!" he cried, "escaped!"

"Thank Heaven, then," said Mr. Bevan, "that this roof has not been desecrated by an act of violence. Oh, Sir George, it is a mercy that time has been given to think he has escaped."

"I'll follow him, were it to perdition."

Sir George was about to open the window and rush into the garden, thinking, of course, it was by that means by which the vampyre escaped, but Mr. Bevan laid his hand upon the smooth gravel path that was immediately below the casement.

"Behold," he said, "one of the first results of an autumnal night. That this coating of fleecy sleet, you see, is undisturbed; it fell about midnight; nine hours have since elapsed, and you perceive there is no foot mark upon it, and in what direction would you chase Varney the Vampyre while he has such a start of you?"

Infuriated with passion, as was Sir George Crofton, the reasonableness of this statement struck him forcibly, and he became silent. A revulsion of feeling took place; he staggered to a seat, and wept.

"Yes, he is gone," he said. "Yes, the murderer of my child is gone; vengeance is delayed, but perhaps not altogether stopped. Oh, Mr. Bevan, Mr. Bevan, why did you tell me he was here?"

"I do now regret having done so, but I believed him to be here, and his departure is as mysterious to me as it can be to you."

Mr. Bevan cast his eyes upon the table, and there he saw a large packet addressed to himself. Sir George saw it too, at the same moment, and pointing to it, said, —

"Is that the vampyre's legacy to his new friend?"

"Sir George," said Mr. Bevan, "let it suffice that the packet is addressed to me."

All the good breeding of the gentleman returned, and Sir George Crofton bowed as he left the room, closely followed by the clergyman, who was as much bewildered by the disappearance of Varney as even Sir George could possibly be. He had a most intense desire to examine the packet, with the hope that there he should find some explanation or solution of the mystery; but not being aware, of course, of what it contained, he could not tell if it would be prudent to trust Sir George at that time with its contents.

As may be well supposed, there was a sort of restraint in the manner of both of them after what had happened, and they did what was very rare with them both, parted without making any appointment for the future.

But whatever might be the feelings of Sir George Crofton then, a little reflection would be quite sure to bring him back again to a proper estimation of what was due to such a friend as Mr. Bevan, and we cannot anticipate any serious interruption to their general friendly intercourse.

The moment the clergyman found himself alone, he with eager steps went into his study, and eagerly seized upon the packet that was left to him by the vampyre, the outside of which merely bore the superscription of — "These to the Rev. Mr. Bevan, and strictly private."

With eagerness he tore open the envelope, and the first thing that attracted his attention was a long, narrow slip of paper, on which were written the following words: —

"It was not my intention to trespass largely upon your hospitality; it would have been unjust — almost approaching to criminality so to do. I could only think of taking a brief refuge in your house, so brief as should just enable me to avail myself of the shadows of night to escape from a neighborhood where I knew I should be hunted.

"The few hours which I have quietly remained beneath your roof have been sufficient to accomplish that object, and the we papers that I leave you accompanying this, contain the personal information concerning me you asked. They had been previously prepared, and are at your service.

"To attempt to follow me would be futile, for I have as ample means of making a rapid journey as you could possibly call to your aid, and I have the advantage of many hours' start; under these circumstances I have no hesitation in telling you that my destination is Naples, and that perhaps the next you hear of me will be, that some stranger in a fit of madness has cast himself into the crater of a burning mountain, which would at once consume him and all his sorrows.

"VARNEY THE VAMPYRE."

One may imagine the feelings with which Mr. Bevan read this most strange and characteristic epistle — feelings that for some moments kept him a prisoner to the most painful thoughts.

All that he had hoped to accomplish by the introduction of Varney to his house was lost now. He had but in fact given him a better opportunity of carrying out a terrible design — a design which now there really did not appear to be any means of averting the consummation of.

"Alas! alas!" he said, "this is most grievous, and what can I do now, to avert the mischief — nothing, absolutely nothing. If it be true that he has, as he says he has, the means of hastening on his journey, all pursuit would be utterly useless."

This was taking a decidedly correct view of the matter. Varney was not the sort of man, if he really intended to reach Naples quickly, to linger on his route, and then there was another view of the subject which could not but occur to Mr. Bevan, and that was, that his mentioned destination might be but a blind to turn off pursuit.

Chapter CCXIII.

VARNEY GIVES SOME PERSONAL ACCOUNT OF HIMSELF.

Never had Mr. Bevan in all his recollection been in such a state of hesitation as now.

He was a man usually of rapid resolves, and very energetic action; but the circumstances that had recently taken place were of so very remarkable a nature, that he was not able to bring to bear upon them any portion of his past experience.

He felt that he could come to no determination, but was compelled by the irresistible force of events to be a spectator instead of an actor in what might ensue.

"I shall hear," he thought, "if any such event happens at Naples as that to which Varney has adverted, and until I do so, or until a sufficient length of time has elapsed to make me feel certain that he will not plunge into that burning abyss, I shall be a prey to every kind of fear; and then again as regards Sir George Crofton. What am I to say to him? Shall I show him this note or not?"

Even that was a question which he could not absolutely decide in his own mind, although he was strongly inclined to think that it would be highly desirable to do so, and while he was considering the point, and holding the note in his hand, his eye fell upon the other papers which had been enclosed with it, and addressed to him.

Hoping and expecting that there he should find something that would better qualify him to come to an accurate conclusion, he took up the packet, and found that the topmost paper bore the following endorsement: —

"SOME PARTICULARS CONCERNING MY OWN LIFE."

"There, then," said Mr. Bevan, "is what he has promised me."

It was to be expected that Mr. Bevan should take up those papers with a very considerable amount of curiosity, and as he could not think what course immediately to pursue that would do good to Varney or anybody else, he thought he had better turn his attention at once to the documents that the vampyre had left to his perusal.

Telling his servant, then, not to allow him to be disturbed unless the affair was a very urgent one indeed, he closed the door of his study, and commenced reading one of the most singular statements that ever created being placed upon paper. It was as follows: —

*D*uring my brief intercourse — and it has always been brief when of a confidential nature with various persons — I have created surprise by talking of individuals and events long since swallowed up in the almost forgotten past. In these few pages I declare myself more fully.

In the reign of the First Charles, I resided in a narrow street, in the immediate neighborhood of Whitehall. It was a straggling, tortuous thoroughfare, going down to the Thames; it matters little what were my means of livelihood, but I have no hesitation in saying that I was a well-paid agent in some of the political movements which graced and disgraced that period.

London was then a mass of mean-looking houses; with here and there one that looked like a palace, compared with its humbler neighbors. Almost every street appeared to be under the protection of some great house situated somewhere in its extent, but such of those houses as have survived the wreck of time rank now with their neighbors, and are so strangely altered, that I, who knew many of them well, could now scarcely point to the place where they used to stand.

I took no prominent part in the commotions of that period, but I saw the head of a king held up in its gore at Whitehall as a spectacle for the multitude.

There were thousands of persons in England who had aided to bring about that result, but who were very far from expecting it, and who were the first to fall under the ban of the gigantic power they had themselves raised.

Among these were many of my employers; men, who had been quite willing to shake the stability of a throne so far as the individual occupying it was concerned; but who certainly never contemplated the destruction of monarchy; so the death of the First Charles, and the dictatorship of Cromwell, made royalists in abundance.

They had raised a spirit they could not quell again, and this was a fact which the stern, harsh man, Cromwell, with whom I had many interviews, was aware of.

My house was admirably adapted for the purposes of secrecy and seclusion, and I became a thriving man from the large sums I received for aiding the escape of distinguished loyalists, some of whom lay for a considerable time *perdu* at my house, before an eligible opportunity arrived of dropping down the river quietly to some vessel which would take them to Holland.

It was to offer me so much per head for these royalists that Cromwell sent for me, and there was one in particular who had been private secretary to the Duke of Cleveland, a young man merely, of neither family nor rank, but of great ability, whom Cromwell was exceedingly anxious to capture.

I think there likewise must have been some private reasons which induced the dictator of the Commonwealth to be so anxious concerning this Master Francis Latham, which was the name of the person alluded to.

It was late one evening when a stranger came to my house, and having desired to see me, was shown into a private apartment, when I immediately waited upon him.

"I am aware," he said, "that you have been confidentially employed by the Duke of Cleveland, and I am aware that you have been very useful to distressed loyalists, but in aiding Master Francis Latham, the duke's secretary, you will be permitted almost to name your own terms."

I named a hundred pounds, which at that time was a much larger sum than now, taking into consideration the relative value. One half of it was paid to me at once, and the other promised within four-and-twenty hours after Latham had effected his escape.

I was told that at half-past twelve o'clock that night, a man dressed in common working apparel, and with a broom over his shoulder would knock at my door and ask if he could be recommended to a lodging, and that by those tokens I should know him to be Francis Latham. A Dutch lugger, I was further told, was lying near Gravesend, on board of which, to earn my money, I was expected to place the fugitive.

All this was duly agreed upon; I had a boat in readiness, with a couple of watermen upon whom I could depend, and I was far from anticipating any extraordinary difficulties in carrying out the enterprise.

I had a son about twelve years of age, who being a sharp acute lad, I found very useful upon several occasions, and I never scrupled to make him acquainted with any such affair as this that I am recounting.

Half-past twelve o'clock came, and in a very few minutes after that period of time there came a knock at my door, which my son answered, and according to arrangement, there was the person with a broom, who asked to be recommended to a lodging, and who was immediately requested to walk in.

He seemed rather nervous, and asked me if I thought there was much risk.

"No," said I, "no more than ordinary risk in all these cases, but we must wait half an hour 'till the tide turns. For just now to struggle against it down the river would really be nothing else but courting observation."

To this he perfectly agreed, and sat down by my fireside.

I was as anxious as he to get the affair over, for it was a ticklish job, and Oliver Cromwell, if he had brought anything of the kind exactly home to me, would as life order me to be shot as he would have taken his luncheon in the name of the Lord.

I accordingly went down to the water-side to speak to the men who were lying there with the boat, and had ascertained from them that in about twenty minutes the tide would begin to ebb in the center of the stream, when two men confronted me.

Practiced as I was in the habits and appearances of the times, I guessed at once who they were. In fact, a couple of Oliver Cromwell's dismounted dragoons were always well known.

"You are wanted," said one of them to me."

"Yes, you are particularly wanted," said the other.

"But, gentlemen, I am rather busy," said I. "In an hour's time I will do myself the pleasure, if you please, of waiting upon you anywhere you wish to name."

The only reply they made to this was the practical one, of getting on each side of me, and then hurrying me on, past my own door.

I was taken right away to St. James's at a rapid pace, being hurried through one of the court yards; we paused at a small door, at which was a sentinel.

My two guides communicated something to him, and he allowed us to pass. There was a narrow passage without any light, and through another door, at which was likewise a sentinel, who turned the glare of a lantern upon me and my conductors. Some short explanation was given to him likewise, during which I heard the words His Highness, which was the title which Cromwell had lately assumed.

They pushed me through this doorway, closed it behind me, and left me alone in the dark.

Chapter *CCXIV.*

A SINGULAR INTERVIEW, AND THE CONSEQUENCES OF PASSION.

*B*eing perfectly ignorant of where I was, I thought the most prudent plan was to stand stock still, for if I advanced it might be into danger, and my retreat was evidently cut off.

Moreover, those who brought me there must have some sort of intention, and it was better for me to leave them to develop it than to take any steps myself, which might be of a very hazardous nature.

That I was adopting the best policy I was soon convinced, for a flash of light suddenly came upon me, and I heard a gruff voice, say, —

"Who goes there? come this way."

I walked on, and passed through an open door way into a small apartment, in the center of which, standing by a common deal table on which his clenched hand was resting, I found Oliver Cromwell himself.

"So, sirrah," he said, "royalists and pestilent characters are to ravage the land, are they so? answer me."

"I have no answer to make, your highness," said I.

"God's mercy, no answer, when in your own house the Duke of Cleveland's proscribed secretary lies concealed."

I felt rather staggered, but was certain I had been betrayed by some one, and Cromwell continued rapidly, without giving me time to speak.

"The Lord is merciful, and so are we, but the malignant must be taken by the beloved soldiers of the Commonwealth, and the gospel God-fearing men, who always turn to the Lord, with short carbines, will accompany you. The malignant shall be taken from your house, by you, and the true God-fearing dragoons shall linger in the shade behind. You will take him to the river side, where the Lord willing, there will be a boat with a small blue ensign, on board of which you will place him, wishing him good speed."

He paused, and looked fixedly upon me by the aid of the miserable light that was in the apartment.

"What then, your highness?" I said.

"Then you will probably call upon us tomorrow for a considerable sum, which will be due to you for this good service to the Commonwealth; yes, it shall be profitable to fight the battles of the Lord."

I must confess, I had expected a very different result from the interview, which I had been greatly in fear would have resulted, in greatly endangering my liberty. Cromwell was a man not to be tampered with; I knew my danger, and was not disposed to sacrifice myself for Master Latham.

"Your highness shall be obeyed," I said.

"Ay, verily," he replied, "and if we be not obeyed, we must make ourselves felt with a strong arm of flesh. What ho! God-fearing Simkins, art thou there?"

"Yes, the Lord willing," said a dragoon, making his appearance at the door.

Cromwell merely made him a sign with his hand, and he laid hold of the upper part of my arm, as though it had been in a vice, and led me out into the passage again where the sentinels were posted.

In the course of a few moments, I was duly in custody of my two guards again, and we were proceeding at a very rapid pace towards my residence.

It was not a very agreeable affair, view it in whatever light I might; but as regarded Cromwell, I knew my jeopardy, and it would be perceived that I had not hesitated a moment in obeying him. Moreover, I considered, for I knew he was generous, I should have a good round sum by the transaction, which added to the fifty pounds I had received from the royalists, made the affair appear to me in a pleasant enough light. Indeed, I was revolving in my mind as I went along, whether it would not be worth while, almost entirely to attach myself to the protector.

"If," I reasoned with myself, "I should do that, and still preserve myself a character with the royalists, I should thrive."

But it will be seen that an adverse circumstance put an end to all those dreams.

When we reached the door of my house, the first thing I saw was my son wiping his brow, as if he had undergone some fatigue; he ran up to me, and catching me by the arm, whispered to me.

I was so angered at the moment, that heedless of what I did, and passion getting the mastery over me, I with my clenched fist struck him to the earth. His head fell upon one of the hard round stones with which the street was paved, and he never spoke again. I had murdered him.

I don't know what happened immediately subsequent to this fearful deed; all I can recollect is, that there was a great confusion and a flashing of lights, and it appeared to me as if something had suddenly struck me down to the earth with great force.

When I did thoroughly awaken, I found myself lying upon a small couch, but in a very large apartment dimly lighted, and where there were many such couches ranged against the walls. A miserable light just enabled me to see about me a little, and some dim dusky-looking figures were creeping about the place.

It was a hospital that the protector had lately instituted in the Strand.

I tried to speak, but could not; my tongue seemed glued to my mouth, and I could not, and then a change came upon my sense of sight, and I could scarcely see at all the dim dusky-looking figures about me.

Some one took hold of me by the wrist, and I heard one say, quite distinctly, —

"He's entirely going, now."

Suddenly it seemed as if something had fallen with a crushing influence upon my chest, and then a consciousness that I was gasping for breath, and then I thought I was at the bottom of the sea. There was a moment, only a moment, of frightful agony, and then came a singing sound, like the rush of waters, after which, I distinctly felt some one raising me in their arms. I was dropped again, my limbs felt numbed and chill, an universal spasm shot through my whole system, I opened my eyes, and found myself lying in the open air, by a newly opened grave.

A full moon was sailing through the sky and the cold beams were upon my face; a voice sounded in my ears, a deep and solemn voice — and painfully distinct was every word it uttered.

"Mortimer," it said, for that was my name, "Mortimer, in life you did one deed which at once cast you out from all hope that anything in that life would be remembered in the world to come to your advantage. You poisoned the pure font of mercy, and not upon such as you can the downy freshness of Heaven's bounty fall. Murderer, murderer of that being sacredly presented to your care by the great Creator of all things, live henceforth a being accursed. Be to yourself a desolation and a blight, shunned by all that is good and virtuous, armed against all men, and all men armed against thee, Varney the Vampyre."

I staggered to my feet, the scene around me was a churchyard, I was gaunt and thin, my clothes hung about me in tattered remnants. The damp smell of the grave hung about them, I met an aged man, and asked him where I was. He looked at me with a shudder, as though I had escaped from some charnel house.

"Why this is Isledon," said he.

A peal of bells came merrily upon the night air.

"What means that?" said I.

"Why this is the anniversary of the Restoration."

"The Restoration! What Restoration?"

"Why of the royal family to the throne, to be sure, returned this day last year. Have you been asleep so long that you don't know that?"

I shuddered and walked on, determined to make further inquiries, and to make them with so much caution, that the real extent of my ignorance should scarce be surmised, and the result was to me of the most astonishing character.

I found that I had been in the trance of death for nearly two years, and that during that period, great political changes had taken place. The exiled royal family had been restored to the throne, and the most remarkable revulsion of feeling that had ever taken place in a nation had taken place in England.

But personally I had not yet fully awakened to all the horror of what I was. I had heard the words addressed to me, but I had attached no very definite meaning to them."

Chapter CCXV.

VARNEY'S NARRATIVE CONTINUED.

*M*r. Bevan paused when he had got thus far, to ask himself if he ought to give credence to what he read, or put it down as the raving of some person, whose wits had become tangled and deranged by misfortune.

Had the manuscript come to him without other circumstances to give it the air of truthfulness, he would have read it only as a literary curiosity, but it will be remembered that he had been a spectator of the resuscitation of Clara Crofton, which afforded of itself a very frightful verification of Varney's story — a story so horrible in all its details, that but for the great interest which it really possessed, he would have deeply regretted the mixing it up in his memory with brighter subjects.

There was something yet to read in the papers before him, and thinking that it was better to know all at once than to leave his imagination to work upon matters so likely seriously to affect it, he resumed his perusal of these papers, which might be considered the autobiography of Varney.

I have already said that I was not yet fully alive to the horror of what I was, but I soon found what the words which had been spoken to me by the mysterious being who had exhumed me meant; I was a thing accursed, a something to be shunned by all men, a horror, a blight, and a desolation.

I felt myself growing sick and weak, as I traversed the streets of the city, and yet I loathed the sight of food, whenever I saw it.

I reached my own house, and saw that it had been burned down; there lay nothing but a heap of charred ruins where it once stood.

But I had an interest in those ruins, for from time to time I had buried considerable sums of money beneath the flooring of the lowest apartments, and I had every reason to believe, as such a secret treasure was only known to myself, that it remained untouched.

I waited until the moon became obscured by some passing clouds, and then having a most intimate knowledge of the locality, I commenced groping about the ruins, and removing a portion of them, until I made my way to the spot where my money was hidden.

The morning came, however, and surprised me at my occupation; so I hid myself among the ruins of what had once been my home for a whole day, and never once stirred from my concealment.

Oh, it was a long and weary day. I could hear the prattle of children at play, an inn or change-house was near at hand, and I could hear noisy drinkers bawling forth songs that had been proscribed in the Commonwealth.

I saw a poor wretch hunted nearly to death, close to where I lay concealed, because from the fashion of his garments, and the cut of his hair, he was supposed to belong to the deposed party.

But the long expected night came at last. It was a dark one, too, so that it answered my purpose well.

I had found an old rusty knife among the ruins, and with that I set to work to dig up my hidden treasure; I was successful, and found it all.

Not a guinea had been removed, although in the immediate neighborhood, there were those who would have sacrificed a human life for any piece of gold that I had hoarded.

I made no enquiries about any one that had belonged to me. I dreaded to receive some horrible and circumstantial answer, but I did get a slight piece of news, as I left the ruins, although I asked not for it.

"There's a poor devil," said one; "did you ever see such a wretch in all your life?"

"Why, yes," said another, "he's enough to turn one's canary sour, he seems to have come up from the ruins of Mortimer's house. By-the-by did you ever hear what became of him?"

"Yes, to be sure, he was shot by two of Cromwell's dragoons in some fracas or another."

"Ah, I recollect now, I heard as much. He murdered his son, didn't he?"

I passed on. Those words seemed to send a bolt of fire through the brain, and I dreaded that the speaker might expatiate upon them.

A slow misty rain was falling, which caused the streets to be very much deserted, but being extremely well acquainted with the city, I passed on till I came to that quarter which was principally inhabited by Jews, who I knew would take my money without any troublesome questions being asked me, and also I could procure every accommodation required; and they did do so, for before another hour had passed over my head, I emerged richly habited as a chevalier of the period, having really not paid to the conscientious Israelite much more than four times the price of the clothing I walked away with.

And thus I was in the middle of London, with some hundreds of pounds in my pocket, and a horrible uncertainty as to what I was.

I was growing fainter and fainter still, and I feared that unless I succeeded in housing myself shortly, I should become a prey to some one who, seeing my exhausted condition, would, notwithstanding I had a formidable rapier by my side, rob me of all I possessed.

My career has been much too long and too checkered an one even to give the briefest sketch of. All I purpose here to relate is how I became convinced I was a vampyre, and that blood was my congenial nourishment and the only element of my new existence.

I passed on until I came to a street where I knew the houses were large but unfashionable, and that they were principally occupied by persons who made a trade by letting out apartments, and there I thought I might locate myself in safety.

As I made no difficulty about terms, there was no difficulty at all of any sort, and I found myself conducted into a tolerably handsome suite of rooms in the house of a decent-looking widow woman, who had two daughters, young and blooming girls, both of whom regarded me as the new lodger, with looks of anything but favor, considering my awful and cadaverous appearance most probably as promising nothing at all in the shape of pleasant companionship.

This I was quite prepared for — I had seen myself in a mirror — that was enough; and I could honestly have averred that a more ghastly and horrible looking skeleton, attired in silks and broad-cloth, never yet walked the streets of the city.

When I retired to my chamber, I was so faint and ill, that I could scarcely drag one foot after the other; and was ruminating what I should do, until a strange feeling crept over me that I should like — what? Blood! — raw blood, reeking and hot, bubbling and juicy, from the veins of some gasping victim.

A clock upon the stairs struck one. I arose and listened attentively; all was still in the house — still as the very grave.

It was a large old rambling building, and had belonged at one time, no doubt, to a man of some mark and likelihood in the world. My chamber was one of six that opened from a corridor of a considerable length, and which traversed the whole length of the house.

I crept out into this corridor, and listened again for full ten minutes, but not the slightest sound, save my own faint breathing, disturbed the stillness of the house; and that emboldened me so that, with my appetite for blood growing each moment stronger, I began to ask myself from whose veins I could seek strength and nourishment.

But how was I to proceed? How was I to know in that large house which of the sleepers I could attack with safety, for it had now come to that, that I was to attack somebody. I stood like an evil spirit, pondering over the best means of securing a victim.

And there came over me the horrible faintness again, that faintness which each moment grew worse, and which threatened completely to engulf me. I feared that some flush of it would overtake me, and then I should fall to rise no more; and strange as it may appear, I felt a disposition to cling to the new life that had been given to me. I seemed to be acquainted already with all its horrors, but not all its joys.

Suddenly the darkness of the corridor was cleared away, and soft and mellow light crept into it, and I said to myself, —

"The moon has risen."

Yes, the bright and beautiful moon, which I had felt the soft influence of when I lay among the graves, had emerged from the bank of clouds along the eastern sky, its beams descending through a little window. They streamed right through the corridor, faintly but effectually illuminating it, and letting me see clearly all the different doors leading to the different chambers.

And thus it was that I had light for anything I wished to do, but not information.

The moonbeams playing upon my face seemed to give me a spurious sort of strength. I did not know until after experience what a marked and sensible effect they would always have upon me, but I felt it even then, although I did not attribute it wholly to the influence of the queenly planet.

I walked on through the corridor, and some sudden influence seemed to guide me to a particular door. I know not how it was, but I laid my hand upon the lock, and said to myself, —

"I shall find my victim here."

Chapter CCXVI.

THE NIGHT ATTACK. — THE HORRIBLE CONCLUSION.

I paused yet a moment, for there came across me even then, after I had gone so far, a horrible dread of what I was about to do, and a feeling that there might be consequences arising from it that would jeopardize me greatly. Perhaps even then if a great accession of strength had come to my aid — mere bodily aid I mean — I should have hesitated, and the victim would have escaped; but, as if to mock me, there came that frightful feeling of exhaustion which felt so like the prelude to another death.

I no longer hesitated; I turned the lock of the door, and I thought that I must be discovered. I left it open about an inch, and then flew back to my own chamber.

I listened attentively; there was no alarm, no movement in any of the rooms — the same death-like stillness pervaded the house, and I felt that I was still safe.

A soft gleam of yellow looking light had come through the crevice of the door when I had opened it. It mingled strangely with the moonlight, and I concluded correctly enough, as I found afterwards, that a light was burning in the chamber.

It was at least another ten minutes before I could sufficiently re-assure myself to glide from my own room and approach that of the fated sleeper; but at length I told myself that I might safely do so, and the night was waning fast, and if anything was to be accomplished it must be done at once, before the first beams of early dawn should chase away the spirits of the night, and perhaps should leave me no power to act.

"What shall I be," I asked myself; "after another four-and-twenty hours of exhaustion? Shall I have power then to make the election of what I will do or what I will not? No, I may suffer the pangs of death again, and the scarcely less pangs of another revival."

This reasoning — if it may be called reasoning — decided me; and with cautious and cat-like footsteps, I again approached the bed-room door which I had opened.

I no longer hesitated, but at once crossed the threshold, and looked around me. It was the chamber of the youngest of my landlady's daughters, who, as far as I could judge, seemed to be about sixteen years of age; but they had evidently been so struck with my horrible appearance, that they had placed themselves as little as possible in my way, so that I could not be said to be a very good judge of their ages or of their looks.

I only knew she was the youngest, because she wore her hair long, and wore it in ringlets, which were loose and streaming over the pillow on which she slept, while her sister, I remarked, wore her hair plaited up, and completely off her neck and shoulders.

I stood by the bed-side, and looked upon this beautiful girl in all the pride of her young beauty, so gently and quietly slumbering. Her lips were parted, as though some pleasant images were passing in her mind, and induced a slight smile even in her sleep. She murmured twice, too, a word, which I thought was the name of some one — perchance the idol of her young heart — but it was too indistinct for me to catch it, nor did I care to hear; that which was perhaps a very cherished secret, indeed, mattered not to me. I made no pretensions to her affections, however strongly in a short time I might stand in her abhorrence.

One of her arms, which was exquisitely rounded, lay upon the coverlit; a neck, too, as white as alabaster, was partially exposed to my gaze, but I had no passions — it was food I wanted.

I sprung upon her. There was a shriek, but not before I had secured a draught of life blood from her neck. It was enough. I felt it dart through my veins like fire, and I was restored. From that moment I found out what was to be my sustenance; it was blood — the blood of the young and the beautiful.

The house was thoroughly alarmed, but not before I had retired to my own chamber. I was but partially dressed, and those few clothes I threw off me, and getting into my bed, I feigned to be asleep; so that when a gentleman who slept likewise in the house, but of whose presence I knew nothing, knocked hardly at my door, I affected to awaken in a fright, and called out, —

"What is it? what is it? — for God's sake tell me if it is a fire."

"No, no — but get up, sir, get up. There's some one in the place. An attempt at murder, I think, sir."

I arose and opened the door; so by the light he carried he saw that I had to dress myself — he was but half attired himself, and he carried his sword beneath his arm.

"It is a strange thing," he said; "but I have heard a shriek of alarm."

"And I likewise," said I; "but I thought it was a dream."

"Help! help! help!" cried the widow, who had risen, but stood upon the threshold of her own chamber; "thieves! thieves!"

By this time I had got on sufficient of my apparel that I could make an appearance, and, likewise with my sword in my hand, I sallied out into the corridor.

"Oh, gentlemen — gentlemen," cried the landlady, "did you hear anything?"

"A shriek, madam," said my fellow-lodger; "have you looked into your daughters' chambers?"

The room of the youngest daughter was the nearest, and into that she went at once. In another moment she appeared on the threshold again with a face as white as a sheet, then she wrung her hands, and said, —

"Murder! murder! — my child is murdered — my child is murdered, Master Harding," — which I found was the name of my fellow-lodger.

"Fling open one of the windows, and call for the watch," said he to me. "and I will search the room, and woe be to any one that I may find within its walls unauthorized."

I did as he desired, and called the watch, but the watch came not, and then, upon a second visit to her daughter, the landlady found she had only fainted, and that she had been deceived in thinking she was murdered by the sudden sight of the blood upon her neck, so the house was restored to something like quiet again, and the morning begin now near at hand, Mr. Harding retired to his chamber, and I to mine, leaving the landlady and her eldest daughter assiduous in their attentions to the younger.

How wonderfully revived I felt — I was quite a new creature when the sunlight came dancing into my apartment. I dressed and was about to leave the house, when Mr. Harding came out of one of the lower rooms, and intercepted me.

"Sir," he said, "I have not the pleasure of knowing you, but I have no doubt that an ordinary feeling of chivalry will prompt you to do all in your power to obviate the dread of such another night as the past."

"Dread, sir," said I, "the dread of what?"

"A very proper question," he said, "but one I can hardly answer; the girl states, she was awakened by some one biting her neck, and in proof of the story she actually exhibits the marks of teeth, and so terrified is she, that she declares that she shall never be able to sleep again."

"You astonish me."

"No doubt — it is sufficiently astonishing to excuse even doubts; but if you and I, who are both inmates of the house, were to keep watch tonight in the corridor, it might have the effect of completely quieting the imagination of the young girl, and perhaps result in the discovery of this nocturnal disturber of the peace."

"Certainly," said I, "command me in any way, I shall have great pleasure."

"Shall it be understood, then, that we meet at eleven in your apartment or in mine."

"Whichever you may please to consider the most convenient, sir."

"I mention my own then, which is the furthest door in the corridor, and where I shall be happy to see you at eleven o'clock."

There was a something about this young man's manner which I did not altogether like, and yet I could not come to any positive conclusion as to whether he suspected me, and therefore I thought it would be premature to fly, when perhaps there would be really no occasion for doing so; on the contrary, I made up my mind to wait the result of the evening, which might or might not be disastrous to me. At all events, I considered that I was fully equal to taking my own part, and if by the decrees of destiny I was really to be, as it were, repudiated from society, and made to endure a new, strange, and horrible existence, I did not see that I was called upon to be particular how I rescued myself from difficulties that might arise.

Relying, then, upon my own strength, and my own unscrupulous use of it, I awaited with tolerable composure the coming of night.

During the day I amused myself by walking about, and noting the remarkable changes which so short a period as two years had made in London. But these happened to be two years most abundantly prolific in change. The feelings and habits of people seemed to have undergone a thorough revolution, which I was the more surprised at when I learned by what thorough treachery the restoration of the exiled family was effected.

The day wore on; I felt no need of refreshment, and I began to feel my own proper position, and to feel that occasionally a draught of delicious life-blood, such as I had quaffed the night before was fresh marrow to my bones.

I could see, when I entered the house where I had made my temporary home, that notwithstanding that I considered my appearance wonderfully improved, that feeling was not shared in by others, for the whole family shrunk from me as though there had been a most frightful contamination in my touch, and as though the very air I had breathed was hateful and deleterious. I felt convinced that there had been some conversation concerning me, and that I was rather more than suspected. I certainly could then have left the place easily and quietly, but I had a feeling of defiance, which did not enable me to do so.

I felt as if I were an injured being, and ought to resist a something that looked like oppression.

"Why," I said to myself, "have I been rescued from the tomb to be made the sport of a malignant destiny? My crime was a great one, but surely I suffered enough, when I suffered death as an expiation of it, and I might have been left to repose in the grave."

The feelings that have since come over me held no place in my imagination, but with a kind of defiant desperation I felt as if I should like to defeat the plan by which I was attempted to be punished, and even in the face of Providence itself, to show that it was a failure entailing far worse consequences upon others than upon me.

This was my impression, so I would not play the coward, and fly upon the first flash of danger.

I sat in my own room until the hour came for my appointment with Mr. Harding, and then I walked along the corridor with a confident step, and let the hilt end of my scabbard clank along the floor. I knocked boldly at the door, and I thought there was a little hesitation in his voice as he bade me walk in, but this might have been only my imagination.

He was seated at a table, fully dressed, and in addition to his sword, there was lying upon the table before him a large holster pistol, nearly half the size of a carbine.

"You are well prepared," said I, as I pointed to it.

"Yes," he said, "and I mean to use it."

"What do they want now?" I said.

"What do who want?"

"I don't know," I said, "but I thought I heard some one call you by name from below."

"Indeed, excuse me a moment, perhaps they have made some discovery."

There was wine upon the table, and while he was gone, I poured a glass of good Rhenish down the barrel of the pistol. I wiped it carefully with the cuff of my coat, so there was no appearance upon the barrel of anything of the sort, and when he came back, he looked at me very suspiciously, as he said, —

"Nobody called me, how could you say I was called."

"Because I thought I heard you called; I suppose it is allowable for human nature to be fallible now and then."

"Yes, but then I am so surprised how you could make such a mistake."

"So am I."

It was rather a difficult thing to answer this, and looking at me very steadily, he took up the pistol and examined the priming. Of course, that was all right, and he appeared to be perfectly satisfied.

"There will be two chairs and a table," he said, "placed in the corridor, so that we can sit in perfect ease. I will not anticipate that anything will happen, but if it should, I can only say that I will not be backward in the use of my weapons."

"I don't doubt it," said I, "and commend you accordingly. That pistol must be a most formidable weapon. Does it ever miss fire?"

"Not that I know of," he said, "I have loaded it with such extraordinary care that it amounts to almost an impossibility that it should. Will you take some wine?"

At this moment there came a loud knocking at the door of the house. I saw an expression of satisfaction come over his face and he sprung to his feet, holding the pistol in his grasp.

"Do you know the meaning of that knocking," said I, "at such an hour?" and at the same time with a sweep of my arm I threw his sword off the table and beyond his reach.

"Yes," he said, rather excitedly; "you are my prisoner, it was you who caused the mischief and confusion last night. The girl is ready to swear to you, and if you attempt to escape, I'll blow your brains out."

"Fire at me," said I, "and take the consequences — but the threat is sufficient, and you shall die for your temerity."

I drew my sword, and he evidently thought his danger imminent, for he at once snapped the pistol in my face. Of course it only flashed in the pan, but in one moment my sword went through him like a flash of light. It was a good blade the Jew had sold me — the hilt struck against his breast bone, and he shrieked.

Bang! bang! bang! came again at the outer door of the house. I withdrew the reeking blade, dashed it into the scabbard just in time to prevent my landlady from opening the door, which she was almost in the act of doing. I seized her by the back of the neck, and hurled her to a considerable distance, and then opening the door myself, I stood behind it, and let three men rush into the house. After which I quietly left it, and was free.

Chapter CCXVII.

VARNEY DETAILS HIS SECOND DEATH.

*T*he clergyman was perfectly amazed, as well he might be, at these revelations of the vampyre. He looked up from the manuscript that Varney had left him, with a far more bewildered look than he had ever worn when studying the most abstruse sciences or difficult languages.

"Can I," he said, — "ought I to believe it?"

This was a question more easily asked than answered, and after pacing the little room for a time, he thought he had better finish the papers of the vampyre, before he tortured his mind with any more suppositions upon the subject.

The papers continued thus, and the clergyman was soon completely absorbed in the great interest of the strange recital they contained.

I cared nothing as regarded my last adventure, so that it had one termination which was of any importance to me, namely, that termination which insured my safety. When I got into the street, I walked hurriedly on, never once looking behind me, until I was far enough off, and I felt assured all pursuit was out of the question.

I then began to bethink me what I had next to do.

I was much revived by the draught of blood I had already had, but as yet I was sufficiently new to my vampyre-like existence not to know how long such a renewal of my life and strength would last me.

I certainly felt vigorous, but it was a strange, unearthly sort of vigor, having no sort of resemblance whatever to the strength which persons in an ordinary state of existence may be supposed to feel, when the faculties are all full of life, and acting together harmoniously and well.

When I paused, I found myself in Pall Mall, and not far off from the palace of St. James, which of late had seen so many changes, and been the witness of such remarkable mutations in the affair of monarchs, that its real chronicles would even then have afforded an instructive volume.

I wandered right up to the gates of the royal pile, but then as I was about to enter the quadrangle called the color court, I was rudely repulsed by a sentinel.

It was not so in the time of Cromwell, but at the same moment I had quite forgotten all that was so completely changed.

I always bow to authority when I cannot help it, so I turned aside at once, without making any remark; but as I did so I saw a small door open, not far from where I was, and two figures emerged muffled up in brown cloaks.

They looked nothing peculiar at the first glance, but when you came to examine the form and features, and to observe the manners of those two men, you could not but come to a conclusion that they were what the world would estimate as something great.

Adventure to me was life itself, now that I had so strangely shuffled off all other ties that bound me to the world, and I had a reckless disregard of danger, which arose naturally enough from my most singular and horrible tenure of existence. I resolved to follow these two men closely enough, and yet, if possible, without exciting their observation.

"Shall we have any sport?" said one.

"I trust that the ladies," replied the other, "will afford us some."

"And yet they were rather coy, do you not think, on the last meeting, Rochester?"

"Your majesty —"

"Hush, man — hush! why are you so imprudent as to majesty me in the public streets. Here would be a court scandal if any eaves-dropper had heard you. You were wont to be much more careful than that."

"I spoke," said the other, "to recall your majesty to care. The name of Rochester, which you pronounced, is just as likely in the streets at such a time to create court scandal as that of —"

"Hush, hush! Did I say Rochester? Well — well, man, hold your peace if I did, and come on quickly — if we can but persuade them to come out, we can take them into the garden of the palace; I have the key of that most handy little door in the wall, which has served us more than once."

Of course, after this, I had no difficulty in knowing that the one speaker was the restored monarch, Charles the Second, and the other was his favorite, and dissolute companion, Rochester, of whom I had heard something, although I had been far too short a time in the land of the living again, to have had any opportunity of seeing either of them before, but since they had now confessed themselves to be what they were, I could have no sort of difficulty in their recognition at any other time.

I had carefully kept out of sight while the little dialogue I have just recorded took place, so that although they more than once glanced around them suspiciously and keenly, they saw me not, and having quite satisfied them that their imprudent speech had done them no harm, they walked on hurriedly in the direction of Pimlico.

Little did Charles and his companion guess how horrible a being was following close upon their track. If they had done so they might have paused, aghast, and pursued another course to that which was occupying their attention I had a difficult part to play in following them, for although the king was incautious enough to have been safely and easily followed by any one, Rochester was not, but kept a wary eye around him, so that I was really more than once upon the point of being detected, and yet by dint of good management I did escape.

Pimlico at that time was rather a miserable neighborhood, and far, very far indeed from being what it is now, but both the king and Rochester appeared to be well acquainted with it and they went on for a considerable distance until they came to a turning of a narrow dismal-looking character bounded on, each side not by houses but by the garden walls of houses, and to judge from the solidity and the height of those walls, the houses should have been houses of some importance.

"Bravo, bravissimo!" said the king, "we are thus far into the enemy territory without observation."

"So it seems," replied Rochester; "and now think you we can find the particular wall again."

"Of a surety, yes. Did I not ask them to hang out a handkerchief or some other signal, by which we might be this night guided in our search, and there it flutters."

The king pointed to the top of the wall, where a handkerchief waved and something certainly in the shape of a human head appeared against the night sky, and as sweet a voice as ever I heard in my life, said, —

"Gentlemen, I pray you to go away."

"What," said the king; "go away just as the sun has risen?"

"Nay, but gentlemen," said the voice, "we are afraid we are watched."

"We!" said Rochester, "you say we, and yet your fair companion is not visible."

"Fair sir," said the lady, "it is not the easiest task in the world for one of us to stand upon a ladder. It certainly will not hold two."

"Fair lady," said the king, "and if you can but manage to come over the wall, we will all four take one of the pleasantest strolls in the world; a friend of mine, who is a captain in the Royal Guard, will at my request, allow us to walk in the private garden of St. James's palace."

"Indeed."

"Yes, fair one. That garden of which you may have heard as the favorite resort of the gay Charles."

"But we are afraid," said the lady; "our uncle may come home. It's very improper indeed — very indiscreet — we ought not to think of such a thing for a moment. In fact, it's decidedly wrong gentlemen, but how are we to get over the wall?"

The party all laughed out together.

Chapter CCXVIII.

THE PALACE GARDEN IN ST. JAMES'S.

*I*t was certainly a very ingenious speech which the lady on the wall had given utterance to, and sufficiently exemplified how inclination was struggling with prudence. It was just the sort of speech which suited those to whom it was addressed.

After the laughter had subsided a little Charles spoke, —

"By the help of the ladder we have," he said, "you can easily leave where you are, and as easily return, but I perceive you lack the strength to lift it over this side so as to descend."

"Just so," said the lady, in a low voice.

"Well, I think that by the aid of my friend Smith here, I can get up to the top of the wall, and assist you."

Charles, by the aid of Rochester, contrived to scramble to the top of the wall, to the assistance of the two damsels who were so fearful, and yet so willing, to risk a little danger to their reputations, for the purpose of enjoying a walk in the king's garden at St. James's.

The idea came across me of doing some mischief, but I did not just then interfere as I wanted to see the result of the affair. The ladder was duly pulled over by the monarch after both the ladies had got on the top of the wall, and while Rochester steadied it below they descended in perfect safety, and the party walked hastily from the place in the direction of St. James's.

I followed them with great caution, after having removed the ladder to the all of a garden several doors from the proper one. They went on talking and laughing in the gayest possible manner, until they reached Buckingham house, and then they took a secluded path that led them close to the gardens of St. James's.

Some overhanging trees shed such an impervious shadow upon all objects that I found I might as well be quite near to the party as far off, so I approached boldly and heard that the ladies were beginning to get a little alarmed at this secret and strictly private mode of entrance to the garden.

"Gentlemen," said one, "don't go into the garden if you have no proper leave to do so."

"Oh, but we have," said the king. "Lately I have had proper leave I assure you; it did happen that for some time the leave was taken away, but I have it again along with a few other little privileges that I wanted much."

"You need fear nothing," said Rochester.

They all four stood in a group by the little door, while the king fumbled about with a key for some few minutes, before he could open the lock. At length, however, he succeeded in doing so, and the door swung open. The king dropped the key and was unable to find it again; so leaving the door as close as they could, the party passed onwards, and I soon followed in their footsteps.

The place was profoundly dark.

I could feel the soft grating of fine gravel under my feet, and feeling that such a sand might betray me, I stepped aside until I trod upon a border, as I found it to be, of velvet turf. The odor of sweet flowers came upon my senses, and occasionally as the night wind swept among the trees, there would be a pleasant murmuring sound quite musical in its effect.

The soft soil effectually prevented my footsteps from being heard, and I soon stood quite close to the parties, and found that they were at the entrance of a little gaudy pavilion, from a small painted window in which streamed a light.

The ladies seemed to be rather in a flutter of apprehension, and yet the whole affair no doubt to them presented itself in the shape of such a charming and romantic adventure, that I very much doubt if they would have gone back now, had they had all the opportunity in the world so to do.

Finally they all went into the pavilion. I then advanced, and finding a window, that commanded a good view of the interior I looked in and was much amused at what passed.

The place was decorated in a tasteful manner, although a little approaching to the gaudy, and the pictures painted in fresco upon the walls were not precisely what the strictest prudery would have considered correct, while at the same time there was nothing positively offensive in them.

A table stood in the center, and was covered with rich confectionery, and wine, while the lamp that had sent the stream of light through the painted window was dependent from the ceiling by three massive gilt chains.

Take it for all in all, it certainly was a handsome place.

The king and Rochester were urging the ladies to drink wine, and now that for the first time I had an opportunity of seeing the countenances of the different persons whom I had followed so far, I confess that I looked upon them with much curiosity. The ladies were decidedly handsome, and the youngest who had fallen to the lot of the king was very pretty indeed, and had a look of great innocence and sweetness upon her face. I pitied her.

The king was a small, dark, sharp-featured man, and I thought that there was an obliquity in his vision. As for Rochester, he was decidedly ugly. His face was rather flat, and of a universal dirty looking white color. He certainly was not calculated to win a lady's favor. But then for all I knew, he might have a tongue to win an angel out of heaven.

Such a capacity goes much further with a woman who has any mind than all the physical graces, and women of no mind are not worth the winning.

Chapter CCXIX.

AN ADVENTURE. — THE CARBINE SHOT. — THE DEATH.

"Nay," I heard the king say, "they ought, and no doubt do, keep choice wine here; drink, fair one."

The young girl shook her head.

"Nay, now," said Charles with a laugh, as he finished off himself the glass that the young girl took so small a sip of, "I will convince you that I think it good."

The lady with whom Rochester was conversing in a low tone, had no such scruples, for she tossed off a couple of glasses as fast as they were tendered to her, and talked quite at her ease, admiring the pavilion, the pictures, the hangings and furniture, and wondering whether the king ever came there himself.

Rochester began mystifying her, talking to her in a low tone, while I turned my attention to the king, and the younger, and certainly more estimable female of the two.

The king had been talking to her in a low tone, when she suddenly started to her feet, her face flushed with anger and alarm.

"Louisa," she said, "I claim your protection; you were left in care of me. Take me home, or I will tell my uncle how you basely betrayed your trust, by persuading me there was no harm in meeting those gentlemen."

"Pho! The child's mad," said Louisa.

"Quite mad," said the king, as he advanced towards her again; she fled to the door of the pavilion. I knew not what impulse it was that urged me on, but I left the window hastily, and met her, she fell into my arms, and the light fell strongly upon me as I confronted the king.

"The guard. The guard," he shouted.

"Louisa pretended to faint, and the young girl clung to me as her only protector, exclaiming, —

"Save me! save me; Oh save me!"

"The garden door is open," I whispered to her, "follow me quickly, not a moment is to be lost." We both fled together.

I was about to pass through the doorway, when a shot from one of the guards struck me, and I fell to the ground as if the hand of a giant had struck me down. There was a rush of blood from my heart to my head, a burning sensation of pain for a moment or two, that was most horrible, and then a sea of yellow light seemed to be all around me.

I remembered no more.

It was afterwards that I found this was my second death, and that the favorite, Rochester, had actually directed that I should be shot rather than permitted to escape, for he dreaded more than the monarch did the exposure of his vices. I do not think that Charles, in like manner, had he been at hand, would have had my life taken, although it is hard to say what kings will do or what they will not when they are thwarted.

Chapter CCXX.

THE TOTAL DESTRUCTION OF VARNEY THE VAMPYRE, AND CONCLUSION.

*T*he manuscript which the clergyman had read with so much interest, here abruptly terminated. He was left to conclude that Varney after that had been resuscitated; and he was more perplexed than ever to come to any opinion concerning the truth of the narration which he had now concluded.

It was one week after he had finished the perusal of Varney's papers that the clergyman read in an English newspaper the following statement.

"We extract from the *Algemeine Zeitung* the following most curious story, the accuracy of which of course we cannot vouch for, but still there is a sufficient air of probability about it to induce us to present it to our readers.

"Late in the evening, about four days since, a tall and melancholy-looking stranger arrived, and put up at one of the principal hotels at Naples. He was a most peculiar looking man, and considered by the persons of the establishment as about the ugliest guest they had ever had within the walls of their place.

"In a short time he summoned the landlord, and the following conversation ensued between him and the strange guest.

"'I want,' said the stranger, 'to see all the curiosities of Naples, and among the rest Mount Vesuvius. Is there any difficulty?'

"'None,' replied the landlord, 'with a proper guide.'

"A guide was soon secured, who set out with the adventurous Englishman to make the ascent of the burning mountain.

"They went on then until the guide did not think it quite prudent to go any further, as there was a great fissure in the side of the mountain, out of which a stream of lava was slowly issuing and spreading itself in rather an alarming manner.

"The ugly Englishman, however, pointed to a secure mode of getting higher still, and they proceeded until they were very near the edge of the crater itself. The stranger then took his purse from his pocket and flung it to the guide saying, —

"'You can keep that for your pains, and for coming into some danger with me. But the fact was, that I wanted a witness to an act which I have set my mind upon performing.'

"The guide says that these words were spoken with so much calmness, that he verily believed the act mentioned as about to be done was some scientific experiment of which he knew that the English were very fond, and he replied, —

"'Sir, I am only too proud to serve so generous and so distinguished a gentleman. In what way can I be useful?'

"'You will make what haste you can,' said the stranger, 'from the mountain, inasmuch as it is covered with sulphurous vapors, inimical to human life, and when you reach the city you will cause to be published an account of my proceedings, and what I say. You will say that you accompanied Varney the Vampyre to the crater of Mount Vesuvius, and that, tired and disgusted with a life of horror, he flung himself in to prevent the possibility of a reanimation of his remains.'

"Before then the guide could utter anything but a shriek, Varney took one tremendous leap, and disappeared into the burning mouth of the mountain."

THE END

Lightning Source UK Ltd.
Milton Keynes UK
UKOW04n0604301013

220038UK00001B/3/P